ALSO BY ELLE KENNEDY

MISFIT

A PREP NOVEL

ELLE KENNEDY

Bloom *books*

Published by Bloom Books, an imprint of Sourcebooks
P.O. Box 4410, Naperville, Illinois 60567–4410
(630) 961-3900
sourcebooks.com

Cataloging-in-Publication Data is on file with the Library of Congress.

Printed and bound in the United States of America.
VP 10 9 8 7 6 5 4 3 2

CHAPTER 1
RJ

"EAT UP, BUD. I'M GETTING MARRIED."

Those were the first words to exit Mom's mouth when I walked into the kitchen this morning. Naturally, I assumed I was still dreaming. That wasn't *really* my mother making pancakes at the stove, casually talking about her spontaneous marriage. Clearly I was embroiled in one of those off-kilter dreams where nothing made any sense.

But nope, I was awake. Awake and apparently in the midst of Mom's midlife crisis. I knew she was dating some new guy these past few months, but it's not like I gave it much thought. My mother's relationships never last.

And yet here I am, barely eight hours later, pressed into an ill-fitting tux and pushing lumps of salmon around my plate beside a similarly blindsided stranger I'm supposed to call my stepbrother.

Meanwhile, our respective and alleged adults grope each other around the dance floor, creating nightmare fuel to some graphic '90s R&B slow jam.

Fuck me with a sledgehammer.

"Maybe it was the fish," Fennelly says next to me, looking a little green, "but I'm starting to feel like something crawled in my stomach and died."

Or maybe it's his dad getting handsy all over my mother in front of a roomful of minimum-wage waiters who aren't getting tipped enough for this shit.

"When the apocalypse comes," I mutter at my own slow, painful torture, "and some dude with a baseball bat is standing over me asking if I have any last words for my maker, I'll tell him I've stared into the face of darkness and fear has no power over me."

Fenn grins and knocks back another glass of champagne like he was raised on the stuff straight out of his mother's tits. They ought to get him a hose. Or an IV.

I haven't decided what I think of him yet. We met for the first time at the altar only an hour ago, standing on either side of the aisle while our parents made their vows to an otherwise empty room. I'm still trying to get a read on this blond pretty boy with the outline of a flask protruding through his pocket.

His name is Fennelly Bishop, which is a fucking stupid name, but then again, I'm not one to talk. Like me, he rebels against the name, and told me to call him Fenn. I suspect he's an athlete, or at least good at sports, because he's got that tall, muscled build that doesn't look like it came from a gym. Although I guess he could have a super-expensive personal trainer on retainer, some burly dude who shows up at his huge mansion and gets paid $200K a year to keep this blue-eyed rich boy in peak shape. They're money people, Fenn and his dad. It wafts off them. The way he sticks his pinky out and leans back in his chair, legs splayed, as though we're all here to serve and amuse him with our quaint peasant talents.

"When I write my memoirs," he says, unraveling the bow tie around his neck, "I'll remember this as the day I learned what the opposite of porn is."

I snicker quietly. Dude's funny, I'll give him that.

Fenn barely has to raise his empty glass in order to get a refill from one of the half-dozen waiters in tuxedos skulking in the shadows of this swanky country club ballroom. It's the kind of place where the silverware is made from actual silver. Someone rushes over and offers to pour, but Fenn swipes the bottle instead. Part of me wonders if I'll have to leave here through a metal detector. The country club is in Greenwich, apparently not too far from David's mansion, which I assume is a palace, based on this club's sizable membership fee. We're worlds away from the lower-middle-class suburbs where Mom and I live on the other side of the state.

"Chick over there? She's looking at you." Fenn nods past my shoulder.

Nobody ever said I was polite, so I turn around to follow his gaze. A short brunette in a server's outfit flashes me a coy smile before raising one brow.

I turn back. "Nah, I'm good," I tell him.

"I don't know, dude." Fenn cocks his head in appraisal. "She's kinda cute. I don't think anyone would notice if you took her into the cart house or something."

The last thing on my mind is hooking up. It'll take weeks for me to be able to unsee the display of parental vertical sex currently assaulting my eyes. Fenn must read the notion on my face because he chuckles and pushes a stray glass of something at me.

"Yeah." He shakes his head. "Neither the time nor place. Sorta like having a wank when I know my dad's in the next room. Can't get hard. Doesn't seem right, you know?"

The guy's too into sharing.

"Lucky for me," he adds with a shrug, "he's not around much."

From the dance floor, my mom waves at us. Then she promptly forgets our existence again when Fenn's father cups her ass over her white satin gown. He gives it a hearty squeeze, and I almost hurl. As far as weddings go, this one is an understated affair. There are more staff at this thing than guests. Just the four of us, all dressed up for this cozy little exercise in psychological warfare.

"This is painful," I groan into the glass of whatever I don't taste as I swallow. "It's like watching a sex scene on TV next to your parents."

"Nah, like watching your parents in a sex scene on TV next to your parents." Clearly disgusted but oddly entranced, Fenn can't look away. He washes the thought down with a gulp of champagne.

"I'm both ashamed and disgusted with myself."

As an act of mercy, Fenn shoves the bottle at me. "Here, man. Never too early to develop problematic coping mechanisms."

I tip the heavy bottle to my lips. "Cheers."

The thing about expensive champagne, it drinks fast. I barely notice Fenn pass off the empty bottle for a second. Our parents continue rubbing against each other in slow motion to a soundtrack of retro cringe. Meanwhile, the sadistic DJ is on his phone checking Twitter, oblivious to our pain.

"This is weird, right?" Fenn is now busy making deformed origami from an embroidered cloth napkin. "I mean, if the two of them died right now. Let's say a chandelier mercifully falls on their heads while we're sitting here. And a shard of glass flies across the room to slit my aorta and I nearly bleed out before slipping into a coma—you would legally have to decide when they unplugged me."

"What the fuck are you talking about?"

The guy chugs a bottle of champagne and thinks he's Nietzsche.

"I'm saying, that's a lot of responsibility. Being family. What do we even know about each other?" He pauses, puzzling over my face so long I get uncomfortable and lean away. Drunks are known for sudden outbursts. "I've already forgotten your name," he says to his own astonishment. "Shit, I actually forgot it."

I can't help but grin. "RJ," I supply, just as another slow jam fills the ballroom. Christ. Enough. I want to murder this DJ. He must be doing this on purpose.

"Is that short for something?" Fenn asks.

"Like, did my parents just pick their favorite letters of the alphabet while the doctor was dangling me upside down by my foot?"

"Did they?"

"Nah. It's short for Remington John." I pull out my phone,

shielding the screen slightly as I find a MacBook on the Wi-Fi network. Call it an educated guess, but I surmise the machine going by "Grandmaster Gash" belongs to the tool in the headphones who's running the music.

"*Remington* John?" Fenn snorts loudly. "How blue collar," he remarks, an undercurrent of rich-boy prick bubbling to the surface.

Distracted, I open Spotify in the background and try to remember what we're talking about. "My dad had a thing for David Carradine in the '80s. I don't know. What the hell kind of *Sound of Music* name is Fennelly?"

He shrugs, unbothered. "My dad would probably say it was an old family name. But I'm pretty sure my mom got it off a baby blog."

In the middle of an especially torrid display to Chris Isaac's "Wicked Game," Weird Al suddenly comes blaring through the audio system.

The DJ throws off his headphones and nearly falls over on his stool trying to figure out why he can't get control of his playback.

"The hell just happened?" Fenn glances at me, then at my phone. "Did you do that?"

I roll my eyes. "I wish. I'm just checking texts over here."

I drop the Wi-Fi connection and pocket my phone, allowing the DJ to take back control as Mom and David saunter over. Sweaty, smiling, and with no remorse for their actions.

"Time to cut the cake, don't you think?" Mom's smile is sincere and joyful, which cracks through a sliver of my bitter cynicism at this spontaneous upending of both our lives. Then she notes the two empty bottles of champagne and raises an eyebrow at me.

I give her a what-can-ya-do shrug. Sorry not sorry. I mean, shit, they should have handed out Vicodin party favors. That dance floor routine alone was like KGB waterboarding torture.

"You were right." David, my mother's new fully articulated checkbook, accepts the scotch on the rocks deposited into his hand by a dutiful waiter. He takes a quick sip. "We would have done better to spring for a band."

"Not too late to throw this shindig in the back of the jet and head to Vegas," Fenn says, a mocking note to his voice.

It doesn't escape me that he says *the* jet. Not "a" jet, as in any old jet. But THE jet, implying the Bishops are in possession of their own private plane. Fuck me. What world is this and how did I end up here?

When Fenn lifts his empty bottle to signal for another, his dad waves off the waiter. Fenn narrows his eyes. "What, aren't we celebrating?"

David spares a brief look at his son. "I think maybe you've celebrated enough."

"I'm going to pop over to the restroom," Mom says. She steps closer to brush lint off the lapel of my tux, lingering over me too long with glassy eyes. I hate it when she gets sentimental. Not my vibe. Especially when I'm being subjected to her fleeting whims of self-indulgent calamity. "You boys behave yourselves while I'm gone."

Nope. I put my fucking foot down at being referred to collectively as her *boys*.

Once she's gone, David hovers awkwardly, first checking his watch and then glancing at his phone. He scans the room as if searching for something requiring his urgent attention, but no such luck. He's stuck with us, these two disenchanted youths waiting for him to walk away so we can get to the bottom of another bottle of champagne.

"So…" Man, he's drowning. This is becoming embarrassing for all of us. "You two getting along? Getting to know each other?"

"*You* two getting to know each other?" Fenn shoots back.

I damn near do a double take at the venom in his voice. For the past couple of hours, Fenn's been laid-back, easy to talk to. But maybe that easygoing attitude and quick grins are only reserved for people who aren't his father.

His dad coughs and adjusts the buttons on his tux. "Yes, well. I know this was sudden—"

"Explosive diarrhea is sudden," Fenn cuts in, his pale blue eyes going glacial. "You had time to order flower arrangements. Which means you had time to come to your senses." He glances at me. "No offense."

I just shrug. Hey, man. I'm a hapless bystander to this tornado.

"Listen, Fennelly. I understand—"

"I'm here, okay?" Fenn ices his dad out with a flat expression and dismissive tone, and now I feel like I'm intruding in whatever bullshit they've got between them. "Let's not pretend this whole thing isn't a clusterfuck of selfishness."

Every line and muscle on David's face becomes strained. His resemblance to his son is striking. They've got the same build, the same ice-blue eyes and sandy hair. And David's one of those dudes who barely ages. He could probably pass for Fenn's older brother. Same way people always mistake my mom, with her long dark hair and flawless skin, for my older sister.

"Fennelly." David sighs at his son. "Could you try, huh? Just a little? For a couple more hours."

Fenn pulls out his phone to scroll through his texts. "Whatever."

David's attention shifts to me. I don't know if he's looking for sympathy or solidarity, but when I don't offer either, he sets his jaw and disappears to check on the cake.

I don't know what I think of David Bishop yet. As far as first impressions go, this isn't a stellar start. Until a few hours ago, I didn't think of him much at all. He was just the new random dude my mother was seeing who I didn't ever expect to meet. Before Mom was suddenly dropping a set of department store cuff links in my hand, I had no reason to believe this guy would be any different from the litany of other brief but intense relationships Mom cultivated and lost in quick succession. I stopped trying to connect or even remember their names a long time ago.

"Sorry," Fenn says to me. "I guess that was awkward."

He guesses? I snort out loud. "So, you two are close."

"Dude. Nothing says *I forgot you're still here* like sending the jet at four o'clock for a six o'clock wedding. There was a tailor with a fucking sewing machine hemming my pants at thirty thousand feet."

"Harsh." I let out a breath. "I'd ask what your father's intentions are with my mother, but I guess we've skipped right past that to *do you want the top or bottom bunk?*"

"Oh, fuck," he says, sort of dry heaving in disgust. "I just realized your mom was probably a flight attendant on that plane. I probably jerked off in the same bathroom they banged in."

"Jesus, Bishop. Keep your traumas to yourself, yeah?"

I'm gonna need a therapist after this goddamn wedding.

Fenn takes a swig from his flask. "So what's your deal?"

"My deal?"

"Sure. What are you into? What do you do when not getting hijacked into shotgun weddings?"

"Don't even joke." If my mother tells me she's pregnant, I'm hopping a train to the West Coast.

The waiters come by to change the place settings. They pop a new bottle of some sweet-smelling dessert wine, which Fenn helps himself to tasting.

"You're going to be a senior, too, right?" he pushes. "Where do you go to school?"

It's a bit more complicated than that. "I don't, technically."

"Aw, shit. You're not one of those homeschool kids, are you?" He leans away from me as if just remembering we'd both had our lips on the same champagne bottles tonight. "You've had all your shots, right?"

"I was at a public school in Windsor last semester. But it was suggested I take an early summer break."

"You got expelled." His expression is mildly impressed. "Did you deserve it?"

"It's a matter of perspective." That principal had it out for me from the first day I stepped through the doors. She took one look at my record and had her mind made up. Not that I did much to convince her otherwise.

"What'd you do?"

"My friend Derek boosted a teacher's car from the school parking lot during a fire drill."

Fenn cracks a smile. "Nice."

"Bunch of us went joyriding through the neighborhood until the school resource officer set up a roadblock in front of the Taco Bell."

"Like at gunpoint?"

"They threw out stop sticks that Derek mostly avoided, but we still blew out a tire."

"Suburbia is wild."

It's also complete bullshit.

I don't even know a kid named Derek.

But I don't trust anyone who wants to know me, and I'm not about to hand over that kind of ammunition to some rando. A marriage certificate doesn't make us allies.

When Mom gets back, she and David gather us around a two-tier white wedding cake and proceed to make us watch them feed each other. Then they get choked up over more teary declarations of grotesque joy, and all I'm thinking about is how to pull one of these waiters out back because someone's gotta have a joint on them. Though I'd settle for a spoonful of arsenic at this point.

"I never imagined I'd be standing here," Mom starts, raising a glass.

Not for lack of trying, I almost blurt out.

I manage to hold my tongue, but come on. It's the truth. Mom's had more boyfriends than oil changes. She spent my entire childhood dating men who weren't interested in putting a ring on it. Despite her best efforts, she was either relegated to mistress territory, or just jerked around until they found someone who was more "wife material." Mom's job as a flight attendant pays well, but a lot of dudes just aren't interested in marrying a chick with baggage. The baggage in this case being yours truly. After all the bullshit she'd been fed by guys over the years, I guess it makes sense she up and married the first one who'd offered. And I suspect the "knowing him less than three months" part was offset by the "he's filthy rich" part.

Not that I'm calling my mom a gold digger—I can't begrudge the woman a little financial stability. But she does have a type. And I doubt we'd be standing here so soon if David didn't have the equivalent GDP of a small island nation.

Still, I don't hate that she looks happier than I've seen her in a long time. Maybe it's the mood lighting, or the white cocktail dress, but she's especially beautiful tonight. For a working single mom who's been putting up with my delinquent ass for eighteen years, she cleans up nice. So maybe I can't begrudge her a little spontaneous self-indulgence.

"I still can't believe this is all really happening." She dabs a napkin under her eye, clearing her throat. "I'm thrilled to have a new son, Fennelly. And I can't wait to get to know you better."

She then goes on about family and love, telling me how David and I are going to become just the best of friends and he's such a great father figure—though Fenn might have other thoughts.

I mean, let's pump the brakes a little. This is the first time I've ever been in the same room with the guy. He seems normal enough. Nice, I guess. Loaded, of course. But I haven't done the appropriate legwork yet to determine where the bodies are buried, and I'm not about to start calling him Dad.

"I never imagined I'd remarry," David says when it's his turn to speak, clutching my mother closely while sparing a glance at Fenn. "Then you smiled at me, gave me a little wink, and it was like having a first crush all over again. Every time I look at you. Every time I hear your voice. I'm falling in love for the first time."

From his chair, Fenn rolls his eyes and drawls, "If only Mom knew she was standing in the way of your true love, she could've skipped the eleven agonizing months of chemo, am I right?"

"Fennelly," David growls sharply.

I'm about ready to duck when Mom grabs David's lapels, keeping him close to her side. "It's okay, honey," I hear her murmur to him. She turns to address Fenn. "I can't imagine how difficult that is to live with," she tells him with a sad smile. "I know your dad cherishes your mother's memory, and I would never disrespect that. I hope we can work on being friends."

Fenn doesn't make eye contact. He's on an island. I have no idea what keeps him glued to this spot when it's obvious he'd rather jump through a window to get out of here.

"It'll be an adjustment," David starts again. "We're all figuring it out together. It's my hope, however, you both understand how much Michelle and I love you." He signals to a waiter who emerges from the corner of the room with a silver tray. Two small green leather boxes sit atop it. "Since today is for all of us, I thought a small gift to commemorate the occasion was appropriate."

David hands a box with a crown embossed in gold to each of us. I eye it warily, fighting the urge to say "nah, I'm good," until I notice Mom imploring me with her gaze. Stifling a sigh, I open the box. Next to me, a bored Fenn does the same. Inside the boxes are matching Rolex watches.

David's excitement makes up for the total lack of enthusiasm on Fenn's and my part. "That's a meteorite face and white-gold case with a metal blade overmolded in a flexible black elastomer," he tells us, as if I understand a word of it. He's literally speaking gibberish. "They're designed for endurance race-car drivers, but I thought it might be a bit more practical and sporting for young men."

"Yeah, no, very practical, Dad." Fenn snaps the box shut but stops just short of chucking it over his shoulder. "How long do you think it'll last at RJ's public school before he's held up at gunpoint in the lunchroom?"

I snort a laugh that gets me a flash of the evil eye from Mom. "What? He's not wrong." Then I remember I'm supposed to be on my best behavior. "I mean, thank you. I'll, uh, be careful."

Mom and David exchange a quick, desperate look. At this point they're muscling through this thing as Fenn and I become more unruly due to our waning patience. Neither of us wants to be here, and I think we're both questioning why we've tolerated it this long.

"On the subject," David says then, nodding at my mother. "I have one more surprise, if it's all right."

Mom smiles at him, that smitten glow returning to her face. "Oh, honey. What have you been up to?"

"Well, I've made some arrangements, and I've managed to secure a spot for RJ at Sandover Prep next semester."

Is he joking?

Prep school?

Yeah, I don't see that working out. Being surrounded by a bunch of posh little bastards in bow ties drinking lattes made of their nanny's breast milk? No thanks. I suddenly wonder if it's too late to hop that train out of town. Flag down a Greyhound, even. I could find my place among the skate park beach people in Venice, maybe polish up on my pickpocketing while surfing the café public Wi-Fi for easy marks. Anything beats being shipped off to douchebag school.

"David, really? That's wonderful." Mom's way too excited about this when she meets my gaze with a desperate insistence. "Isn't it wonderful, RJ? This is going to be such a great opportunity for you."

In other words, *could you try not to get kicked out of this one?*

"Oh yeah, it's a real opportunity," Fenn echoes mockingly, looking amused by the announcement. "Sandover Prep is known for its stellar academics and model students and—oh wait, stupid me. I must be thinking about some other prep school." He glances at my mother, whose expression has gone uneasy. "Sorry to inform you, Dad's new wife, but Sandover's where all the delinquents are sent." Laughing carelessly, he pokes himself in the chest. "Case in point, me."

Mom's gaze swivels to David, who is quick to intervene. "Fennelly is being hyperbolic. Sandover is one of the top schools on the East Coast. Its alumni include two former presidents and dozens of Rhodes Scholars. I promise you, RJ will be receiving the best possible education there and will pretty much be guaranteed admission into any college of his choice."

As David continues to reassure her, Fenn leans toward me with a bitter smirk and a soft taunt. "Congratulations, brother. Welcome to fuck-up school."

CHAPTER 2
SLOANE

NOT A DROP OF RAIN HAS FALLEN ON NEW HAMPSHIRE IN WEEKS. Even the grass is gasping. As I maintain a brisk and steady pace, the earth crunches under my sneakers, dry and brittle. It's like running across rice paper. The trees on either side of the trail provide shade, but little relief. Penny and Bo, our golden retrievers, are good sports, even if their panting is more labored than usual.

"Maybe we take the short way 'round, yeah?"

When I don't respond, my sister throws an elbow, jarring me from my thoughts.

"Sorry," I tell her. "I drifted off there for a second."

"She's got the sun madness," Casey mocks, keeping pace beside me.

This heatwave is relentless. I can almost feel the gray matter melting inside my skull as we jog the well-worn dirt path on the empty wooded grounds of Sandover. In a few days, this place will be overrun by adolescent males and their pubescent shenanigans. Until then, we have the exclusive run of the place. Our personal estate of green lawns, brick, and ivy.

With campus empty, though, it's easy to feel like ghosts here, haunting the abandoned courtyards, secluded from sight and beyond reach. Unsure we're even real until the luxury cars pull up and whistles chase me back over the hill and through the trees.

"To think," I say, clapping at Bo and Penny to coax them into keeping up with us when their heads droop. They drift closer to Casey like I'm the wicked stepsister. "There are girls out there who would slit their best friend's throat to live on an all-boys campus."

Casey snorts. "They can have it. I give them a week before the smell runs them off."

She's not wrong. By September, there's a distinct odor that gets baked into these walls, into every room and corridor. I don't care how many janitors and buckets of ammonia they throw at it. Boys are animals and there's no getting around it.

Still, occasionally, the view isn't terrible.

"What about St. Vincent's?" I ask my sister. "Think you're ready?"

"Sure." Her answer is a little too quick.

"It's okay if you're—"

"No, I know. It's whatever, right?" She flashes a smile and flicks sweat off her forehead. "Fresh start. I'm excited. I just want school to start already. All this anticipation."

I'm not sure if the sugar coating is more for her benefit or mine. Fact is, we're both relieved to get away from Ballard Academy and all that bullshit. I haven't even spoken to Mila or any of my old friends all summer. Not that I was holding my breath for an apology. Mila and the girls can choke on their gluten-free vegan protein bars, for all I care.

"It's okay to say you're not okay," I tell Casey. Despite what she says, I know she's not. Going to St. Vincent's may seem like a solution, but the rumors and gossip don't end at Ballard. It hurts to know that this will follow her.

She gives me that sunny smile that's so uniquely Casey. "You worry too much."

I don't know how she still smiles. Where the sunlight comes from, or how she's protected that brightness through it all. If I went through what she had, I'd have sunk so deep, so dark, they'd be finding trapped miners before they got to me.

"I enjoy it. It's practically a hobby. Like collecting rocks or something. I take my precious little worry pearls out of their pouch and polish them."

Casey laughs and it makes me sad all over again. Although her laughter sounds the same, I can't help but think it's a lie. She doesn't want to let her big sister see the cracks, not when she's spent months carefully gluing the pieces back together.

"You're exhausting." She shoulders me off the path, and then, with a whistle to the dogs, she takes off at a sprint, kicking up dust in my face. "Race you."

My phone vibrates, so I let her get a head start while I pull it out of my back pocket. I figure it's our dad, demanding to know why I dragged his sweet, precious Casey out into the heat, but a glance at the screen reveals an even more annoying caller.

My ex.

Despite my better judgment, I answer it. "What do you want, Duke?"

"So you didn't block my number." He's got this assuredness in his voice that reminds me why I've been ignoring his texts. Duke is the kind of insufferable ass who winks at you with a mouthful of blood as he asks for more.

"That can change, if you prefer." I make sure my tone is as cool and indifferent as possible.

"I missed you," he says, undeterred. "Can't wait to see you when I get back."

Ha. Like I should be flattered. I've heard his bedroom voice before, the one that calls at three in the morning trying to talk me into sneaking into his dorm. Two years of our on-and-off relationship has inoculated me to his persuasions. We're currently off, and I plan on keeping it that way. Duke might be hot, but we were way too toxic together. There's only so much make-up sex you can have before you start to wonder if maybe it's possible to hook up *without* breaking up every other second.

"Sorry," I inform him. "Save your excitement for the Ballard freshmen and townies."

"Hey, don't bite. I'm being nice."

"This isn't a thing anymore, Duke. Let it go."

Casey comes back for me, rolling her eyes when she realizes who it is.

"You say that now," he insists. "But we both know you can't stay away from me. See you soon, babe."

I hang up on him, growling at the phone. Dude is a piece of work.

"You'll be back together by dinner," Casey tells me.

"He can eat shit."

"Heard that before."

"Duke's first love is himself. He's never getting divorced."

"Heard that one too."

This time I growl at *her*, which just makes her laugh.

Despite what she thinks, I'm done with him. A girl can only ride that carousel so many times. As a matter of fact, I think I'm skipping the whole amusement park this year. Going on a boy hiatus. A dick detox. I'm a senior now. It's been all fun and games, but now it's time to get serious about my grades and landing a scholarship. Pretty good isn't good enough if I want a shot at running division one track in college. And God knows an admissions rep isn't interested in my keg-stand record or my all-star beer-pong titles. I need to focus this year.

Which means no more Duke.

No more sneaking out and partying with Silas and the boys.

No more doing the bare minimum in the classroom because I'm too impatient to get outside on the track.

I just turned eighteen. I'm basically an adult now—or at least I'm trying to be. And I can't afford any distractions this year.

When we get home, the dogs bound through the door ahead of us, practically colliding at their water bowls.

"Girls?" Dad's voice carries into the front hall from the kitchen.

Casey glances at me. "Uh-oh. What's burning?"

We kick off our shoes and follow the acrid smell to the tendrils of smoke wafting from the oven. Dad's standing over the stove with a pot on every burner.

"Potatoes might have gotten away from me," he says ruefully. He catches Casey with a kiss on the cheek as she pulls a bottle of water from the fridge. "You look a little pale, sweetheart. You feeling all right?"

"I'm fine." Casey chugs some water. "Just hot out there."

His attention snaps to me across the counter. "You shouldn't push her so hard. Can't expect her to keep up with your pace."

I shrug. "She's the one who wanted to race me back."

"I had you." Casey does a taunting little dance, her strawberry-blonde ponytail swishing around.

"You had nothing. I could have beaten you running backwards."

"Sloane. I expect you to be a little more thoughtful." Dad gives me the sour face. He's the only one with a problem, but somehow, it's my fault. "I don't want to see anyone coming back here with heatstroke."

By "anyone," we both know he means Casey. Because she's the baby. The fragile one who hasn't been ruined and hardened beyond repair.

"Seriously, Dad," Casey tries to intervene. "Relax. Someone's gotta keep Sloane fresh for tryouts."

"Come here and taste this." He offers her a spoon, entirely dismissing her assurances.

In our father's eyes, Casey is made of glass and I'm made of stone, and there's nothing anyone can say to convince him otherwise. Even before Casey's accident, he took for granted that I didn't need coddling, that I'd always tough it out and be the strong one.

Unfortunately, the pressure to always be "the strong one" is unbearable. I feel like I'm taking up all the slack, plus dealing with my own shit, while he resents every little show of vulnerability as some personal slight against him.

It's not a sustainable status quo and I'm very near fed up.

Thankfully, college is just around the corner. One more year, and then I can finally put myself first. Get some distance from the constant scrutiny and find out what it feels like to be my own person again.

My phone buzzes in my pocket again, and I don't have to check it to know it's Duke with another pathetic attempt to wear me down.

Not this time.

New year, new game plan.

No distractions. And absolutely no boys.

CHAPTER 3
RJ

"So you're really leaving, huh?"

Julie tugs on a pair of boxer briefs that might have belonged to me at some point, then slips a loose T-shirt over her head. Her gaze remains locked with mine the entire time. She wants me to watch her get dressed. It's her little way of putting some punctuation on it. On us.

"So I'm told." Sitting on the edge of her bed, I pull my jeans on. "Bummer."

She hunts around the room for a lighter, then opens a mint tin to pull out a joint. She sparks one end and blows the embers before stomping them out on the hardwood floor. I've always liked the way she looks when she closes her eyes and inhales.

She blows the smoke out her open window and offers me a hit. As I take it, she bites her lip and sweeps her chocolate-brown eyes over my bare chest. Not even ten minutes ago, her tongue was traveling over every inch of this chest.

"I wasn't totally bored of this arrangement yet," she admits.

I exhale out the window. "All good things…"

Taking the joint from my lips, she comes to sit on the bed against the headboard while I find my shirt and put on my shoes.

"Yeah, okay," she answers. "I know the brush-off when I hear it."

"Whatever. We both know you'll barely miss me." She's never been the emotional type, and I don't expect she'll start now. She just likes giving me a hard time.

"I might," she protests, and I grin at that. "It does suck you won't be around for senior year."

"Yeah. Well, getting expelled took care of that."

"It was a bonehead move." She laughs at me. "Fucking amateur hour."

"Easy, cupcake."

Julie scoffs at my warning. "'Oh, look at me, I'm a solid C-student hacking my grades to give myself straight As. Hope no one notices.'"

"All right, I got greedy. I admit it. Lesson learned."

Honestly, I didn't think a few overworked, underpaid public school teachers with three jobs and two hundred students would be paying attention. Or even give a shit. It's not like I did it for myself, really. I thought it would be a nice birthday present for my mom. Make her feel good about herself, like I wasn't a complete screwup. I should've just gotten her some flowers. Or at least not tampered with the one class taught by the teacher who hated me more than paper cuts.

"Do yourself a favor." Julie snuffs out the joint and lights some incense on the nightstand. "Try to stay out of trouble."

I shrug. "That's impossible."

We say goodbye with a hug. It's more efficient this way. Clean and quick, no sense pretending either of us had a lot of emotion invested in this. Even if it wasn't just sex, I've changed schools enough to learn how to leave. When you move around a lot, you don't bother with many attachments. Everything ends.

At our little house on Phillips Avenue, I kill the engine of my old Jeep to find movers loading up a truck parked on the street. Before I even reach the front door, I can hear the screech of packing tape being pulled from the roll. Moving is practically a ritual in this family. The scent of cardboard. Empty rooms. Tiny particles caught midair in slanted sunbeams. These things are more familiar to me than chicken soup.

"Oh, RJ, there you are." Mom emerges from among the towers of boxes. She checks her watch with a frown. "The movers have been here for hours. Where were you?"

"Saying my goodbyes."

"Well, hurry up." She plants a thick black marker in my hand. "I need you to figure out what you want to bring to Greenwich, what to ship to New Hampshire, and what's getting donated."

"Donated?" I didn't know we were liquidating.

"Sure." Mom blows hair out of her eyes and wipes the sweat from her brow. She's got an almost frantic, giddy energy about her that is harshing my buzz a bit. "David already has furniture a hell of a lot nicer than this ratty old stuff. We're getting a fresh start. Clean slate."

"Okay, well, I'll leave you and your clichés to your work. I'm gonna throw some clothes in a bag and call it good."

"No, I'm serious. You'll need to do a little more than that." She all but drags me to my room, which the movers have already started dismantling into open boxes. "Labels. On everything, okay? Whatever you want sent to Sandover, make sure to mark it."

"Right. What about belts and shoelaces? Should I ship those? Don't want to get them confiscated by the warden."

Her face falls, and I know instantly I've stepped over the line. I don't always mean to be such an ass. Not to her, anyway.

Mom softens her tone. "Is that how you feel? Be honest, are you mad at me because I'm sending you to boarding school?"

"I was joking. It's fine."

"No, talk to me." She tugs my arm to sit on the bed beside her.

When I don't speak, she brushes my hair back, searching my face. Christ. It's always awkward when she gets all maternal on me. It's just not her natural state. Which isn't to say she's an awful mother.

We've always gotten along well. But as far as family ties go, ours have never been the strongest, what with her being gone a lot and generally being more interested in herself than anything I had going on.

I get it, though. She never set out to have a kid at nineteen. Shit happens. That she didn't leave me on a bus or outside a fire station is more than my dad ever gave us. So I can't really complain. But these heart-to-hearts don't come naturally to either of us. When the rare one occurs, it feels like we're impersonating characters we've seen on TV.

"This isn't punishment, you know? I'm not trying to get rid of you. David thought this would be a good experience. Maybe keep you out of trouble," she tactfully adds.

"Seriously, it's not a big deal." Given the choice, I'd rather not be trapped in that mansion with the two of them going at it all the time, worried about whether my mom had just been railed on the breakfast counter. "Besides, I'm used to being on own."

My childhood is a graveyard of microwave dinners and pizza boxes. You quickly learn to be self-sufficient when your mom is hopping all over the country as a flight attendant. I was thawing leftovers while she was hitting on bachelors in first class.

Guess it worked out for her after all.

"Well, luckily you won't be on your own at Sandover. You'll have Fennelly there with you," she says cheerfully. "He can show you the ropes."

I'm pretty sure the only place Pretty Boy will be showing me to is the liquor cabinet.

"And try to be patient with him, okay?" she continues. "David says Fennelly is still a bit put off by our marriage."

I can't help but laugh. "Put off? Mom, the dude's probably been up every night since the wedding googling how to get an annulment without you guys knowing."

Her smile falters. "He'll come around. Right?" I don't know if she's asking or telling.

"Sure," I lie. "Eventually."

"Maybe you can work on him, make him realize this new arrangement isn't all bad." She lifts a brow at me. "And as for you, maybe tone down the whole loner misfit vibe and try to make some friends?"

"I have friends," I grumble.

"Internet people don't count, RJ. Would it kill you to be more sociable?"

Sociable? Why the hell would I do that? I much prefer my "loner misfit" life, as she phrased it. Really, what's not to like? I make bank online. I'm good-looking enough that I don't have issues getting chicks, so hookups are plentiful. I don't need to buddy up to my classmates and pretend to give a shit about their sports teams and college plans. Sure, some might say I have major trust issues, but fuck 'em. I'm a lone wolf. Always have been, always will be.

"You're going to do great, bud." She kisses my temple and squeezes my face. "I have a good feeling about this. Okay?"

I give her the reassuring smile she wants. Mostly because I don't have the heart to tell her that if history is any predictor, we've got tickets to the shit show waiting at the box office.

CHAPTER 4
FENN

ALL THE FREAKS AND DEMONS COME OUT FOR AN END-OF-SUMMER house party. I've seen more nipple piercings than bikini tops, and I'm pretty sure that was Lawson I watched follow the Sear sisters into the back seat of his dad's Mercedes G-Class with a bottle of mezcal and a bag of coke. If we survive the night, senior year is going to be absurd.

Though I've known him for a few years now, I've only been in Lawson's Southampton house a couple of times. I don't think I've even seen every room. The estate is massive, that old-money Americana with all its palatial luxury. It has two pools, for Christ's sake. To this day, nobody can ever get a straight answer about what Lawson's dad does exactly. Well, other than being a grade-A prick. From what I've managed to glean, Mr. Kent is some kind of legal "consultant" who also dabbles in finance and has advised two White House administrations. Fingers in many pies and pockets.

"You lose your drink?" My buddy Silas finds me making my way back toward the sound of voices from one of the eleven bathrooms I had to hunt down to find an empty one. He puts a crystal tumbler in my hand. "Someone broke open the wine cellar."

I chuckle. "Man, Lawson's dad is going to take ten years off his life."

"For real. Where the hell is he, anyway? I haven't seen him since he lit that bonfire on the tennis court."

"He's in the garage, in the middle of a Sear sandwich."

Silas nods, because of course. Not that the guy isn't up for a good time, but he's as close as it gets to a chaperone at these things. There's no stopping a little property destruction or noise complaints, but Silas generally tries to keep the bodily harm and maiming to a minimum when he can. And to keep Lawson from decisions he'll regret. As if that's possible. The pay is shit and the hours suck, but Silas keeps at it anyway. He's a good dude, which is more than I can say for the rest of us.

We make the rounds through the house, every room a different Lynchian exploration of the adolescent condition. A couple of Ballard girls in cutoffs and tattoos invite us to a game of life-size chess with priceless sculptures they've collected from around the house. Silas nearly chokes on his anxiety getting away from them.

"You can't save him from himself," I remind Silas. Lawson is a creature of chaos. There's no harnessing that storm.

"Maybe. But I don't have to help make it worse."

We end up back at the lap pool where an otherwise tame tournament of naked chicken is underway. Just to get his mind off things, I introduce us to some fresh talent.

"Where do you go to school?" I ask the pair of nearly identical blondes. To be fair, I'm not quite seeing straight. In this light, I only see tits and hair color.

"Dalton," one says.

"In the city."

I lift my tumbler to my lips. "What grade are you in?"

I can see the inclination to lie before one of them loses her nerve and spits it out. "We're sophomores."

Silas shoots me a warning stare, signaling to abort.

"How do you know Lawson?" I ask suspiciously.

The girls look at each other and giggle in that mystical secret girl language. "From the city."

For fuck's sake. Lawson's already been here. Not that we haven't crossed paths before, so to speak, but I just can't get into it once I know he's already been with them.

"He does know everyone," I answer. "Silas isn't normally this talkative, by the way. I'm sorry he's monopolizing the conversation."

He flicks me off with a sarcastic grin.

Silas technically has a girlfriend, but she isn't here, and I've never been convinced those two are remotely compatible. They're more like two married people who've been together so long that breaking up seems like more effort than it's worth.

"How was your summer?" Silas reluctantly asks as an icebreaker when I nudge him. He can hate me now, but the guy needs to relax.

"I was obsessed with the summer Olympics," one of the chicks says. "Like, I spent six straight hours watching Korean archery and whatever. It's addictive."

"Hey, you know Silas here is a swimmer?" I tell her. "Show her your abs, bro."

"Stop," he chides me.

Her eyes go wide. "Oh, seriously? Swimmers are so hot."

I feel him groaning in his head. I almost expect him to push me into the deep end. But I catch a hot little brunette in a black bikini watching me from across the pool and zone out of the conversation until Silas pulls me away to pretend to refill our drinks at the keg.

"That was fucking brutal," he moans, scrubbing a hand over his close-cropped hair. "Do me a favor? Stop doing me favors."

"Oh, come on. Just a little kibble to take the edge off. You don't have to bang her. What's a BJ between strangers?"

"Dude, seriously, get a hobby."

"Where's Gabe when we need him? You wouldn't be such a buzzkill if he were here." I speak without thinking, only to instantly regret it. I don't need the reminder that life's been total shit since Gabe was sent away. He and I had never gone this long without talking, and it's fucking surreal that he's not here right now. The two of us have been tight since kindergarten.

"Still haven't heard from him?" Silas tips his head to study me.

"Nope. I texted his dad last week and got a reply a couple days ago basically telling me to piss off and lose his number."

"I don't get it." Silas has made attempts to contact Gabe as well, never getting any further than the rest of us. "Granted, Mr. Ciprian was never your biggest fan. But it's still messed up he won't even tell us where Gabe is. What happened to him. Like, he could have been hit by a bus for all we know. There one day, gone the next."

"It's a military school—we know that much," I remind Silas.

There's a wet *smack* that pierces my eardrums so loudly I flinch. It's Jesse Bushwell doing a belly flop off the roof of the pool house. There's stunned silence when his body just kind of floats there for a second. Then an eruption of cheers when his head pops up and he throws his arms in the air in triumph, his stomach looking like a porn star's ass in a spanking video.

"We do know he's at least alive, right?"

I glance back at Silas, nodding. "I managed to get a hold of his brother over the summer, but even Lucas doesn't know what place they shipped Gabe off to. He hasn't been home."

"I mean, I care about the guy too." Silas doesn't come about his tone of judgmental disapproval on purpose. He can't help having an overdeveloped sense of morality. "Not to sound glib, but the drug dealing was bound to catch up to him."

We're interrupted again, this time when someone turns up the music coming from the in-ground audio system. It was loud before. Now it's deafening. A moment later, Lawson makes a reappearance, wearing nothing but a pair of swim trunks and a cocky grin. The Sear sisters are nowhere to be found, but no worries—our buddy isn't alone for half a second before some chick sidles up to him. Another half-second and she's running her manicured fingernails all over his bare chest. I swear, dude's got game even when he's not playing.

Silas follows my gaze and shakes his head when we see the girl hold out her palm to offer Lawson whatever party favor she's enjoying. Gray eyes gleaming, he drags a hand through his messy hair, shoving it away from his forehead before he pops the tiny pill under his tongue and slings a muscular arm around the girl's waist. The guy just hooked up with two other chicks and is already on his third, and it's barely past midnight. Fuckboy doesn't begin to describe Lawson Kent.

"Gabe's about to get a new roommate in whatever hole his dad threw him in," Silas says with a sigh. For tonight, it seems, he's given up the leash and is resigned to let Lawson run wild. Sometimes you gotta know when you're beat.

I chug the rest of my drink, feeling glum again. "Fuck Gabe's dad. Hell, fuck all dads."

"Oh, yeah." A mocking grin spreads across his face. "I totally forgot! How was the wedding? Manage to catch your stepmom's name before they said their I do's?"

"Missy? Michelle? Who knows. I was high when I got there and drunk by the time we left. Told my dad's secretary to put it in a memo."

The chick seems nice enough, for a flight attendant who popped up out of nowhere. Call me crazy for being a little suspicious at the speed of this marriage. All I can say is, my dad better have secured her signature on a prenup before he married his fucking stewardess.

"What about your new stepbrother?"

"He's all right, I guess. Chill. Sort of aloof, if anything. Turns out he's taking Gabe's spot in the dorm, so we'll be roommates."

Silas grins, and I don't think I like him having a laugh at my expense. "Nothing like a little forced bonding to bring a family together. What'd he do to end up on the Island of Misfit Boys?"

"Just your standard grand theft auto," I say with a wink. "So you two should get along great."

"Yeah, screw you."

That smacks the smile off Silas's face. He tends to get a little touchy about the time he got expelled from Ballard for getting wasted and crashing the principal's car into the goalpost on the football field. How he managed to aim the car at the smallest target on an empty field, I don't know. Just lucky, I guess.

My phone goes off in my pocket, and I pull it out to see a text that makes my pulse quicken.

Casey: So when are you getting back to campus? We need to hang out.

"That your new roomie?" Silas taunts.

"Nah. Just Casey." Once again I speak without thinking, forgetting that my boys don't actually know about this particular friendship of mine.

"Seriously?" Silas cocks an eyebrow at me. Damn, it really is no fun being on the rotten end of those looks.

"What?"

"Fuck you, 'what?' She's a good girl, Fenn. And a junior."

"It's not like that." I shrug. "We've been talking a little over the summer, that's all. Not a big deal."

"So you're friends now?"

"Why's that weird? We connected after her accident. You were there with me, remember? When we dropped by to see how she was doing?"

He flinches at the memory. Casey's accident always triggers that response in people. It puts a heaviness in my gut that hasn't subsided even a little since last semester. If anything, the pit gets deeper.

"Didn't realize you were getting her fucking number when I turned my back for a second." He pauses ominously. "Sloane won't like this."

"Sloane knows all about our friendship and she's cool with it."

I'm only half lying. Yes, Casey's sister knows we're friends. But she sure isn't cool with it.

Silas rolls his eyes. "Yeah, no. I wasn't born yesterday. Sloane is probably throwing a fit."

"Oh no! And we can't upset your best friend Sloane," I say sarcastically. "God forbid."

He frowns for a beat, before shaking his head in resignation. "Just try not to break that poor girl's heart, man."

"It's nothing, Si. Just chill."

He watches me warily. "I want to believe you."

"So do it."

"Thing is, I've known you a minute."

Awesome. Nice to know even one of my best friends thinks I'm a selfish bastard. "I'm not putting the moves on Casey. She's the furthest thing from my type."

In fact, Miss Brunette in the Black Bikini meets my eyes as she grabs two bottles of beer and disappears around the side of the house.

Don't mind if I do.

"Now if you'll excuse me," I tell Silas. "I'm being summoned by someone who *is* my type."

He shouts "safety first" after me, and I give him the one-finger salute as I walk off.

No one understands better than I do how poisonous someone like me would be for a girl like Casey. I just don't have the nerve to tell her.

Or maybe I'm just the selfish bastard Silas thinks I am.

CHAPTER 5
RJ

IT'S LIKE SOMETHING OUT OF A HORROR MOVIE. THE LAND ROVERS unloading students and cardboard boxes against the backdrop of an orange sky. Pan to the bell tower as night falls and close in on the lonely freshman being stalked through the courtyard by a shadowy figure with a meat hook. Just saying, there's a reason so many of these movies take place at secluded prep schools in the exclusive New England enclaves.

"Let us know if you forgot something," Mom says, combing her fingers through my hair like I'm a pet she's dropping off at the vet. "We'll have it overnighted."

"Use the credit cards if you need something in the meantime," David tells us.

It's Friday afternoon and our parents are dropping Fenn and me off in front of the senior dorm. They insisted on making the trip with us, a fact Fenn protested until the moment the car pulled up to the curb.

"Yep, top marks, David." Fenn doesn't spare a glance from his phone to get in another jab at his father. "Dad of the year. You can go now."

It's been like that since we left the house. And by house, I'm referring to the disgustingly lavish Greenwich mansion where my mother and I now reside. Granted, I was only there two days before it was time to leave for New Hampshire, so, really, I barely got a chance to peek into all ten bedrooms and twelve bathrooms. For all I know, the rest of the house is a dump. I mean, I only spotted *one* thousand-dollar espresso machine in the chef's kitchen that was bigger than our old house in Windsor. Who are these peasants?

Mom's been floating on cloud nine since the move. She'd served rich folks in first class my whole life, and now she's one of them and loves every second of it. I can't even count the number of times she whispered, "I feel like a princess" into my ear while David's household staff served our dinner last night.

Me, I just felt out of place. My scuffed-up Converses don't belong on marble floors. My stubble-covered face shouldn't be peering into gold-gilded mirrors in my own private bathroom with a jacuzzi tub. And I didn't even have time to dwell on the total lifestyle rehaul before being carted off again.

"If you need anything, let us know." David looks to me now, because his son can't be bothered to acknowledge him. "Call any time, day or night. We're here for you."

"Come on." Fenn slings his leather duffel bag over his shoulder and gives me a nod. "We're on the third floor."

Mom grabs me for one last hug. She gets a little red in the eyes, but I suspect the tears will clear up the second those two are alone. Maybe shipping me off wasn't her idea, but she got on board with it quick.

I'll say this much—of all the prisons I could have ended up in, Sandover Prep is not the worst.

Inside, everything is mahogany and leather. Paintings in gilded frames line the wide corridors, which feel more like a museum than a cage for high school deviants. It's a long way from the lowest-bidder corporate design solutions of the typical public school or state college dorm.

"There's a common room through there." Fenn points toward it when we reach our floor. "They call it the Lounge. One of two shared bathrooms over there."

Fenn nods as we pass a dude with messy shoulder-length hair and a movie-star face. Shirtless and wearing only a pair of black silk boxers, he's hanging out of his doorway with an unlit cigar in his mouth and a snifter in hand like he's hosting a Playboy Bunny party in there. The guy quirks a brow, amusement dancing in his silvery eyes when he notices me. I have a feeling he won't be the first to question what a punk like me in ripped jeans and an old band shirt is doing in a place like this.

"And this is us." Fenn stops at the third door from the end of the hall.

The room is bigger than I expected. It has a large sitting area in the middle, with a couch, couple of armchairs, and sixty-five-inch TV. On either side of the room are two full-size beds, tall dressers, desks, and matching closets. Everything is trimmed in wood and hideous wallpaper of a duck hunt or something. The boxes we sent ahead last week are already here, stacked up behind the leather couch.

"We get decent Wi-Fi?" I ask Fenn.

"Sometimes? I don't really spend enough time in my room to notice."

I scan the spacious area. I guess I can always run an Ethernet cable when I find the router. The first box I crack open has my computer gear. As my new stepbrother watches in dismay, I waste no time installing my monitors and booting up my machine to make sure the movers didn't kick the thing all the way from Connecticut to Sandover.

"What's all this about?" Fenn hovers over my shoulder. "Please don't tell me you're one of those Twitch bros."

"Nah, I'm not a gamer."

"What's this shit for then?"

"Side projects."

"Lame." He kicks my rolling chair, pushing me away from the desk.

If I weren't on my best behavior, we might have a problem. Dude doesn't need to get the impression he can do that twice. But I let it slide—this time.

"You're new here, so let me help you out," he says. "We can't have you getting a reputation as a loser on day one."

"I couldn't give a shit about my reputation." It's not like I landed in this place for being a social climber.

"Yeah, well, you don't know any better." He throws open our door and jerks his head at me. "Things work different around here. So get your ass out of that chair, *Remington*. Gotta show my new stepbro off to the rest of the floor."

I swallow a sigh. Whatever. I have the rest of the semester to sit in this room bored out of my mind. Might as well get the lay of the land.

For the next twenty minutes, Fenn introduces me around our floor. I meet guys with names like Xavier, Shepley, and Tripp, who all look the same to me, a blur of designer clothes and expensive watches. Eventually we end up back at the Playboy room, where I'm introduced to Lawson, who's finally put on some pants. He's still shirtless, but at least his package isn't in my line of vision anymore.

"Hey," he says. "Welcome, make yourselves at home."

"RJ, this is Lawson. Don't take pills from him."

Lawson grins at Fenn. "Fuck off."

The guy is tall, around my height, with a few lines of text tattooed on the left side of his ribcage. I can't make out the words, but I imagine it's something angsty and irrelevant. With his big frame and tousled hair, Lawson gives off a real Tim Riggins from *Friday Night Lights* vibe. And I'm only familiar with goddamn Tim Riggins because Julie used to make me watch the show between rounds of sex while I protested the whole time. I fucking hate sports.

"Hey, I'm Silas."

I hadn't noticed the second guy sitting on his bed. He's one of those people your eye loses in the scenery if they stop moving. Cropped hair, hazel eyes, generically handsome features. When he stands, though, he's taller than he looked. Both he and Lawson have an athlete's build. I peg them as rowers maybe. Something posh. I can't imagine either of them in any kind of contact sport.

"So. RJ." Lawson offers me a drink from a liquor cart sunken inside the sofa under the seat cushion. "What's your deal?"

Why does everyone keep asking me that? "Don't have one."

Lawson glances at Silas. "So coy." Then he throws himself in one of the armchairs, feet up on the coffee table. "None of us ended up here by accident. We all get into something."

I shrug.

"Hey, if you run, it'll only make me chase you." Lawson picks a half-smoked cigar out of an ashtray on the table and lights it.

"Stop flirting," Fenn tells him.

"Just making friends, Fennelly. Jeez." Lawson studies me again, amused. "Whatever your side hustle is," he warns me, "keep it close to the vest. You don't want Duke peeking at your cards."

I can't help but laugh at that. "You have a den mother?"

"A housefather, actually," Silas says ruefully. "Mr. Swinney."

"Don't worry. Roger's a puppy," Lawson adds.

"About as intimidating as a goldendoodle with cataracts." Fenn's voice is absentminded. He's on his phone again. He's been texting with someone named Casey all afternoon, but when I asked if she was his girlfriend, he recoiled in horror. I guess *girlfriend* is a bad word around here.

"Duke is another senior. Fancies himself a rottweiler." Lawson pauses. "Although I guess he is one. He's definitely got the bite to back up that bark. But I don't want to get ahead of myself. You'll run into him sooner or later."

So apparently Duke is what passes for the muscle around here. I'll have to see what I can dig up on him, find out how much real trouble he's capable of. Either way, I'm not about to be intimidated by some soft-ass prep school rich boy.

"Well, Remington." Lawson grins at me, and I glare at Fenn for outing me. "Welcome to Bendover Prep. Turn your head and cough. It'll only hurt a little."

Charming.

A short while later, we make our way to the Lounge with the rest of the guys on the floor for a mandatory house rules meeting. The halls already stink of pot, and I think I saw a still in one room on the way over here, which I assume is more of a hobby than necessity. Seems like there isn't any security to speak of, in terms of sifting out the contraband.

"All right, gentlemen, quiet down."

A man in a brown blazer and glasses stands at the front of the room. Frazzled and unkempt, he looks like he got dressed in his car. He clears his throat a few times, failing to get the attention of the three dozen guys piled on the couches and scrolling on their phones.

"Come on, eyes up," he pleads. "This will only take a minute." If anything, the room gets louder. "Please, the sooner we start, the quicker this will be over with."

It goes on like that for several minutes. I'm an asshole, so I'm struggling not to laugh at his plight. The poor dude even leaves at one point and comes back to give it another go. Until Silas, either out of pity or boredom, finally gets everyone to shut up long enough for the housefather to say his piece.

"Seriously?" I whisper to Fenn, as Roger Swinney recites a list of rules. "Eleven o'clock curfew on weeknights?"

"Nah, it's more like a loose suggestion. Just don't get caught."

"What about the headmaster? I've got a meeting with him later."

If Mr. Swinney is any indication, the faculty around here doesn't have a firm grip on the inmates. More like a truce.

"He's not a pushover, but not like a hard ass either. He's the type who wants to be everyone's guidance counselor." Fenn rolls his eyes before his expression turns serious. "The only real rule—stay away from his daughters. He'll have you on a spit if you go anywhere near them without his permission."

When the locals grow restless, the housefather gives up trying to keep their attention and dismisses us all.

"Dinner out tonight?" Lawson offers as we head back to our rooms. "Announce ourselves to the townsfolk in proper fashion?"

Why do I get the impression for him that means nailing the blacksmith's daughter on the church steps?

"Pass," I tell them. "Maybe next time."

"Remington is antisocial," Fenn informs his buddies.

No, Remington just has research to do and would prefer some privacy.

But I keep that revelation to myself. These guys don't need to learn I'm about to unearth their deepest, darkest secrets. What they don't know can't hurt 'em, et cetera et cetera.

Well, unless I decide to hurt them with whatever I discover.

Either way, it's time to get a closer look at my cellmates.

CHAPTER 6
RJ

I'VE NEVER BEEN OFFERED TEA FROM A MAN IN A CARDIGAN BEFORE. The headmaster invites me into his office, and we sit in a couple of high-back leather chairs while he crosses his legs and holds the cup and saucer like he's Mr. Fucking Rogers or some shit. Even at nearly nightfall it's still gotta be eighty degrees outside, but he looks like he's ready to cozy around the fireplace with NPR.

"We're pleased to welcome you to Sandover, Mr. Shaw. I understand you don't care to be called Remington."

"RJ's fine." If he calls me Sport, I'm outta here.

"As you wish." He takes another unbothered sip, eyeing me over the rim of the prissy teacup. "What would you say your goals are this semester, RJ?"

"Goals?"

"How do you intend to spend your time with us? What do you hope to accomplish?"

I'm pretty sure this is a mind game, even if I don't know its purpose yet.

"Graduate, I guess. That's the point, isn't it?"

"At minimum, yes. But I'd hope you could find other ways you also might enrich your experience here. Make the most of this opportunity. Have you considered where you'll apply to college?"

"Can't say I have."

College was never something that was high on my priority list. If I'm being honest, it seems like a complete waste of time and money. Considering where my interests lie, I can't see what college would have to offer that I can't manage to figure out on my own.

"I'd encourage you to investigate some of the many extracurriculars available. They do tend to keep our students out of trouble," he says with that polite pointedness that somehow makes it ruder.

"I'm not much of a joiner. Clubs aren't my thing."

"So I understand."

Ha. If he thinks getting a look at my records is a threat, he underestimates me. As if I'd ever go into any new interaction completely blind—I started my homework weeks ago. Oh, yes, I've been reading up on Headmaster Tresscott. Father of two. Wife deceased. Suffers from an incurable hero complex. The man fills the void of his soul by trying to save the wealthy wayward youth who get stashed here like boxes of winter clothes in the attic. He doesn't scare me, and his boring speech does nothing to pump me up.

"We maintain a high academic standard at this institution. Sandover sends our graduates to elite universities and ensures they're well-prepared for the rigors of higher education. This isn't a place to simply pass the time."

I don't know. Seems to me the reputation of "elite institutions" is based on the hollow shell of legacy admissions and wealth. It's just a bunch of fancy people getting together to perpetuate the myth for the protection of their own image. If I threw on a Harvard sweater, no one would know the difference.

Still, I smile and nod because mouthing off on day one makes me an enemy, and I don't need the extra scrutiny.

"So we're clear…" he says, setting aside his drink. "Hacking, or any other type of invasive and duplicitous activities, won't be tolerated here. We expect our students to embody our values of dignity, respect, and honesty, without exception. Sandover is a second chance.

For many, a last chance." His dark-gray eyes sweep over me. "What you choose to do with it is up to you. As long as you're here, you will abide by our rules."

Uh-huh. For all his talk about values and what he will or will not tolerate, I'm fairly confident it's a bunch of bullshit. During my research, I managed to peek at some faculty records. Near as I can tell, it's impossible to get kicked out of Sandover. So Tresscott can say what he wants about rules and responsibility, but I know better. Whatever infractions these Sandover boys commit are nothing enough zeros can't solve. Mommy and Daddy cut another check, and all's forgotten. It's the oldest truth there is—wealth is immune to consequences.

"Let's level with each other, yeah?" The thing I hate most about rich people and those that surround them is all the polite pretension. "I didn't ask to be here and wasn't given a choice. I don't plan on being a pain in your ass. If that changes…"

Tresscott watches me carefully.

"Well, we're only upright animals in fancy clothes, right? Can't fight the forces of nature."

"No," he says, picking up his cup and saucer again. "I suppose not."

"So can I go now?"

"One last thing. Are you an athlete, Mr. Shaw? I didn't see any sports in your transcripts."

"Not my thing, no." Since freshman year, various coaches have hounded me to try out for one thing or another. Always telling me I've got the build for it. But team activities aren't my jam. Forced camaraderie is my worst nightmare, and I've heard enough locker room horror stories to prefer to meet my hazing in the daylight.

"You'll have to enroll in phys ed, then," he informs me. "It provides a rotation throughout the semester in several athletics."

Great. That's going to be a problem. I'll need to see what I can do about opting into something solitary. Track, maybe. I'm a decent runner. At home, I used to run all the time. It started with having to get out of the house when Mom brought her boyfriends around and closed her bedroom door, but eventually it became a habit. A couple of miles at first, then longer distances. It helps me clear my head.

After Tresscott lets me go, I wander the grounds for a while, finding the marked trails around the outskirts of the campus that wind through the surrounding forest. It's nearly dark and I don't want to be stumbling around trying to find my way back to the dorm after sunset, so I start back in that direction when I notice a narrow dirt path disappearing deep into the trees. It's unmarked and looks less worn by foot traffic than the other routes, which instantly sparks my interest. I decide I've got enough time for a quick pit stop. A hundred yards in or so, there's an old flowerbed overgrown with weeds; right beyond it is a wooden bench in the center of a small clearing.

It's not a bad place to have a smoke, and I waste no time rolling a quick joint. Sitting on the bench with my legs stretched out in front of me, I inhale a deep drag and try to decompress for a minute.

I'm used to upheaval. After five schools in three years, you either learn resiliency or find yourself disappearing beneath the waves. It feels like I've been treading water my whole life, but, hell, if nothing else, it's taught me I can count on myself. There's no need for me to rely on anyone else, because at the end of the day, I'm the only one who has my back. And whatever comes, I've always got another move.

A rustling noise jars me from my thoughts, shifting my attention in the direction of it. I hear the racing footsteps battering the dead leaves and dry grass just before she comes around the bend. A leggy chick with dark hair tied up in a sweaty knot. She nearly runs past me before jerking her head and sliding to a halt.

"Hey," I say lightly.

"You're not supposed to be here," she huffs out, hands on her hips and chest heaving to catch her breath.

"Yeah. I keep telling them that."

Her cropped T-shirt hangs off one shoulder. My eyes get trapped tracing her ass in a pair of tiny running shorts that cling to her sweat-slick skin. This girl is so hot, it almost hurts to look at her. And it's not just the smoke-show body. Her complexion, even coated with a sheen of sweat, is totally flawless, incandescent, the type of skin you see in makeup ads. Her dark-gray eyes are framed by full, thick lashes, and her lips have that cupid's bow thing going on, that sexy curve that puts all sorts of dirty ideas in my head.

I don't know which scenario is more appealing—having those lips pressed against mine in a hot kiss or wrapped around my dick while I come on her tongue.

Annnd, shit, I need to banish those thoughts ASAP before she notices my jeans are looking a bit too tight all of a sudden.

"No." She stands upright, scowling. "I mean this trail is out of bounds. You're trespassing."

I can't help but give her another lingering once-over. "You sure you're not the one in the wrong place? Isn't this an all-boys school?"

"My dad works here. Who the hell are you?" The girl could light fires with those eyes. Burn down small towns with her glare.

"Not very friendly, are we?" I can't help but mock.

"Not usually, no. Answer me."

Oh man, I have a serious thing for angry chicks. I don't know what it is about a girl with a chip on her shoulder who looks at me like she wants to kick my teeth in, but it makes my dick twitch.

"My name's RJ," I answer dutifully. "I'm new."

"No shit." She cocks her head, impatient. "What decaying suburban sidewalk did they scrape you off of?"

Fuck, sweetheart. Say less.

When I see her eye my joint, I hold it out to her. "Want a hit?"

She works her jaw, that intense gaze sizing me up. Then she snatches it from my hand to take in a couple deep drags, proceeding to blow the smoke in my face as if I'm not already turned on.

"Do I get your name?" I ask her, fighting a grin.

"No." She hands the joint back.

I suddenly hear Lawson in my head. *If you run, it'll only make me chase you.*

"Well, shit. What do I write when I'm carving our names in a tree?"

"Wow." She barks out a laugh. "Do you know you said that out loud? 'Cause that was embarrassing."

"Nah. It's pretty hard to insult me," I tell her.

"I'd try if I cared."

Everything about her tells me to fuck off, but she's still here. And I'm not sure what it says about me that I kind of like the abuse. I'd let this chick walk on my face with a pair of combat boots. The hostility just makes me imagine loud, hair-pulling sex.

"We could grab some dinner and you could give it your best shot," I offer.

"Sorry. I don't go out with randos I meet in the woods."

"You run into a lot of those out here? Because I could walk you home. You know, for protection."

She scoffs, rolling her eyes. "I can take care of myself."

"Then walk me home."

The slightest tug of a smile curves her lips and disappears just as quickly. Oh yeah, she definitely likes me.

"Watch out for the raccoons," she warns as she starts to walk away. "Some idiot spent a semester dosing them with LSD, and now they're like deranged little science experiments with opposable thumbs and no regard for human life."

She's probably kidding. I think.

"Same time tomorrow?" I call after her. "I'll supply the refreshments."

She doesn't bother to look back. "Have a nice life, rookie. Good luck in Boys Town."

She's out of sight in seconds as I realize she's left me in near total darkness. It's as if she yanked the sun out of the sky to spite me.

It's fucking hot.

That girl's the poisoned tip of a dart, and I'm so into it I can't wipe the smile off my face. I guess this place won't be a total bummer after all.

If I manage find my way back to civilization.

CHAPTER 7
SLOANE

I DON'T KNOW WHAT TO MAKE OF THE GUY ON THE TRAIL. OR WHY he looked at me like we've always known each other. Back home, I take a quick shower to wash off the sweat from my run. I'm brushing out my hair at my desk when Casey pokes her head in my room. She makes herself comfortable by plopping down on my bed to watch me with the gleam of a burning query dancing in her eyes.

"What?" I catch her stare in my mirror, instantly suspicious.

"Good run?"

"Fine. What's with the smile?"

"You were gone a long time." Her conspiratorial grin absorbs her face. "One might think you didn't go for a run at all, but instead went to see, oh, I don't know, maybe someone whose name starts with a D and ends with an –uke?"

"One might be dead wrong," I answer with a snort. "I told you, Duke and I are done."

"Then what took you so long?"

"There was some random guy on the trail. I thought a townie had wandered onto campus, so I stopped to interrogate him."

"Ha!" she pounces. "So you *were* talking to a boy."

"Wasn't much of a conversation."

It destroyed my whole run, in fact. Like a burst of buckshot right through my chill. My trail is my sanctuary, where I go to turn down the volume on my thoughts and escape whatever is piling up in my head. It's my unreachable dimension. An escape hatch from my life. A perfectly preserved oasis of peace. And here's some inter- loper, some tourist, helping himself to my forest of solitude? And then he's got the nerve to flirt with me, and what, I'm supposed to find it charming? Fuck off, trespasser.

"So was he a lost townie?"

"No, apparently he's new."

Although his major malfunction is yet to be determined. Most of them are the standard-issue rich delinquents showing up with aggressive alcoholism and untreated drug addictions. Whether my dad likes it or not, Sandover is the quiet, picturesque diversion program that keeps the hit-and-run drivers, bar fighters, dealers, and gamblers out of prison and the tabloids.

"But you were out there for a while." In Casey's imagination, the mundane moments of my life are somehow filled with scandal. "Didn't you learn anything about him?"

"His name's RJ. That's about it. I didn't stick around for his biography."

Most people who know me would say I have a talent for being off-putting. I sort of pride myself on my ability to send boys running for their lives. I don't know if this one was dumb or had a death wish, but he wasn't budging.

"Initials are so mysterious," Casey declares.

"If you say so."

"Is he hot?"

"He's not a hideous forest troll, I guess."

On first impressions, sure, he was nice to look at. Fine. He was *very* nice to look at. Something about his hair reminded me of getting undressed. The way it looks after a guy pulls off his shirt. He had dark hair too. I like guys with dark hair. And even with him sitting down, I could tell he was tall, his body ripped. I'm a big fan of those qualities too.

But that doesn't mean I get all dewy-eyed over every tall, dark, and handsome guy I come across. Especially when they have those up-to-no-good eyes. The ones that wink at you with a smile while they're holding up a bank. Getting mixed up with another bad boy is not part of my senior plan.

"Coming from you, that's a huge compliment," Casey accuses. "Admit it, you think he's hot."

"I said he's not hideous."

"Come on, you can do it. Tell me you think he's hot." My sister is clearly enjoying watching me squirm.

"Oh my God. He's hot. There. Happy now?"

She smiles smugly. "Quite."

"You're such a brat."

"Takes one to know one," she says in a singsong voice, and I promptly give her the finger.

"Honestly, I'm more interested in why I haven't heard of him yet," I admit, more to myself than her, as I lie down on the floor with my foam roller to work out some tightness in my legs. "Who is this guy? Where'd he come from? Who's his family, you know? It's like he fell out of the sky. Something about him… He was kind of insufferable, but not with the same smarmy, overindulged ego of most of those pricks. It was like his own special concoction of irritating."

Casey crawls to the end of the bed, peering over the edge so she can see my face. "Those are a lot of questions for someone who said she's swearing off boys this year."

"Doesn't mean I'm trying to date him. He's an unknown. You know me, I don't like question marks."

Guys around here like to sneak up on you with those charming smiles and lying white teeth. They possess just enough breeding and manners to get your guard down, but really, they're wolves in designer jeans. And I'm nobody's mark.

"I don't know..." She bites her lip at me. I don't like it when her wheels start turning. "Sounds to me like he got under your skin maybe."

"You're grasping."

"If you say so."

My phone buzzes on top of my dresser. "Grab that, will you?"

She hops off the bed and checks my phone screen. "It's a text from Silas."

I sit up and skim the message, which is basically just letting me know he's back on campus. I tell him to come over. We didn't see each other all summer, and I've missed him.

Among the trash of high society that gets flushed downstream to Sandover, Silas Hazelton is the rare exception, a genuinely nice guy who isn't working on his twelve steps or growing into a future sociopath. How he maintains his kindness in that cesspool of self-indulgence is a mystery, but he's the only honest boy at Sandover. Which is why he's also the only one Dad lets in the house.

Silas: On my way.

When I answer the door ten minutes later, Silas greets me with, "Hey, stranger." He's wearing khakis, a white T-shirt that clings to his rock-hard abs, and a cheeky smile.

We're such close friends, sometimes I forget he's kind of a snack. But with those dimples and his swimmer's build, I can't deny he's looking yummy.

"You're in a good mood," I tease as he pulls me toward him.

"Missed your face." He gives me a tight hug and kisses my temple. Of the truly great hugs in the universe, his are up there.

"Silas, welcome back." Dad noses in, standing in the foyer with a cup of tea. Just his subtle way of making sure I haven't developed a sudden and uncontrollable sexual attraction to one of my best friends. "Settling in all right?"

"Yes, sir. Can't say I miss the smell in the junior dorm. The senior building is a rose garden compared to last year's rooms." Silas is basically catnip for parents, way too good at the small talk.

Dad chuckles. "We put a fresh coat of paint in over the summer."

"Get in some fishing during the break, sir?"

"Not as much as I'd have liked."

They chat about fishing for a bit, my dad thrilled to have another dude with whom to discuss the boring topics his daughters don't give a shit about. And despite the drunk driving incident that landed Silas at Sandover, he's never been in trouble, so I guess that's why Dad has a soft spot for him. Figures he's a good influence on me.

Dad tolerated Duke. Barely. We were at each other's throats for weeks when I first got together with Duke, until I finally made my dad realize it was better to know who I'm spending time with, and let it happen where he can mostly keep an eye on us, than have me sneaking around behind his back with random strangers. I'm not sure Dad appreciated the ultimatum, but he came around to the idea. He still hated Duke's guts, though.

"The trout were a bit smaller than—"

"Cool, thanks, Dad," I interrupt. "He doesn't want to hear about your trout."

Silas is too polite to rescue himself, so I grab him by the arm and pull him toward the staircase. Dad skulks around at the foot of the stairs for a moment before retreating to the den. And in about ten minutes, he'll casually walk past my bedroom door and pretend not to eavesdrop, and I'll pretend not to know. It's practically a routine now.

"So…" We plop down on the bed, and I turn on the TV to give us some noise protection. "You're back."

"Afraid so."

"And how was the *Vineyard*?"

He rolls his eyes at the way I emphasize the word. I can't help giving him some shit over being a hoity little nerd, running around the island in polos and Sperrys like a preppy golf cart mafia. Silas is obnoxiously close with his perfect *Full House* family, who spend their summers boating and hosting lobster boils. It's adorable and disgusting.

"It was good."

I study his face, noting the reddish tinge to it. "Did you actually get a tan?"

"My sisters let me fall asleep on the floating dock," he grumbles, "and I woke up looking like human jerky. Last week was my molting season."

"Poor baby." I do feel bad for him. Silas can get a sunburn just sitting too close to a window. "Have you seen Amy yet?" I ask.

He hesitates, a response I've noticed more often lately. He and Amy have been together since freshman year when they both started at Ballard Academy, where we all met. He'd never say it himself, but I've started to wonder if he isn't still with her out of habit more than interest.

"She doesn't get in until later. We'll probably meet up over the weekend."

"How's that going?"

"Yeah, good."

I stay quiet, letting him try to convince himself first. When it doesn't take, he shrugs.

"She wanted to come out to Martha's Vineyard, but her parents wouldn't let her. They were on her grandparents' ranch for a big family reunion or something. She didn't take it well," he admits.

"If you're not careful, you're going to wake up married to her."

"Why do you do that?" A sigh punctuates his frustration as he sits up.

"What?"

"You know what. You're always picking at things."

"How?" I try not to laugh when he scowls at me, and fail miserably. "I'm just saying, if you're not going to stick your oar in the water, you're at the mercy of the current."

"Yeah, and how's things with, oh, wait, you don't have a boyfriend.

Because you're off self-centered douchebags with hyperinflated egos this week, right?"

"Touché, dickwad."

Silas smothers a grin. "How was Colorado?"

"Ugh. Nightmare. We get there and find out my aunt just got dumped by her boyfriend, so I spent six weeks on her roller coaster of grief. I ate three gallons of mint chocolate chip and had eight pedicures, Silas. Do you understand me? More people have touched my toes than a truck stop gas pump."

He snickers loudly. "Seems like there's a side hustle in a combination of those interests somewhere."

I swipe him over the head with a throw pillow. He bats it away.

"What?" He laughs. "Just, you know, if you need money for running shoes or whatever."

"Speaking of running, actually. I was on the trail today and ran into one of your strays."

"My strays?"

"Looked like a senior. Some guy named RJ."

He nods with recognition. "Yeah, I met him during move-in. That's Fenn's new stepbrother."

My jaw drops. "Oh, shit. I forgot about the whirlwind wedding. But you didn't tell me he was coming here. What'd he do?"

It's the first question everyone asks. What heinous affront to civil order did the new kid commit to be remanded to this ivory penitentiary? For the guys, it's their way of sizing each other up and finding their position in the power structure. For me, it's mostly curiosity and so that I know who to steer clear from.

"He told Fenn some story about joyriding in a teacher's car," Silas answers. "After meeting the guy, Lawson is suspicious."

"Joyriding? Sounds kind of tame." As far as offenses go, it's hardly the worst.

"Or it's flat bullshit," Silas says with a shrug. "Covering for something worse. He was cagey. Not super sociable either."

"Yeah, I talked to him a little. He seemed awfully sure of himself for someone who has no idea where he is."

"Wouldn't be the first to show up in denial."

He makes a good point. Everyone copes with incarceration differently. Some cling to their old lives, while others learn to embrace the suck. RJ struck me as someone capable of the latter, but he was a bit too chill about it all. A few weeks of dealing with Duke and his crew, and RJ might be singing a different tune. Sandover has the power to eat a guy alive if he doesn't adapt fast.

"What else have you heard about him? Fenn give you the download?"

Silas flinches at the question, oddly put off. "Why do you care?"

"I don't. Not really." My brow furrows. "Why do you?"

"It's just weird, is all. I didn't see your name on the welcome committee roster." He offers another shrug, this one teeming with apathy. "Like I said, the guy's cagey. Evasive. I got a bad vibe."

The groove in my forehead deepens. His reaction is especially strange because, as a rule, Silas likes everybody. Well, until they give him a good reason not to, and even that takes some doing. He's put up with Lawson for years, and that guy's a walking true crime podcast.

We stare at each other for a moment, as if we suddenly don't recognize the other. An odd standoff ensues, before the awkwardness gets so torturous, I open my mouth just to make it stop.

"Sorry I asked." It's my turn to shrug. "Anyway, I really don't care about Fenn's new stepbrother. I was just curious."

Silas relaxes, and the subject shifts back to our summers, his time at the Vineyard. Except RJ lingers in the background, more unknowns now milling about in my head, kicking at the walls. It's annoying as hell, the fact that we spoke for all of ten minutes and yet he's gotten under my skin.

This guy's already becoming more trouble than he's worth.

CHAPTER 8
SILAS

Sloane says I'm one of her best friends, but sometimes I wonder if she knows what that means. She's one of those people who are hard to get close to. You think you know them, that you're in there, but then they rearrange the furniture, and you realize you were only ever talking to a reflection of a reflection in a hall of mirrors, still totally out of reach.

Not that I want her within my reach. At least not in *that* way, I remind myself as I trudge down the path toward campus. Despite what Lawson thinks, I'm not playing a long game with the intention of getting in Sloane's pants. Sure, I may have entertained the idea a time or two back in the day when we were at Ballard Academy. But Sloane and I never went there. She met Duke, and then I met Amy, and whatever attraction I felt had fizzled out.

I mean, obviously I still think she's hot, but…whatever. Why am I even thinking about this right now? We're just friends.

Back at my dorm, I get a text and know before I glance at the screen it's Amy wondering why I haven't texted her yet. Over the summer we developed a schedule, a routine of appointment texts and phone calls to appease the strain of distance. Which is fine. I don't mind. Except lately I've run out of words to use. I cringe at myself repeating the same Pavlovian responses, unable to break the pattern. I'm like a robot scanning her texts for keywords and accessing a programmed reply.

Amy: Saw Sun today. She says hi.
Me: Hi.
Amy: She hacked all her hair off and pierced her nose. Looks like she did it herself with a bread knife and a knitting needle. I feel so bad for her. She's going to get destroyed on Monday.
Me: That sucks.
Amy: Yeah, she's in rebellion mode. Murphy sent her a dick pic meant for someone else. There was still lipstick around it. He tried to play it off, but...

I stare at the latest text, wondering why we're dissecting the appearance and love life of some chick I barely know. I've only met Sun like once. What do I care?

The window rattles across the room. A second later, a girl in a short skirt and tank top tumbles inside. She picks herself up, giggling, as tiny bottles of liquor fall out of her hands and clatter on the wood floor like a melody of tinkling piano keys.

She gathers the bottles as if she's shoplifting, then tosses her dark hair back to look up and find me watching her. I don't know what I expect, but she smiles at me.

"Hi there."

Then Lawson barrels through the window next. "See? That wasn't so hard."

"Your friend's cute," she says, still eyeing me.

"I keep telling him that," Lawson drawls. "But he's no fun."

"We could make it a party." Window Girl shakes a handful of mini vodka bottles at me. "If Friend wants to join."

"Friend does not," I tell Lawson with a pointed glare.

"You said you were going out."

"It was a short visit."

He shrugs with an unapologetic smile because Lawson is never sorry.

It takes them no time to down a couple bottles and then start making out on Lawson's bed across the room from mine. Breathy noises and the soft squeak of bedsprings greet my ears.

Amy: You still there, baby?
Me: Yeah, sorry. Lawson just walked in.

Window Girl is probably the prettiest townie in her school. I bet she's popular and in love with life. She'll make friends at a good state college and graduate with prospects of a decent job that will propel her to a comfortable if unremarkable life in the suburbs with a husband of average achievement. And sometimes, when she's out drinking with the girls, she'll see a handsome younger man give her a courtesy smile over a shot of tequila and she'll remember the time she climbed through some hot rich boy's window.

Lawson won't remember her face by morning.

Window Girl glances at me over his shoulder when they unlock their mouths long enough to come up for air. Half her shirt is hiked up so the bottom of her bra is showing. Her hand reaches toward me.

Amy: You could ask for a different roommate.
Me: I know.

"Come here," she says, watching me from under heavy-lidded eyes. "You don't have to just watch."

"No thanks," I mumble.

And then I grab my shoes and leave.

Lawson is a weirdly unifying individual, in that he's almost universally regarded as a living, breathing red flag. Most of the time he's either being a selfish prick or dragging me into some bullshit I didn't ask for.

The thing is, I know where it comes from. I've known Lawson since the third grade, and I can honestly say not many people would be even remotely functional dealing with what he's been through with his family. His mother divorced his dad when he was little, then took off and left him with Satan. No exaggeration—his dad is the meanest, cruelest person I've ever met in real life. A few years back, an article came out about how more people die by suicide at Roman Kent's company than a Chinese electronics factory. The guy is supervillain-levels of vindictive. And he seems to concentrate that evil energy squarely on his son.

So I guess, yeah, in a way I feel for Lawson. Who knows how I would have turned out if my family was a malevolent chaos circus. The bitch of it is, despite all the ways he's gotten me in trouble over the years, the guy is loyal. He sticks up for his friends and never turns his back. If you're getting your ass kicked, he'll be there taking the beating with you.

As much as he's a pain in the ass most of the time, I feel like somebody's gotta stick beside him. Might as well be me.

But that doesn't mean I don't want to wring his neck half the time.

I get another text as I'm wandering along the path between the senior dorm and the pool house. It's nearly pitch black, save for the dim orange footlights and occasional firefly hovering above the grass. I wish I were back in my room, watching mindless YouTube videos or playing a video game, but I'm not in the mood to witness another one of Lawson's self-destructive episodes.

> Amy: I miss you. Feels like we've barely talked all summer.
> Me: Miss you too. You'll see me soon.

As I pass the trail that leads to Sloane's house on the edge of campus, I suddenly laugh out loud at how totally predictable it was she'd manage to find the fresh meat before the semester's even started. Already sniffing around RJ as if she didn't just dump Duke because she allegedly came to her senses about dating douchebags who treat her bad. Sloane is similar to Lawson in that she's also her own worst enemy. The girl is a heat-seeking missile for the dipshit high school bad-boy types who will either break her heart or dick her over.

She's a smart person, probably the cleverest I know, so I can't for the life of me figure out why she lets herself get taken for the same scam every time.

But whatever. Not my problem. If she wants to set herself up for a fall, that's her prerogative. We've been friends long enough that I know better than to believe she listens to anyone else. Even when they're trying to stop her from making a huge mistake.

CHAPTER 9
RJ

IT'S A SICK JOKE. I SURVIVED THIS LONG WITHOUT GETTING TRAPPED in a team jersey or club T-shirt, stayed one step ahead of an orange jumpsuit, only to get led down a blind alley and straight into a blazer and striped tie. When David first mentioned Sandover, I hadn't realized I'd end up wearing a school uniform with loafers and fucking button-downs every day. If I'd known that, I would've skipped town without so much as a note on my pillow.

"Screw this thing." I yank the blue and green tie from around my neck and chuck it at the floor. "If I wanted to dress like a flight attendant, I'd go as my mom for Halloween."

"Dude, it's not that hard." Fenn picks up the tie and tries to wrap it around my neck as I lean away out of pure spite. "Come here, ya big baby."

Biting my tongue, I stand still while he ties it loosely.

"See? Easy. When you take it off, just loosen it and pull it over your head. I'm not doing this every morning."

"Thanks, Mom."

He flips me off. "Eat my ass."

Nothing has ever felt so defeating as staring at myself in the mirror in this stupid navy-blue uniform with the gaudy gold crest on the pocket. It's like someone's reached in and plucked my soul from my chest while I stand there a hollow husk, dead-eyed and slack.

"Don't worry, you should have plenty of time to learn to tie it while you're hiding in here every weekend."

"Being alone is not the same as hiding," I tell him while we put on our socks and shoes.

"We got here three days ago, and I haven't seen you leave this place once except to go to the dining hall, and then you won't even stick around to sit with us. All you do is sit on the computer. I get it, bro, porn can be fun—like that MILF stuff? Where the young stud walks into the kitchen after baseball practice and his cougar stepmother is all like, *I'm so lonely, Jonathan. Your father doesn't fulfill my needs. Please give me your dick.*"

I stare at him. "Are you speaking from personal experience here? Do you moonlight as some dude named Jonathan who serves old broads?"

"I fucking wish. Anyway, how much jerking can you do before your dick rots and falls off?"

"You let me know when you figure that out," I shoot back on our way out the door.

"Seriously, man. If you crawled out of your hole occasionally, you might realize there's an excellent talent pool out there. Could give lefty a break now and then."

"God, I can't imagine how gut-achingly boring sex is with New England townies and stuck-up prep school girls."

"Not with that attitude."

We swing by the dining hall to grab a muffin and coffee then head to our first class Monday morning. Fenn hasn't stopped giving me shit about turning down invites over the weekend. He keeps hounding me to make friends, but I don't see the point. Under normal circumstances, I wouldn't associate with these people, and vice versa. Why pretend otherwise?

While we walk, Fenn gets a text, grinning at his phone before showing it to me. "See that? This is what I'm talking about."

I take a quick look. It's a headless girl in a burgundy school uniform flashing an upshot of some under boob.

"A friend of yours?" I ask in amusement.

"For a night. But I don't do seconds."

Shrugging, he deletes the text and shoves his phone back in his pocket. I do hope those tits find their Prince Charming someday.

"So, if you're not some sick niche porn addict, what are you doing on that computer all day?" he asks, still sounding frustrated by my total disinterest in hanging out with him, his friends, and his random nudes-sending townie chicks.

"Research," I answer vaguely.

Lots of guys nod and say hi to Fenn as we cross campus toward class. Clearly he's considered popular in this tiny, privileged bubble. Me, I've never had much use for the cool kids and their admirers. I can't think of much else more embarrassing than high school hero-worship.

"Research for what?"

"Personal projects."

"Ooh," he says, mocking me. "How mysterious. What, are you selling organs on the black market? Running a shady crypto empire?"

"Sure, if you like."

"You're really going to keep secrets? From your own brother?" he says, feigning outrage.

I just shrug, hiding a grin. Truth is, secrets are my superpower. And while he's been nagging me about going out and getting to know each other, I've been learning everything I need to know about my new stepbrother and the other inhabitants of Sandover Prep.

It took me no time at all to hack Fenn's Sandover transcripts and have a look in his DMs. He sure spends a lot of time talking to that Casey chick. And it's like he's two different people. There's some downright raunchy shit in there with random hookup chicks, and then he and Casey are talking about TikTok musicals or some dumb thing. If he's playing a long con on her, it seems like a ton of effort for minimal reward. I'm almost tempted to warn the poor girl. She seems sweet. But I'm not about to get that involved in someone else's life.

In my world, knowledge is the real power. And I'm damn good at mining it. But as it stands right now, I'm nowhere close to trusting Fennelly Bishop enough to let him know the extent of my capabilities. People don't tend to react well to learning their illusions of privacy are paper windows.

After calculus in the morning with Fenn, I end up lab partners with Silas in physics. Silas is startled to find I'm perfectly capable of understanding the day's tasks, but not as startled as our teacher. Come to think of it, the calc teacher also seemed confused that I understood what inverse functions are. I'm sensing the teachers expected me to be a barely literate caveman, regarding the public education system only slightly above those places you take your dog to make them stop peeing on the furniture. I suppose they're not entirely wrong. I was in AP classes like three schools ago before all the expulsions caught up with me and they stopped letting me enroll. Despite their opinions about my intellect, I've never found school all that difficult, just excruciatingly dull. I have little patience for the conventional classroom experience. It makes me too restless.

After lunch, I spot Lawson when I walk into my modern lit class. From the back row, he kicks a chair at me to insist I sit beside him. The guy's a royal prick, but I sort of dig it. He doesn't care what other people think of him. Hell, except for the ways they can amuse him, I don't figure he thinks about anyone else much at all. That, I respect. At least with him, he wears it all on his sleeve.

"And how are we enjoying our first day in Shangri-La?" he asks, watching me with a lazy smile. His blazer's draped over the back of his chair, tie loosened.

He does have this unsettling quality about him, though. When he looks at you, you know he's considering your fate. How he might write you into his plot. We're all characters in his riddle of mischief and malice.

"Stood outside for twenty minutes waiting for a golf cart to pull up, but it never came."

"Yes, well, the chauffeurs' strike has made pedestrians of us all. Unions truly are the bane of civilized society."

I'm fairly sure he's only half kidding.

For real, though, I don't know how I'm going to last the month wearing a suit with this weather. It's like taking a stroll through a fat man's ass crack in a sauna out there. What's the point of a fancy school and all this money if we can't at least get some scooters in this bitch?

"Fenn says you were jerking it in your room the whole weekend." Lawson glances over, flashing a magnanimous smile. "If you need help picking up girls, all you gotta do is ask."

I roll my eyes. "I pick up fine, thanks."

"You sure? I'll set up some introductions. There's this one girl, Rae, a senior over at Ballard." His eyes glaze over a little. "Man, I'd sell my soul to Satan to fuck her again. But she's like our boy Fenn—one and done, you know? She doesn't do seconds. Says it's the only way to avoid forming attachments."

My mouth quirks in a reluctant smile. Sounds like a girl after my own heart. "Attachments blow," I agree.

"You want her number, then? Swear to God, her body is unreal—"

"Good afternoon, gentlemen."

Lawson lurches upright in his seat, his attention snapping to the front of the room. "What is all this?"

"I'm Mr. Goodwyn." The teacher approaching the desk at the head of the class is a tall, clean-cut dude who looks like he spent his summer behind the register of a J.Crew in an outlet mall. The rolled-up sleeves of his white button-down reveal a pair of muscular arms without a hint of sagging skin or liver spots. He stands out like a sore thumb among a mostly geriatric faculty.

"They're letting freshmen teach senior lit now?" Lawson cracks. It gets muffled laughter from the rest of the class.

"I'm handing out copies of the syllabus with a picture of my driver's license attached," Mr. Goodwyn responds, unfazed. "Please take one and pass it back."

Mr. Goodwyn's young. Mid-twenties going on sixteen. Clearly he's heard it enough to have a sense of humor about it.

"How is *Dante's Inferno* modern literature?" Lawson calls out after glancing at the syllabus.

"Among other works, we'll be examining Dante's influence on the hero's journey and modern novels like Richard Matheson's *What Dreams May Come*," Mr. Goodwyn says while writing page numbers on the whiteboard.

"Oh, yeah." Lawson smirks. "I saw that one. Jennifer Connelly goes ass-to-ass on a double-sided dildo with a hooker."

The room collectively chokes on its laughter. Mr. Goodwyn pauses at the board, his back to us.

"You're thinking of Darren Aronofsky's film *Requiem for a Dream* based on the novel by Hubert Selby Jr." Mr. Goodwyn turns around and sits on the corner of his desk. "Interestingly, also released in 1978, the same year as Matheson's *What Dreams May Come*. Both intimate and intense psychological explorations of the human descent into hell, literal and figurative."

"Fascinating." Lawson is temporarily quieted but undeterred, answering with a mildly threatening grin for failing to get a rise out of the teacher. "Looking forward to it."

If that exchange had taken place at some of my old schools, the kid would've been tased by a two-hundred-pound cop and dragged out on a trail of piss. This is more entertaining.

Lawson spends the rest of the class testing his boundaries, poking around at the edges of what Mr. Goodwyn will tolerate before breaking into a cold sweat or tossing him out. By the time class mercifully ends, I've gotten the impression the rest of us are intruding on some weird foreplay happening between those two.

Later, walking out of our history class at the end of the day, Fenn crumples up our essay rubric and tosses it over his shoulder. "This is bullshit. Who assigns a paper on the first day?"

Ten chapters and two thousand words by Friday. Like we don't have other classes to worry about.

"A sadist," I reply. I shift the strap of my Sandover-issued messenger bag to my other shoulder. "And what does this place have against backpacks? Why do I have to carry a purse over here? Motherfucking sadists, the lot of them." I shake my head. "See you back at the dorm."

"What? Hell no." Fenn pulls on my man-purse when I try to duck out. "You're coming with me."

"Where?"

"I've got soccer practice. You should come hang out."

"Like sit in the stands with the girlfriends and groupies? Yeah, pass."

We exit the rear of the building toward a side of campus I haven't explored yet. Huge old-growth trees shade the lawn and brick paths toward a complex of sports fields. Even in the shadow of the massive oaks, it's hotter than the hood of an Indy car out there and my socks become soaked with sweat. I peel out of my blazer and yank my tie off. Fenn shakes his head, knowing he'll be watching me mess with it again in the morning.

"All right. Stop," he orders. "Stop walking. We need to have a chat."

I swallow a sigh. "Do we?"

"Yes," he says, crossing his arms over his chest.

"Christ, you're such a drama queen. Fine. Go."

"You're a good-looking dude," he starts.

"Are you hitting on me?"

"You wish."

My sigh slips out.

"I'm just saying, you're good-looking, which means there's no excuse for you to be a lazy, low-effort, antisocial asshole. You could be pulling chicks left and right if you made an effort. Like, those ripped jeans and hoodies you wear? I get it. Rebel without a cause. Cool. But I've got a rep to maintain—"

"Wait, this is about you?" I cut in, my tone dry.

"Of course it's about me." He sounds frazzled. "I can't be brothers with the weird loner. It would be one thing if you were ugly— then everyone would see your antisocial self and think you're alone because *I* want nothing to do with *you*. Know what I mean?"

"Not really."

"But no, you have to be fucking good-looking. So now everyone is shaking their heads thinking, why won't this guy chill with Bishop? Well, fuck you, Remington. Not on my watch. Would it kill you to make an effort?"

"Why do I care about your rep?"

"You don't care about anything," he gripes.

He's not wrong. I've never cared too deeply about shit, except maybe my tech. Break my monitors, and watch me care a hell of a lot. But everything else, friends, school, chicks… I go with the flow, never investing too heavily in one particular thing. And what's so wrong about that? I mind my business and do my thing. If more people followed my lead, maybe we'd be closer to achieving world peace or some shit.

"Come meet the guys," Fenn says irritably. "Be goddamn social for a change. I'm not letting you sit in our room like a sociopath all semester."

Another breath lodges in my throat. He's a dog with a bone about me making friends. I couldn't give a shit, but fine. If it'll get Fenn off my case for a few days, I'll make an appearance then slip away when he's not paying attention.

"For a little while," I agree.

It's a trek to the soccer field and there aren't any faculty around, so I pull a joint out of my bag.

"Dude, seriously?" Fenn side-eyes me.

"You don't smoke?"

"Sure, at parties or whatever. Not before practice. And definitely not out in the open."

"It's medicinal. I can't tolerate you preppy fucks for more than eight hours sober."

"Listen." He stops and gives me an impatient sigh.

"Awesome. Another chat?"

He ignores the jab. "There's a way things are done around here. Guys do what they do, but at the appropriate time and place. It's not cool to be walking around stoned all the time. We don't flaunt it."

"You keep forgetting, I'm not one of you. Not trying to be," I remind him.

This is just another school in a long list for me. The only difference is the tax bracket. Doesn't change who I am.

"Be whatever you want. But have some tact."

My instinct is to tell Fenn to get bent. What the hell do I care about their arbitrary customs? I can't see how it affects me in the slightest or what interest of mine it serves to assimilate. But then there's this nagging voice in my head that reminds me he isn't just a roommate. We're chained together now, both victims of the same sick joke our parents played on us. And I don't hate the guy, so why make an enemy when he wants to be an ally? For now, at least. I'm still not about to place my blind trust in him.

"I'm trying to help you," he tells me, as if he sees the indecision working its way through my head to a conclusion.

So, I tuck the joint behind my ear. Call it a compromise. "Don't ever say I'm unreasonable."

Fenn rolls his eyes at me but is sufficiently appeased.

We head toward the training facility where the gym and locker rooms are. Outside, a group is messing around with a soccer ball, doing a few minimally impressive tricks.

"Oh, this'll be fun," Fenn mutters as we approach them.

One of the guys pops the ball in the air toward Fenn, and he dribbles it on his knee a couple times before kicking it back.

"Who's your new boyfriend?" someone calls.

Fenn just rolls his eyes again. I don't think much fazes this guy. Well, other than the fact that I refuse to pledge my social obedience to him. He definitely doesn't love that. "Guys, this is RJ, my stepbrother."

"You got a doctor's note for that, stepbrother?" A guy with a tight T-shirt who looks like he's compensating for a tiny dick with chest presses nods at my joint.

"Yeah, it's right here." I reach into my pocket and pull out my middle finger.

It gets a laugh from Fenn, but Mr. Pecs over here isn't amused.

"Your brother hasn't figured out how things work around here," he says to Fenn while creeping into my personal space.

Fenn shrugs. "Don't know what to tell ya, Duke. He's got a willful streak."

Duke. So this is the crime lord of Boys Town. I don't know why I hoped he'd have at least a cool scar or something. The guy's tall and ripped, but so are those *Riverdale* dudes, and I'm fairly sure I could take an Archie Andrews-looking motherfucker.

"You're new here," Duke starts, posturing up with his arms crossed. "So I'll lay it out for you. If you're thinking of dabbling in any kind of volume business, I get a cut. There's no action on this campus that doesn't go through me."

"Is this a shakedown? I never saw *Goodfellas*."

His answering chuckle is loaded with arrogance. "You know, it's always the funny ones who break first."

"Am I funny?" I glance at Fenn. "I was going for rudely dismissive."

Duke's voice gets quiet even as he affects a smile to prove to his friends he's unbothered by my indifference to him. "You're gonna figure out quick, I'm the guy you don't want as an enemy."

I don't know. I've been to a lot of schools and seen every kind of bully adolescent America has to offer. From what I can see, he's not so unique. The bully at my last school had a neck tattoo, a throwing knife collection, and a stabbing problem. I make a mental note to text Julie and find out if ol' Gavin was finally arrested for something.

"Got it," I tell Duke. "But see, you don't even know me. So which guy do you suppose I am?"

He narrows his eyes.

Guys like Duke, they don't know yet how much they have to lose. Or how easy it is for someone to take it—if properly motivated.

Because I'm the guy you don't want to give a reason.

Ignoring my question, Duke shifts his gaze to Fenn. "Bring your brother to the fights Saturday night," he says as he and his buddies walk away. "Love to see him there."

Fenn shakes his head at me once they've gone. "Went exactly like I thought," he muses, more to himself than to me.

"Fights?" I echo, only mildly curious.

"You'll see."

We go to the side entrance of the building for the locker rooms, and I realize where I am now. Just across the lawn, past a small grove of trees, is the narrow dirt path where I encountered the angry girl.

"I met a chick out there the other day," I tell Fenn.

Confused, he follows my gaze to the woods. "Were you out there building a fort or something?"

"I was wandering around and followed the path to find a place to smoke. This girl comes running up and basically told me next time I'd be shot on sight."

Fenn pushes open the door to the building. "Ah, yeah. That trail's off limits. Leads to Sloane's house." He glances at me over his shoulder. "Best to keep your distance."

"She was hot, though. Like in a step-on-your-balls-and-make-you-call-her-mistress kind of way."

He snorts a laugh. "You poor dumb bastard."

"Why, who is she?"

"Sloane Tresscott. She's the headmaster's daughter." He's still chuckling to himself as he strides forward. "As in the one person on this campus you actually can't fuck with."

CHAPTER 10
SLOANE

THE FIRST DAY OF SCHOOL SUCKED. I WALKED OUT OF ST. VINCENT'S after the last bell ready to chalk it up to jitters, a bad mood, or not enough sleep. Call it a fluke and try again. Only today isn't looking much better. The teachers run this place like a Russian gymnastics camp. Get caught breathing too loudly in class, and it's fifteen lashes and a day in the stockade. I thought all those clichés about Catholic school were only true on TV, but it turns out they take all this saints and angels stuff super seriously.

Which wouldn't be so awful if the other girls were at least tolerable. But they're not. Everyone I've met so far is either infatuated with their own reflection, too good for the room, a straight-up raging cunt-monster, or the reincarnated soul of a forty-year-old virgin pilgrim searching for sluts to hang. I made the apparently heinous sin of putting on a little makeup and wearing my skirt above the knee, so just walking the halls I'm catching daggers from the judgey swamp creatures who lurk here.

I don't know why I thought an all-girls school would be a good idea. It's like taking all the catty bullshit from a coed high school and distilling it into an estrogen-supercharged toxic cocktail of bitchiness. But maybe it's just me.

Not like there were a lot of options after Dad pulled us out of Ballard. Casey's accident freaked him out so badly that he didn't want her within a hundred yards of that campus ever again. St. Vincent's is the last private school within a commutable distance to Sandover, and since Dad would rather force his own faculty to homeschool us than send us to public school, here we are.

After class, I stop by my locker to see a couple of girls with flat hair watching me. Like they've been waiting. It gets my back up right away, and I'm reminding myself to take my rings off if I have to start swinging.

"I heard," the first one says too loudly, eyeing me over the other girl's shoulder, "her sister went crazy."

"It's true," the other says, and turns around to look me dead in the eyes. Her name's Nikki. She was in my first period, and I knew the second she watched me walk into the room that she was going to make me kick her ass.

I suppose it was wishful thinking to hope the rumors wouldn't make it all the way to St. Vincent's. At Ballard, it was impossible to shut them down—God knows I tried. But despite my best efforts, the most traumatic event of my sister's life turned into the second most traumatic event of her life. Sympathy from her peers? Yeah, right. Casey didn't get any of that once the rumor mill got to work. She became the crazy, drugged-up sophomore who tried to drown herself for attention. As if Casey would ever be capable of something like that.

"My cousin goes to Ballard and said the crazy bitch drove her car into a lake at prom," Nikki says gleefully. "Like how fucking extra can you get?"

My hand drops from my locker as I give Nikki an overly sweet smile. The Ballard assholes drove Casey out of school, but I'll be damned if I let the St. Vincent's assholes do the same. "Sounds like your cousin's a stupid bitch who should learn to keep my sister's name out of her mouth."

She smiles back, smug and self-satisfied in her cruelty. "But it's true, right? She, like, had a psychotic break."

"Did she?" I say softly, closing the distance between us to speak just to her, despite eyes lingering on us as others pause to witness. "What if it was the other sister who plunged her car in the lake? What would make her do such a strange thing? Someone like that would be unhinged. Utterly unpredictable. Capable of anything, really. Even sudden bouts of blind rage and intense violence. Without proper medication and treatment, I certainly wouldn't want to provoke someone like that, you know, become the thing that sets them off again." My smile widens. "Who knows what they'd be capable of, right?"

"Uh, okay." Nikki releases a nervous laugh, noticing she's gained the audience she thought she wanted but less certain of her motives now. "Are you threatening me?"

I slam my locker shut and smile at her. "No, sweetie. A good Catholic girl doesn't need to make threats. God will strike her enemies down for her."

At that, I walk off, leaving her to consider the repercussions of messing with my sister. I don't give a damn what anyone says about me. Come for Casey, though, and I'll ruin your life and everything you care about. I am not the one to fuck with.

"That was maniacal." A short girl with a nose ring swoops in beside me as I walk toward the cafeteria.

"Was it?" There are a thousand ways to get shivved in a school like this, and I don't trust a friendly smile any more than I can spend it.

"Nikki's going to have PTSD from that."

"She should learn to pick her targets more carefully."

"I'm Eliza," she says. "You're new."

"So much for keeping a low profile."

"It's a small school. You were always going to get noticed."

Something about her energy makes me like her, despite my

cautious suspicions. She's got a calm confidence and easy chill that saps the sting from my blood.

"You want to bail on lunch and take the nickel tour?" she asks.

It's a better offer than what's waiting for me in the cafeteria: a hundred whispering girls concocting more outrageous stories about my sister and placing bets on my next blowup. Casey has second lunch, so I can't even check in on her. It's giving me anxiety, if I'm being honest. Since the accident, we've barely spent a day apart. I thought I was growing exhausted with the nanny routine, but now I find myself preoccupied with wondering if she's faring better than I am so far.

"My sister's not crazy," I inform Eliza, flicking up one eyebrow. "Just to get that out of the way."

"Didn't think she was," Eliza answers lightly. "I know better than to believe a word any of those gossiping witches say."

"Good."

Following Eliza, we end up out beyond what I thought was the southern boundary of campus. Out here, the vegetation has been left to its own wild devices to move in on the old gray stone building, climbing its pocked walls. There's a steeple overhead with an opening where a bell would be. With a coaxing nod, Eliza pries open the heavy wooden door that's swollen and warped after years of rain and humidity inflicting damage on its frame.

"I didn't know this was here," I remark.

The old chapel is dark and musty inside. It still holds its wooden pews and hymnals, although scorched and fragile. Pages strewn on the ground crumple with the vibrations of our footsteps that mingle with the prints written in the dust on the floor.

"There was a fire. Decades ago," Eliza says.

"And they just left it here?"

"Yup. Story goes they were having choir practice, and a nun and some students were trapped inside. Died right here," she adds, standing behind what's left of the crumbling altar. "The families sued, and the fight lasted for years. They never bothered to tear it down. I come here to smoke."

Vines creep in through cracks in the walls, weeds growing up through the floors. It's as if the earth is slowly taking it back. Only dim light manages to break through the stained-glass windows.

"This way," she says, leading me to a suspect wooden ladder. Someone's propped it up against a wall to get up to the empty belfry.

Eliza gestures for me to climb first. From the bottom, she holds the ladder to keep it steady.

I reach the top where the sunlight is nearly blinding after coming up out of the dark chapel. I feel around through hot white light for the ledge and grab on, feeling the ladder creak under my feet.

I sit on the ledge as my eyes adjust. First to colors, then shapes that emerge where the flares of sunlight fade. Clouds bring fleeting shade that allows me to realize just how high this is and the vast breadth of the campus below.

Eliza easily finds her way to sit beside me. There's a slight breeze up here, but it offers no relief from the humid blanket of heat that clings to us. I don't know if it's the weather or the height, but my stomach churns. The ground below seems suddenly unsteady.

"You good?" she asks with a grin.

"I am now. I figured there was like a thirty percent chance you were bringing me up here to push me off."

"And now?"

"Like six percent."

Eliza barks out a sharp laugh. "Nice."

We eventually get around to that cigarette. She smokes cloves, which I love for the taste but can only tolerate in small doses before my throat catches fire. By the time lunch ends and we need to head back, I've decided I like her.

"You'll do," I announce.

Eliza tips her head to look at me, amused. "I'll do how?"

"As a friend. We're going to be friends."

That gets me a wave of laughter. Shutting the door behind us, she leads me away from the old chapel, still giggling to herself.

"I'm honored," she says, but I think it's only half sarcasm. "Although I should warn you—I'm a very bad influence."

"Bring it, you bad bitch."

We start giggling again, and I realize I'm actually in a good mood. At school. At *Catholic* school. And just as the thought surfaces, I get a text from a number I don't recognize.

> Unknown: Got your name. And your number. Fenn says hi.
> —RJ

I don't know whether to laugh or curse. So I do both.

Eliza looks over curiously. "Boyfriend?" she asks.

"Cute stalker."

"Yeah?" She glances at my screen. "How cute?"

"A lot more than he has any right being," I grumble.

And his persistence makes him even more attractive. He definitely gets points for the effort to track me down, even if it's slightly creepy. I need to have a talk with Fenn about handing my number out to random strangers.

> Me: Tell Fenn to sleep with one eye open.
> RJ: I tricked him out of it. His only sin is being simple.
> Me: And yours is being a walking red flag.

"Is this a thing or…?" Eliza asks, reading over my shoulder.

"Haven't decided yet." I mean, I have. Of course I have. I already decided I'm not getting wrapped up in more bullshit boy drama this year.

But texting isn't dating.

> RJ: You could tell me to lose your number.

Me: You could prove your devotion and hold your breath till
I call.
RJ: Our spot, tonight after dinner? I'll bring dessert.
Me: You mean my spot.
RJ: I'll hit any spot you like.

Eliza snorts. "He's trying so hard. But I bet he does oral."

"Yep, okay. We don't even know the guy. Let's pump those brakes."

Me: Stay off my trail.

This guy thinks he's clever. That he'll wear me down with enough charm and flirting until I can't remember why I left him holding his joint in the woods. And maybe the old me would've fallen for it.

But the new me refuses to fall for flirty banter and a pretty face.

CHAPTER 11
RJ

TUESDAYS WE ENGAGE IN TEDIOUS PHYSICAL ACTIVITY. TODAY THE PE teacher has us at the indoor pool doing laps. If it's between an hour here versus two miles dripping sweat on the track outside like my skin's going to melt off, I don't mind it so much.

"Any of you not know how to swim?" the teacher asks, biting his whistle with the side of his mouth as we all stand in our shorts at the edge of the pool.

One pasty, freckled kid raises his hand. The teacher grabs a bulky neoprene vest off a shelf on the wall and tosses it at him.

"There. You can doggy paddle on the side."

He tells us to call him Brek. I don't know if that's a first name, last, or more a state of mind. But he manages to look less interested in being here than the rest of us. I take a guess he's a forty-something former Olympic whatever, who, after he washed out of a division one school and did a stint in rehab, called in a favor to get this job and now regrets whatever vices brought him here to babysit a bunch of rich malcontents.

"The rest of you'll be doing a 200-meter freestyle relay followed by a fifty-meter sprint. Four to a lane. Line up." His whistle screams in the hollow, cavernous building.

I have no concept of how far that is until the first swimmers are in the water, going back and forth. Four laps each. I get a little winded watching them and decide to put myself in the anchor position for my lane. I need to psyche myself up for this a little. Not like I don't exercise—I run, lift weights—but swimming is a whole different thing when you have to time your breaths and propel your whole body through the water.

Brek blows his whistle to tell us to get up on the platforms. Then without really thinking about it, I dive in the water once the guy before me touches the wall. My mind blanks and I go on instinct. I haven't even been in the water in probably a year, but it comes back to me. I find my stroke and set my pace. The first turn is tricky because I only mimic what I've seen on TV of real swimmers. I botch it a little then figure it out on the next one. After the third turn I'm waiting to feel the pain in my muscles or the burn in my lungs. Before it comes, I drive my fingertips into the wall and realize it's over.

Four laps done. Too easy.

After the relay and we've had a minute to catch our breath, we all line up for the sprint. Brek pulls out his little stopwatch then blows his whistle. I'm in the third heat, and something strange happens when I'm standing at the edge. My hands go a little numb. My pulse picks up. I find myself rocking back and forth. I realize when I explode off the platform that I want to kill this swim. There's no prize or bonus points for coming in first, but for some reason I really give a shit about getting to the other end of this pool as fast as I can. I kick like hell. Feel the strain in my wrists from pushing the water behind me.

When I slam into the wall and throw my hair out of my eyes, I glance around and realize I'm a body length ahead of the tidal wave of the other guys.

That felt pretty fucking good, actually.

As I'm toweling off, I notice an older guy talking to Brek. He's tall and built, with a deep tan. He's got a whistle around his neck and a Sandover Swimming shirt on. They catch me looking and wave me over. Against my better judgment, I walk toward them.

"That was a decent time you put up," the man tells me. "You ever swim competitively?"

"Not really my calling."

"You've got the size and build for it. How tall are you? Six-one, two?"

"Six-three."

"Weight?"

"How should I know? Who weighs themselves?"

He narrows his eyes at me. "We've got practice about to start. Why don't you stick around and try out for the team?"

"Yeah, thing is, I already have plans to slam my dick in a car door, so I'm gonna have to take a rain check on that."

"All right, Shaw." Brek waves me off with a grimace. That'll teach him to try to include me in shit. "Hit the showers."

Better men than Brek and Bobby Breaststroke over there have tried and failed to put my name on a team roster. At this point, it's a matter of principle.

By the time our class is out of the showers, the swim team is in the locker room getting dressed for practice. Silas nods as we pass each other on his way out to the pool.

"Fenn's brother," Lawson shouts across the room at me. "You lost?"

I throw my bag down beside his on the bench in front of the lockers. "This isn't the library?"

"They still have those in public school? Thought they'd all been converted to armories."

"Something like that."

"So I heard you took a shot at Sloane," he says, tugging a swim cap over his head. "How'd that go?"

Fucking Fenn, man. He gossips like a girl.

"We have an unspoken bond," I answer.

Lawson cracks a smile. "Dead on impact, then."

"Nah, I just need to find my in with her."

"Yeah," he drawls. "You do that."

I know girls like Sloane. They want to make you run at the sword to get to them on the other side. The gushing wound proves you mean it. That's usually way more effort than I'm willing to devote to get laid, but the difference is, this time I think she might be worth it. I have no idea what's got me so hung up on this chick, but it's like a dare I can't say no to. She doesn't think I've got the stamina, so I'll prove her wrong. Even more than a conquest, though, something tells me she and I aren't so different. If given the chance to have a proper conversation, we might even get along.

"Don't sweat it," Lawson says, closing his locker. "She's a ballbuster. The girl gets off on it. The glacier that carved the Grand Canyon couldn't wear her down."

"Speaking from experience, huh?"

"There's no shame in the game, as long as you know when to quit."

No offense to Lawson, but it's good to know Sloane has higher standards.

I'm a glutton for punishment lately, so I text her on my way to the dining hall.

Me: That dessert invitation is still open.

I take it as a good sign she doesn't leave me on read.

Sloane: I bet it is.
Me: So go out with me.
Sloane: Find a new hobby.
Me: I like this one.
Sloane: Haven't had enough rejection?
Me: Not yet.

I'll get her there. It takes time to build a rapport, and around here, I've got nothing but time.

Back at the dorm, I find Fenn on his laptop in front of the TV.

"Now who's the shut-in?" I taunt, throwing my stuff down next to my bed.

"Have to work on this damn history essay." Keys click furiously as he talks. "Coach needs my help with soccer tryouts this week, so I don't have much time to work on it."

"Oh, right. Yeah, I finished that last night."

"What?" He jerks his head at me. "Seriously?"

"Sure."

"How the fuck, man?"

I take my own laptop to one of the armchairs. "Grabbed one off the internet."

"Dude, the school uses plagiarism software. You'll get caught."

"Not the way I do it."

He eyes me skeptically. "Yeah, and how's that?"

There's risk in letting Fenn in on my methods. Sure, he's all "family first" now, but there's no guarantee he wouldn't turn on me at any time, given a good enough reason. But weighing the reward, he *is* my best connection to a new and fruitful customer base. What's the worst that could happen? I get kicked out of another school? I'm an old pro at that.

"Simple," I tell him. "All these plagiarism software checkers connect to online databases of submitted source material. I figure out which one the school is using, hack into their server, and delete that specific essay."

His eyebrows shoot up. "You can do that?"

"It isn't hard. I had a nice little side gig going at my last couple schools. I could hook you up."

"Hell yeah." He slaps his laptop shut. "But seriously, you can't get caught."

"Never have."

It's one of my more elegant hustles. The massive volume of sources contained in these databases is their selling point, but it's also their weakness, because it makes intrusion and deletion practically undetectable. And since my business is by nature a small operation, the risk is minimal.

It's perfect, really.

Fenn watches me while I start searching for a suitable essay to give him. "So this is what you do in here all day. Hacker shit?"

"More or less."

"Still nerdy as hell," he says, grabbing the TV remote to find something to watch with all his newfound free time. "But maybe not a lost cause after all. I guess now I'm fifty percent more cool with the idea of having you for a roommate."

I don't have the heart to tell him this won't last. Because honestly, I can't see myself being at this school for too long. I'll get kicked out eventually. And even if I do graduate, he'll be going to some Ivy, and I'll be doing my own thing. Maybe we'll convene for holidays if our parents are still married, but the jury's out on that one too.

Still, the next time he's bothering me to go out, I'm going to count this as bonding time.

CHAPTER 12
FENN

"Come here, you little cockwaffle."

I peel off my headphones, jostled from my trance thanks to RJ's angry outburst.

"Little further." RJ jerks the controller, rocking as he sits on the couch. "Left. *Left, damn it.*" He kicks the coffee table in frustration and tosses the Xbox controller. "This game is stupid," he grumbles at me. "Why'd you get me on this?"

I glance down to notice I've been stuck on the same page of my physics textbook for nearly an hour. It's Wednesday night, and I sat down after dinner to get some work done, but instead, I've bounced between compulsively checking my DMs and drifting off inside my head.

"No one's forcing you to play it," I say, absentminded. "Just turn off the game."

"No." He stubbornly juts his chin and picks up the controller. "I refuse to be bad at this."

"You do you, baby girl." I start scrolling through my DMs again.

"I'm sorry, did you just call me *baby girl?*"

I look up from my phone. "Did I?"

"Yes."

"Then, okay, you answered your own question." I delete a couple messages from a Ballard chick looking for a repeat hookup.

RJ stares at me for a moment before sighing and resuming his game.

I close my DMs and rub my forehead, wishing I could be rid of all this restless energy. Don't know what's wrong with me. I woke up thinking about Casey and haven't managed to shake the urge to see her all day. We were messaging last night, but I haven't heard from her since my last response. It wasn't important, just some random comment. Lately, though, I'm like an addict. Hanging on those little flashing bubbles.

I'm becoming obsessed and it's kind of a problem. I could seriously ruin this girl if she doesn't hurry up and figure out I'm no good to have around. Casey is as gentle and innocent as they come, a unicorn in the muddy swamp of the prep school circles. Not to mention she's only a junior. So I've got no business letting her be corrupted by my tendency for debauchery and self-destruction.

And yet. Here we are. Here *I* am, texting her every day and wanting to see her when I know my dirty hands shouldn't be anywhere near someone so pure.

Only problem is, I'm a greedy coward who can't stay away.

I toss my phone aside, pick up my textbook, and order myself to concentrate.

Then I see my screen light up under the duvet. It's a response from Casey to my last DM. Just an "LOL," but the way my pulse quickens, you'd think she sent a nude.

I check the time and realize it's after ten. Biting my lip, I stare at the screen for what feels like eternity.

Screw it. I send her a text.

If I had any self-restraint, I wouldn't be such a bastard.

Me: Want to be a little bad?
Casey: Depends...

Me: Sneaking out. Meet up?

Casey: On the trail.

Me: See you soon.

"Where are you going?" RJ's suspicious voice stops me as I'm heading for the door.

"Going to see a girl." I glance over my shoulder. "You okay with that, Daddy?"

He rolls his eyes and goes back to the video game he sucks at.

It's not curfew yet, so I don't have to use stealth to leave the dorm. I just walk out, hands shoved in the pockets of my jeans, heart rate accelerating the nearer I get to the outskirts of campus.

Funny thing is, Casey and I had hardly ever spoken before her accident this past spring. She was just Sloane's little sister. The cute, sweet, bubbly cheerleader. Always there in the background. Then afterward, we grew closer. Silas wasn't so off-base with his accusations; the day we stopped by the Tresscott house, I gave Casey my number when Silas and Sloane left us alone in the kitchen. I don't know what compelled me to do it. Maybe because she looked so beaten and forlorn, that red gash on her forehead still not fully healed.

I'd kept it light, sympathetic. Told her, *hey, if you ever need to talk, I'm a great listener.*

I never expected her to actually text me. And I damn well shouldn't have texted back. But she did, and so did I, and, somehow, we became friends.

Pretty much from the end of April until she left for Colorado this summer, we spent nearly all our time together, taking walks with her dogs on the trail between her house and the main campus. I don't know that I was great company, but the time seemed to lift her spirits during her darker moments.

The headmaster wasn't a fan at first. His instincts for danger are clearly more developed than hers. But he couldn't ignore that spending time together really seemed to help dig Casey out of the hole she fell into after the accident. Under strict guidance that we only see each other for afternoon walks within shouting distance of the house, he allowed it.

Guess he should have known better.

It was only a matter of time before I had Casey sneaking out of the house after curfew to go gallivanting in the middle of the night with my sorry ass.

Tucked into the trees that wrap around campus, a dirt path leads to Casey's house. A year ago, I would have been stumbling around in the dark getting my legs chewed up by thorns and poison ivy. Now I can practically find my way with my eyes closed.

Just a few feet from the edge of her yard, near enough that the porch lights from the house peek through the leaves, Casey stands in the glow of her phone's flashlight. Her head lifts with a smile when she sees me coming.

Without a word, she throws her arms around my waist for a hug. It makes me sick that she's happy to see me. There's always some part of me that hopes this time she'll have come to her senses. This time she'll tell me to piss off. Instead, she holds me tight, and I can't help but welcome the heat of her pliant body and inhale the scent of her hair. It always smells like lavender.

"Nice jammies," I tell her.

Lately, evenings are still warm and humid, and Casey showed up in a matching pink PJ set: short-sleeve button-down top and shorts. She looks fucking adorable.

"Oh." She laughs at her outfit. "Thanks. I figured if anyone saw me leaving, it would look more suspicious if I changed clothes."

I lift a brow. "Careful. I think I'm starting to have a bad influence on you."

"Hmm. Yeah, I'll keep an eye on that."

She looks good. Like generally happier and more at ease than the last time we'd met. And vastly improved from spring. She'd been so ravaged back then, dealing with nightmares nearly every night. I guess I would be too if I almost drowned and woke up on the bank of a lake without any idea what happened. That shit's fucked up.

"How's things?" I ask her. "New school treating you okay?"

Looking away, Casey nibbles her lip. "Meh. Not great, honestly."

"You're not liking St. Vincent's?"

"So far, not a fan."

"Why, what happened?" An instant jolt of anger hits my blood.

"It's been a tough week." Her face falls, sadness and gloom again taking over. It's heartbreaking. "Nobody really talks to me, but I hear what they're saying."

"Like what?"

"Just rumors, you know. Somebody heard from somebody... So yeah, it seems my popular days of cheerleading and yearbook committee are a thing of the past. I'm not making many friends over there."

"Fuck 'em. They sound like a bunch of dumb cunts."

"Fenn." She chastises my word choice, but I'm not wrong. And the hint of a smile tugging at her full pink lips tells me she agrees.

I poke her in the side, smiling playfully. "I could find some sixteen-year-old girl boxer to kick their asses for you. I mean, I'd offer to do it myself, but the optics..."

"Send me to school with my own brute squad, huh?"

"Sure, why not?"

"Maybe you could teach me some moves." Eyes twinkling, she mocks a few jabs at the air. "I could get super fit and start wearing black eyeshadow."

"With these skinny little wrists? I think you're more suited to the art of psychological warfare." My smile falters. "Seriously, though. Anything I can do to help with the school situation?"

"No, there's really nothing to do except suck it up. They'll get bored of me eventually." She nudges me with her elbow and manages a brief smile that I wonder if she coaxes more for my benefit.

The main thing I've learned about Casey after spending all this time getting to know her, is that she always puts other people first. Always considers their feelings before acknowledging her own. This girl is constantly reassuring everyone else—her dad, her sister, me. Hell, if she and those St. Vincent's cunts were ever dragged into the head nun's office, Casey's the chick who would defend her bullies and ask the higher-ups to show some mercy.

I want to say that kind of attitude is obnoxious, but the truth is…it's inspiring. It gives me the tiniest flicker of hope that maybe humanity isn't doomed.

Me, I was doomed a long time ago. Probably long before I met Casey, but what I'm doing with her sure as shit won't help me find any atonement. I'm a bastard for letting her believe we're friends.

"Busted."

Casey and I both jerk to attention, quickly turning toward the rustling trees. My stomach instantly drops at the sight of Sloane.

CHAPTER 13
SLOANE

I'D ALMOST RATHER CATCH MY LITTLE SISTER ON A ROCK BAND'S tour bus than skulking around the woods in the middle of the night with Fenn. He's probably got a worse reputation than a rock star for using and discarding girls. Outmatched only by Lawson, and that's not great company.

"Care to explain yourself?" I ask coolly.

"We were just talking," Casey insists.

"I'm asking him." Because he knows better. I've graphically detailed what I'd do to his scrotum if I ever find out he's got bad intentions toward my sister.

"Wow, where's the time gone?" he says. "Got dark quick, huh?"

Sarcastic little shit. "You can't be here. If our dad knows you're dragging her out after dark, he'll go ballistic."

An indignant Casey cocks her head at me. "Fenn didn't drag me out. I asked him."

"Uh-huh. I bet."

I don't buy that for a second, which is only more proof that he's rubbing off on her. Fenn might be hot, and a lot funnier than you'd expect, but I've never trusted the guy. I didn't think it was such a great idea for Dad to start letting those two hang out following Casey's accident, but after a few weeks I couldn't deny that her mood had improved. Whatever effect he had on her, it was working. But now Fenn's getting too comfortable. He needs to occasionally be reminded there are boundaries—and consequences to not respecting them.

But my sister isn't backing down. She gives me a faint smirk. "I must have imagined all those times you were slipping out to see Duke after curfew."

"That's different."

"How?"

"You know how." Because she better not be sleeping with Fenn, for one thing. "And because you're not me."

"Whatever."

I resist the urge to roll my eyes at her flippant dismissal. She can be pissy with me all she wants. I know what the Sandover boys want from a girl like Casey, and it isn't platonic picnics under the stars.

"Guess I'll talk to you later," she finally says to Fenn, when she realizes I'm not going to budge. Ignoring my frown, she steps forward to give him a hug before heading back toward the house.

Fenn tries to ease away too, but I stop him with a glare. "You stay," I order.

He halts. "All right. Let's hear it."

I square up to him, one hand planted on my hips. "I mean it, Bishop, no more sneaking around or secret midnight meetings."

"It's barely after ten," he cracks with a crooked grin.

Maybe some girls find it endearing, but I'm not one of them. I glare harder.

"All right, fine. Fuck, Sloane. Relax. Won't happen again."

He runs a frazzled hand through his pale hair, drawing my gaze to the toned biceps beneath his snug black long-sleeve. It serves to remind me that Fenn's a dangerous guy. Six feet tall, fit, too attractive for his own good. A boy like him could break my sister's heart without even trying. Which is only more reason to keep a close eye on him.

While I've got him here, though…there is something he can help me with.

"So, what's the story with your stepbrother?" I demand.

"I don't know." Fenn's brow furrows, but he elaborates when I don't respond. "He's basically a loner. Never wants to go out or even make friends. Keeps to himself, mostly. I can't drag two words out of him half of the time."

"That's funny. He won't shut the hell up in my texts."

"Really?" He appears surprised, which means RJ hasn't been pressing him for information.

"Yes, really. It's annoying as fuck."

"Bullshit." Fenn flashes that lopsided grin. "You love the attention."

"No," I deny, while the voice in my head taunts *yes you do.*

"Sure, Sloane, you keep telling yourself that." Smile fading, he shoves his hand through his hair again. "Now you tell me something—should I be worrying about those girls at St. Vincent's? Sounds like Casey's getting bullied."

"That's not your problem. I can handle it."

"Yeah?"

"Oh yeah. I already went at it with one chick who was talking shit. She's probably going to need a therapist after our conversation."

"Good. Keep at it."

"Of course." If there's one thing Fenn and I have in common, it's being protective where Casey's concerned.

I don't mind going to bat for my sister. Happy to cut a bitch. But keeping up the persona, being this model of an invincible force in everyone else's eyes—it's exhausting. Dad and Casey lean on me, expecting me to shoulder their burdens, and meanwhile I'm looking around and there's no one ready to catch me when it gets too heavy. But I can't tell them any of that. Casey would be overwrought with guilt. Dad would probably lecture me that I'm letting him down. As for friends, that's something I'd never share with Silas or anyone else—nobody is allowed to see me looking vulnerable. Ever.

Still. It would be nice, I think, to have just one person I could say that to.

After Fenn's gone, I stay outside for a moment, breathing in the warm night air. I'm just turning back toward the house when a text lights up my phone.

Mila: We still not talking?

Speaking of "friends."

I continue walking, ignoring the text. But I keep my read receipts on for certain people, and Mila is one of them. I want her to know I'm reading her messages and choosing to ignore them.

Observant as always, my former best friend doesn't miss the slight.

Mila: Come on, babe. Bygones etc?

I leave her on read again. Mila and I have known each other since freshman year, which means she knows exactly what I'm like. Sloane Tresscott doesn't have much use for second chances. You hurt me or my family, you're dead to me. When I'm filling out those college applications and one asks me what my greatest strengths are? Easy.

Running.

Never showing weakness.

And my unwavering ability to hold a grudge.

CHAPTER 14
RJ

Sloane is my white rabbit.

I know this fixation is problematic, and yet I can't fight the feeling that she wants to get caught. So I follow the breadcrumbs.

Sure, I could go through the trouble of developing the necessary relationships to interrogate every acquaintance she has on this campus and glean enough information to help me get a date with the girl. But fuck, that seems like an awful lot of effort.

Now that I know her last name, breaking into her accounts is simple. At first I just scrolled her feeds from my own accounts, but it turns out Sloane is the one hot girl on the planet who doesn't post her entire life on social media. Not a single bikini pic or bedroom selfie. Which is a damn shame, because I have a feeling she looks fantastic in a bikini, and I wouldn't be against seeing her bedroom… Sadly, her main feeds are a barren landscape, so I had no choice but to dig a little deeper.

Okay, fine, I had a choice. I *chose* to take a quick peek behind the curtain. I know it's an invasion of privacy, but…only a little one. It's not like I'm digging for dirt or trying to scrape her nudes. I make a pointed effort to stay out of her DMs—I don't read a single message or even peek at the senders. Instead, I concentrate on figuring out what makes Sloane tick.

Lawson insists she's untouchable, which sounds like quitter talk to me. I can't resist a puzzle, and this one is especially intriguing. If my reward is getting her in bed, even better.

Throughout the morning on Thursday, I piece together little tidbits about Sloane. The posts she likes. The stuff she's into. Like some band she saw three times last year, following them across New England. Or the inordinate amount of time she spends researching running shoes. Eventually I shift my attention to actual work, finding myself in the computer lab after my last class because the dorm internet is at a crawl, and I have shit to do. Like printing the history essays Fenn and I have due tomorrow. Only this damn printer keeps saying the paper tray is empty when I've added paper to the thing twice.

"Come on, you piece of shit. What do you want from me?" I give it the ol' engineer's tap, which only makes it sputter a noise I haven't heard it make before.

"It's always doing that." A dark-haired kid walks up and gets on the floor to reach behind the machine and unplug it.

"I probably should have started with that, huh?"

"Nah, this requires more than just unplugging. Watch, it's a whole thing," he says after plugging it back in. He stands to monitor the display screen as it boots up. "They haven't updated the firmware on this thing since like, 2003, so it's always freaking out for no reason."

As I watch, he goes through a series of menus and error codes to manhandle the printer into believing it has sufficient paper to print.

He nods, pleased with himself. "That should work. For now, at least."

"Thanks." I go back to my computer to start the print job again. Sure enough, the printer starts humming happily and spitting out pages.

The kid follows me, lingering over my shoulder. He looks younger than me, maybe a sophomore or junior. "You've never been in here before."

"No."

"I'm Lucas." Then he pauses in wait, and I stifle a sigh and force myself to introduce myself.

What the hell is up with everyone at Sandover being so intrusively friendly? I thought they were all supposed to be delinquents. "RJ," I say.

Lucas notices my laptop sticking out of my bag and his expression lights up. "Did you build that yourself?"

"Huh? Oh. It's a custom case I had this guy build me in exchange for hacking his boyfriend's phone to find out who he was cheating on him with."

"Seriously? That's cool."

"You into this stuff?"

"Yeah. I mean, I'm not like an expert or anything, but I dabble. Read a lot, mostly. My dad would bury me in the backyard if I actually got caught, you know?"

Despite my initial reluctance, we end up chatting for a while. Turns out he's a junior, and he's been obsessed with computers and writing code since he was twelve. Lucas is modest, but he knows his stuff, not like a lot of posers you find online trying to pass themselves off as some second coming of The Condor. It's almost always some twelve-year-old who'd just spent the weekend watching *Hackers*.

"There you are," Fenn announces, walking into the lab. "Dinner, dude. Let's go."

"Hey, Fenn." Lucas nods at him while I grab our papers from the printer.

"Here, shithead." I toss Fenn his essay. "Enjoy your A."

"And you're sure this'll work?"

"If you did what I told you and made it sound more like you wrote it, then yeah. No sweat."

"If what'll work?" Lucas asks, peering at the pages.

"Nothing." Fenn rolls up the essay. "Mind your business."

"I'm done here anyway." I throw my essay and laptop in my backpack.

"Good. Come eat with us. You can't spend every night eating in the dorm. It's creepy." Fenn glances at Lucas. "Let's go. You can come too. We can try to figure out where the fuck your dad stashed your brother."

Lucas's face grows pained. "Dad won't budge, man. He says we're 'no contact'—I guess that's some kind of therapy term? We're no contact until Gabe proves, and I quote, that he's ready to be a respectable member of our family. Even Mom won't tell me where they sent him."

I follow the exchange, only half lost. I know from snooping through Fenn's digital life that Gabe is Gabe Ciprian, Fenn's best bro since grade school. I just hadn't realized the guy's father was in the mafia or some shit.

"Anyway, I gotta go." Lucas shrugs. "I'm going over to Casey's house for dinner. See you guys later."

Fenn's expression falls and his mouth flattens as he watches Lucas leave.

Lifting a brow, I follow him to the door. "What's up?"

"Huh?" He snaps out of his dead-eyed stare.

"You look like you're about to challenge a junior to a duel at noon."

"No one's ever allowed at their house," he says, his eyes flashing with annoyance. "Except for Silas, who's close with Sloane, and then this fucking kid for some reason."

"So?"

"So, Casey's dad barely tolerates us going for a walk and only as long as the sun's up. We have to stay on the marked trails where the school has cameras."

"Harsh."

"It's medieval. The dude is ridiculous."

I don't have any useful advice for him, unless he wants some help disabling the security cameras. Then I realize, this could be an in for me. I know from hacking Fenn's phone that he's tight with Casey. He doesn't talk about her much to me, but maybe there's an angle here I might be able to exploit to get closer to Sloane.

"So, what's with their dad?" I ask while we stop by our room to change out of our uniforms. "Why's he biblically strict with them? Is it just the headmaster job following him home or something more?"

Fenn goes silent for a long moment. His expression is unreadable, as if he's deciding whether to answer me. He sits on the edge of his bed, bending over to put on his shoes, and doesn't look at me when he finally speaks.

"Tresscott was always protective of them—like, he'd threaten to castrate anyone who came within twenty feet of the headmaster cottage. But it was never to this level."

"So, what happened to get it to this level?"

"Prom," Fenn says flatly.

I grin. "We have prom at an all-boys school?"

"No, it's at Ballard Academy. Sandover guys can buy tickets to any social event at Ballard, so a bunch of us went to the junior prom this past spring. Sloane brought Casey, but then kind of lost track of her during the night." He lets out a long, weary sigh. "Far as we know, someone drugged Casey's drink. She disappeared at some point and wound up driving her car into the lake out behind the abandoned boat house. Nearly drowned."

"Jesus. That's heavy. Was she hurt?"

"A gash on the head, a concussion, and some bruises. She was pretty shaken up after that. Still is."

"Did they catch the guy who drugged her?"

"She didn't remember anything. There were security cameras, but the school said they were down for maintenance, so they didn't capture what happened. That was it."

Fenn's mood sours. He doesn't speak again while we walk to dinner, stuck in his own head. Me, I'm wondering why this major accident wasn't in any of the local papers. If there'd been articles written about it, they would've come up in my dig on the headmaster. No reporter would pass on a story that juicy, which tells me someone made an effort to keep it *out* of the papers.

And I'm probably not the first to point this out, but the cameras being down during a major school event and someone nearly dying is one hell of a coincidence. Then again, this was months ago, so I'm sure the family shook that tree.

At dinner with Silas and Lawson, I'm the one getting interrogated.

"Saw you talking with Coach Gibson," Silas says over his rice pilaf. "Are you thinking about jumping in the pool with us?"

I grunt out, "Not a chance," and take another bite of lemon chicken.

My strategy for surviving these forced interactions is to always keep food in my mouth so I'm not compelled to offer much more than grunts in response. Despite what Fenn says, I don't need friends. I'm not one of those people who needs the reassurance of constant human contact. I prefer to be alone if I have the choice.

"Coach has a hard-on for him," Lawson tells Fenn, before grinning at me. "Absolutely salivating at getting you in a Speedo."

I cock a brow. "You're not selling it well." Team sports fly in the face of everything I believe in, but especially nearly naked team sports.

"Besides, his full-time job lately is stalking Sloane," Fenn cracks.

"We're getting to know each other."

"Right. You're getting to know the hundred different ways she can tell you to fuck off."

Lawson speaks over the rim of his glass, boredom in his voice. "Cut your losses. You're never getting a date with her. She's beyond your reach."

"Push her too far," Fenn adds, "and she'll have your skin hanging on her bedroom wall."

I glance at Silas, waiting for him to chime in. He doesn't. "What, no dose of pessimism from you?"

He shrugs, donning a thoughtful look as he brings his fork to his lips. He chews, swallows, then offers another shrug. "Doesn't matter what I say. You'll keep chasing her regardless. They all do."

I eye him back, equally pensive.

"Look, part of Sloane will always be out of reach. Like, you can never pin her down. That's the appeal. Dudes become obsessed with her, want to win her over, but it'll never work. Sloane always wins in the end."

"We'll see," I say confidently. Although Silas's take on her is surprisingly deep. Intimate, almost.

Fenn said they were close, but I suddenly wonder if he has a thing for her. My brief research dive into Silas Hazelton revealed the consummate good boy. Well, excluding whatever mysterious transgression got him expelled from Ballard and shipped to Sandover—if there's a paper trail about that, I hadn't uncovered it yet. He's squeaky clean, otherwise. Top swimmer with Olympic potential. Cute doormat of a girlfriend. Text message exchanges that sound almost scripted. I hadn't found a single love poem dedicated to Sloane Tresscott on his computer or any telescopic-lens photos of her jogging in a sports bra, so if Silas is lusting over her, he's playing it close to the vest.

As for Sloane, the way I'm reading it, she's sent me an invitation to her labyrinth. All that remains is for me to navigate my way through. It's about the journey.

And I'm always up for adventure.

"He's already made friends with Duke." Fenn exchanges a look with Lawson, the two of them in on a joke I'm not privy to.

"Bet that went well."

"RJ's such a people person, after all."

Lawson grins at me. "This should be fun."

After dinner we end up in the dorm's common room for a game of pool. Other than the trail where I met Sloane, the Lounge is probably the only place on campus I don't entirely hate. It's like a rich dude's man cave in here, full of leather couches, wood paneling, and a fridge and snack bar that mysteriously gets restocked daily despite me never seeing anyone except our housefather puttering around in the building.

Tonight, someone swapped out all the sodas in the fridge for some fancy craft beer I've never heard of. Fenn's already on his second bottle and we just started playing. And if I thought hustling these guys was a viable business model, they quickly dispel that notion. These rich boys are decent enough to make it competitive as Fenn and I play Silas and Lawson two-on-two.

"No, bullshit. You didn't call your shot." Fenn shoves Lawson from the table when he tries to line up a second shot.

"Didn't I? I'm certain I did."

"I heard it," Silas says from the corner.

"You said three in the corner. You don't get to take seven in the side."

"Three? Nah, I don't remember saying three. Definitely said seven."

"You can take that seven and use it as a butt plug."

Standing nearby, Duke and some of his hangers-on watch us until Lawson relents and Fenn takes his turn.

"Who's winning?" Duke asks me. He saunters over casually, as if he hadn't vaguely threatened to put me in a pair of cement shoes last time we met.

"We are." Fenn bends over the table and aims his cue.

"Let me get next," Duke says.

Fenn sinks the eight ball with a *thunk* to end the game. "These guys might want a rematch."

"Four-on-four, then."

"Kinky." Lawson winks at them. "I'm game."

"Great." Duke throws his arm over my shoulder. "This one's on my team."

Oh, joy.

A few rounds in, it feels like I'm on a shitty blind date with someone who won't take the hint. Duke doesn't shut the hell up trying to make small talk with me. It's baffling. Like some Dr. Jekyll and Mr. Asshole bullshit going on. My silence and lack of eye contact somehow encourages him. He chats on about the World Cup, tells me about his workout routine, gripes about how his ex is such a cocktease. Meanwhile, I stand there not caring about soccer or steroids, and wondering who the hell could be shallow or dumb enough to date a guy like Duke Jessup.

"What do you say we raise the stakes?" Duke asks before the next game. He stands at the far end of the table chalking his cue. "Hundred bucks each?"

"Careful, Duke," Fenn warns. "You're only up one. Not the time to get cocky."

"What's the matter, don't think your brother can cover the bet?"

"Do you take food stamps?" cackles one of Duke's boys, whose name I can't be bothered to remember.

"Can he get it on an installment plan?" Another one with a crooked nose laughs.

"How does it work?" Duke sinks his next shot. Four and nine in the corner pocket. "Does your mom hand out your allowance, or do you have to suck stepdaddy's dick yourself?"

"You talk too much," I say, not rising to the bait. Meanwhile, I'm making a mental note to move Duke to the top of my background check list. It's always useful having ammunition on an asshole.

"Is that so?" Duke misses his next shot, much to my amusement. "Come on. Don't be a chickenshit. Put your money on the table. Whoever sinks the eight wins the money."

I shrug. "I'm good."

"Tell you what, I'll even float you."

Sitting on my stool, I watch Silas land one then a second shot. I don't so much as look in Duke's direction. "Yeah, not interested."

"What is your deal, bro?" He's smiling, but when Duke gets up in my face, he's not so friendly anymore.

"Don't have one, bro." I gaze past him, over his shoulder, to continue watching the game behind him.

"You know, you've got a real bad attitude. I thought you would have figured out by now to show some respect."

I can't help but flash a careless grin. "Don't know what to tell you. I guess I'm a slow learner."

"Hey, Duke. If you're in the mood to hit on someone all night, I could use a good lay." Lawson leans against the doorway, red-eyed and jittery despite his lazy grin. He'd slipped away a few minutes ago and came back wired.

"Sorry, Kent, even if I did swing that way, I wouldn't touch your one-inch pole with a ten-foot one," Duke calls back, and I can't deny I do enjoy the pole line. Assholes shouldn't be allowed to be funny. "Who knows where that dick's been."

"I can tell you where it's been," Lawson says helpfully. "Last night it was hitting your sister's G-spot."

Beside me, I hear Fenn sigh. "Not the goddamn sister again," he mumbles.

"Excuse me?" Eyes blazing, Duke charges at him. "Come on, dipshit. Say it again." He grabs Lawson's shirt while the other guy laughs.

"I said, I drilled your little sister last night."

Silas, who'd been silently going about his evening in the corner, throws himself between Lawson and Duke's fist.

"All right, enough. Game's over." He shoves Lawson, who continues to slur taunts, back out into the hallway. "He's a shithead, okay?" Silas tells Duke to disarm the situation. "What do you expect?"

Duke flicks his hard eyes over Silas. "You better get your boy. One of these days I won't have such a good sense of humor."

At that blowup, the night is done. Silas locks Lawson in their room while Duke storms off with his crew. I get the sense Silas has a lot of nights like this, babysitting his roommate. But hey, it made for better entertainment than pool, that's for sure.

Maybe this place won't be a total drag after all.

CHAPTER 15
LAWSON

THERE'S A MOMENT THAT HAPPENS WHEN MORNING FIRST pierces the veil of sleep. I lie there, listening for the sirens and sounds of decay, wondering what disturbances had transpired overnight. And then I feel disappointed, because the world is just as I fucking left it.

When I was little, movies had us believing the apocalypse was imminent and dystopia just around the corner. Any day we'd wake up to society in shambles and anarchy in the streets. The desolated remains of humanity.

Instead, the alarm on my phone orders me to shit, shower, and shave for another day of tedious monotony. Forever on this Ferris wheel of disappointment.

"Get up, man." Across the room, Silas is already moving around. "You'll be late again."

"And yet, I can't muster a solitary fuck about it."

"Come on, Lawson. I'm not doing this every day. Get your ass out of bed."

"Give me a good reason."

"Give yourself a reason." His tone is lined with aggravation. He's already sick of my shit and it's only the end of our first week. Silas is losing his touch. When we met, I could stretch his patience for at least a semester.

I sigh. "I'd kill for a suicide."

"Dude." Silas stops to chastise me with a glare. "That's morbid."

"Fine. Maybe we could start a rumor that the fencing coach is running a sex cult of freshmen out of his basement."

"You need a hobby."

"What do you think I'm spitballing here?" I swallow a groan, wishing I knew how to explain it. The boredom, and what it does to me.

Trust me, boredom is not an ideal condition for someone with my taste for self-destruction. It's a gun on the mantel that's always pointed at my head.

I need constant amusement. I need distraction and perpetual motion. Left to my own devices, I tend to get restless and make a mess of things. Stagnation drags me back inside my own head where I'm reminded why I don't care to spend much time in there. Turns out, we don't get along, me and myself.

"I'm taking a sick day," I tell Silas, watching him walk around in a towel. I let myself linger on the water still dripping down his muscular back for only a moment before redirecting my gaze at the ceiling.

Despite himself, Silas chuckles. "Laziness isn't a medical condition."

"I suffer from terminal boredom."

"And that's fatal, huh?"

"Could be."

"Then the cure..." Silas insists, dropping his towel in front of the closet before pulling on some boxers. "Is getting your ass out of bed. I promise nothing interesting will happen if you stay in here jerking off all day."

"All right, deal. You jerk me off and I'll get dressed."

That gets me a snort. "In your dreams."

Sometimes. I mean, I can't lie—it's definitely crossed my mind more than once. What it might be like to hook up with Silas. If he weren't straight. But my destructive streak stops just this side of ruining our friendship by nudging that line. Apparently it's the one thing I hold sacred enough not to set on fire. Anyone else, though? Bring it. When your partner pool is twice the size of most people's—and with my hedonistic tendencies—sex becomes an endless playground. Male, female, threesomes, orgies, indoors, outdoors…I'm always game.

"Meet you at breakfast. Hurry up." His shirt still unbuttoned, his jacket and tie in his hand, Silas picks up his backpack to leave.

I don't bother to shave and make it to the dining hall with just enough time to sit with a coffee and danish, somewhat surprised to see RJ has graced us with his presence. The guy looks genuinely pained to subject himself to the interaction of other humans. From what Fenn says, he'd have more luck bonding with his stepbrother if Fenn were a chatbot.

Still, I respect the mystery. Wouldn't it be something if the dude turned out to be some black-market kingpin? Running guns and girls to the seediest creeps on the internet. My cameo in a Netflix documentary could be good for a laugh.

"You were on one last night," Fenn tells me when he comes back with another bowl of cereal.

I furrow my brow. "Was I?"

"Yup. You decided to pick a fight with Duke."

I crack a smile. It sounds vaguely familiar. "How'd that go?"

Silas grumbles something under his breath.

Before I could press for more details, a short guy with too much gel in his hair walks up to our table. Matt something or other. I'm shit with names. Probably because I'm usually drunk, high, or a combination of both during most introductions.

"Hey, Fenn. This your brother?" Matt asks.

RJ's gaze lifts from his scrambled eggs. He casts a suspicious look at Fenn, who just shrugs in response.

"Right, yeah. I might have mentioned to a couple of people you could offer some homework help," Fenn confesses.

I grin at the almost complete lack of remorse on Fenn's part. Like me, he's more of a beg forgiveness than ask permission kind of guy.

"You sell essays, right?" The dude leans over our table, whispering while his shifty eyes scan the room. "I need one for English on—"

RJ sighs and returns to his breakfast, head down. "Text Fenn your info."

"Oh, yeah. Cool. Thanks, man." Matt struts off looking like a guy who bought his first dime of weed at the bike racks.

Children.

"You know that kid?" RJ asks Fenn.

"He's fine. Not the brightest, but he won't snitch."

"By 'a couple of people,' how many more ambushes like that can I expect?"

"Maybe more than a couple," Fenn relents, his grin sheepish.

I snicker softly. Fenn isn't the most discreet person I know. He's probably already told half the school his stepbrother is running an essay factory.

"Not that I don't wholly approve of this little enterprise," I tell them. "Honestly, big fan. But you might consider being a little less conspicuous." I give a quick nod, drawing their attention to Duke and his salivating junkyard dogs, who are watching us from across the dining hall.

"Not my problem," RJ mutters around a slice of toast.

I glance at Silas, who intervenes on my behalf. People usually take Silas seriously, whereas with me, they see a screwed-up fuckboy whose opinion isn't worth shit. I don't mind. Saves me a lot of boring conversations.

"Look," Silas starts, using his Mr. Serious voice on Fenn's stepbrother, "I know Duke comes off like a big talking clown, but he's not messing around when it comes to his business. All commerce and vice runs through his shop, no exceptions. He doesn't make enemies unless he has to, but trust us, he'll absolutely enforce those policies if you press him."

"Yeah, still not bothered." For once, someone considers Silas's advice as useless as mine. Totally indifferent, RJ finishes his breakfast and slides back from the table with his tray.

"Dude," Fenn says, making one last attempt at educating his stepbrother, "these aren't empty warnings. You *should* be bothered. Last guy who defied Duke ended up in the hospital with internal bleeding."

That gets RJ's attention. Well, sort of. He half cocks his head, which tells me he's at least paying attention. "How'd Duke escape without punishment?"

I snicker softly. "We all escape without punishment here, man. Our parents are filthy rich."

"Duke's vicious," Fenn says grimly. "He's capable of inflicting some serious damage."

"Did the internal bleeding guy survive?" RJ asks.

Fenn frowns. "Barely."

RJ seems to think it over. Then he says, "I'm not worried."

Whether it's hubris or ignorance, RJ is greatly underestimating not only Duke's resolve, but his grip on this school. Duke might be dumb, but he makes up for it in cruelty.

Still, there's something admirable in RJ's stubbornness. I appreciate his absolute lack of fucks. Not that I'd call us friends. His near-total refusal to engage socially makes that a wee bit difficult, but I've taken a liking to him. He's a wild card, and those are always the most fun.

After lunch, RJ takes the seat next to mine in English. "Hey," he grunts.

"Hey. You do the reading?"

He shrugs and fishes a copy of *On the Road* out of his bag as Mr.

Goodwyn launches into his discussion for day. It appears our teacher hasn't shaved since Monday morning, covering up that soft-skinned Good Boy with a bit of ruggedness. It fits. I picture him growing up somewhere cold. On a farm with cows and a goat he named at birth. A Midwestern milk-drinker lured to the East Coast and the promise of the big city, only to wash out to our little country hamlet.

"Mr. Kent."

I lift my head. "Huh?"

Mr. Goodwyn sits on the corner of his desk in a plaid Banana Republic button-down with his sleeves rolled up to reveal toned, tan forearms. His inquisitive green eyes are focused on me, waiting for a response.

"Sorry, didn't catch that."

He holds up his worn paperback. "Angst and longing."

"Aren't we all."

Sputters of laughter briefly deflate his irritation.

"In the reading, Mr. Kent. *On the Road*."

"Right. That's the one where Marylou is jerking off two guys in a car."

"I believe I'm sensing a pattern, Mr. Kent."

"No, I'm sensing a pattern," I counter. "Are we going to read anything this semester that doesn't include graphic sexual content?"

While Mr. Goodwyn tries to appear unperturbed every time I bring up sex, I sense his simmering unease. But clearly I hold his intrigue, because although he could dismiss me any time he likes, he doesn't. I might not be the most academically engaged, but I do consider myself a student of human nature, and I certainly know sexual tension when it's watching me like a nervous man at the end of the bar twirling his wedding ring in his pocket. Is Mr. Goodwyn batting for the home team? A switch-hitter, at least.

I'd fucking bet on it.

"You've seen the film adaptation, no doubt. I don't suppose you've actually read the text," he says, taking a seat behind his desk.

"Can't, I'm afraid. I made a pledge."

A slight smile pulls his lips, despite himself. "Is that right?"

"As a white male of privilege, it's my social responsibility to decolonize my bookshelf. I've already met my quota of dead white guys for the year."

"I see." Mildly amused, if only because he hasn't heard that excuse before, he again opens his paperback copy and begins writing on the board. "Then at least pay your classmates the respect of quietly following along."

My gaze tracks the motion of his hand, then lowers to his ass. All sorts of ideas skip through my head, none of them respectful. I begin to imagine what's happening under Mr. Goodwyn's button-downs and khakis. I bet he's one of those nice boys with a six-pack and ten-inch dick. Sensitive, rugged, and a raging-huge hard-on.

As he turns from the board to face the class, those green eyes collide with mine for just a second. A fleeting look, but it's rich with possibility. Seems I was a bit hasty to dismiss this semester as a lost cause. Silas was right. Today was worth getting out of bed.

And Sandover's faculty has undergone a significant upgrade in other departments too. As a laugh, I signed up for an Intro to Fine Arts class, figuring some watercolors and pottery would be a minimally taxing way to grab an A. But the nearsighted, half-deaf old bag who'd taught here for three decades finally retired or dropped dead. In her place, they lured a young redhead with a set of tits that would take your eye out from across the room. Last class, she wore a paint-covered olive jumpsuit with a tight shirt barely holding back those pointed nipples. Today, it's a gauzy white dress that doesn't disguise the fact I can see the color of her freckled pink flesh through the fabric when the afternoon light hits her exactly right.

"Nice to see everyone again," she says when everyone's seated. "I'm still learning all of your names, so if you've forgotten..." She writes her name again over the ghost of white chalk still on the board. For an art teacher, she has indecipherable handwriting. "I'm not picky, so you can call me Gwen, Ms. G, Mrs. Goodwyn—whatever you're comfortable with. And if you'd rather I use your nickname or a middle name, please tell me."

Gwen Goodwyn. For a second, I'm sure I heard her wrong. I squint at the board, again trying to make sense of the chicken scratch. I thought she'd introduced herself last class as Gwendolyn. Granted, I was still stoned at the time. Easy enough mistake to make, I suppose.

But goddamn. If this is who Mr. Goodwyn's fucking, I'd pay money to watch.

The image of Ms. G's cute round ass in the air, taking it from behind while he wraps her long, curly hair around his fist, both of them watching as I jerk off, nearly gets me sporting a tent in class.

Or the three of us in a car set out across the American West. Naked on the hot leather seats. His dick in my hand while she's thrusting against my fingers.

Oh, fuck me. This is exactly what I needed to jar me from my boredom spiral.

I become fixated on the idea until Silas is standing in front of me, slamming a locker in my face.

"Where'd you go?" he asks when my eyes focus on him. We're in the locker room where I've been standing with my goggles in my hands for an indeterminate time.

I sweep my tongue over my suddenly dry lips. "I think I'm going to seduce my teacher."

"The hell are you on about?" He sighs and throws a towel over his shoulder. From the door, Coach shouts for us to all hurry up and get in the pool.

"Turns out there's a Mr. and Mrs. Goodwyn," I say slowly, my mind working over the implications.

"I'm not following. Which one are you seducing?"

A faint grin tugs on the corners of my mouth. "Both."

CHAPTER 16
SLOANE

IT'S ALMOST TOO HOT TO RUN. THE AIR CONDITIONING AT SCHOOL has struggled all week to keep up with the boiling heat that's settled over us, refusing to relent. Maybe the only positive of St. Vincent's draconian skirt requirement: at least we get plenty of ventilation.

After Casey and I get home from class, I toss my uniform on the floor and pull on a tank and a pair of running shorts. I lace up my shoes practically midstride and then I'm out the door. Lately, I can't wait to hit the trails and get some miles under my feet. Just let the day drip from my pores while my playlist silences all thoughts but breathing and keeping pace.

About a half-mile from the house, I smell him before I come around the bend.

The trespasser.

Yup, here he is again, sitting on the bench, smoking like it's his personal headshop. I pull up short and catch my breath. RJ doesn't look up from his phone as he takes the joint from his lips and holds it out toward me.

"Thought I told you—"

"We both know I'm not gonna listen," he interrupts. "So let's skip ahead to you telling me what time to pick you up tomorrow."

I tip my head at him. "Still living in the land of delusion, huh?" When I don't take the joint, he pulls a drag and shrugs.

"I'm almost rooting for you."

RJ grins to himself and slides his phone in his pocket. "I know."

It's an entirely different thing meeting him in the daylight. The last time we were standing here, he could have been anyone. Some mangled figure in the darkness trying to lure me to his murder basement. Now, tucked in the forest shade from the too-bright sun, he's definitely not a monster. It's his hazel eyes, though, that capture my attention most. Flecks of brown inside a moss-green ring. Bright against the locks of chestnut hair the fall across his forehead.

"Why aren't you out with everyone else?" I don't know him at all, but I do know trouble when I see it. He's absolutely the type to be getting up to no good. "Most of the guys go into town on Friday nights." Which basically amounts to getting drunk and hitting on townies' daughters and the unfortunate wayward private school girls who wander into their lecherous paths.

"I don't care much for most people."

"Yeah? I'm just lucky, then, I guess."

"You're different."

Despite myself, a little flicker of pleasure tickles through me. "How's that?"

"You've got a better ass." A devilish grin spreads over his face. It's a nice smile. Honest. If completely full of itself.

"Walked right into that one, didn't I?" I say with a sigh.

"It's fine to say you're fishing for compliments. I don't mind."

He's got a bottle of water with him. That, I will take a hit of. I sit down beside him and chug about half of it.

"Sure, help yourself," he drawls.

I don't miss the way his gaze focuses on my mouth as I drink his water. "So, what, you didn't get invited to hang out with the cool kids?"

"Nah. I just prefer to be by myself."

I'm following the contours of his forearms as he raises the joint to his lips when it occurs to me, I'm spending more time than is prudent cataloguing his features. He doesn't strike me as an athlete of any kind, although he's lean and toned.

When I catch myself staring, I find a fascinating trail of marching ants on the ground to watch instead.

It was a lot easier to ignore him when RJ was only a blank face in my head.

"Fenn said you've changed schools a lot."

"Five times in three years," he confirms. "This makes six. Mom was always chasing some guy across the country. So here I am."

"That sucks."

"It's whatever. Eventually you learn there isn't much point to making friends. Everything's temporary. You just end up with a bunch of people in your timeline you follow out of some misplaced compulsion to like their posts and appear interested in their bullshit. No thanks."

It's weird, but in some ways, I recognize parts of myself in RJ, both of us keeping other people at a distance while living most of our lives in our own heads. Both of us guarded and maybe a little misunderstood.

Or maybe I'm reading way too much into his whole loner persona.

"I changed schools this year too," I admit.

RJ again offers me the joint, and this time I take a quick drag. "How's that going?"

"It blows. I go to a Catholic girls' school—"

"Yeah?" He perks up, raising a cheeky eyebrow.

"Trust me, it's the opposite of sexy. Imagine a Victorian orphanage for the Amish but where they beat you with guilt and unsalted food."

"I don't know… That could be sexy."

"You want to borrow my skirt and attend in my place, be my guest."

"See? Already getting you undressed."

"It's cute you think you'd even know what to do with this," I hit back.

"Please, sweetheart. Try me."

He swipes the tip of his tongue across his teeth as he smirks. Just a subtle reflex that for a moment pulls me in.

"In your wet dreams."

"Constantly."

I roll my eyes and steal another drag of his joint.

The way the boys were talking about him, they painted RJ as some maladjusted social defect, sitting in his room reading incel manifestos. Turns out, he has a personality. He's funny. Knows how to flirt. Stupidly hot. That initial intrigue I felt that first time is still present, something that hints at what's still under the surface we're skimming. I'm not about to call it a spark, but maybe a tiny glow of interest. A teeny-tiny urge to get to know him better.

"So the running," he says. "That your thing?"

"I run track, yeah. I'm aiming for a scholarship, but I sort of let my grades slide last year."

"If you ever need a tutor…"

I swallow a laugh. "Right, sure."

"I think you'd be surprised."

"Yeah, I bet. The secret delinquent genius."

"If you think insults will put me off…"

"No, that's what I like about you. You don't try to impress me."

"Should I?"

"Why would you, when you've got this whole mysterious scumbag thing going for you? Just be yourself, right?"

That earns me a deep laugh. Oh no. I like the sound of his laughter. It has the sexiest pitch to it, quickening my pulse a little.

"How about you let the mysterious scumbag take you out tomorrow night?"

RJ aims his cocky grin and charming hazel eyes at me, and I

have no doubt it's worked wonders for him in the past. Sadly for him, I'm not just another easy mark.

"How about no," I answer graciously.

"Help me out then. I'm supposed to go to 'the fights.' Whatever that is."

Ha. I tamp down a giggle, not wanting to give anything away. But it looks like RJ has managed to get absorbed into the social structure of Sandover whether he likes it or not. This should be good. For a laugh, at least.

"I wish you well." I finish off his bottle of water and bend over to tighten my laces before standing. I still have a few miles ahead of me before nightfall, along with a pile of homework I'm determined to finish. That scholarship isn't going to win itself.

"Want to give me a hint what I'm in for?" His expression is hopeful.

I could. But what would be the fun in that? Some rites of passage are for the traveler alone.

So I simply flash him a sanguine smile and say, "You'll see. Wouldn't want to ruin the surprise."

CHAPTER 17
RJ

On Saturday night, Fenn and I cool our heels in our room waiting for the babysitter to pass out. The way Fenn explained it, the housefather has a routine you can set a watch to: He makes a lonely dinner in his apartment downstairs, turns on a couple of hours of true crime shows or that History Channel alien bullshit, guzzles a few black and tans, and then falls asleep in his armchair, snoring over the TV.

"Dude, I swear this chick's body was unreal." Fenn bounces a tennis ball off the ceiling while lying on his bed. "Like some regressive comic book shit."

"Cool," I mutter while at my computer responding to messages.

Fenn's been going on about the girl he hooked up with last night for like twenty minutes. This after he let some Ballard girl blow him before making an excuse to bail on her and bounce to a different bar. I stopped paying attention when he wanted to tell me about the mechanics of sixty-nineing in a Porsche.

"You ever let a girl finger your ass?" he's saying now. "I haven't, but she offered, and I was like, what the fuck? Who wants to be on the receiving side of that? I mean, to each their own or whatever, but some things are sacred. Let me have this one tiny space to myself, you know? I just met you. We are not that close."

"Uh-huh."

I fully support a healthy sexual appetite, but Fenn is sort of a glutton for pussy. At the rate he's going, he's bound to reach a point of diminishing returns. Or a broken dick.

"Hey." He tosses the tennis ball at me. It hits the wall barely a foot to the left of my monitors. "What are you doing over there?"

I shoot him a look of warning. "Keep your toys on your side of the room or we're gonna have a problem, *Fennelly*."

"Oh, go cry to your mommy about it, *Remington*," he says, mocking me. "Seriously. You got a cyber nerd girlfriend on this or something?" Then he snickers. "Sloane would be relieved."

"Funny."

"When are you going to give up and stop embarrassing yourself? She's not caving."

"I've barely started." It's not in my nature to admit defeat.

"All right, seriously." Fenn gets up to hover over my shoulder. "Who are you talking to?"

"Other hackers from the boards," I answer absently, tapping out a quick message to some guy from Denver who I enjoy talking shop with. "People always hit me up for tips or resources. Ask for advice."

"So, you're a big deal nerd guru to these people?" Fenn's tone is equal parts impressed and disgusted.

I shrug. "Sort of." Obviously I haven't been around as long as some of the old-school dudes, but I've been in the community since I was a little kid. I've built a reputation.

Fenn's checking his phone now. "Well, it's time to unplug, bro. That's not real life. *This* is real life."

About an hour after curfew, Fenn and I sneak downstairs, past Mr. Swinney snoring in his armchair over *Ancient Aliens*. At the junior dorm we meet up with Lucas, the kid who helped me sort out the printer in the computer lab, then set out in the dark to the far north end of campus. Fireflies dot the black as the lights of campus dim behind us and the grass reaches higher up our legs.

"Where the hell are we going?" I ask, my fingertips grazing the weeds as we walk.

"You'll see." Fenn leads us with the light of his phone down an overgrown trail pitted with rocks and random potholes.

"At least clue me in on what this is all about. I don't like surprises."

"You're no fun," he sighs. "The fights are an underground tradition. Call it unsanctioned athletics."

"For guys with loose morals and deep pockets," Lucas chips in, his voice dry.

"A sturdy chin doesn't hurt either."

I nod. "Rich Boy Fight Club. Got it. Could have just said that." Wealthy people are always repackaging poor-folk shit and calling it clever. "Does the faculty know about this? Tresscott?"

"Probably," Fenn answers. "Kind of hard not to be suspicious when you've got dudes showing up to class with shiners and busted lips. But if they do know, they look the other way."

"Oh, Headmaster Tresscott definitely knows," Lucas says, grinning. "I swear he let it slip at dinner one time. But I have a feeling he allows it because he thinks it's a good way for us to let off steam. Maybe he hopes it'll cause less trouble for his staff."

I don't miss Fenn's cloudy expression when Lucas says the words "at dinner." My stepbrother's still got a major thorn in his paw about the fact that Lucas gets unlimited access to Sloane's little sister while Fenn is kept on a tight leash.

"You ever fight?" I ask Fenn.

"Sometimes," he says, now staring straight ahead as he picks up the pace. "If I feel like releasing some aggression."

"Dude, Fenn's vicious," Lucas tells me. "You should've seen what he did to Duke's wingman this one time."

Fenn snickers without turning around. "Who knew an ear could bleed that much?" He shakes his head in disbelief. "That was a total fluke hit."

"Yeah right," Lucas accuses. "You went there on purpose."

Fenn glances over his shoulder to flash an innocent smile. "I would never clock a man in the ear. That's just cruel."

I can't deny that their banter succeeds in raising my interest levels about these "fights." Just slightly. I'm still not on board with the whole being social thing. But it's hard to imagine my pretty boy stepbrother beating the shit out of anyone, let alone Duke's goon Carter. That's definitely something I'd pay money to see.

"How long has Rich Boy Fight Club been going on?" I ask curiously as we push our way through the darkness.

"It started years ago," Fenn says. "Hell, probably decades. Sometimes guys from other schools come to mix it up. The real action is on the sidelines."

I'm almost afraid to ask what kind of scratch these dumb fucks are throwing down to watch each other bleed.

"Gabe told me one time he saw like fifty grand change hands in one night," Lucas says.

"Gabe...that's your brother, right?" I prompt. "Fenn's old roommate?"

"Yeah." Lucas deflates somewhat, dropping his head to watch his feet disappear through the tall grass. "Our dad sent him to military school this year."

I raise a brow. "What happened? He get caught betting the Bentley on a couple sophomores knocking each other's teeth out?"

"Have you heard from him?" Fenn jumps in, turning to study Lucas.

"Nah, man. I told you, it's like Dad threw him in solitary or something. I haven't spoken to him since the van came and picked him up." Lucas glances at me. "He got caught dealing."

"Your dad didn't say anything else about why?" Fenn gets weirdly insistent, pumping Lucas for information, even though the junior is obviously not in the mood to talk about it. "You didn't hear them arguing or anything?"

"No, dude. You know my dad. The quieter he gets, the worse it is. Gabe came home that night, and the next morning his bags were on the porch."

"And Gabe really didn't say anything to you before he left? How he got caught."

Lucas becomes visibly reluctant to participate in this investigation, and I kind of feel bad for the kid getting grilled by Fenn. I know Gabe is his best friend, but Christ, dude, you don't have to waterboard his little brother. Let him come up for air.

"How much farther?" I prod to change the subject. "I can't see a damn thing out here—"

I barely finish that sentence when a whistle calls out to us and breaks the darkness.

Fenn turns to grin at me. "We're here."

Through the silhouette of trees, we come to a clearing where a dilapidated greenhouse is lit by a few dim lanterns inside. The panes are cruddy with years of pollen and decomposing foliage collecting on the roof. Shrubs and vines hug the perimeter, climbing up the walls and breaking through the glass.

"School closed it up decades ago and left it abandoned," Fenn says as we approach the shadowy figures standing outside. "Rumor is a groundskeeper used to bring kids here."

"I always heard it was a woman, and she killed herself because a teacher got her pregnant and wouldn't marry her," Lucas says.

Charming.

When we walk up, Lawson is taking bumps of coke off the back of his hand while Silas is texting on his phone, pretending not to notice.

"Welcome to the festivities, gentlemen," Lawson drawls. "I hope all your affairs are in order."

"Ah, God. What's that smell?" I groan as the odor of rancid

garbage and dead animals burns my nostrils. It gets stronger near the entrance.

Silas lifts his head from his phone. "About forty years of mold, rotting plants, racoon shit, and sweat," he answers dryly.

"Just wait." Lawson smirks, somehow enjoying this. "It gets worse."

We make our way inside, where the bodies are packed in like slabs of meat in a truck. It was humid outside, but in here, I can barely breathe through the thickness of sweat and testosterone. Condensation drips in greenish-yellow trails down the glass as if it were raining.

I don't know what I expected. Maybe dipshits in polo shirts slap-fighting for their daddies' car keys. But this is intense. Guys are walking around shirtless, smacking themselves in the face to get pumped up. Cracking their knuckles and eyeing the crowd for victims. As I walk through the crowd, I see faces in the shadows salivating for carnage.

Damn, these dudes really came to beat the shit out of each other. All around me, hands are flashing wads of cash and flipping through handfuls of hundred-dollar bills like they're tossing singles at a strip club.

Without any ceremony or pretentious pomp, two skinny shirt-less guys meet in the center of the concrete floor, shaking out their arms before launching at each other like their plane went down two weeks ago in the frozen wilderness and they've run out of caviar and protein bars. It's bloody and primal. Splashes of red stick to the bottoms of their feet and trace their dance as they move, creating footprints in the mud of dirt and body fluids.

The sounds of bone-on-bone and the smack of flesh against wet flesh make me wince. That squishy, puckering noise of landing a blow on an already broken, tender face.

At some point, they're not even breathing air anymore. Just exhaust and marrow.

When the former champ collapses and his noodle arms can't lift his body weight from the muck, they declare the mangled thing standing over him the winner. Five hundred, a thousand moves from one hand to another within the crowd, dozens of bets trading a month's tuition without a thought.

"Gonna get your hands dirty, New Kid?" Carter slides up beside me in the mayhem.

I spare him with a cursory look. "Nah, I think I'm going to hang on to my teeth. Might need them some day."

Another guy steps up to fight the winner. Which hardly seems like a fair deal when the winner gave everything he had in the last bout and is barely on his feet. Unfazed, the tall, lean senior strips off his T-shirt and steps into the circle.

"Worried you might embarrass yourself?" Carter bumps my shoulder to try getting a rise out of me. "Nobody expects the new guys to win. But you might figure out you like it."

"Yeah, what's not to like? Letting some asshole take out his daddy issues on my face. Sounds like fun."

The new fighter pumps the crowd for approval and applause before dancing around, daring the other guy to hit him. At one point he puts both hands behind his back and sticks his face out to his reluctant opponent, who at least knows better than to take the bait. The guy can barely see through the swelling and blood in his eye. Still, when his new opponent lashes out with a jab, the skinny guy lands a devastating uppercut that draws a gasp from the spectators, and the fight begins in earnest.

"That's coward talk," Carter informs me. "What, you afraid to get hit?"

"Nah, I'm good." If I could be goaded into a bare-knuckle brawl by the dumbest kid in remedial preschool, I wouldn't have this well-developed sense of superiority.

As a matter of fact, after the initial shock-and-awe campaign wears off, watching dudes go at each other for shits and giggles gets a little tedious. There's only so much porn and gore a person can watch before it loses the effect. I guess illicit violence doesn't get me hard. Maybe it's a money thing. I wouldn't understand.

So, I tell Carter to fuck off and head for the exit, searching the jam-packed space for Fenn or Lucas. Hell, I'd even welcome a high-on-coke Lawson at this point. But they've all been swallowed up by the crowd. I fish my phone out of my pocket and type a one-handed text to Fenn, telling him I'm bailing.

Before I can slip out, however, Duke corners me near the door. He's wearing gray track pants and his trademark white T-shirt that shows off every ridge and ripple of his chest. I'm surprised he's even wearing a shirt. He's the guy who always needs to be flashing his abs to the world.

"Not leaving yet, are you?" he mocks. "We're just getting warmed up here."

"Yeah, I don't think I'm straight enough to get the appeal." I think it over. "Or maybe I'm too straight to watch half-naked dudes pretend-fuck each other for ten minutes."

"That's hilarious," he says, rolling his eyes. "Speaking of hilarious—I heard a funny story about you recently. That you sold essays to a couple seniors last week."

I offer a shrug. "So?"

"So, I thought I made myself pretty clear. Any side action goes through me. That's the way it works around here."

That gets him another shrug. "Yeah, I'm not into it."

"Not into it," he repeats, crossing his arms over his chest. Duke keeps his composure with this play at civility, but below the surface, I know he's fuming. Just itching to throw me in the center of the circle and go a few rounds. "Maybe you didn't understand, but participation isn't optional."

Frustration rises inside me. Forget this nonsense already. "Look, man. I'm not interested. This is my gig and I'm not asking permission or forgiveness. Deal with it."

"You still don't get it." He muscles up to me, dark eyes gleaming. "I run this shit. All of it. You either get with the program or you find out how hard your life gets."

I flick my gaze to his. "Do I look like I respond to threats?"

"I can give you a preview right now if—"

Duke's ready to take a swing until Fenn dives between us. "All right, party's over," my stepbrother announces. His tone is light, but it's betrayed by the hardness of his face. "Time to blow this Popsicle stand."

"Your brother's testing my goodwill," Duke snarls.

"Yeah, he's an insolent little fucker, huh?" Fenn throws his arm over my shoulder and proceeds to practically drag me outside. Lucas and a distracted-looking Silas trail behind us, but Lawson is nowhere to be seen.

"You don't have to do that," I tell Fenn. "Duke doesn't scare me."

"Dude, I get that you don't understand it, but seriously, you shouldn't antagonize him. It's not a problem you want."

"He can bitch and moan all he likes; he's not squeezing a cent out of me."

Outside, I breathe in some much-needed fresh air, happy to leave the scent of blood and sweat behind me. While Silas texts somebody, Fenn pulls out his trusty flask and takes a quick sip. When he holds it out, I accept it and slug back some bourbon that goes down so smooth I'm pleasantly surprised.

"Who died and made that asshole king, anyway?" I mutter, passing the flask to Lucas. "And why does everyone put up with it?"

Silas finally peers up from his phone. "Tradition," he answers. He rolls his eyes. "Any time you're trying to figure out why some stupid shit is happening at Sandover, the answer is always tradition."

"It's a tradition for a juiced-up psychopath to profit off hard-working entrepreneurs?" I grumble.

Fenn snorts. "Pretty much. But this year it's a lot more entertaining," he says with a laugh. He drains the rest of the flask before tucking it into the back pocket of his thousand-dollar jeans. "What with you not falling in line. Poor Duke doesn't know how to handle someone like you. He's probably crying himself to sleep every night."

"Or plotting your demise," Silas says, grinning at me.

I'm unbothered. Let Duke plot and scheme. I'm doing the same over here on my end. Or trying to, at least. My background search into Duke hadn't turned up anything juicy yet. Just the usual basic bullshit. Filthy rich parents. One older brother who's an upstanding and contributing member of society. Little sister who attends some disgustingly posh prep school out of state. The two of them are close, judging by his social media.

As far as I can tell, there's nothing overtly nefarious in his family life. Which means I need to keep digging. I'm confident I'll find something on him eventually. Guys like Duke always have a skeleton or two in their closet. Only a matter of time before one comes tumbling out.

I glance at Fenn, then Silas. "I still can't gauge your relationship with the guy. You're not friends."

"Friends?" Fenn echoes. "Nah. We're cordial. There's no point agitating Duke unless it's for something important, a hill you want to die on, you know? For the most part, we do our own things."

Silas shrugs his agreement. "He gives us wide berth because we don't try to mess with any of his rackets."

"Rackets. God, he's such a douchebag." Lucas laughs. "I don't know what Sloane ever saw in the guy."

I blink.

Then blink again.

"Wait, what?" I blurt out.

While Lucas seems confused by my outburst, Fenn and Silas exchange an amused grin. "Shit, Lawson's going to be so disappointed," Fenn says solemnly. "He really wanted to be the one to break the news."

"Sloane dated Duke?" I growl.

Fenn is clearly fighting back laughter. "Oh yeah."

"For two whole years," Silas adds helpfully.

In one of the rare instances of my life, I'm actually struck speech-less. No smart-ass remark to be found.

Sloane? And *Duke*?

What in the actual fuck?

CHAPTER 18
SLOANE

"Hey, you up?" I tap on Casey's door Sunday morning. She hadn't come down for Sunday morning breakfast, which is unlike her. "I'm going for a run. You want to come?"

There's no response.

"Case?" I poke my head in her room to see she's still in bed.

She rolls over, bundled in her covers. "What time is it?"

"You still sleeping? It's after ten."

"Sorry." She yawns, rubbing the crust from the corner of her eye. "Didn't realize."

A wave of concern washes over me. "Are you feeling okay? Coming down with something?"

I take a spot on the edge of her bed as she sits up against her pillows. Casey pulls away when I try to feel her forehead.

"I'm fine." Brow furrowed, she doesn't look at me. "Just didn't sleep well."

"What's up?"

Her fingers pick at the buttons on the duvet while she decides whether to tell me what's really going on with her. I give her the space, because I know if she's going to say anything, it'll be in her own time.

"I guess…" She sighs. "I've been having nightmares again."

It's an absolute dagger through my chest. "About the accident?"

"Of drowning."

The D-word carries heavy connotations in this house. Even before prom night.

I wasn't there when Mom died. Casey and I stayed behind with our dad while Mom went to the Cape with our aunt and some of their girlfriends. It was supposed to be a fun weekend girls' trip. Instead, it ended in tragedy. A total fluke accident that ended with Mom slipping and falling overboard. Her limbs getting tangled in ropes of seaweed that pulled her under the surface. A stunned Aunt Monica told Dad it all happened so fast. Mere seconds. The blink of an eye. Gone. Dead.

Years later, I can't even hear the word *drowning* without my mind conjuring up gruesome images of Mom gasping for air as she got sucked underwater.

My body feels cold, tense. "Did something trigger the nightmares this time?"

Casey shrugs, then lifts her bloodshot eyes to mine. She's pale and exhausted, creases from her pillow still carved in her skin. Her hair is sweat-matted to the side of her head, and her sheets are tangled around her legs from a harrowing night fighting for her life. I would give anything to trade places with her and take on her demons. It kills me that I can't. That I have to stand by helplessly watching her suffer.

"Just being at school, I think. Hearing everyone whispering about it behind my back. Over the summer I kind of got to ignore it, but then we came back. And even though it's a new school, it feels the same."

I try to mask my anger, but it burns hot in my gut. Gossip is an irresistible force in perpetual motion, and while I've done my best to put the fear of death in anyone with my sister's name in their mouth, it clearly hasn't done much good. Casey will continue to be at their mercy, at least until someone else's life is destroyed for public amusement and the rumor of the month sucks up all the air in the room, making them forget about her.

"Did you remember anything else?" I hate to ask. It feels invasive every time. But ever since she was found on the edge of the lake that night, we still have so many unanswered questions.

The investigation had stalled before it started. Cameras were down, and no one saw Casey get into the car or how it became half-submerged in the lake. How she ended up on shore soaking wet and unconscious.

That's the most frustrating part of it—how are we supposed to help her fully heal and find real closure when we don't even have the whole story?

"See something new this time?" I push when she doesn't respond.

Casey shakes her head, lips sealed tight, before finally letting out a quiet breath. "Every time," she says softly. "I feel the water climbing up my neck. It's cold and I'm wondering where it's coming from. Then I open my eyes and I'm trapped. Sinking. I can't feel my body. My limbs won't respond, and nothing feels real. I try to hold my breath but the water's reaching my lips and it's dark and I can't find my way out. Then someone's telling me it's all right. I'm going to be all right. I open my eyes and I'm on the ground, freezing, with everyone shouting and standing over me. That's it."

My heart aches, a hot throbbing mass squeezing painfully in my chest. Because she looks like our mom. Strawberry-blonde hair and a slight nose. A swipe of freckles under her eyes. I've heard Casey tell this story, nearly word-for-word, a dozen times. And every time I can't help seeing our mother.

"Do you want me to call Dr. Anthony? If you wanted to talk—"

"No." She averts her gaze again. "It's fine. It'll work itself out of my system eventually."

"But you know you don't have to suffer, right? We're all here to help you."

"I know." But she's obviously done talking. She's an island. No one can reach her if she doesn't allow it.

Casey was only five years old when our mom drowned. She and I huddled on the couch at our old house in Massachusetts, clinging to each other's clammy hands, while Dad stammered through how to tell us that Mommy was never coming home. It took the better part of a month to realize what it meant. In practical terms. Suddenly she wasn't there to pull us out of the bathtub and comb our hair. To pour milk in our cereal. To wear her clothes and sit on her spot on the couch.

No one taught us how to navigate this world as women. What it meant to be a girl in high school. Now Casey's my responsibility and I feel entirely unqualified. How do I coach her through another trauma when I'm not sure any of us have recovered from the first?

In the kitchen, Dad is still sipping tea and reading the news on his iPad. When he asks about Casey, it's hard not to take it as an accusation.

"She's not still sleeping, is she?" He checks his watch. "Did she seem under the weather last night?"

"No, she's not sick." I put the breakfast bar between us, leaning against the counter for support because more than hearing it from Casey, I hate having these conversations with him. "She's having the nightmares again."

Dad puts down the tablet. "Did she talk about it?"

"A little. There weren't any breakthroughs."

In the immediate aftermath of the accident, Casey withdrew from everything. She retreated into herself and shuffled around here like a ghost, if we saw her at all. We spent several unbearable weeks gently nudging communication until she was verbal again. Now I see those days reflected in Dad's worried stare when he meets my eyes. It's like both of us are always holding our breath that something doesn't trigger her to regress back into her darkness.

"She's going to need your help adjusting to her new circumstances now that you're both back in school."

"I know that." Unbeknownst to him, I've spent the week committing multiple counts of misdemeanor assault to try clearing a path for Casey to have a normal semester at school.

"We shouldn't take for granted the progress she's made to this point. More likely the next few months will be the most difficult of her recovery, so we can't let our guard down, Sloane."

"I'm not."

I swallow the lump of frustration that jams in my throat, but it's so hard not to let my emotions spill over. Trauma within a family always creates a cascade effect of collateral damage. For us, it's this widening schism between Dad and me, a result of his deep disappointment and distrust. Months later, we still don't know who drugged my sister and put her in that car. And in an absence of answers, Dad blames me. *I'm* the one who brought her to that dance and promised to look after her. *I'm* the one who abandoned her to get back on my on-again, off-again bullshit with Duke.

I was supposed to be watching her, and instead, she almost died. Dad's never forgiven me for that, and I don't know if he ever will.

What I do know is that I'll never forgive *myself.*

"Are you all right?" he asks. "Is there something else we should talk about?"

It's an empty question. He doesn't want to know how I'm doing—his gaze is already dropping to his tablet even as he voices the obligatory question. Since Mom died, I've been expected to fill her place, to take care of Casey and hold the family together. I'm supposed to be the strength the rest of them rely on, and it's a burden I bear in silence, because I don't get to show weakness. Our family is a house of cards built on my shaky palm. If I so much as blink, the whole thing falls apart.

"Nope," I answer. "All good."

Dad's attention returns to his news feed, and I mask my weariness and leave to sweat it all out on my run. For the next hour, I push my legs faster until the heavy, damp air burns in my lungs and my muscles scream for relief. I thrust myself at the miles and terrain, hearing nothing but my footfalls, so that when I lean panting against a tree trunk, doubled over, I'm too exhausted to think.

I'm cooling down, trying to regulate my breathing, when a text pops up on my watch.

RJ: At the spot for a smoke. Join me?

I should say no. I mean, first and foremost, I'm in my laundry-day workout clothes and haven't washed my hair in two days. But the real issue is, I have no business getting involved with him. Casey needs me. I've got my hands full with school. The last thing I should expend energy on is the incorrigible antisocial new guy.

Even if he is suspiciously gorgeous. And kind of funny.

And he does get good weed.

Not that I'm going to make that a habit.

Weirdly, the thing I find most interesting about RJ is that he doesn't fawn all over me, tossing hollow compliments like bread for ducks. A part of me doubts he's actually interested in a serious romantic entanglement. At this point it's our inside joke. Our bizarre secret language. Half a dare, half suicide pact.

So I don't reply and make my way back home. Just happens I have to pass the bench anyway.

"You run a lot, huh?" he says when I show up, and offers me a hit.

"That's kind of the point, yeah."

"It's working for you." He gives me an appreciative wink. The guy could flirt with a tree stump.

Taking a long drag, I sweep my gaze over him, wishing I didn't enjoy the sight so much. But this is the first time I'm seeing him in his street clothes, and I really like it. His jeans are faded and worn in, with a rip at the knee that draws my attention to his long legs. A black T-shirt hugs his chest and shows off sculpted biceps I didn't expect. His personality doesn't give off guy-who-works-out vibes, but his body says otherwise.

"You like what you see?" RJ slants his head, sounding amused.

I blink, inwardly cursing myself for getting caught checking him out. Denying it will only make me appear weak, so I own the ogling.

"The view's not bad," I concede, passing the joint back.

"Well, look at that. Progress." He chuckles softly, those hazel eyes flickering with heat. "What's your favorite part of me?"

"Don't push your luck, sweetie."

He ignores that. "Arms, right? You look like the kind of girl who's into arms. Either that, or my ass. You an arms girl or an ass girl, Sloane?"

I lift a brow. "Neither. I'm partial to the dick."

His expression goes a little hazy. "Fuck," he groans. "Why'd you have to say that?"

"What," I say innocently, "you're not confident about your dick game? Pity."

RJ's gaze transforms from hot to molten. "Sweetheart, my dick is always the most confident motherfucker in the room."

As he raises the joint to his lips, I don't miss the way his other hand does some strategic rearranging down below. This conversation is getting him hard.

Just like that, my throat runs dry. Damn it. I know I'm the one who opened this door, but now I'm really regretting it. I can't sit next to RJ and his semi. It's just going to make me want to reach over and touch him. To unzip his jeans and slip my hand inside and hear him moan when my fingers encounter his hot, male flesh.

My entire body begins to tingle, bringing a jolt of anxiety. Oh my God. How am I lusting this hard over this guy?

"I don't see any black eyes or bloody knuckles," I say, desperate to change the subject. "How'd it go with the boys last night?"

"Funny you should ask. I ran into your ex-boyfriend. Think he likes me."

"I bet."

"Tell me something," he says, blowing embers off the end of the joint. "What is it with hot chicks and egomaniacal douchebags? Like, historically. What's the biological imperative there?"

"So, you two really hit it off, huh?" I'm not sure why I like that he isn't a fan of Duke's, but it puts the first genuine smile on my face I've had all day. It's sort of cute in a petty way.

RJ watches me carefully. "You still into it?" he asks.

I roll my eyes. "Not even a little."

"Good. Then go out with me. There's a Sleater-Kinney cover band playing a bar in town tonight. They probably suck, but—"

"Shut up. You know Sleater-Kinney?"

"Sure. They're one of my favorite bands."

I just gape at him. "You're putting me on. Fenn or Silas told you to say that."

RJ cocks his head at me. "Why?"

"Sleater-Kinney is seriously one of my favorite bands. I once basically stole my dad's car and followed them across four states for like a week."

He grins. "Really? That's awesome. Most people I know have never heard of them," he says. "Guess we have something in common after all."

Perish the thought. Still, his taste in music does speak highly of his character.

"Come on. It's one night." RJ has persuasive eyes. They possess a hypnotic quality, both devious and dependable. "Have a drink and show me around town. Consider it a public service for the less fortunate."

Yeah right. RJ is no charity case. Whatever he is, I know I haven't seen his true stripes yet. He's still camouflaged, out here in this borderland between our real lives. Nothing's authentic until we meet each other in the real world, until I discover who he is in public when other people can see him too. Because more than anything, he has my curiosity.

"Fine," I cave. "But I'll have to sneak out. If my dad finds out, he'll lose it and you'll be in deep shit."

"Don't threaten me with a good time."

"Don't you have a housefather or something? How are you even going to get off campus?"

RJ cracks a thief's smile. "Don't worry, I got it sorted. Just be ready to go at eleven."

CHAPTER 19
RJ

"Settle something for us," Fenn orders when I slide into the seat next to him in the dining hall. I made it for lunch minutes before the kitchen closed. Thank God, because I'm hungry as hell from that joint I just shared with Sloane.

I set my tray down and waste no time digging into my meatloaf. "What?" I grunt between bites.

Fenn points his fork at me. "Man-bun: douchey or cool?"

"Douchey," I say instantly.

Across the table, Silas dons a triumphant look. "See?" he tells his roommate.

"Aww, don't do me like that, Remington," drawls Lawson, who's currently sporting the aforementioned man-bun. "DiCaprio wears a man-bun sometimes."

"DiCaprio is a douche," I reply.

"Blasphemy. Dude's like fifty and banging twenty-year-old supermodels. He's who I want to be when I grow up."

That makes Fenn think for a moment. "I guess I'd start wearing a man-bun if it got me some supermodels," he relents.

Silas gapes at him. "I can't believe you just said that."

"I think the more pressing question is, how do we feel about ponytails?" Lawson asks, leaning back in his chair.

I make a gagging sound, with Silas and Fenn nodding in agreement.

"Gross, bro."

"Unless you're in a metal band," Silas counters. "But even then, that's pushing it."

"It'd better be a damn good metal band," I agree.

"Look at us!" Fenn says happily, gesturing toward me. "We're bonding!" He glances at the other two. "I've been trying to bond with this asshole for weeks. He refuses to bond."

Just like that, I clam up. Because he's right. We're borderline bonding here, and I need to nip it in the bud before something crazy happens—like I become actual friends with these guys and join their pussy posse.

Oh shit, didn't DiCaprio have a pussy posse back in the day?

What have I become?

"Speak for yourself," Lawson says over the rim of his water glass. "Your stepbro and I are old friends. We're always bonding in lit class, right, Remy?"

I fix him with a deadly glare. "Call me that again and I'll sneak into your room tonight and—"

"Suck me off? Excellent. I'll leave the door unlocked."

Silas snickers. "You walked right into that one."

"Murder you," I grumble. "I was going to say murder you."

Lawson just waggles his eyebrows at me.

I let out an aggravated sigh. "Fuck off, man-bun."

After lunch, Fenn and I head back to our room, where I settle at my desk and check on some outstanding projects. I keep hitting dead ends in a couple of my background digs, particularly my deep dive into our housefather.

"You ever notice how Roger leaves here around the same time every Sunday afternoon and doesn't come back until after curfew?"

"Huh?" Fenn is on the coach, starting a video game. "Yeah, I guess."

"What do you think he's up to?" I pull up another window on my computer. "The guy doesn't have a family stashed off campus, right?"

"I don't know." His delayed answers come between button mashes. "Don't think so."

"Could be a girlfriend. Or elderly parent?"

I've been tracking his travels, but according to the map, there's nothing out there but empty fields and abandoned warehouses. A single paintball range and ropes course is the only operational business nearby, but it closes before sundown. Swinney has no reason to be there late at night.

"Dude, what are you babbling about?" Fenn tosses the controller down and comes to read the monitor over my shoulder. "What's so interesting about Roger?"

"Look." I bring up the map. "Every Sunday he drives out to the middle of nowhere, a couple hours from campus, stays there all night, then drives back. But there isn't shit out there. Not even a seedy motel to take a hooker."

"Maybe they stay in the car."

"But he doesn't make any stops on the way. Straight there. Straight back."

"All right, so what? It's Roger. Maybe he's UFO spotting."

Huh. Hadn't considered that. "Or burying bodies."

"Also a solid guess." Fenn takes a seat on the end of my bed. "Wait, how did you even know about this?"

"Hacked his phone. It tracks his most visited locations."

"Dude, that's fucked up." But he laughs when he gives it some thought. I tend to find most people value privacy in principle more than practice. "What else did you get?"

"About Roger? Nothing interesting." I glance over my shoulder. "But I did get a look at a draft police report of Casey's accident they didn't release to the public."

"You hacked the police department?" he demands.

"Technically I guessed the password. Their security is shit."

His smile evaporates and darkens into a deep scowl. "Why would you do that? That's risky shit, bro."

"Like you said, it's a mystery. I don't like unresolved questions."

"What'd it say?" he asks.

"Not much. The investigating officer was skeptical of Casey's story, but that was about it. Doesn't seem like he gave it much effort, honestly."

Fenn rises to get a drink from the mini fridge. "You're diabolical, but I kinda like it," he says, and tosses me a soda. "Go on, then. Let's have it. You hacked my accounts by now, right?"

"Only a cursory background check."

"Bullshit." He waves toward my monitors. "I see what you do in here, and none of it is fucking cursory."

A grin breaks free, tugging at the corners of my mouth. "Your sexting skills could use some work."

He narrows his eyes. "Bullshit," he says again.

"Your dick pics are decent, though. Really good use of lighting and common objects for scale."

He brightens. "Thanks."

"I was being sarcastic."

"Nah, you were impressed. Don't deny it. It's okay—I know I have a good cock. I'm packing." His expression brightens even more. "Please tell me you snooped into Lawson's DMs too."

"Oh yeah." I shudder, because I still haven't recovered from *that* trip down the hedonistic rabbit hole.

"Does he pull as many chicks as he brags about?" Fenn demands.

"Dude. You don't even know. He's texting like three different girls *and* a guy or two on any given day. I don't know where he finds the energy."

Fenn offers a solemn nod. "Sport fucking is a full-time job."

I snicker.

He once again plops down on my bed. "So, what's the plan tonight? You want to go stake out Roger and find out what he's up to?"

Tempting.

But I say, "Can't. Got a date with Sloane."

He snorts a laugh. "Yeah, I'm sure."

"Really."

Fenn almost does a spit-take of his soda, slapping his hand over his mouth until he's swallowed. "Bad idea. You're seriously playing with fire here."

"So you've said."

"I'm serious. We're family now, and since I don't know how I'd explain going home for Thanksgiving without you, I need to reiterate that Sloane is Duke's ex. He's killed for less."

I grin again. "That's half the fun, isn't it?" Sloane's a prize in her own right. But if I can smear it in Duke's face, all the better.

"I admire your dedication," Fenn says, shaking his head in resignation. "Hope she appreciates what you're risking to get with her."

"I still don't get why any of you actually take that dude seriously. Just tell him to piss off."

"I already told you, he's capable of serious violence. It's not worth it for me to provoke him. I don't need the hassle, and I don't care enough to antagonize him."

"So you're just cool with him thinking he runs the school?"

"He doesn't *think* he runs it. He *does* run it," Fenn says with a dry grin. "That's just the way it is. It's not like Duke woke up one day and declared himself king of the mountain. There's a lineage."

Rich kids and their rituals. It's exhausting. They fucking love a pageant.

I lean back against my chair. "This is going to be dumber than it sounds, isn't it?"

"Back in the day, it was Duke's brother running the show. Brett. He started the fights as something to do in the dead of winter when the campus is boring as fuck, and then monetized it by setting up bets and taking a cut off the top. Then he took a cut of everything else on campus. When he was graduating, he named a junior to take up the mantle."

"If this ends with some *Game of Thrones* cousin-kisser shit, I'm out."

"Sophomore year, Duke decided he wanted the job. But you can't just take it. There's rules."

"Rules?" I swear, this school is one massive migraine.

"For Sandover leadership. Rules are, you gotta fight to a knockout. Which Duke is damn good at. So you know how that turned out."

I tip my head. "Anyone ever challenge the Mad King's reign?"

"A few times. They always lose. People usually give them a hard time for a while then forget about it. Duke doesn't. He'll pretend like all's forgiven, but that's only so you don't see it coming when he sticks the knife in. There's a reason no one crosses him. It's not just because broken bones hurt."

"Yeah, well. If there wasn't any risk in rebellion, it wouldn't be cool, am I right?"

"Listen, dude. Duke's never gotten over losing Sloane. She's the face that launched a thousand ships."

"Not seeing a downside…"

Sighing, Fenn shrugs. "I'm just saying, tread lightly."

"I'll take it under advisement. On a related note, can you hook me up with a car to borrow for tonight? I heard Silas say he has one, right? Not sure I know him well enough to ask, though." At Sandover, the guys are allowed to have cars—and personalized parking spots, of course—but I've discovered that most of them don't bother bringing their rides to campus. They all have chauffeurs on speed dial.

As if to punctuate that, Fenn pulls out his phone and types something. My own phone buzzes a second later.

"Number for a private car service," he explains, giving me a faint grin. "This one's on me, Romeo."

CHAPTER 20
RJ

Sneaking out of the dorm around eleven, it occurs to me
that I might have walked into a trap. What if I'm an unwitting victim
of a long con? Here I am, the clever fuck who gets a date with Sloane
Tresscott only to figure out too late she's been putting the screws to
me. Which is why, as I'm crossing campus toward our spot on the
trail, I give myself sixty-forty odds of Sloane standing me up. Or
maybe sending a text with something like, "LOL, eat shit, asswipe."

But the odds are in my favor. Traipsing down the dirt path, I
come around the bend to get a flashlight in the face.

"You're late."

So she does care.

"I bet you were early," I say, shielding my eyes from the light.

"I was thirty seconds from going home."

"Then I was right on time."

The light disappears and I'm momentarily lost in the dark.

"This better be worth it," Sloane grumbles.

I hide a smile. I've only just gotten here and already she's over
it. Sloane's not going to make this easy on me, nor would I want her
to. From the second we met, she's been intent on throwing me off
kilter. Keeping me unsteady, ready on my toes, like I'm on the side

of a building waiting for her to sneak up from behind and shove me. It's not boring, and that's what makes it great.

"I'd say you look nice tonight," I tell the outline of her silhouette, "but my retinas are still recovering."

Sloane scoffs. "Yeah, save it for the townie you'll be making out with in the bathroom while I'm paying the tab."

"Speaking from personal experience?"

"When you grow up around prep school boys, you keep your expectations low," she replies.

Not exactly a glowing endorsement of Duke. Which bodes well for me.

"I'm not one of them," I remind her. "Take off the dorky uniform and I'm still nobody from nowhere."

"You say that now. Give it time."

Sloane walks quickly, making us take the long way to avoid cameras. She's a thief prowling the museum under laser beams and over pressure sensors. A practiced escape artist. She stays a step ahead of me while we make our way across campus to the gates where the car is waiting. I finally get a good look at her outfit, and my cock nearly tunnels its way out of my jeans. Her legs are endless in those tight, black leggings, and the top she picked is a cropped halter held together by flimsy strings I want to rip off with my teeth. She's not wearing a bra either. Kill me now. There's no way I'm making it through tonight without thinking about her nipples the entire time.

Catching my glazed expression, Sloane raises a brow. "You okay there, RJ?"

It's hard to swallow through my cotton-stuffed throat. "Just wondering who I blew in a past life to deserve this outfit of yours."

"Who says it's for you?" She offers a cheeky smile, then disappears into the back seat of our town car.

God help me. This girl is pure fire.

Sandover is about a fifteen-minute drive through the middle of nowhere to the tiny downtown district of Calden that consists of a few shops and restaurants. The lone bar is open till two every night. The way Fenn tells it, carding is antithetical to their business model. Rather than drunk locals, the real money is in underage rich kids rolling up in their chauffeured Bentleys to blow their trust funds on eight balls with Johnnie Walker chasers.

Nice gig if you can get it.

The car drops us in front of a neon-lit red shack built of vertical wood siding and shoestrings. The doorway is decorated with vintage brewer memorabilia, and a hand-painted wooden sign above the door has a flying saucer on it. Inside, it's one flannel shirt away from a 1994 high school reunion. There are more neck beards and unironic ponytails than I've ever seen in the wild.

The band is already into their set, playing to a house mostly distracted by darts, pool, or foosball. Christ. Now I know what a Gen X identity crisis feels like. There are pop sci-fi-themed murals on the walls, cult movie relics, and furniture that smells like it was fished out of the discard dumpster outside a Goodwill. A group of over-forties plays a role-playing game in the back corner beside a pinball machine. Bikers with fresh, small-batch meth stuck under their fingernails glare at us from the far side of the bar.

"Not what you were expecting?" Sloane smirks and saunters up to the bar.

"Hell no. What is this place?"

"Charming, right? Welcome to Calden."

Sloane is a knockout on any occasion. Sliding up to the bar in this hipster hillbilly sausage fest, she doesn't even need to be braless to get the bartender's attention. The guy is already diving toward her, tongue practically on the floor. She orders us a couple beers, then hands me one.

"Hope you don't feel emasculated," she says as she directs us to a table.

"It takes more than a lady ordering her own drink to threaten my manhood."

But I get it. Sloane's determined to let me know I'm on her turf. She's holding the reins to this date and I'm along for ride. Knowing her, she intends to put me through the wringer and see what's left when I come out the other side. But whatever tests she can engineer, I'm ready. I wouldn't have started the chase if I didn't know what I'd do when I caught her.

"So what do you think?" I nod toward the band, who are set up on the floor against the far wall, framed by the restrooms and kitchen on either side. This place is a dump. But it's growing on me?

"They're loud," she says.

I nod in agreement. "They do seem to think decibel level is a replacement for talent."

That makes her snicker. "I mean, he's almost getting the lyrics right."

"Words are hard," I say solemnly, which earns me another laugh, this one lighting up her entire face. Christ, she's gorgeous.

Then, as if realizing she'd lowered her guard for an entire second, Sloane's gray eyes narrow at me. "Be honest." She sits across from me at the table, which won't do if I'm going to steer tonight toward something more productive than an expensive interrogation.

"What?"

"I said—"

I lean in, pretending not to hear until she huffs and slides her chair next to mine. So fucking easy.

"Tell me the truth," she says. "We're only here because you want to piss off Duke, right?"

"I asked you out before I ever knew about you and Duke," I point out. "So, no, that's not why we're here."

"Yeah?" Her eyes can be damn potent when she turns on the intensity. "You're saying there's no part of you that enjoys getting to Duke?"

"Being honest?" I shrug. "Sure. His power trip rubs me the wrong way. So maybe I don't mind shoving his face in it."

"Thought so. I appreciate the honesty."

"But." I lift a brow. "I asked you out because I want to get to know you." I pause. "And because you're a drop-dead stunner."

She cracks an embarrassed smile and turns her face to cover her flushed cheeks as she takes a swig of her beer.

"So for me, I don't really see a downside there. Call it a win-win."

"Fuck off," she says over the rim of the bottle. It's adorable the way she rolls her eyes because she can't take a compliment. Nothing more offensive than someone being nice to her.

"Yeah?" I grab my beer and half stand like I'm ready to bail. "I can get out of here if you—"

"Stop it." She laughs despite herself. "Sit down."

It works, though. Chips away at the glacial layer of primordial ice around her. Sloane wants to come off like being here is some major imposition, but I can't help feeling, somehow, she's the one who asked me out. She walked me into her snare and I'm exactly where she wants me, even if admitting it would nearly kill her.

"You know, it's weird," I remark. "I never saw myself dating a jock."

"One date." She points the lip of her bottle at me. "Not dating."

"Give it time."

After another swig, Sloane seems to settle in. She relaxes a bit into her seat and stops acting like she's conducting a job interview. For the first time, it feels like we're having a real conversation and not circling each other in a standoff.

"And if this was the cafeteria," she asks. "What table would you be sitting at?"

"Me? Nah, I don't subscribe to the table-based profiling system."

"No, you're right. I picture you smoking under the bleachers with the other misfits."

"Because if we can't be reduced to a member of the Breakfast Club, what's the point, right?"

"Oh, so he's a sensitive misfit."

I love the way she laughs. Her mouth turns up on one side and her eyebrow arches. It's stupid how sexy that is. If Sloane threw a wink my way, that look could have me robbing a bank. She's got a smile that begs to cross the desert in a convertible with a sawed-off shotgun in her lap and a suitcase full of cash in the back.

"All right, your turn." I set my elbows on the table and dare her to hold eye contact. "Tell me something real about yourself."

"Real, huh?" She ponders her response while cautiously sipping her beer. "Like what?"

"Anything." It's all been surface level with us so far. Which is fine enough for figuring out whether you want to hook up with a chick. Now that I've got her here, I have to admit I'm curious. "What's the worst thing that's ever happened to you?"

Sloane's playful smile retreats behind her implacable mask of cool assuredness. She sets her bottle aside and stands.

"I've got a better idea."

There's a small empty space between the band and tables. She's the only one interested in scuffing it up as she backs away from me to dance to the off-key rendition of a song I probably wouldn't recognize even if I'd ever heard of Sleater-Kinney.

"I don't dance," I mouth to her over the straining sound system.

With hands framing her lips, she shouts at me. "If you want another date, you do."

Fuck me.

I abandon my beer and join her on the makeshift dance floor. But whatever I do on there, I couldn't defend it as dancing in a court of law. I do my best to follow Sloane's lead, though I'm sure it looks better on her.

"I almost feel bad," she shouts against my ear over the distorted guitar ten feet from my other eardrum. "You're not good at this."

"Hey, if making an ass of myself is what it takes…"

Maybe it's a little appreciation and a lot of pity, but Sloane leans into me. She presses her hands against my chest. Runs them up to grip my shoulders. She smells good and it knocks me off my game for a second. I'm suddenly lost in the nebula of lights reflecting on her hair that's dark brown in daylight but now shines jet black under the cheap stage lights that were probably salvaged from a kids' party DJ garage sale.

"If you're full of shit, you're pretty good at it," Sloane tells me while slithering her perfect body against me. As if I'm not already counting back from a thousand because sporting a hard-on would get my dick snapped off.

"What part of anything I've said sounded like I wasn't dead serious?" I ask her.

Sloane's shining, sly glare doesn't give me an inch. "All of it."

"Goes to show you don't know me very well."

"That's the question, isn't it?" Her hands find their way up my neck, brushing the hair at the base of my skull. "How do I know who you really are?"

"Sounds like you don't trust me." My head lulls into her hands and my eyes nearly shut completely. I almost forget we aren't alone, disarmed by her seductive manipulations. This chick makes it tough to keep my wits about me.

"Should I?" she challenges.

"One way to find out."

I expect her to laugh. Maybe roll her eyes and shove her hand in my face. Instead, I think she shocks both of us. Sloane slides her fingers into my hair and grabs my head to pull me in. With my hands gripping her hips, I kiss her. Fully and with more hunger than even I meant to.

It's intense and digs something up inside me that's at once picturing clothes on the floor and bare skin, but also hair on my pillow in the morning. It scrambles my head.

I don't hear her moan so much as feel it vibrate against my mouth. That just gets me hotter, my hips moving forward, just slightly, so she can feel what she does to me. Another moan tickles my lips, and then her tongue is slicking over mine, her fingers tangled in my hair, her warm body pressed tight to mine.

Between her exploring tongue and her nails biting into my scalp, the entire world fades away. I forget my own name. Until our lips part and our eyes meet. Both surprised. Confused, maybe. Then embarrassed when we realize we're standing alone in the middle of the bar in near silence. The band members have abandoned their posts. There's just pinball music and the *thunk* of darts finding their targets in the background, the din of conversation totally oblivious and unconcerned with the massive shift in the status quo we've just experienced.

This girl is an earthquake.

I'm still rattled when we take our conversation and another round of beers to a more private table in a shadowed corner. We don't talk about the kiss or that I'm still staring at her, wondering what the fuck this chick did to me like I've just remembered another life where we were star-crossed lovers separated by war.

I'm stuck in my own head until I notice Sloane picking at the label on her beer and the way her mouth makes a sad, wistful smile.

"Silas or whoever probably told you I'm obsessed with Sleater-Kinney, right?" She doesn't look up from her pile of paper scraps forming on the sticky tabletop. "They were my mom's favorite band."

"Yeah?"

Sloane nods absently. "Or at least, she had a lot of their records. When I was little, I'd sneak into the den and go through her record boxes and pretend to play them." She glances up to offer a brief self-deprecating smile. "I was like five, so I didn't really know how to use the thing. Then she'd find me and pull out this one that had a sleeve that was falling apart. We'd sing along and jump around the room, screaming at the top of our lungs to girl punk. She was so cool to me in those moments. And now that I'm older, I realize that was part of her before me and Dad and Casey ever came along. So, yeah. There's your 'something real.'" Sloane shrugs to herself, as if she's almost afraid to look at me for a response. "I guess it rubbed off on me. Listening to them, I mean. I guess I feel closer to her. It helps me remember her."

I'm stunned for a moment, absorbing what she's just told me. It took some serious emotional heavy lifting for her to lay that on the table. I think it might be the first honest moment between us, a small glimpse at the authentic person beneath all the bravado and misdirection. And it's kind of heartbreaking. Like, all right, sometimes I'm a bastard, but I get this is a precious thing for her and whatever I've done right, she decided to share it with me.

A small pang of guilt swirls around in my gut at the reminder that I lied about liking her favorite band. That I only knew the damn band existed because I hacked her. But I do my best to ignore the uncomfortable sensation. It's not like I used Sloane's dead mom against her on purpose. And it all worked out, didn't it? She's having a good time and, if I'm reading her right, had one more chance to relive a happy memory. All's well that ends well, right?

"I bet you take after her more than you realize," I tell her, which gets a shy smile in return. "Your mom sounds like a cool chick."

"She was." Whatever memory flashes behind Sloane's indiscernible gray eyes, she blinks, and it's gone. She lifts the bottle to her lips and takes a long gulp. "So thank whoever clued you in. Far as first dates go, this one was a sure thing to get on my good side."

"Enough for a second date?"

Her coy glare returns and all sentimentality evaporates. "Getting ahead of yourself much?"

"Eh, I like my chances."

"God, you're so sure of yourself."

Sloane rolls her eyes, but she doesn't object when I drag her chair closer to kiss her again. Our lips meet, tongues touching for one tempting, agonizing second before she pulls back.

"You're a good kisser," she whispers, her soft breath tickling my face. "But not—"

"Swear to God," I interrupt, "if you say 'but not as good as Duke,' I'm never sharing my weed with you again, Tresscott."

Her laughter heats my neck as she buries her face there and convulses. "Down, boy. All I was going to say is, but it's not how I expected you to kiss."

"What'd you expect?" I ask roughly. I rest my hand on her hip, lightly dragging my fingers over the exposed skin between her waistband and top. I don't miss the way she shivers.

Her expression takes on a pensive gleam. "Slower, lazier. I figured you'd treat kissing the way you treat everything else, like you couldn't care less. But it's not like that."

"Trust me, I care very much about kissing you."

Those sexy lips curve. "Yeah? Then do it again."

She doesn't have to ask me twice. I lean in, my mouth a scant inch from hers before something else occurs to me. "Goddamn it," I curse.

"What?"

"He doesn't have a tiny dick, does he?"

Sloane startles. Then she snorts. "Wait, you mean Duke?"

"Yeah," I say miserably. "I've taken great pleasure in the thought that all those bench presses and biceps curls are to compensate for a little dick, but now that I'm thinking about it—"

"Why are you thinking about my ex's dick when you're kissing me?" she demands in exasperation.

"—I'm realizing there's no way you would've stuck around for so long if he was rocking a small package. So that means it's not tiny, right?"

Her lips are twitching wildly. "No, rookie, I'm afraid not."

"Bastard."

She laughs, then raises herself off her chair and slithers into my lap. "Luckily, you don't seem to have any problems in that department either," she murmurs, and then she rubs her perfect ass over my growing erection and kisses me again, and damned if I don't see stars.

It's like we don't know how to temper ourselves. The instant we touch, something consumes us. Total blackout. Her nails biting into my skin. My teeth scraping her tongue. She pulls my hair at the roots and I'm about to rip her pants off if not for the split-second of clarity that reminds me we're in public and I still barely know this girl. She's hypnotizing.

"They're going to kick us out of here," she whispers against my lips before shoving her tongue in my mouth again like she paid for it.

"They should," I rasp back. "We're completely indecent."

But we don't stop, not until the manager of the bar eventually stomps up to our table and politely announces it's time to go.

Later, after the car drops us back at campus, I walk her all the way back to the path despite her protests. "I can find my way home in the dark," she grumbles.

"I know you can. But I'm being a gentleman. Would you just let me be a fucking gentleman?"

Her quiet snort echoes between us.

"And now she's laughing at me," I narrate out loud.

"She is," Sloane agrees.

"Watch it, cupcake. Or I'll do something crazy. Like hold your hand. Or text you good night when I get home."

She stops walking, her eyes shining in the sliver of moonlight that pierces the darkness. "You wouldn't dare." Then she gives me a quick kiss and disappears through the trees toward her house.

I'm grinning like an idiot the entire walk back to the dorm, where I quickly pull out my phone just to prove that I do indeed dare. A quick glance reveals Fenn is asleep and snoring softly on his side of the room. Poor baby. Must be exhausted from all the blowjobs he probably received tonight.

I tap out a quick text.

Me: Had an amazing time tonight. You're incredible. Good night, Sloane.

My screen lights up instantly, summoning that stupid grin again. I'm damn glad Fenn isn't awake to call out my sappy self.

> Sloane: Don't go getting all romantic on me, rookie. It's beneath you.
> Me: You like it.
> Sloane: Not one bit.
> Me: All the bits.

There's a short delay before another message pops up.

> Sloane: I guess... I don't entirely hate it. Good night, RJ.

CHAPTER 21
SILAS

"Fuck, man, I can't do it. When I go in, just let me drown." Lawson is doubled over, practically dry heaving beside me at the edge of the pool at Monday's practice.

In the water, the team is swimming two lanes of four-by-one-hundred medley relay. Brandon and Carter are dolphin kicking their way to the final lap of the breaststroke before Lawson's supposed to dive in for the butterfly. This is the fourth time today Coach has made us swim this relay and we're all feeling the hurt. I sucked in more water than air on my last lap. My arms are noodles. Heavy and limp.

Coach blows his whistle for the next swimmers to step on their platforms and Lawson shoots me a parting glance. A disconcerting smirk, as if he's found his epiphany the second before he takes a swan dive off a tall building.

"We are going to perfect these transitions if it kills us," Coach shouts. "Patience, precision, perfection."

"The beatings will continue until morale improves," Lawson mutters, adjusting his goggles over his eyes as he gets onto the platform.

He strolled into the locker room this afternoon with his

headphones and sunglasses on. Coach knew right away he was still hungover from the weekend. If he ever sobered up. When I woke up Sunday morning, Lawson was tangled up in his bed with two naked chicks he brought home from the bar in Calden. First thing he did after opening his eyes was snort a line and then climb under the covers to go down on both girls, who proceeded to moan so loudly, I'm shocked they didn't wake Mr. Swinney. Not that Roger cares enough to reprimand any of us.

Needless to say, I went to grab breakfast early yesterday. Real-life porn isn't my thing, especially when it stars my friends.

Still, Coach would've taken it out on all of us today regardless of Lawson. The fact that the whole team is sloppy and dragging ass today is fuel on his fire.

When Carter touches the wall, Lawson throws himself off the starting platform and does a header straight to the bottom of the pool. Then, he folds his legs yoga-style and proceeds to meditate, sitting beneath the surface. It takes a few seconds before Coach realizes Lawson isn't coming up.

Again, the whistle screams through the building and the water goes calm as the other swimmer drags himself out of the pool, panting hard.

"Hazelton." Coach barks my name. "Get his ass out of there."

Goddamn it. Smothering a sigh, I dive in and more or less have to wrestle Lawson to the surface.

"Aw, I knew you cared," he teases me as we climb out of the water.

"You two, front and center." Coach calls us from the other side of the pool. "The rest of you chuckleheads hit the showers."

"See what happens?" I give Lawson a shove when he's reluctant to line up for his ass-reaming. "You pull some bullshit and I get chewed out for it."

"Like you're not teacher's favorite."

"Not the point."

We go stand in front of Coach, who's got his clipboard clutched in his tight fist, like a receipt of all our failings.

"Make me understand it." He barely contains his frustration behind the sarcasm. Digs his thumbs into his eye sockets. "Because Hazelton has improved his splits at every practice. But, Kent, my grandmother with a metal hip could post a better time doing a doggy paddle."

"I bet your grandmother is ravishing in a Speedo, sir."

"Do us all a favor?" Coach uses the dad voice. The one he whips out when he's *not angry, just disappointed.* "If you don't want to be here, spare the rest of us the effort."

"Don't listen to him," I quickly interject before Lawson can deliver some snide retort he can't walk back. "He's an asshole when he doesn't sleep well." I nudge my roommate's shoulder. "Right, asshole?"

Lawson takes pity on me. Rather than really shoving his foot in his mouth, he winks at me and smiles. "Just a wreck without my beauty sleep, Coach."

"Uh-huh. Get out of here," Coach dismisses him, but asks me to hang back a minute.

We've had too many of these talks.

"Despite how he comes off, Lawson really does want to swim," I assure Coach. "I know his attitude sucks, but if you can get past that…"

"Yeah," he groans, unconvinced. "So you keep telling me."

"He just finds it easier to make people hate him."

"I'm not interested in fixing the kid's head. If he wants to swim and learn to be part of the team, I can help him there. Kent's got all the natural talent to be a force in this sport. If he can get out of his own way."

"I think he knows that." I also think it scares him, but I don't say that out loud.

"So do you. Having that natural talent, I mean." His frustration dissipating, Coach leads me to the bench against the wall and gestures for me to sit beside him. "If you want to swim collegiate, you're good enough to go anywhere you want. I can make those calls, Silas. But you need to decide what's most important: your future, or your friend. If you're not careful, you're going to end up on the bottom of the pool with him."

This isn't the first time we've had some version of this conversation. Hell, it took plenty of convincing to get Lawson on the team to begin with. He has that effect on people—near-instant animosity. Because he doesn't let most people know him the way I do.

Still, that doesn't mean the routine doesn't get old. It's exhausting sometimes.

"I get you, Coach. I'd appreciate anything you could do to help me out with colleges. I promise I won't let you down."

"If you want to thank me, talk to that other friend of yours. Shaw. I think he's got something we could work with. Get him in here to try out."

RJ? I almost burst out laughing. I know Coach saw him swim, but Fenn's stepbrother is even less enthusiastic about the team than Lawson.

"I barely know the guy," I admit. "I'm not sure I have any pull there."

Coach gives me a slap on the back that leaves no room for discussion. "You'll figure it out."

In the locker room, Lawson's waiting for me with a frown.

"Some people have no sense of humor, huh?" He sighs when I don't respond. "My bad."

"Don't apologize if you don't mean it."

I grab my towel to go shower, but Lawson blocks my path.

"Oh, come on, man. I mean it, okay? I'm sorry you had to take one on the chin for me. All right?"

"Are you? Because that'd be a first."

He looks momentarily wounded. There's an instant pang of

regret that I've gone too far this time. But there's a bigger part that knows I'm right.

Lawson puts on his sunglasses and unaffected grin. "Feel better?"

"It's fine. Just let me shower so I can get out of here."

"Whatever. I'll leave you to your thoughts, then." He backs off and shuts his locker to walk away.

I remember then I'm still wearing my swim cap and goggles on my head, so I throw them in my locker and take a second to type a quick text to Sloane.

> Me: Lawson's one stunt away from getting us both relegated to a community college intermural swim team next year. Had to sit through another parent-teacher conference after he staged an underwater protest.

I feel shitty as soon as I hit *send*. Most of the time, Lawson's antics don't faze me. He's just looking for attention or validation. He's bored and restless and doesn't understand limits. Mostly, he's always trying to remind people how much he doesn't need them so he can't be hurt when they leave. It's a coping mechanism that's turned to white noise in my head. Other times, though...

My phone buzzes in my locker as I'm about to close it.

> Sloane: Just finishing up at the track. I'll come by.

CHAPTER 22
SLOANE

Silas is in a mood when we meet up after his practice. The unfortunate consequence of being Lawson's wet-nurse is having to clean up his shit.

"How mad was your coach really?" I ask as we walk across campus toward his dorm.

"I don't know," he says with a shrug. "Like at some point we're all culpable, right?"

"It's still a choice. For example, I choose not to make Lawson my headache and it works out fine for me."

That summons a slight smile from him. "Seriously, though. How much can Coach expect from the guy when he's put up with him this long?" Silas rationalizes more for his own benefit than mine. "If he was going to kick him off the team, he probably should have done it the time the bus got searched by the highway patrol when someone at our meet told them Lawson was dropping acid between heats."

"Is that true?"

"Which part?"

I shake my head, torn between laughing and groaning. "Dude is too much."

He's also some sick marvel of biology—the shit he gets away

with while still performing at peak athletic ability is insane. Because that's the trick. It's why Lawson runs around getting away with murder: everything comes so fucking easy to him. If he actually applied himself, he'd be an Olympic-level swimmer. And he's sharp as hell. Would break the SATs if he felt like it. I'd hate him if he weren't so easy to pity.

"After Coach's pep talk, he told me I could make it up to him by getting RJ on board."

My heart skips a beat at the sound of RJ's name. Oh no. I've been trying not to think about him all day and failing miserably. Now that he's a topic of conversation, it's impossible to push him from my mind.

"What, really? Like join the team?" I suck back a laugh. "Where did that come from?"

"Yeah, so the other day, his PE class was in there doing laps. Coach saw him and now he's got a major crush."

"Wow..." It's hard to swallow my laughter. This can't be real. "Not that I know him well, but I think RJ'd rather gag on a toilet brush. He doesn't seem like the sporty type."

"I don't fucking know what Coach is thinking." Silas sighs. "Part of me wonders if this is a desperate move to have someone in his back pocket in case Lawson bails altogether. But RJ? The guy's not a team player. Hell, he doesn't even want friends."

"Yeah, so, speaking of which..." I hadn't planned to mention anything, but since Silas brought him up, I'm dying to get some perspective on the situation. "We went out last night."

"Wait, huh?" Silas squints against the sun, holding his hand over his face. "You're talking about RJ?"

Something in his voice makes me self-conscious. "Yeah. No big deal or whatever. We went to the bar." I pause. "We sort of hooked up."

He seems almost confused, cocking his head at me. "Really?"

"Well, no, not that far. We made out in the corner to a terrible cover band."

"Okay..."

Wary, Silas continues walking in silence. I can't tell what he's thinking. I don't have a great read yet on how the other guys rate RJ. Well, other than they all think he's an antisocial shut-in who may or may not have a criminal record across six states. Casey said Fenn was talking about sweeping the dorm for FBI bugs, and I think he might be only half joking.

"I know," I say awkwardly. "He's not my usual type. The whole apathetic bad boy thing gets tired. But also, in a weird way, I wonder if we're too much alike?"

After all, we can't both be the bitchy one who won't make conversation at parties. So guarded we'd rather keep everyone at arm's length than risk the disaster of someone figuring out who we really are.

Silas gives me half a nod to say he's following, but doesn't offer a pity laugh.

"Seriously. We're similar, no? In theory."

"Sure. You've got two people who don't really like people," he answers to prove he's listening.

"That's stupid, right? A straw house in a tornado."

There's a beat. "But you like him."

"I don't not like him."

Let's not get carried away, after all. It was a good kiss. Several good kisses. Okay, fine, it was more than good. I completely lost my head last night. I got lost in the heat of his mouth and the hungry sweep of his hands on my lower back, caught up in the shocking excitement of realizing that, oh shit, I might be into this guy.

If I didn't have any self-control, I could see a version of last night that ended with condom wrappers. The fact that RJ is hot is not in dispute. We have some sick sort of chemistry that I don't totally understand. But it was opening up to him about my mom that's been weighing on me since I woke up this morning. I've never told anyone that story, least of all on a first date. Duke and I never had the deep conversations, but that was the point. No one dates a guy like Duke—brash and boisterous—because they want to stay up late trading traumas. He was a good time and didn't push my boundaries. Kept it fun and on the surface where it's simple.

RJ, he's complicated. I know if I go down this road, I'm not going to like everything I find. About either of us. Not to mention it's going back on the one promise I made myself for this year. Eye on the prize and no distractions. I don't want to be one of those girls who give up on themselves to chase a boy.

And yet there's this compulsion. A completely irrational need to see what happens.

"I think I want to go out with him again." I feel dumb even having this conversation out loud. "Is that a horrible idea?"

Silas is quiet for a while, approaching the senior dorms. The longer the silence persists, the more certain I become he thinks I'm an idiot. But I'm not looking for his approval so much as his advice. And when the advice comes, it startles me.

"If you want to see him again, do it," Silas finally says. "Who's stopping you?"

Me, I guess. And at the moment, I can't think of a good enough reason why I shouldn't go out with RJ.

So, what the hell.

"Yeah, okay," I say slowly, my cheeks feeling weirdly hot. I hope I'm not blushing. I never blush. "I will see him again."

And then, proving he has the worst possible timing on the planet, the front doors of the dorm swing open and my ex-boyfriend strides out.

"Babe," Duke says, his face lighting up. "Fucking finally."

Silas looks like he's trying not to laugh.

"Sorry to break it to you, but I'm not here to see you," I tell my ex. "I was just walking Silas home."

Duke shrugs, his chiseled features completely unbothered. "Whatever. Now that you're here, we need to talk."

Silas glances at me. *Want me to stick around?* is the unspoken query.

I respond with an *all good* smile, and he leaves me with a quick hug and ducks inside. Alone with Duke, I give my ex a long once-over. I can't deny he looks good. Duke is tall and muscular, his broad shoulders filling out his Sandover blazer so damn nicely. But I also can't help comparing him to RJ. They're about the same size, same build. Both attractive in their own right. The main difference is, Duke never roused any deeper feelings from me. He was great in bed, absolutely. Funny with the one-liners, sure. But I was never tempted to dig deep with him, to poke around in his psyche, in his soul. I never cared about that with Duke.

With RJ, I want to know everything about the guy. And that's a bit terrifying.

"Sloane, come on," Duke says darkly. "How long are you going to hold out on me?"

"I'm not holding out. I told you, I'm done."

He moves closer, flashing the sweet, disarming grin that once upon a time would've worn me down in a heartbeat. "You saying you don't miss me?" His voice lowers to a smoky pitch. "Not even a little?"

"Not even a little," I say flatly.

The smile fades. "You're lying. And in case you were wondering, I miss you too."

Weariness creeps in and weighs down on my chest. "I can't do this right now, Duke. We're not going out anymore, okay?" To soften the blow, I add, "I can't focus on relationships this year. I'm trying to get a scholarship. So, please, just back off. I can't do this."

Before he can object, I give him a patronizing pat on the arm and stalk off, leaving him in my wake. Luckily, he doesn't chase after me. Which is somewhat of a surprise, because Duke's not the kind of guy who backs down so easily.

As I'm cutting across the lawn toward home, I encounter yet

another obstacle—my dad spots me from the courtyard and waves me over with a scowl.

Stifling a sigh, I jog toward him.

"What are you doing wandering campus?" he demands with far more indignation than seems reasonable.

"I wasn't wandering. I left the track and walked Silas back to his dorm after practice."

"You know I don't like you on campus during school hours."

"Technically…"

"Sloane." He narrows his glare and lowers his voice.

"Okay. Fine. But it's not like I'm vandalizing property or overthrowing the government. Silas and I were just taking a walk."

The strain in his cheeks eases and he lets out a sigh. "No, you're right. I know I don't need to worry about you. Tough as nails, this one." His expression softens a bit. "Did Casey mention having any more nightmares last night?"

Because it always comes back to her. Wouldn't want to get distracted from his single-minded concern for only one of his daughters. I feel like most parents might find a way to throw more than a few scraps of attention to *both* their kids, but what do I know about parenting.

"I don't know," I answer. "She didn't say anything."

"I need you to keep an eye on it for me. She talks to you. Casey wants to lean on her big sister."

As if I haven't been there for her every day since the accident. But in his mind, I'm always failing both of them.

I speak through the lump of resentment obstructing my throat. "Yeah, Dad. Of course. I've got it covered."

CHAPTER 23
RJ

"WHAT DO YOU THINK THE AUTHOR IS DESCRIBING HERE?" ON Tuesday, Mr. Goodwyn sits on the edge of his desk, paperback novel in hand. He's rolled his sleeves up, so we're really in for it today. The guy gets fucking giddy for class participation.

"They're having dinner," someone answers from the front row like a good little dog.

"Yes, but remember we're talking about subtext. So with that in mind, the author is giving us clues to their intent. What are some of the words that stand out to you in this scene?"

"Slit." Lawson chews on the end of a pen beside me.

"All right." Pleased to get some engagement in the discussion, Goodwyn jumps off the desk to scrawl the word on the white board. "What else?"

"Rigid," Lawson says. "Meat."

The class is quick on the uptake and mumbles out some laughter while our teacher fearlessly adds the word to the list.

"Mr. Kent." He turns around to level a playfully chiding look at Lawson.

"Yessir?"

"We're always grateful for your insights. How do you read the subtext of this scene and the author's intent?"

"Kind of sounds like they're saying the narrator wants to fuck their family."

The laughter isn't shy this time. Mr. Goodwyn gives him a tolerant smile before holding his hands up to quiet the room.

"Perhaps you could find more eloquent vocabulary and tell us what clues you see in the text?"

"Listen, we still don't know if this is really their family, right?" Lawson says. "The main character shows up and suddenly the mom is opening up boxes of clothes in the attic from college and the dad is a depressed shut-in probably sharpening axes in the garage. But we get to this dinner and it's like eight pages of describing the wet fleshy meat or whatever. That reads to me like sexual tension."

I'm not totally oblivious to subtext either. Though lately I'm more interested in the apparent flirtation happening between Lawson and our esteemed English teacher. These two go at it every class like the rest of us aren't even here.

Sloane: Could be worse. At least you don't have to attend chapel. I can livestream Sister Katherine's lecture on modesty for you.
Me: Hard pass. I'm watching Lawson seduce our English teacher. Kinda hilarious.
Sloane: That boy is so slutty it's almost impressive.

With Mr. Goodwyn otherwise distracted, I've been texting with Sloane. We text nonstop now, despite her insistence that I haven't earned a second date with her yet. Operative word being *yet*. I'm becoming addicted to our chats, and I have a feeling she is too, though she'd probably never admit it, not even at gunpoint. Which, of course, is why I like her so much.

Sloane: By the way... Heard you're shopping for Speedos.
Me: WTF?

> Sloane: Rumor has it you're joining the swim team.
>
> Me: Like hell. I'm not about to strut around in public with my junk stuffed in a pair of nut-huggers.
>
> Sloane: Don't sell yourself short.
>
> Me: You don't have to buy a ticket, cupcake. You can just ask.

"Are we distracting you, Mr. Shaw?"

I glance up from my phone to see Mr. Goodwyn with his arms crossed. Busted.

"He's searching incest porn." Carter twists around from the chair in front of me to deliver the taunt.

"Nah," I say. "Just looking up a good sex addiction therapist for Lawson."

Lawson winks at me. "I'd like to see them try."

Duke's best friend and favorite lapdog sneers when he doesn't get a rise out of me. Honestly, I wonder how sincere his hatred is if he can't muster a better effort. This is some amateur-level bullying. I'd expect more from a private school hoodlum.

"All right, people. Back on task." Goodwyn retreats to his desk again, sorry he bothered. Secretly, I think our teacher enjoys the *Lord of the Flies* dynamic of this overindulged group of self-obsessed dicks with teeth.

After class, Lawson and I are heading in the same direction. I've got gym next and the dread is real.

"They've got us playing field hockey today," I groan, checking the schedule on my phone. "Kill me."

"You know the way to end your suffering." Lawson slides on a pair of sunglasses as we step outside into the blistering sunlight. "Just give in, man."

"Not you too." Seems like everyone is prodding me about this swimming bullshit today.

"Hey, it couldn't be easier. A few seconds in the water and you're a legend. Stay in your lane and only worry about yourself. Simple."

"Come on, it's a little more complicated than that."

Lawson flashes that lazy grin of his. "Really? You think they'd trust me in there doing rocket surgery? We're not handling plutonium, man. It's just swimming."

I can't argue him there. I've only known him a couple of weeks and I've already seen him strolling into class hungover and strung out more than once. If he can muster the capacity to bang out a few laps in the pool, it can't be that hard. At the very least, it's got to be less painful than gym, right?

I let Lawson go ahead when my phone vibrates and I see my mom's calling.

"Hey, Mom."

"Hey, buddy. Glad I caught you."

"What's up?"

"Nothing." There's a pause, and for a second I'm furiously running around in my brain trying to figure out what I've done. "Feels like we haven't talked in ages. You still at school?"

My first instinct is that she's checking to make sure I'm physically still on campus and haven't managed to get my hands on my tuition and skipped town. Then I realize she means am I still in class.

"Yeah. On my way to gym."

"Okay. I won't keep you. Just wanted to check in and see how things are going."

Won't keep me, my ass. She's a talker, so before she lets me get a word in, Mom's telling me all about redecorating David's house and picking out new furniture. How much fun she's having getting to know everyone at the country club. Apparently David bought her sailing lessons and a golf instructor. He'll turn her into an acceptable wife in no time.

"Sounds like you're having a good time," I remark with more evident resentment than I intend. But if she notices, she doesn't let on.

"We're so happy," she gushes. "He's wonderful."

Whatever. I suppose I don't hate that she's enjoying herself, or that he makes her happy. There are worse things that could happen.

"What about you?" she eventually gets around to asking. "How's school going?"

"Good." My answer is automatic. I don't give it much thought. Then as I linger on it, I realize I even mean it. "I like it here, I guess."

"Really?" Her excitement is loud and evident through the phone. "Oh, RJ. I'm so glad. I knew this would be good for you if you gave it a chance."

I don't share her certainty that this was always going to pan out. Against all odds, I've managed to find things not to hate about Sandover.

The freedom, for one thing. Most of the time we're all left to our own devices with only minimal supervision. Plus the food is excellent. Nothing like the cafeteria slop courtesy of the lowest-bidder government contract supplier in public schools.

And there's Sloane. The easter egg I never expected out here in the rich kid rehab.

Don't get me wrong, I still don't see myself chumming it up with Fenn and the other guys. I'm only here for a year and this place has done nothing to change my outlook on transitory friendships. I came here for a diploma, not a lobotomy. But I can't deny that I don't entirely mind my stepbrother. Hell, even Lawson is growing on me.

"Tell me everything," Mom pleads.

"There's not much to tell." I pause. "I mean…I've sort of been thinking about joining the swim team."

A long beat of silence follows.

Then I hear the distinct sound of my mother laughing at me through the phone. It sounds choked, as if she's trying to cover it up, but there's no mistaking her sheer amusement.

"Thanks for the vote of confidence," I tell her. "That's some top-notch parenting."

"You're serious?" She stifles herself, her tone becoming firm.

"RJ, you're not a team player, buddy. Some people aren't cut out for it. That's fine. You know I've never tried to push you out of your comfort zone."

Right, except for sending me off to some vine-covered hamlet of wealthy screw-ups and future criminal CEOs.

"But I'm glad you're thinking about finding a hobby. I just don't see this one working out, if I'm honest. Remember the last time we went to the lake? You spent the whole time in the car on your phone."

My mom tries her best, but she's never been the overly maternal type. Honestly, it's my fault for expecting her to take an interest in my activities. We don't become delinquents because we come from such strong, functioning households. But maybe just this once I wanted to hear a little parental encouragement.

Then again, spite is a powerful motivator.

Challenge accepted.

CHAPTER 24
SLOANE

"GOD HELP ME IF I EVER NEED TO KNOW HOW TO FIND THE CALCIUM carbonate level of a crab shell." Eliza sits beside me at our lab table, visibly wilting from boredom while the sister drones through the instruction sheet at the front of the class.

I laugh. "Here. Let me show you an old Ballard life hack."

I pull out my phone and Google calcium carbonate chemistry lab. Several PDFs show up in the search results. A quick look shows similar values on each, which I take as sufficient evidence they're likely correct. With the quick scrawl of my pencil, I start filling in our worksheet for the crab shells, eggshells, and various other test subjects on our table.

Eliza grabs my phone. "Why is somebody named RJ sending you pictures of his underwear?"

"What?" I snatch it back, staring at the screen. "Oh my God. It's a Speedo," I say in delight.

RJ: I'm sure I'll regret this.

I giggle to myself. "A guy I know at Sandover just crumbled to peer pressure to join the swim team."

This is priceless. I can't believe he went through with it. Fenn is never going to let him hear the end of it. I quickly send a response.

Me: Ready for your first shaving party? You can borrow my razor.
RJ: Fuck that. I'm not shaving anything.
Me: It'll do wonders for your muscle definition. Have you seen Silas's abs??
RJ: You can just say you want to see me with my shirt off.
Me: Trust me, you've never felt anything better than clean bedsheets on freshly shaved legs.
RJ: Speaking of getting your legs under my sheets...
Me: Nice try.
RJ: Meet me tonight.
Me: Careful. Don't want to sound desperate.
RJ: Sloane. Baby. Playing hard to get is less convincing after you spent the night with your tongue down my throat.

I feel a blush warm my cheeks. Damn it. He raises a good point. Still, I can't cede the upper hand. That's not how I roll.

Me: With that attitude, could be the last time...
RJ: You're killing me.

"Heads up." Eliza elbows me, whispering. "Incoming."

Sister Margaret strides down the aisle between lab tables to glare at me. I tuck my phone in my lap.

"Eyes up front, ladies. No phones in class."

"Her weirdo sister is probably at lunch having a nervous break-down over her mashed potatoes." Nikki's friends all laugh as she shoots me a snide smirk.

"Silence, Ms. Taysom."

I return Nikki's smirk, mockingly asking, "Why don't you get a therapist for your personality disorder and spare the rest of us, for Christ's sake?"

The sister huffs and crosses herself before turning her blistering gaze back to me. "Detention, Ms. Tresscott. Not another word."

Whatever. I hate that chick. I'll take detention any day of the week if it means getting the last word against Nikki.

When Sister Margaret returns to the front of the room, I say fuck it and send a quick reply to RJ.

Me: Meet you at the spot tonight.

———————

After detention, Casey is waiting for me in the parking lot to drive home. I ask how her day went, but she doesn't have much to say. I take that to mean there hasn't been a dramatic improvement since last week's rocky start.

"So, hey," I say, keeping my gaze on the road. "I need you to cover for me tonight."

"Oh yeah?" She turns in her seat with a conspiratorial smile.

"I'm meeting RJ on the path later."

"Sneaking out, you mean."

"Whatever. Just in case Dad—"

"Yep, I got it. Operation Rendezvous is in effect."

"You're such a nerd."

She leans back in her seat, quite amused with herself. "The no-boys rule didn't stand a chance, huh?"

I heave a loud sigh. "Fine. Maybe I sort of like the guy."

"Well, duh."

It came on like one of those month-long flus. Or mono. The symptoms so subtle at first, they were nearly imperceptible. Then you get that tickle in your nose. The scratch in the back of your throat. Before you know it, you're huddled in bed under a mountain of tissues, and you've caught a full-blown crush. I can't stop thinking about the damn guy. Last night before bed, I just lay there for an hour fantasizing about kissing him again. Which eventually led to other sorts of fantasies, all of them involving RJ's mouth on various parts of my body and my mouth on one particular body part of his. I made myself come thinking about sucking him off, his fingers fisting my hair as he shuddered from release.

I roll down the window, suddenly feeling too hot in the car.

In the passenger seat, Casey reaches into the backpack at her feet and pulls her phone out, grinning to herself.

Suspicion flutters through me. "Who's that?" I demand.

"Fenn. Just asking how school's going."

So him, she'll talk to.

My gaze remains fixed straight ahead, because I don't want her to see my distrustful expression and think I'm grilling her when I ask, "What's that all about?"

From the corner of my eye, I watch Casey pull an innocent face. "What's what?"

"You spend a lot of time talking to him."

"We're friends."

"Friends," I echo, wary.

"Yes, Sloane. Friends. I'd think that would make you happy. It's not like I have a lot of those these days."

I know she doesn't mean it, but her words cut deep. Reminding me that if I'd been there for her like I'd promised, none of this would've happened.

"But Fenn? I mean, of all people."

"He's sweet." She doesn't look at me, but I see her smiling to herself while peering out the window. As if this car is big enough to hide that besotted smile. "And he makes me laugh."

The kiss of death, right there.

"So you like him," I push.

"I didn't say that."

She didn't have to. Casey can talk to me like we've never met, but I'm not so dense I don't notice my own sister watering the seeds of her little crush garden.

"Anyway, he's probably dating someone, right?" she says.

Fuck my life.

"Fenn doesn't date," I remind her pointedly. "He plows through hookups like he's going for a world record and never talks to them again. Not the type of arrangement you want anything to do with, Case."

"I'm not saying I would," she snipes back with more attitude than she's mustered in months. I'd almost be proud of her if she weren't talking about becoming a notch on Fenn's belt.

"Good. Then don't."

At my sharp rebuke, she sulks in her seat, all full of contempt and righteous indignation. I'm the bad guy who never lets her have any fun. As if I've never been where she is.

"Trust me," I tell her, trying to sound like her big sister and not her mother. "You don't want to catch feelings for a guy like Fenn. It's the last thing on their mind. At this age, they're incapable of participating in a real relationship. It's all prologue to getting laid and then forgetting your name. It'll never mean the same to them that it does to you."

Before I even finish the thought, I realize just how true it is. It's good advice.

Not just for her, but for the both of us.

CHAPTER 25
RJ

I DON'T KNOW WHAT HAPPENED. I THINK I BLACKED OUT AND WOKE up in Coach Gibson's office with him shaking my hand. Then, somehow, I ended up at the pool in a navy Speedo, with Silas and Lawson in my ear giving me advice I'm too delirious to understand.

Now, it comes back to me in a rush of regret. Asking to be excused from gym to go find Coach Gibson in his office. Agreeing to formally try out at practice. Because apparently I'm on a mission of self-destruction.

"This was a bad idea," I mutter to Silas, who's beside me at the starting platform.

"There's nothing to it," he assures me. "Just don't forget to breathe."

"Almost no one shits the pool their first time," Lawson deadpans.

"Great. That's helpful."

A whistle screeches, piercing my eardrums. The echo rings inside my skull.

"I don't even know how to dive off this thing," I whisper to Silas. The entire swim team is lined up behind me, arms crossed and eyes narrowed. The worst part is that Carter is on the team, so he'll no doubt report my every dumb screw-up to his lord and savior Duke.

"Bend over like you're tying your shoes. Stick your ass out and grab the front."

"Imagine you dropped the soap in the prison showers."

"Seriously, dude." I glare at Lawson. "You're terrible at this."

I get in position and take a deep breath. Though I'm not certain how I got here or why, I recognize the jittery sting in my toes. It's not the swimming that worries me. Or even making an ass of myself. I suddenly realize that what it boils down to is: I hate doing anything I can't be great at. If I'm not the best, why bother? Maybe that's why I tend not to stray too far outside my comfort zone.

Goddamn it. My guidance counselor two schools ago would probably call this a character-building moment.

Coach Gibson blows the whistle again, and like a Pavlovian response, I jolt off the platform. I don't know all the rules and mechanics of competitive swimming, so Silas told me to ignore the technical and instead aim for speed. Quickness off the platform and split times between laps is what really matters today. So I push through the water with as much force as I can muster, grabbing the water with both hands and kicking like something's chasing me.

When I hit the wall after the turn and throw the water out of my eyes, Silas gives me a discreet thumbs-up. I climb out of the pool and accept a towel from Lawson. No one gives much away in their faces until Coach nods at his stopwatch.

"That'll do. Go pick out a locker, Shaw."

Maybe part of me is disappointed. If I'd botched it and not made the team, I could have said I never wanted it anyway. But now, I might actually have to try. I fucking hate trying. But it's too late to back out now. My dumb ass is doing this, whether I like it or not.

In the locker room after practice, I get dressed beside Silas and Lawson.

"Not bad for a novice," Lawson tells me. He glances at his roommate. "Bro, how hilarious would it be if he places in the state rankings at his first meet?"

"Yeah, sure," I answer with heavy sarcasm.

"He's not far off." Silas sits on the bench to pull on his socks. "You're fast. Just have to see if you can maintain that speed with the right form."

"Fuck form. Be legends," Lawson says, sliding on his sunglasses.

I don't put much stock in what they're saying, mostly because this is a temporary arrangement. One season. Just to get the hell out of gym and field hockey bullshit. Lawson was right—swimming is a solitary thing. Me against myself. No playbooks, no rules. Hell, if I suck, maybe I won't even swim. I could take a nap while getting credit to ride the bench. Easy. I'm cool putting my pride aside to coast through the semester.

"Hey, so someone mentioned shaving," I say, remembering Sloane's mocking text. "That's not really a thing, right?"

Silas cracks a smile. "Oh, it's a thing. Have to take every advantage you can get."

"Or if waxing is your preference…" Lawson says helpfully.

A shudder runs through me. "Even my legs?"

"Everything the water touches." Lawson pulls a disposable razor out of his gym bag and tosses it on my backpack. "Technically, the balls are optional. But think fast, swim fast, I always say."

Silas shrugs. "Girls like it."

Awesome. Like the Speedo isn't embarrassing enough.

Last week Lucas had mentioned a programming issue he's having and asked if I could try talking him through it, so after practice I head to the computer lab to meet up. I'm a few minutes early and take a seat at a machine in the back of the room to wait for him. There's hardly ever anyone in here. Today, it's just a couple underclassmen downloading torrents and talking too loudly for me to ignore their boring conversation. When I hear Duke's name, I get a little more interested.

"Why does he care?" the skinny ginger asks.

"I don't even know. Something about Duke's cousin being friends with the guy?"

"What happened, exactly?"

"Last weekend Liz is all like, 'Oh, I'm not feeling well. I'm not going out.' Then Sean says he saw her out with that asshole from Ballard again. I call her out on it, and she still won't admit it, but now is like, 'I think I'm too busy with school to have a boyfriend.'"

That, or maybe she didn't appreciate his voice-impression of her. I don't even know the girl, and I'm offended for her.

"That's convenient, Liz," the friend says mockingly.

"Right? So I told Caleb, I'm gonna figure out a way to fuck this dude's shit up. Then all of a sudden, Duke's sticking his nose in it, saying the guy is off limits."

"It's bullshit." I'm not sure if Ginger is reacting to the story or the content filter that pops up on the screen to kick them off the torrent site. "Duke was unbearable last year. Now he's gone totally power-mad."

"Someone needs to kick him off his high horse."

"Have you seen his fights? Doesn't look likely."

"We could always hire a ringer."

My attention is rerouted when Lucas walks in. He briefly scans the room until he spots me, then walks down the aisle of desks to sit beside me and pull out his laptop.

"Hey. Thanks again for doing this," he tells me, pulling up his script for me to examine. "I've been messing with it all week and I keep making it worse."

"No worries." I take a minute to scan the code, and it becomes evident pretty quickly where he screwed up. With a few keystrokes, I make the necessary changes and run the script to test that it functions.

He gives a self-deprecating laugh. "Of course, you figure it out in ten seconds. I should've seen that."

"It's a common mistake. Don't beat yourself up." Lucas is smart, and he's got a knack for this stuff. I've just been at it a lot longer. "Sometimes it takes another set of eyes to catch it."

"Hey, did you see this?" He pulls up a blog post on his laptop about a recent hack of some chud message board. The hackers posted the user metadata and ten years of messages to a public forum outing a bunch of Nazi assholes. The blog identifies the hackers as a group called the Infinite Wisdom of the Cosmic Turtle.

"I think I know one of them," I tell him. "We've traded a few exploits on the forums."

"Dude, that's badass. You're like a legit hacker guru."

"Say that a little louder, will ya?"

Lucas smothers a contrite smile. "What was your best hack? Or your favorite, at least? Anything I would have heard of?"

I shake my head ruefully. Me, I'm not in it for the fame. Some people are chasing glory. Others are on a soul mission. But I'm not an activist or fame whore. It's a hobby. A useful skill, like lifting heavy shit or running fast. I'm lifting code.

"There's a reason hackers are anonymous," I say. "And that's the way I keep it. I'm not trying to dare the FBI to hunt me down. I don't plan on dying in Gitmo for getting free Netflix."

"Hey."

I glance up to see Ginger and his butt-hurt buddy standing over us. I peg them as sophomores, judging by the unfortunate patches of facial hair and untreated acne.

"What?" I demand.

They shrink back, yet still determined.

"You're a hacker?" the newly single kid asks. "Like if I said I wanted you to dig up dirt on someone?"

The question doesn't surprise me. Lots of people with an axe to grind have found their way to me, looking for revenge by exploiting the secrets and weaknesses of their enemies. Often, they're not happy about what they find. But it pays well, and I'm not in business to worry about outcomes.

"That depends," I say, cocking a brow.

"Name your price."

I love dumb rich pricks.

"Email me the name and background to this address." I take the guy's phone and give him a burner address that can't be traced back to me. "I'll be in touch."

After they leave, Lucas is there staring at me, dumbstruck.

"Is that what it's like?" he marvels. "You do this a lot?"

"When it suits me." I shrug. "Information is good business."

Like sex, drugs, and power, knowledge is one of the oldest commodities. My particular skill set tends to make me the resource of last resort for the petty and vengeful, but that's hardly my concern. The first rule of the information economy is to maintain a firewall between myself and the messy stuff. I'm here for the what, not the why. When a transaction goes badly, it's always the human element that fails.

Most of the time, the system works.

Then again, that's the thing about picking locks and turning blind corners. Even when you're careful, occasionally there's a twenty-gauge shotgun waiting in the dark.

That night, I'm in the dorm, sitting on my bed doing some homework with my headphones on. I don't hear the angry stomp of footsteps charging toward my room. Or the *click* of the handle turning. Only when the door flies open to bounce off the wall, do I look up from my laptop.

I see Duke lunge for me about a second before his right cross cracks against my jaw.

CHAPTER 26
RJ

MY EARS ARE RINGING WHEN I SPIT BLOOD ON THE CENTURIES-OLD hardwood floor. It lands in a thick, red glob, in which I watch the reflection of my bedside lamp topple to the ground as Duke shoves me against my nightstand and I stumble into the wall.

"You think I wouldn't find out?" he shouts at me, pinning my back to the window with my shirt crumpled in his fists.

The drapes cradle my face and I wonder briefly in the haze of chaos screaming through my skull if they're strong enough to catch me from falling three stories when the glass breaks.

The guys were right. I underestimated Duke.

I underestimated him big-time.

And yet even recognizing that, I can't stop my own smart-ass nature any more than I can stop the sun from rising.

"You're gonna have to be more specific," I mumble through the blood still filling my mouth and the searing numbness in my jaw.

"I know where you were this weekend." Duke catches me by the throat when I try squeezing past him. "Arrogant little fuck. Think you can use her to get to me?"

Sloane.

Shit.

"Oh. That." I can't restrain a pained chuckle.

With everything else going on, I'd forgotten that nugget was bound to get back to him. Granted, I didn't spend even a second considering his reaction, but this is worse than I would have imagined.

"Tough breakup?" I ask politely.

Duke throws me off the wall and I crash into the sofa.

"Stay the hell away from her." He's red and seething, full of rage and hormones. "Whatever your stupid plan is, it won't work. I run shit on this campus. That's the way it's gonna stay."

When you sit on a stolen throne, you see enemies everywhere.

"Duke, man. I don't give a shit about your power trip or fucking prep school politics. You don't factor in my world at all."

"I don't factor?" He cracks a malicious smile. "All right. I was polite before for Fenn's sake. We could have worked something out. Now I'm done with diplomacy."

I take advantage of the brief interlude where he doesn't have his hands on me to readjust my jaw. "Not sure we agree on that definition."

"I told you what would happen," he reminds me, his tone icy.

"Yeah." I pull myself upright and wipe the blood off my chin. "My first guidance counselor always said I needed to work on being more present."

"You like being clever, don't ya?"

"Eh." I shrug. "It's a living."

"Smartest guy in the room, right?" He steps up to me, flaring his nostrils.

The thing about prep school bullies, they all think they have this righteous entitlement to take up space.

"So be smart now," he continues, gaze deadly. "I want to hear it."

"Hear what?"

"You're not going to see Sloane again. I don't even want to hear her name's been coming out of your mouth."

"Oh. Yeah, no. I'm not going to do that."

In any income bracket, a bully is still a big dumb animal. We don't run to the fallout shelters for every escaped zoo hippo that goes charging through the town square, do we? No. We call out Fish and Wildlife to shoot its ass full of tranquilizers. I'm not scared of Duke or his threats.

"You realize you can agree now or after you're picking your teeth up off the floor." Duke's barely contained anger pulses in the bulging vein in his forehead. "I'm giving you a chance to take the easy way out. What's some chick worth against a broken nose?"

Some chick? Nice. It really stretches the imagination, what Sloane ever saw in this guy.

"Let me ask you something…" I trail off for a second, mostly for dramatic effect. Sure, there's part of me shouting in vain, ordering me to stop, waving his arms in the air. I do have a healthy aversion to pain. But I'd rather die than give a jackass like Duke the satisfaction. Call it a moral imperative. "What are the chances a girl has ever not faked an orgasm with you?"

I almost intuit the first blow before it lands. I wince and tense for the impact. Give Duke credit, it hurts far worse than I bargained. I almost regret asking for it. Then the second one comes in quick succession, knocking me to the floor on my hands and knees, and it sort of stuns my nerve endings dead. A pool of blood forms below me for a second before my ribs flare in pain when he lands a stiff kick that flips me over.

"This can end any time you want," he growls over me, landing another kick.

Blood coats my throat and bubbles out in a hacking cough when I croak out a laugh. "Already? We're just getting to know each other."

Duke drops to his knees to pummel my face. I've finally had enough when I muster up the strength to throw him off me and scramble to my feet. I've been in my fair share of fights and usually hold my own. But if I'm honest, this is the first time I might have bitten off more than I can chew.

Duke and I wrestle around the room, getting tangled up and trading shots. His land more often than not, and each one leaves me blinking away dark spots from my vision a few seconds longer. The fatigue builds faster than I can shake it off, while he doesn't appear at all winded. Duke's got ten more rounds in him while I'm clinging to the ropes, my midsection beaten to scrambled eggs and my face a swollen mess.

I'm thinking about asking for a time-out and water break when the door swings open and suddenly Mr. Swinney is shouting as others wrap us up to pull Duke and I apart.

"Everyone to bed," the housefather orders. He stands fuming in the center of the room in his pajamas, blood staining the bottom of his slippers. "Lights out in two minutes. No exceptions." He stares down at the mess of trauma smeared on the floor. "And clean this up."

Duke stumbles off with a final murderous glare in my direction. "This isn't over," he warns before Carter forcibly drags him away.

Afterward, Fenn mops up the mess while I lie in bed with two cold soda cans pressed to my face. And another six-pack on my abdomen.

"You get now why I warned you about him," Fenn says, wringing shiny pink liquid from a rag into a bucket. "Why I took you to the fights."

"It's becoming clearer, yes."

"Yeah?" he mocks. "Because it doesn't look like you can see too clearly right now."

I let out a tired groan. "You were right, okay? I was cocky. I ignored your warnings, and this is my reward."

Everything hurts. The pain is like sand in a plastic bag. Press in one spot and a million grains of pain rush somewhere else.

"In my defense," I mutter, "he's a hard guy to take seriously."

"I get it. He's a dick. But he backs it up. You have to stop antagonizing him, bro."

It's sound advice. I know Fenn's just looking out for me. Anyway, it'd be difficult to explain to our parents why he let me get shipped home for the holidays in a box. Then again, I've always been stubborn.

"Yep. I hear you."

As of right now, I'm no longer underestimating Duke Jessup.

While he keeps scrubbing, I pull up Sloane's name in my contacts and give her a call. My hands are too sore to text.

"Hey," I say when she answers. "Listen, I'm sorry to do this, but I can't make it tonight."

From the floor, Fenn shoots me a glare.

"Your lack of punctuality isn't cute," Sloane says on the other end. "I'm already here. You better say you're on your way."

"I mean it. I can't tonight. I—"

"Nice try. You're probably behind me, right? Lurking in the woods like a weirdo. I'm not afraid of the dark."

Fenn mouths *Hang up* at me.

"I'm not messing with you. I swear. Give me a couple days—"

"So you're standing me up." Her tone changes. In an instant the humor is gone, replaced with pure venom. "Seriously, RJ? What the hell?"

"I'm sorry, but—"

"Save it, asshole. I gave you a chance and you blew it. Have a nice life."

"Christ, woman." I growl in aggravation. "Your ex just threw me around my room like a tackling dummy and my face is ten shades of purple, but if you want me to go stumbling around in the dark with both eyelids swollen shut, I guess I don't mind traipsing through poison ivy if it'll shut you up for five seconds."

Fenn snorts out loud.

There's a long pause where I realize I might have stepped over the line a smidge.

"Duke really beat you up?" she demands. "Over me?"

"You might have come up in conversation, yes. Things are still a little foggy, though. Concussion will do that."

"Was it even close?"

I should probably make it sound good, talk myself up, but I don't have energy. And a little pity might help my case. I'm not above it.

"Not even a little," I admit.

"So he didn't scare you off?" she asks.

"What, that? It'll take a lot more than a beating to keep me away from you, cupcake."

In the resulting silence, I can hear her reluctant smile.

"I'll see you tomorrow," she finally says. "You can show me your battle scars."

"See you tomorrow."

Fenn shakes his head, resigned. "Poor dumb bastard."

Nah. I don't know if I'd call myself dumb. Because the way I see it, I still got the girl.

CHAPTER 27
RJ

THE NEXT MORNING I'M SUMMONED TO THE HEADMASTER'S OFFICE, where he has me sit in a leather chair while he heats water in an electric kettle for a cup of tea. It's cop tactics. Leave the suspect to stew for a while before the interrogation begins. Let the tension build while you wonder how much they know. In my case, it could be anything. An elaborate cheating scheme the like of which this place hasn't seen in its long and storied history. Using school property to engage in illicit online activities. Getting cozy with his daughter and underage drinking. Take your pick.

"Do you drink tea, Mr. Shaw?"

I stay cool, watching him conduct an elaborate ritual to prepare a bitter cup of dead-leaf water. "You were going to call me RJ."

"That's right. I remember now. Our first conversation." He takes a seat across from me in the cavernous wood-paneled office. "You promised to keep your nose clean, as it were."

"Is that what I said?"

"To paraphrase."

Tresscott's got an odd demeanor about him. Friendly, and yet vaguely threatening. I can't help feeling like he's set a trap and is watching me sniff the ground, inching closer.

Another cop tactic is leaving enough empty space for the perp to incriminate himself. I've seen enough three a.m. reruns of *Law & Order* to know better than to get caught by some network television-level sleuthing.

"If I'm being accused of something," I tell him, "I'd like to be given the chance to defend myself."

"I'd say you could have used a bit of defense last night," he says, nodding at me. "Judging by those bruises."

Oh, right. The fight. Not sure what it says about me that I'd already forgotten. It's a relief, but I don't let it show. I thought for sure they'd managed to hide a keystroke logger I couldn't find on the computer lab machines.

"Mr. Swinney informs me that you and Duke really had it out."

Goddamn Roger. Fenn said the guy was a mouse. I didn't expect him to go tattling to the headmaster about a simple dorm fight, and now it seems like I'm going to have to do something about that guy. If he's running to Daddy about every little indiscretion, I can't trust what'll happen if he were to stick his nose somewhere else it doesn't belong.

"A little disagreement," I assure Tresscott. "We hugged it out."

One corner of his mouth twitches with the slightest smile as he takes a sip from his mug. "I'm sure." Then he sets the mug aside. "Your teachers tell me you're excelling in class. You received an A on your first essay."

"I try." I mean, not that hard, but we live in a results-based society. People say they care about the how, but no one wants glass walls in a slaughterhouse.

"That you're maintaining your academics is why I've decided to let this incident slide. In the future, I won't be as lenient."

Yeah right. That's not what I've heard. There's a reason the tuition for this place is sky-high. Parents pay Tresscott and his faculty to act as babysitters, not administrators. Which means nobody gets kicked out of Sandover, not if the headmaster wants to keep his cozy salary.

"But I won't tolerate any future fighting. If you can't solve your differences with more constructive means…"

I lift a brow. "Not to nitpick, but Duke started it. Might want to drag him in here next."

"That's hardly the point. And I'll decide what intervention is necessary with Mr. Jessup, if that's all right."

"You're the boss."

I smile and nod, because in the end that's all he wants—my acquiescence to the façade of responsibility. The headmaster gets to feel like he's in control of the situation, me suitably contrite and put in my place, because it reinforces the power structure. But only I know that I had his daughter dragging her nails down the back of my neck this weekend.

Like I said. Information is power.

———————

At lunch, the guys can't wait to give me a hard time.

"You look like you've been hunting a madman through Cambodia," Fenn tells me when I sit down with my tray. He's still marveling at my face, which I imagine is somehow worse than when I woke up this morning.

"What the hell does that even mean?"

"You're sporting war paint," Silas says. "Those bruises are gnarly."

I've never stuck a finger into my own bullet wound before, but the agony of chewing right now has to come close. "You should have seen the other guy," I mutter into my mashed potatoes.

"We did." Lawson laughs. "You even manage to lay a hand on him?"

I show him my swollen knuckles. "I hit something."

Fenn snorts. "Not hard enough."

"I don't know what sort of radioactive spider crawled up Duke's dick hole, but the dude punches hard." I sigh and force myself to take another jaw-jarring bite.

"Now you know why most of us steer clear," Fenn reminds me again. I don't think he'll get bored of *I told you so* anytime soon.

Silas doesn't hide his grin. "You really got your ass kicked."

"If you wanted to skulk away, there's no shame in running." Lawson smirks at me over a Greek salad. "I know people who could get you a new identity. Help you slip out of town."

I shrug. Because it wasn't my first fight. Some of them I won, others I didn't. I didn't feel much different about either result. It's whatever.

"Still think Sloane is worth it?" Silas asks pointedly.

His tone raises my hackles a little. His attitude's been weird for a while, hard for me to make sense of. Sometimes it's like he's trying to be my best friend. Other times, I think he enjoys taking shots at me a little more than the other guys. I'm not sure what that's all about, but I suspect Sloane plays a role in it. Although he hardly ever brings her up, I still can't shake the feeling that Silas has a thing for her, no matter how often he's texting with his Ballard girlfriend.

"If I was going to let Duke scare me off, I wouldn't have asked her out in the first place," I answer lightly.

"How'd that go, anyway?" Lawson asks. "You two search each other for tattoos yet?"

I keep it vague. "We had a good time."

"Yeah?" he drawls, and I realize the original question had been a trap. Another one of Lawson's little games. "I heard you two spent all night at the bar trying to swallow each other's faces."

"No comment." I take another agonizing bite.

"Fuck." Lawson is obvious about adjusting himself as he groans. "I would seriously hit that."

Fenn rolls his eyes. "We know."

"In her daddy's office. Bent over that fucking antique chess set."

Silas bristles. "Could you not? I'm still eating."

Then, because the two of them enjoy poking at Silas, they go into an elaborate description of their weekend exploits. Lawson tells us about some housewife he picked up at a hotel bar in Manchester because she looked like his dental hygienist.

"Are you sure it wasn't her?" Fenn asks with a grin.

"Come to think of it, I don't think I know her name. Could have been."

"That'll make for an awkward cleaning," I say.

"Not as awkward as my last birthday brunch after I fucked my dad's new wife."

I wait for Lawson to laugh and give me the punchline.

He doesn't.

I stare at him. "Oh, you're serious."

He cracks a self-satisfied smile and pops an olive into his mouth. "He had it coming."

And I thought my family was complicated.

CHAPTER 28
SLOANE

RJ IS EARLY AND WAITING AT THE BENCH WHEN I FIND HIM ON THE path after school. He's barely tucked into the sliver of shade under the large branch of a tree. Even the slightest cover from direct sunlight is a relief from the relentless heat.

I see a hundred guys a day in this same school uniform. RJ does something different to it. Jacket off, sleeves rolled up on his white button-down shirt. The striped tie loose around his neck. Joint hanging out of his mouth. He's like a Tarantino character.

His face, though, has seen better days.

"Check you out." I sweep my startled gaze over the multitude bruises in various shades of purple. It's worse than I thought.

"Forgive me if I don't look excited," he sighs. "I can't feel my eyebrows."

"Yeah?" I lean in and make him meet me for a kiss, then pull back just before our lips touch.

RJ groans. "Cheap shot, Tresscott."

"Work for it."

He stomps out the spent joint. Quicker than expected, he lunges for my waist and pulls me to sit on the bench then lays a kiss on me.

It hasn't even been that long, but I'd already forgotten how magnetic that first kiss felt. I'd lost the sensation in the beer haze, convinced myself I'd exaggerated it in my head. But now I remember the overwhelming motivation to jump him. And the tenderness of his lips. Emphatic but not rushed or forceful. If a kiss can be cool, RJ's mastered the technique. Effortless.

"Yeah," he says, his voice thick. "I felt *that.*"

"Here. I brought you something."

I reach for my bag and fish out a gift. A second later, I smash a half-melted ice pack over his eye. The ice didn't stand a chance under the searing sun. My weather app keeps telling me the heatwave will break any day now, but I've seen no evidence of this.

"It didn't survive the trip so well," I tell him, rueful.

RJ beams at me. "It's the thought that counts. See? I knew you were into me."

"I *thought* about filling a Ziploc with glass to punish you for bailing on me."

"Then I appreciate your restraint."

Granted, his excuse for standing me up was justified. But I might still be a little bitter. I don't want him getting the idea to make it a habit. And maybe some of my lingering irritation also has to do with how unexpectedly disappointed I was to realize I wouldn't see him last night. When I wasn't paying attention, I'd started to give a shit about this guy, and I'm not sure I'm okay with that.

There's something about a boy who gets under your skin that you just can't trust.

"Well..." I know he has another joint on him. I wait for him to take the hint and light up a second. "I hope you've used your time wisely."

"Meaning...?"

"I didn't just come here for a social call. Let's see some groveling."

"Right. I was just getting to that."

He passes me the joint while he gives me the abridged version of what happened. That someone at the bar had seen us and the rumor mill quickly spun its way to Duke.

"Serves me right for studying with the door unlocked," he finishes with a shrug.

Some part of me knew this would happen, seeing as how Duke is a macho, territorial dickhead who likes to turn everything into a blood sport. One of the many aspects of his personality I never learned to love.

"I am sorry, though," RJ says roughly. "I wouldn't have bailed on you for anything less than severe head trauma."

His visible regret goes the rest of the way to getting back into my good graces. And I suppose taking an ass kicking for a single date deserves some points. "Fine. You're forgiven. This time."

"Help me understand it. How did you two even happen? Because I'm having a hard time figuring out what you saw in the guy."

I go silent for a moment, mulling over my time with Duke. He was my first proper boyfriend, to use the term loosely. Before him, I'd hooked up here and there, but nobody managed to hold my interest for longer than a weekend or so. Somehow, Duke broke that weekend barrier. Looking back on it, I honestly can't understand why I let him. But whatever. I don't know any girl who isn't at least somewhat embarrassed by the romantic choices they make in high school. I still cringe at my freshman yearbook photo. Mistakes were made all around.

"It was mostly a physical attraction," I confess. "I can't think of a conversation we had that was longer than a commercial break. Not a lot of substance there."

"But you were together for a while," he says, prodding for a more thorough explanation.

"Off and on. Truthfully, it was mostly swinging from hookups to fights. We'd argue about everything. Maybe you've noticed he's sort of insufferable. Hence breaking up every other week."

"But you'd always take him back." An air of annoyance falls over

RJ. His expression hardens, even though he's trying hard to appear unbothered.

"Well, not always. I'm here, aren't I?"

"Duke still seems pretty attached."

"He was always possessive. At first, I guess, I was attracted to it. I thought it was one of the things that made him seem passionate. Now I get he's just a prick."

RJ pauses for a beat. Then, "You two still hook up?"

I can't help but snort at the accusation. "Have you not been paying attention?"

He doesn't react, remaining coldly annoyed. "I mean, I don't know. What I heard in your description just now is you never really liked the guy but if the dick is good…"

"Oh. I get it." I crack a smile and chew on my tongue to bite back a laugh. "You're jealous."

"Nah. Just trying to figure where I stand in all this." He pulls the ice pack off his face. The small bag is now a floppy pillow of warm water.

"Nah," I mimic. "You're jealous."

I think it's hilarious he's having a little tantrum over Duke and me, even if it's totally unwarranted. Trust me, I'm never going back there. Got my hand stamped and a T-shirt. All good, thanks.

RJ voices another flimsy denial. "Nope. Only wondering if these visits from your ex are going to be the status quo."

"Don't worry," I assure him. "Knowing Duke, it'll get much worse."

That gets me a chuckle. "Expensive first date."

"And worth it, right?"

"I'll let you know when my rib heals."

A slow smile crawls across his lips, and he gets that cocky sparkle in his eyes that dares me to do something about it. So, I stand to straddle his lap. Put my knees on either side of him and drape my arms over his shoulders to run my nails over the nape of his neck.

"No, I'm not hooking up with Duke anymore," I say firmly.

He shrugs, but I feel the tension release from his shoulders. "Cool."

"Does this hurt?" I ask, setting my weight on his legs.

"I wasn't kidding when I said I can't tell the difference anymore." But he reaches up to grip my waist, keeping me in place. "I can't believe they let you wear these things to school."

RJ rakes his gaze over my uniform. Like him, I ditched my jacket in the car and untucked my blouse. My tie's a wide loop dangling from my collar. But it's the skirt he lingers on. And the strip of bare leg below the hem.

"I never understood the schoolgirl kink," he says, licking his lips. "I think I get it now."

There's a palpable tension between us. A warm, thick hum surrounding us in this bubble of sexual energy. In his eyes I know he senses the same. His fingertips twitch against my skin. Neither of us sure what to do next or who will make the first move, both of us desperate for something, anything, to happen.

Patience has never been my virtue, so I press my lips to his and slide my tongue in his mouth. I want his hands all over me. I want to feel him against my skin. To know what it's like when he skims the curves of my body. We've never been here before and there's a moment of hesitation before RJ kisses me back with the same insistence. Then his fingers begin to wander, encouraged by the breathy noises I can't control.

"I like you in a skirt," he says, softly squeezing my ass.

"I thought you wanted me out of it."

"If that's an option."

I press down against his lap and feel the bulge between my legs. A sharp hiss sucks the air from me. He's thick and hard, and as much as I want him to slip his hands inside my skirt, I'm eager to live out the fantasy that's been keeping me awake since our date.

When I reach between us and flick open the button of his trousers, he peers at me from beneath heavy-lidded eyes. "Thought I was the one who was supposed to be groveling."

"Oh, don't worry," I murmur, "I'll get you on your knees eventually. Right now I want to be on mine." Smiling, I slide off his lap and kneel in front of him.

His groan echoes in the warm air between us. "Don't start something we can't finish."

I peek up at him, all innocence. "Who says you won't finish?" I drag his zipper down and reach into his boxers.

The second I touch his dick, he curses under his breath, one hand coming to rest on my shoulder.

"Sloane." His voice is hoarse. "You don't have to."

"Shut up and enjoy it."

RJ watches as I wrap my fingers around his shaft and slowly bring my mouth toward him. My pulse quickens at the first taste of him, the first swipe of my tongue over the drop of moisture pooling at his tip. I lick it up, and smile when I feel a shudder go through his entire body.

"You look so hot with your tongue on my dick."

"Yeah? What if I put your dick in my mouth? How will that look?" And then I do it, swallowing up half his length before he can reply.

I can't remember the last time I was this wet while giving a blowjob. Maybe never. My thighs involuntarily clench together as I take my time sucking RJ's dick. My heart is beating so fast I feel like I just ran twenty miles. And the sounds he's making…oh my God, those hoarse breaths and low moans. I'm liable to self-combust.

RJ threads his fingers through my hair, but he doesn't move my head or guide me. He gives himself over to me completely, only thrusting when I teasingly deprive him of my mouth.

"You're perfection," he tells me, his expression blazing with lust.

I stroke him softly then give a sharp squeeze, summoning another moan from him. His hips lift, his dick seeking my mouth again. I want him so badly my body actually hurts. My nipples, my clit, it all hurts.

He's in pain too. I watch him as his features stretch taut, as he bites his lip. His breathing becomes shallow. His entire body is tense. Hips straining, craving relief.

"I want you to come in my mouth," I whisper against his tip, and that's all it takes for his restraint to shatter.

Fingers tightening in my hair, RJ thrusts deep, fucking my fist and my mouth until finally he groans, "Coming," and spills in a hot rush.

I swallow every drop, my clit throbbing so painfully, I have to squeeze my legs together.

When he finally settles, I release him gently and lick my lips, and RJ's agonized groan hangs in the air. "Oh hell, that was so hot... licking your lips like that. Goddamn it, Sloane."

I'm not gonna lie—this guy is great for my ego.

With an impish smile, I daintily rise to my feet and smooth out my skirt. "Don't say I never did anything for you, sweetie."

He croaks out a laugh, his hands reaching for me. "C'mere, you brat. Time for me to do something for you."

My pulse kicks up a notch when I see the molten heat in his eyes. And when he tugs me back onto his lap, my core begins to ache again. His dick is still out. Still hard. But he ignores it, dipping his hand beneath my skirt instead.

"Are you wet?" he whispers, pulling my head down with his other hand so he can kiss me.

"Very," I whisper back, then tease his lips with my tongue.

"Yeah? Let me see." His fingers inch toward my panties. They reach the seam just as his pocket starts to vibrate.

"Ignore it," he mumbles. He clutches me tighter when I break our kiss and pull away.

"No, we should probably stop now. I can't really stay long anyway." I get to my feet and work on straightening myself out. If I don't leave now, I might not be able to control myself. "Casey's covering for me, but my dad will be home soon and start wondering where I am."

With a frustrated sigh and an amusing glare, RJ tucks his dick back in his pants and zips up. Then he pulls his phone from his pocket to read the alert.

"Anyone I should be worried about?" I ask more as a joke, to which he raises an eyebrow.

"Do you want it to be?"

I try to get a glimpse of his screen, but he jerks it away. It was my fault for starting this game. "Well, now I do want to know what you're up to."

"Truth?"

"Well, yeah."

"I've been digging up what I can find on the faculty."

"Seriously?" I thought maybe a girl from back home or some Tinder townie.

"There's this one dude. The housefather of the senior dorm. Mr. Swinney. He's a goofy middle-aged man who wears slippers and watches TV too loudly."

"Sounds nefarious."

"That's the thing. Why would such a painfully boring guy be completely invisible online? Not just scarce. This guy is a ghost."

"Weird."

"It's fucking suspicious," he says.

I know a lot of the Sandover faculty and staff, but I've never met Mr. Swinney. I'm not sure I've ever heard Dad mention him either.

"What if he's here under an assumed name and the mafia is after him?" I offer as an explanation.

"Or," RJ comes back, "he killed his wife and kids in Texas and has been hiding out here under bad suits and thick glasses."

"He was in a polygamous religious cult in the Chilean mountains until he had to take a really long dump then walked out of the bathroom to realize he'd missed the fruit punch accession."

We go on a bit of tangent, devising more elaborate and devious conspiracies that might have brought the elusive Mr. Swinney to our quiet little campus. RJ has an insatiable curiosity, which I find kind of cute. Once his suspicions are tickled, he can't let it go.

Then another notion occurs to me. "When you say digging…"

He shrugs it off like a totally normal thing. "If someone has any presence at all online, I can find them. It's not that hard to break into a person's accounts."

That gives me pause. My head starts spinning with every questionable photo or embarrassing argument I've ever posted. I haven't posted much lately, but I'm not totally invisible either. And, yes, I know the internet is forever, but I generally operate under the assumption that nobody cares about me enough to dig up an Instagram post from middle school.

"Like social accounts?" I ask.

"Sure." He says it so matter-of-factly, oblivious to the alarms blaring in my brain. "Anything. If I wanted to see someone's Snapchat or peek at their Amazon orders…"

"Someone like me?"

I watch the breath catch in his throat. See him swallow to buy time while his mind rushes to formulate an answer that doesn't get him kneed in the crotch.

"Your lack of response is troubling," I tell him, my wariness climbing fast.

RJ licks his lips for a second, then lets out a quick breath. "It's not like that. If you remember, you weren't all that forthcoming the first time we met."

"So you *hacked* me?" I growl. The urge to slug him and put a fresh coat of paint on that black eye is almost irresistible. "That's some dark shit, RJ."

"Listen." He takes a step toward me, but my glare stops him dead. "I didn't read your DMs or anything. I only wanted to get to know you better."

"You can't turn this around like what you did wasn't fucking creepy."

And I don't know what to do with the fact that he believed this was a legitimate way of meeting someone. Behind my back. While I slept. Poking around in the dark.

A rush of anger bubbles in my stomach. "You lied to me."

Then another piece of this sleazy puzzle clicks into place.

"Oh my God. That's why you knew I liked Sleater-Kinney! Because you got it from my social media." I take a step closer, shoving a finger in his chest and barely containing the impulse to shove him on his ass. "You let me talk about my mom."

"That's true," he rushes to say, holding his hands up in surrender. "But I swear, I had no idea what that music meant to you. I wouldn't have—"

"What? Used my dead mother to get a date? But you'll totally betray my privacy and my trust."

I don't know what to do with the rage burning in my chest. It's suffocating. I can't catch my breath. My legs move because I can't stand still, too much adrenaline coursing through my veins.

"Fuck, RJ. You know I actually liked you? Against my better judgment. But you got me."

His face falls, wounded. Good.

"I knew better. I told myself not to let my guard down. I broke my own promise to myself, for fuck's sake. I was supposed to concentrate on school this year, and instead, I've been texting with you in class and acting like some smitten preteen." My voice cracks slightly, which only adds insult to injury. He's not allowed to hear how much this affects me. I clear my throat, arming myself with another harsh look. "You know what I liked best about you? How upfront you were with me. That you were real." I meet his eyes with a bitter smirk. "Turns out, we've never even met."

"Sloane."

His gaze softly pleads for another minute. To spin some yarn about how, when you think about it, the despicable lengths he went to only proves the depths of his sincerity, or some other weak-ass bullshit.

But he can save the words for the next target. I'm already gone.

"Have a nice life, rookie."

CHAPTER 29
SLOANE

I THOUGHT I KNEW WHO I WAS. I THOUGHT I COULD TRUST MYSELF.
Now I'm pulling stuffing out through my burst seams, and it doesn't
look like me. I'm a disheveled toy on the floor watching her vacant
reflection in the mirror.

My sister watches me from my bed, her teeth digging into her
bottom lip. When I stormed into the house after the fight with
RJ, she'd taken one look at my face and corralled me up to my
bedroom before Dad could see me. I'm pretty sure there'd been
tears in my eyes. Actual *tears*. Nobody makes Sloane Tresscott cry.
Asshole.

"If you gave him a chance to explain…" she finally hedges.

"Kind of need you to be on my side with this, Case."

"I am. Obviously. I just think—"

"Whatever you're about to say, write it down on a little piece of
paper, fold it up real small, stick it in your mouth, and swallow it."

"Fine. Jeez."

Lying on my bedroom floor, I close my eyes and try to remember our first conversation. When I clocked RJ as more trouble than
he was worth and then walked away. Turns out that was the last
good decision I made before his whispers soaked into my skin and

sprouted into curiosity, already too late to realize he'd been manipulating me from the start.

"I'm such an idiot. How did I not see this coming?" Bile stings the back of my throat and I gag thinking about what had happened on that path before his phone interrupted us. "How did I ever like him? I fell for my own stalker. I blew him in the woods, Case. Like, just now! I was on my knees with his dick in my mouth."

Casey's cheeks go a little pink, and she looks like she's trying not to laugh. "Oh. Wow."

"Right? Fucking embarrassing."

"Sloane, come on. You didn't do anything wrong." Now she's watching me with a sympathetic if helpless frown. "It sounded like he was really into you. Seems like he still is."

I lurch upright. "He was playing me. Invading my privacy so he could pretend we had so much in common. I can't trust anything he said was ever the truth."

Casey's eyes dart across the room. Her face contorts and I see the strain to bite back the words.

"What?" I demand.

"I am on your side. Just remember that." Her fingers pick at the corner of a pillow while she musters up the courage to spit it out. "And I'm not saying it's exactly the same thing…"

"But?"

"I mean…you've sort of played with guys too. In different ways."

I stare at her, lips tight and jaw clenched. Then, on a long exhale, I flop back to the floor.

"Fine. You've got me there." I frown at her. "But definitely not the same thing."

"Definitely." Casey continues to study me. "Only, maybe that's not the point?"

My phone vibrates again. It's been doing that every few seconds since I got home, a minute or two between attempts at most. The incessant buzz of RJ's hapless pleas for me to hear him out.

"I don't even know what that means. The point is he let me believe he was this genuine, authentic person, no bullshit. Except it turns out the entire basis of our...whatever it was, was formed on a lie."

"I get what he did was terrible." Casey's still trying to find an angle of approach where her balloons of optimism won't get shot out of the sky by rooftop snipers and anti-bullshit missiles. "I do. Still doesn't mean everything about him wasn't true. The person you talked to and hung out with is still the same."

RJ: Sloane. Let's just talk. Please.

This time I take a second to text back, if only to stop him from blowing up my phone all evening.

Me: I don't even know you. There's nothing else to say.

"That person isn't real," I tell my sister, my tone flat. "And so he doesn't exist."

I'm still staring at the ceiling hours later in bed, after all the lights are out and Casey's abandoned her mission of character rehab on RJ's behalf. I turn the last week over in my head a dozen different ways to find the clues I missed, all the moments where a different choice would have saved me the embarrassment of getting had by the scam artist. Flashes of our kisses, his hands, burst through my thoughts. Intruding. Because thanks to RJ, I can't even find peace in my own head. He's invaded that too, refusing to let me sleep and just forget this day. And his face.

On the nightstand my phone lights up. It's around one in the morning and there's another text. My eyes are bloodshot and blurry when I try to read it.

RJ: I'm outside.

Exhaustion stutters my brain's engine and I have to read the text three times before I understand what it says.

Me: That was stupid.

RJ: Probably. But I'm going to start throwing pebbles at your window if you don't come out here.

Nothing about this approach is endearing. In fact, it feels like more of the same manipulation that got us here. Practically, however, if he wakes up the whole house and my dad has to go storming out on the lawn in his house robe, we're all in a shit ton of trouble. So I throw on a hoodie and shoes, then climb out my window. I find RJ standing against a tree at the far corner of the house. He peers out of the shadows when he hears my footsteps.

"Thank you," he says with hesitance in his voice. "I know you don't want to talk to me."

"Great. Good chat."

He rakes a hand through his dark hair, clearly nervous. "But if you'll just give me a few minutes to explain what was going through my head…"

"I don't really care."

Emotionally fatigued as I am, I hate the fact that my first thought is how hot he looks in a black T-shirt and loose jeans with years of memories worn in. His pants are more honest than anything that's come out of his mouth.

"Please." Something in his eyes won't let me turn my back on him. I don't know if I'd recognize his sincerity, but it's close. Desperation, maybe.

"Fine," I mutter. "Make it quick."

We walk under a full moon down a trail that leads from the back of the house toward the lake. For some time, he doesn't speak. At a distance we follow the light of our phones to navigate the fallen tree limbs, rocks, and divots. I'm not sure whether he's gathering his thoughts, or just rehearsing the meticulously crafted load of bullshit he's spent the last several hours drafting in his dorm with the expert assistance of Fenn and Lawson.

The silence is nice, though. I miss the way the forest whispers late at night. When the insect songs have quieted and there's only the warm summer breeze that nudges the leaves. The wings of an owl lifting off from a limb. The faint skittering of tiny rodent feet through the grass. It puts me in a trance, and I don't realize until the silver reflection of the moon on the water catches my eye that we've walked all the way to the lake without uttering a word.

There's an old, rusted paddle boat overturned at the water's edge, where we sit to stare at the ripples traveling the surface of the water. Another minute or so passes before he senses my restlessness and sucks in a breath to plead for his life.

"I am sorry." RJ faces me, but I don't turn to meet his eyes while I fish for a rock in the dirt with my foot. "I've spent all night thinking how you must feel. And I get it. I massively screwed up."

"You were a conniving, sneaky little creeper who invaded my privacy so I'd go out with you." I find a good one and dust the sand off, then fling it at the black, gently lapping tide.

"You're right. And I justified it to myself a dozen different ways."

"Because you knew it was wrong."

"I did."

At least he admits it. I'm all done handing out Brownie points, but he's earned himself another minute of my indulgence.

"Go on." With my foot I scrape the dirt for more rocks.

"In my head, I told myself I only wanted to get a sense of who you were so I could understand how to approach you."

I chuck another rock at the water and watch it skid. "Most people do that by talking, you know. They don't break into people's bank accounts to figure out how much to spend on a birthday present."

"True." He clears his throat to cover a laugh, and so help me I will shove his face in the mud if he so much as chuckles. "Today made me realize something. I think my moral compass has gone a little off-kilter. You know, like I started messing around with computers as a hobby. I wanted to learn more. Then I had to test myself. So this silly thing I got into as a kid took over my life and became this crutch I leaned on for everything. I didn't give it a second thought."

"That's pretty messed up, RJ." I get a couple more skips out of my next rock. The patterns it draws on the water expand and glide toward the darkness in all directions. "But you're the one who let it get out of hand."

"I admit that now. In my defense, I think I became function-ally brain-dead when I first saw you. Like here's this stunning chick who is clever and sarcastic and I'm dying to know her, but I think somewhere along the way I forgot how to just interact with people." He leans forward, dropping his chin in his hands as he rests his elbows on his knees. "You know, moving around, I made it a rule not to get attached to people. Why bother, right? Except part of that was making sure I could reject them before they left me. And I guess the hacking gave me—"

He stops abruptly, and I can't stop myself from glancing over to see what's up. The startled look on his face makes me frown.

"What?"

RJ drags a palm over his forehead, for a moment shielding his eyes from my view. "I think I had an epiphany," he mumbles, sound-ing so unhappy I have to fight a laugh.

But I refuse to reveal a trace of humor right now. He'll think he wore me down, and we're not there at all.

"Hacking gives me access to information nobody else has," he finally says. "And, well, when you know people's secrets, it gives you power. Control."

"The upper hand," I murmur, albeit reluctantly. Because I know all about needing that upper hand.

"Yeah." He nods a couple times. "But finding out people's secrets that way… You think it helps you know them, right? But it doesn't.

It's not real. It's just words or pictures on screens. It's not the same as actually having a person share something with you. That's the real part." Regret softens his profile. "I'm really sorry. I should've waited for you to open up to me on your own time. I thought us having something in common would speed up the process, but that's not how this relationship stuff works, is it?"

"No," I agree wryly. "It's not." I'm out of rocks, so I clasp my hands in my lap. "Want to know the part I hate most about all this?"

He looks up, braced for the worst but somehow resigned.

"Even worse than wasting my time and betraying my trust, I found out this person I was starting to like never existed. Evaporated into the thin air of a thousand tiny lies. I don't know if you under-stand what that feels like."

His voice goes a little husky. "Sloane, come on. I admit I lied about liking the same band, but the rest was true. I'm the same person. Just more flawed than I let on."

"I've been going over things in my head tonight, and it occurred to me that maybe your best trick was that you somehow avoided really telling me anything about yourself."

"It wasn't on purpose."

I believe he believes that, but I know it isn't true. I'm a fairly guarded person and he makes my perimeter look like a chain-link fence. But that's for his therapist to sort out. Can't fix his whole personality in one night.

"If you want me to believe you, then it's time for you to tell me something real. You opened me up and got to walk around inside my head. Now it's your turn."

He bites his lip for a moment. "All right. So. Yeah… I also like to run."

I blink. "Huh?"

"I like to run," he repeats sheepishly. "You know that thing you're so passionate about? Track? I'm actually into it too."

My jaw drops. "Is this a joke? We had something legit in

MISFIT **211**

common this whole time, but you had to go and pretend you liked Sleater-Kinney? What is *wrong* with you?"

RJ's tone becomes rueful. "Haven't we just determined there's plenty wrong with me?"

I huff in aggravation. "You're ridiculous. You asked me about track a bunch of times and never once mentioned you're into it. Sprint or distance?"

"Distance. Started when I was a kid," he says gruffly. "Mom would bring boyfriends home, and I'd get the hell out of there and run around the neighborhood to kill time."

Before he even finishes saying it, I realize exactly why he didn't tell me about his affinity for track. Because that would've meant sharing where it stemmed from, and what I'm learning about RJ is, he'd rather walk barefoot on hot coals than reveal any vulnerability. We are very much alike, he and I.

"Eventually I started to enjoy it," he adds, shrugging awkwardly. "Helps me clear my head."

"That's one of the reasons I love it," I admit. "The head-clearing part." Irritation once again clamps over me. "See how easy that was, RJ? Being fucking real with each other?"

He looks like he's stifling another laugh. "Yeah. I guess it's not awful."

"Good. Now what else?" I push. "Give me something else. Something deeper than a shared sport."

RJ lets out a sigh as he lies back on the overturned paddle boat to stare up at the sky. It's an especially clear night, the stars like buckshot blown through the vast blackness.

"Something deeper," he echoes, his voice even huskier now. Raspy. This is clearly a challenge for him. "All right. My dad used to do magic tricks. That corny sleight-of-hand shit that twists a kid's head in knots. I only have a couple memories of him, though, because he walked out on us when I was a toddler. He showed up probably looking for money and found me instead. Decided he'd make nice and entertain the kid while trying to convince my mom to float him a few bucks. So both the memories I have of him, he's pulling quarters from my ears."

His tone becomes soft and distant, barely disturbing the stillness and the moon mirrored in the lake. RJ tucks his arms behind his head. I lie back beside him, fighting the urge to reach for his hand.

"He was a con man. Fleeced his way across the country squeezing widows for their social security checks or selling some asshole who couldn't afford it on a business plan he didn't own." He glances at me, face still a puddle of blurred, painful colors. "I keep tabs on him. Every few months I search police blotters and booking documents. I checked last month—he's back in prison on his third grand larceny charge. Might never see another day as a free man as long as he lives."

It seems like I should say something. I want to. It's as though part of him is reaching out, aching for someone to grab his hand in the dark and say it's okay, but what do I know about what he's been through? I've also lost a parent, sure. And it's a gaping wound that never heals. Except each one of my brief, incomplete memories of my mother is wonderful. She loved us. Lived for us. I grew up in a functional, happy home where my biggest gripe was not getting to have ice cream for breakfast or stay up late watching TV.

"Mom always told me, mostly when she was mad at him, that I got my resourcefulness from her, but that mischievous streak—that was Dad. I think it sunk in, hearing that. Maybe it made it easier to lie and sneak around, you know? It was in my blood, so what could I do about it? But at the same time, I was terrified. Of being a loser just like him. Going too far and landing myself in prison."

RJ turns to face me fully. The evidence of how rending these memories are for him have become evident in his heavy features, the flat plank of his lips. I'm almost sorry I brought us here, and yet still satisfied that finally I'm beginning to understand him. Not only the facade he presents, but what it's concealing. A hundred puzzle pieces of him snap into place around these formative moments in his life, the relationships and fears that raised him.

"I don't always like myself," he admits roughly. "In fact, sometimes I can't stand myself and it's like I'm trying so hard to make sure no one can see all the ways I'm just like him."

My heart clenches for him. "You're being pretty hard on yourself for a guy in high school. It's not like you killed someone."

"I appreciate that, but it's hardly a consolation. You're right to hate me. What I did was inexcusable."

"It was. And you're nowhere near off the hook for that. I'm still pissed."

What RJ did is so beyond the usual high school bullshit that I'm not sure if I've entirely wrapped my head around how I feel about it. But I do understand that in his mind, there was no malicious intent. He's just got his head on backwards.

RJ sits up. For a moment he stares out at the forest-wrapped darkness and breathes. Then he meets my eyes with real sincerity I haven't seen before now.

"I really like you, Sloane. More than I expected to. And I know I'm an asshole for even asking this, but I promise, if you let me make it up to you, I'll only be honest from here on out. I'll prove you can trust me. Whatever it takes. Even if you need to stay mad for a while."

My first reaction is to stick to my guns and tell RJ he had his shot. That while I forgive, I can't forget. Except when I stare into his eyes, I'm flooded with all the ways he felt familiar from the moment we met. That kissing him feels like the tape ripping across my chest at the finish line, filling me with adrenaline and exhilaration. A loud, insistent voice reminds me of all the ways I'll miss him if I let him go. What I'll never know if I don't try.

"What does a second chance look like to you?" I finally ask.

His lips twitch with the reluctant beginnings of a smile. "I'm not here pouring my heart out for a make-out session at a bar and a BJ in the woods."

"Be specific," I warn him.

His expression relaxes. "I want to hold your hand. I want to text you good night and good morning. I want to listen while you tell me about your day. I want an us."

I'm not sure which one of us is doing it. But we drift closer, tides we can't control pulling us to the place where our lips meet.

It all comes back to me. That giddy excitement and trepidation. The feeling of standing on the cliff, staring down at the waves beating against the rocks. Terrifying but impossible to resist.

Kissing RJ is a thrill I never anticipated, and as his mouth devours mine, the unbidden impulse in my gut tells me exactly what I want.

"A second chance," I say when our lips part and he strokes the side of my face with his thumb. "A last chance."

Fuck my life, but my gut wants him.

CHAPTER 30
LAWSON

I'M NEARLY DONE WITH LUNCH WHEN SOME FRESHMAN STUMBLES up to our table in the dining hall and throws a folded piece of paper at me like it's going to self-destruct.

See me in my office before class.

—Mr. Goodwyn

"Afraid I have to eat and run, gentlemen." I grab my bag and push my chair in as Silas furrows his brow at my sudden departure. "Appears I have a date."

RJ, whose face is much less purple today, rolls his eyes at me. "Use condoms," he grunts between bites of his pasta.

"Nah, rawdog it," Fenn pipes up. "Feels better."

"Or," Silas suggests helpfully, "maybe just keep it in your pants?"

"Where's the fun in that?" I ask my roommate, cracking a faint smile.

The junior faculty offices are clear across campus in an ancient building that smells like Civil War boot rot. A secretary guards the border between the reception area and the offices beyond.

"Mr. Kent." Petra, the seditious little minx who sits behind the desk, flips her red-rimmed glasses up to eyeball me while chewing on a coffee stirrer. "Up to our old tricks?"

"I was summoned," I tell her, flashing a grin while I push my way through the swinging wooden gate that claps as I pass. "You look gorgeous, sweetheart. Don't change a thing."

Her pleased giggle tickles my back.

Mr. Goodwyn's young and still new on campus, so they threw him in a cramped corner office with no window or ventilation. His name—JACK GOODWYN—is written on a piece of paper taped to the door. Exposed pipes rattle overhead every time someone turns on a sink or flushes a toilet. Wouldn't want to get stuck in here during an earthquake.

He hasn't bothered to decorate, and I wonder if it's because he's hoping to soon earn an upgrade or because he's less than committed to his tenure at our fine institution. The mismatched furniture is the best of what the facilities crew could pull out of the discard pile that's tossed together like a haphazard funeral pyre in a storage warehouse behind the gym.

"Mr. Kent." He enters in a frazzled state, hurrying to throw his messenger bag on a dented filing cabinet before standing behind his desk with sweat beading at his hairline. "Petra should have asked you to wait at reception."

I throw myself down in one of the ripped pleather-upholstered chairs that squeaks when I sit. "That Petra. What will she get up to next?"

He clears his throat and swipes the sweat off his forehead while combing his fingers through his hair.

"So…" I watch his gaze sweep over his desk like he's checking to see what's been disturbed while I was left unsupervised. "This is cozy."

Taking a seat behind his desk, Mr. Goodwyn reaches into a drawer for a manila folder. "I asked to see you so we could talk about your homework in my class."

He pushes the folder across the desk for me to open.

I stare at him. "It's empty."

"So now that we're in agreement on that point, let's talk about why you haven't turned in a single assignment."

A rather cheeky, self-satisfied little sparkle appears in his eye. He must have spent the entire harried jog over here devising that clever little empty folder scheme. Maybe even over breakfast.

"Look at that," I drawl. "I wandered straight into your adorable little trap. Well done, sir."

His mouth flattens to a straight line. "Lawson."

"Mmm." I bite my lip at the heated sensation that admonishing tone sends through my groin. "That was nice. I bet your wife likes it when you talk dirty."

He flinches, aghast at the assertion.

"She's a treat, sir. Well done. Let her know the white dress is my favorite."

My dick gives a little twitch at a familiar late-night fantasy. Gwen on her knees, tits out, dress down around her waist, with him standing over her as he comes on her chest.

"This is an entirely inappropriate conversation." A scowl grows deep and firm across his brow. "I realize I've let you indulge a certain preoccupation during class discussions, but—"

"We could entertain other things." I lick my lips and watch him squirm in his chair. I bet he's grateful to be concealed behind the desk. "I assume that's why I'm here."

"I don't think I take your meaning." Oh, yes, he does. "You've had your fun, Mr. Kent. Now I have to reiterate, the syllabus—"

"Mr. Kent again, huh? I liked it better when you called me Lawson." I wink at him. "Jack."

"Mr. Goodwyn," he growls in frustration.

"You don't have to be embarrassed, Jack." I pull my leftover apple out of my bag and take a sweet, juicy bite while I recline in the chair. "Lots of married men are bi."

The side of his neck, just below his jaw, flutters with his quickening pulse. "I don't know what gave you the impression—"

"Don't you?"

His chest rises on a deep breath. Right now, he's tearing through every conversation, every moment of eye contact, for the careless traces he left while he entertained himself with torrid little mindplays of keeping his student after class. I wonder how he pictured it. When he closes his eyes, does he want my dick in his mouth? Or is he pressing me against a bookshelf?

"If you've misconstrued…"

"Hey, hey." Holding my hands up, I lower my voice like I'm trying to coax a frightened kitten from a thorny bush. "I can keep a secret. No judgment here."

"You're my student—"

"And I'm eighteen. What are a few broken rules between consenting adults?"

"I didn't mean—" He stops abruptly, cheeks flushed.

It suddenly occurs to me that he might not have any practice in this particular area of his predilections. A friend in college, maybe. One late night over study notes and coffee, a naughty little romp in the bookstacks. Staring down a life forever shackled to the same pussy and unable to resist knowing what it meant to get it up the ass just once. Then they part awkwardly and never speak again.

"It's all good," I tell him to ease his fears. "I think you'd be surprised how many people around here are living double lives."

Jack Goodwyn's repressed sexual appetites would hardly make the gossip section of the school paper.

"I think, Mr. Kent, you ought to go."

"Sure. If there's nothing else you'd like to discuss." I take another bite of the apple, watching him swallow hard. "I do have one question, though. Does Gwen still go down on you?"

If he's offended by the question, he doesn't verbalize it. Stunned silent, maybe. Or else intrigued. His mind is probably racing with his own forbidden fantasies. Wondering when he might wake up covered in sweat, still in bed with his fist wrapped around his own cock and imagining it's my mouth he's fucking.

"Are you still enjoying the honeymoon period, or has she stopped letting you touch her? Says she has a headache, but you can hear her going at that vibrator in the bathroom every night. Let me know if I'm getting warm."

He finally seems to compose himself, setting his jaw and resting his elbows on the desk. "You have until Friday to turn in your missed assignments or take a zero. My advice? Your energies are better applied on your homework."

"I'll keep that in mind." I grab a pen and a scrap piece of paper from my bag, jotting down my phone number as I stand. "This is my number. Should I leave it here with you in case there are any opportunities for, ah, extra credit?"

His gaze wanders over me before he catches himself and licks the nervous dryness from his lips.

"Sir?" I prompt, fighting a grin. I wave the paper at him. "What should I do with this?"

He hesitates.

Dilemmas, dilemmas. Does he dismiss me and hold on to his plausible deniability, eventually claiming sexual harassment on my part if anyone ever calls him out for flirting in class?

Or does he—

"Leave it with me," he grinds out, reaching for the paper.

I plant my apple on the desk with the note beneath it and give Mr. Goodwyn a wink as I leave.

As I'm passing through the reception area, Petra spins in her chair to closely follow my departure. "Good chat?"

I dole out another wink, nodding vigorously. "Very productive."

CHAPTER 31
RJ

As close calls go, that one was razor thin. I think I'm still hungover from the emotional bender last night became. I don't know what it looked like to Sloane, but it was one of the most uncomfortable conversations I've ever had, like excavating my heart with sandpaper. I've never talked about my dad with anyone before, hardly even my mom.

Strangely, though, I feel better.

I managed to hang onto Sloane by the tips of my fingers, yeah. But it feels like we're closer now. Like we understand each other better. It was messy, and neither of us is unscathed, but there's a bond between us now that I'm not sure we would have gotten to any other way. Fuck, that sounds corny and sentimental, but...whatever. I guess this chick is getting to me.

And I don't entirely mind it.

Sloane: FYI, I changed all my passwords to my dogs' names.
Me: Funny.

Thursday night, Fenn and I are on the couch in our dorm playing video games. I let my guy die and now get to watch Fenn run around trying to salvage the level, while texting with Sloane at the same time.

She's taken to ribbing me about my not-so-slight indiscretion. I know I deserve it. Just have to take my licks until she's worn herself out. In terms of punishments, it's not the worst outcome.

Sloane: You didn't copy my nudes, right?
Me: Which ones were yours? Let me see and I'll tell you if I recognize any.

At least she's got a sense of humor about it.

Sloane: Casey suggested I give you make-up assignments.
Me: Did she? Like what?
Sloane: How would you feel about spending a week in a mascot costume?
Me: You think that's the most embarrassing way I've ever shown up to class? Try harder.
Sloane: So what are we doing this weekend?
Me: We, huh? I thought you said you had that history paper to write.
Sloane: You're more interesting.

As much as my ego enjoys hearing that, something's stuck with me since our fight in the woods. That moment when Sloane admitted she'd broken her promise to focus on school this year. She'd looked so ashamed with herself, and I can't deny it sparked some guilt in me. I, personally, might not give a shit about homework, but Sloane's trying to land a scholarship. I'd hate to be the reason she lost out.

Me: Tell you what. Meet me at our spot tomorrow after school and bring your work. If I see you finish at least a rough draft, I'll allow you to spend time with me Saturday night.

> Sloane: ALLOW me! Gee! Thank you SO MUCH!!

I chuckle at the phone, drawing a sigh from Fenn.

"Your lovey-dovey texting is repulsive," he informs me without taking his eyes off the TV.

> Me: You'll thank me when you're older.
> Sloane: Haha.
> Sloane: Fine. Study date tomorrow after school. Don't be late.
> Me: Wouldn't dream of it.
> Sloane: And don't forget to text me good night.
> Me: Wouldn't dream of that either.

There's a knock at our door and Fenn throws down the controller to answer it. He was getting his ass kicked anyway.

"It's for you," he calls. "Some sophomore."

Fenn leaves the door open and takes his seat back on the couch as I grab a thumb drive from my desk drawer.

"What'd you find?" The eager underclassman reaches out to snatch the drive from my hand, but I don't let him get his sticky little mitts on it yet.

"Payment upfront," I remind him.

He scoffs. "But I don't even know what's on it."

"And it'll cost you five hundred to find out." I don't negotiate with scrawny virgins still asking Santa for their first pube.

He strikes a defiant glare. Then, as if deciding the information is worth the risk, and correctly calculating that I am not the one to fuck with, he flares his nostrils and pulls out his phone. With a huff he transfers the money. I check my own phone to see an alert the transaction's gone through.

"Pleasure doing business with you." I hand him the drive and close the door in his face.

A loud snicker sounds from the couch. "That dumbass really gave you five hundred dollars to find something embarrassing on the guy who stole his girlfriend?" Fenn says, restarting the level.

"Yup. Matters of the heart." I grab a soda from the fridge for myself and toss another to him. "What can you do?"

"I've got to learn some of this computer stuff."

We both look at each other when there's another knock on our door.

"Unhappy customer?" Fenn asks with a sigh.

"Grab the bat."

I gave the kid his money's worth—what's on the drive more than satisfies his request. I'm not in the business of scamming my customers. But every now and then, someone shows up with buyer's remorse and I have to enforce a strict final sale policy.

"If it's Duke," he says, with the metal bat over his shoulder, "this won't help you."

I open the door. Luckily, it's not a disgruntled customer. Just some guy with a box and a clipboard.

"Shaw or Bishop?" he barks.

"Yeah?"

"Sign here." He shoves his clipboard at me with a pen and I scribble my signature. Then he hands me the box and hurries off.

"What's that?" Fenn stashes the bat and comes over to read the label on the box. "Shit. It's from my dad. Must be for both of us."

Inside, we find two identical smartphones in elaborate packaging like something out of *Mission: Impossible*.

I stare at the thing, confused. "I already have a phone."

Fenn tosses his on his desk and walks back to the couch. "He does this. It's probably some exclusive toy no one can get their hands on. But he did. And he wants us to know what a big deal it is."

"What do I do with it?" My old phone works fine. My first instinct is to sell the new one, though I suppose David would notice eventually.

"Keep it. Flush it. Whatever." Fenn mashes buttons on the

controller, angrily muttering at the screen while his tone grows more frustrated. "He's trying to buy you off so you'll like him. That's his M.O. Easier to spend money than effort."

"As long as he's taking good care of my mom, I'm basically indifferent to the man." I shrug. "I mean, he seems like a step up from Ponytail Venture Capitalist. But not as cool as Tech Start-Up CEO—that guy was a total douche, but he let me beta test some sick new apps."

"Wait, these are guys your mom dated?" Fenn sounds amused. "They don't have names?"

"After a while I stopped learning names. Easier that way."

"So what you're saying is, my new stepmother is a slut?"

"Hey." My face hardens with a warning. "Go there again and I'll erase your existence from the digital world. Drain your trust fund too."

He has the decency to look repentant. "Sorry."

"Better be." Nobody talks shit about Mom. She might be self-absorbed at times, but she's still my mother.

On the coffee table, Fenn's old phone starts vibrating. He leans forward to glance at the screen, then grimaces.

"Fuck. Here we go." He puts it on speaker and rolls his eyes at me. "Yeah?"

"Glad I caught you," David says. "RJ there with you?"

Fenn holds the phone toward me.

"Yeah, hi, David," I say awkwardly.

"Great. I've got your mom here with me. You have a chance to open the package I had couriered over?" He must have just gotten the notice it had been delivered. Quite the eager beaver.

I flop down next to Fenn. "Hey, Mom."

"Hi, bud. Hey, Fenn."

"Pretty cool, right?" David sounds far more enthusiastic about the new device than either of us. "It's supposed to become the first smartphone on the moon. I don't how that works, but you'd probably understand the tech stuff better than I do."

"Great, Dad." Fenn flashes his middle finger at the phone. "I can order a pizza from NASA but will it work in an elevator?"

"RJ, they tell me it's got the fastest processor ever designed in a smartphone. Twice that of anything on the market."

"Cool, yeah. Uh, thank you, David."

It feels strange even accepting it. Presents from Mom usually amounted to gift cards or cash. Which I'm not complaining about.

"I'm sure you know how to set them up," David says. "Let me know what you think."

"Yep. Okay," Fenn says, rushing to hang up. "Bye."

"Oh, buddy, before you go." My mom jumps in before Fenn can end the call. "We were thinking it'd be fun to take a family vacation for the holidays. We didn't get to spend much time together, the four of us, before you two left for school. What do you think?"

Fenn puts two fingers to his head, preferring a quick, painless death to the slow, agonizing torture of family bonding time. I'm right there with him.

"Yeah, great, Mom."

I lie, because what else am I supposed to say? Let her knock herself out. Winter break is still a few months away. By then, I can figure out a way out of this.

After Fenn hangs up, we decide to be magnanimous and open up the phones to check them out. For all the hype, they just look like normal phones.

"I've never actually been on a family vacation," I confess as I scroll through the setup process for my new space phone. "Mom's job was to travel, so when she got to be home for a while, the last thing she wanted to do was get on another plane or spend hours in the car."

"We used to go places," he tells me. "When Mom was around. We spent holidays on the Vineyard."

"Of course you did." Posh little shit.

"Those were good memories." Fenn tosses the phone aside to chew on his cheek. He's staring at the TV, but I don't think he's aware of it.

Inside I cringe, because I feel a full-on emotional confession bubbling its way to the surface. Given last night with Sloane, I'm not sure I'm in a great headspace to get drawn into another heart-to-heart. But I would feel like a jerk leaving to take a piss while Fenn's deep in reminiscence, so I have no choice but to grin and bear it.

"My dad was different then," he admits. "Always wanted to have activities planned with us. We'd go fishing or just take the sailboat out. He spent hours teaching me knots that I could never remember."

It's hard to picture the family dynamic he's describing between those two. I've known families who haven't gotten along. Kids who hated their parents. Parents who were mean as shit and couldn't be bothered. What Fenn and David have is almost worse. There's no good reason for them to have a care in the world except some deep underlying animosity that makes Fenn want to plunge chopsticks in his ears at the sound of his father's voice.

"So what happened?" I ask. "Seems like no matter how often you tell him to fuck off, he keeps trying to win you over."

Whatever sentimentality briefly took hold of Fenn's otherwise sour mood, it dissolves in the acid of his resentment.

"After Mom died, he decided not to deal with it. My mom was gone, and my dad disappeared. All he did was work, and when he was home, he did his best to avoid me. Years of pretending I didn't exist. Then suddenly he shows up with a new wife and kid…" Fenn stares daggers through my skull. "This isn't love or kindness or his benevolent generosity, dude. He's trying to distract everyone from the fact that he's a shitty person who doesn't give a damn about anyone else. When this wears off, trust me. He'll go right back to being a selfish prick."

At that, Fenn turns off the game console and puts on a soccer game, turning up the volume. As much as I didn't want to get roped into a therapy session about childhood traumas, I do feel for the guy. Absent fathers do a number on a kid.

"At least your dad never got hauled out of a motel room naked by the FBI."

His head whips around. "What the hell?"

"Oh, yeah. Dad's first arrest was a shit show. They were there to pick him up on wire fraud charges. Found him getting a spray tan because he's gotta convince some mark he's been in Panama the last six months setting up some major development deal."

Fenn whistles softly. "That's attention to detail."

"Second time they hauled him in, he'd been dating the director of the mail department of a payroll processing firm for something like eight months. He needed her to learn about their schedules or systems—whatever. He'd been living with her. Doing grocery shopping and taking her kids to karate. The whole thing was a con, obviously. But, fuck, dude. At least your dad doesn't have a fake family he treats better than his real one."

Fenn watches me for a moment, as if processing the picture in his mind. Then his face crumples and a hysterical laugh jumps out of him. He's suddenly doubled over, can't breathe, laughing in my face.

"So...you know. There's some perspective for you," I tell him, shrugging wryly.

"I'm sorry." His face is red and wet with tears of laughter. "You win, man. That's fucking awful."

"Thanks. Glad I could help."

I've always had a sixth sense for trouble. Like the way diviners smell groundwater or your uncle knows a storm's coming by the creaks in his knee. So the next day, when Fenn and I are in the Lounge shooting pool, I know something's coming for me. I woke up with an itch behind my ear warning me to be on guard.

"You hear that?" I ask him.

"Huh?" Fenn is bent over the table to line up his next shot.

"Did it just get quiet in here?"

He ignores me. More concerned with the careful geometry of sinking the twelve and two in opposite side pockets.

The dorm tends to exhibit the constant hum of a hundred teenage boys roaming around grunting, farting, and fighting. Add to that at least as many televisions, laptops, phones, and anything else that makes a sound, all of it echoing down the halls and traveling through the ductwork. You don't notice how loud it gets until you walk outside and your ears exhale.

So when it's suddenly silent except for the *crack* of Fenn striking the cue ball and cursing under his breath, I know that trouble has found me.

"Round two, motherfucker." Duke comes charging in from the hall with bulging veins. "I'm here to answer your death wish."

"Whoa, Duke. Slow down, big guy." Fenn throws himself in Duke's path, still holding the cue stick in a clear warning. "We're in the middle of a game."

"Fuck your game." He speaks to me over Fenn's shoulder. "Liked the first beating so much, you went begging for a second, huh?"

We realize when he shoves him at us that Duke's dragged the sophomore in with him. Shit. I knew I should have had the talk with that kid about keeping our arrangement on the DL. Some people don't appreciate discretion.

"Who's this?" Fenn plays dumb for as long as it'll keep Duke from throwing furniture at my head.

Duke nods at the sophomore, who looks like he's already changed pants once today.

"Tell him what you did."

Reluctant, the kid glances around the room, his jaw working as if he's gnawing on his own tongue.

"Out with it," Duke snaps, "or a nurse will be pulling billiard balls out of your ass with salad tongs."

"Fuck, man. Okay." The kid takes a steadying breath and only briefly meets my eyes like we're two prisoners standing over the gallows as the nooses are tightened around our necks. "I took the pictures you gave me yesterday and sent them to a few group chats with people I know at Ballard."

"The whole school has seen them," Duke interjects. "The guy's been crucified."

Good.

"Have you seen the pictures?" I step out from behind Fenn, who warns me with his eyes to keep my damn mouth shut. But I have no remorse whatsoever loading that kid's revenge canon and setting him on his merry way.

"I don't have to." Maybe Duke wouldn't be so smug if he had to answer to his indignation in a more public forum.

"If I were you, I'd want to know what I was defending before I went around associating myself with it."

Duke's expression betrays a moment of hesitancy. Now he's wondering if he's made a huge mistake. Maybe I'm naïve, but I'm giving Duke the benefit of the doubt that being a bully doesn't necessarily make him the sort of guy who's palling around with people who wear blackface to parties. Then again, plausible deniability is also complicity. After a beat, he jerks his head at the sophomore and tells him to get lost.

"The point is," Duke says to me, his voice low, "you keep stepping out of bounds. Pretty sure I made the rules clear the last time we had a chat."

"Whatever. My conscience is clear on this one. Call it a public service."

Beside me, I feel Fenn sigh. Because he knows I can't help myself.

"I warned him," Duke tells Fenn. "I spelled it out in capital fucking letters."

"He comes from public school," Fenn pleads. "I don't know. He's got some sort of learning disorder. It's all the lead pipes in the water fountains."

"Nah, bro. We're past favors and forgiveness. He can't keep doing whatever the hell he wants. I've had enough. I want my cut. And I want him to admit I run this place."

"No, you know what?" I'm fed up now. I'm standing right here, but these two are talking about me like parents fighting over a kid throwing a tantrum in the restaurant. "I've fucking had enough. I don't know where you get this maniacal sense of entitlement. Or why the hell everyone else lets a 'roided-out fuckboy tie a bedsheet around his neck and call it a cape, but I'm done playing Lost Boys."

"RJ." Fenn's warning tone begs me to shut up. But I'm on a roll. "Don't."

"Are you challenging me to a rematch?" A sick grin stretches across Duke's face.

I flick up an eyebrow. "Even better. I'm challenging you for your job."

CHAPTER 32
RJ

"Jesus Christ." Fenn throws his hands up and stares at me in disbelief.

"Oh, I love this," Duke says slowly, giving me a dismissive once-over. "I'm in."

"Great. Let's make this happen," I tell Duke, because I'm not sure I'm totally in control of my mouth at this point.

In fact, I'm certain I already regret this. What the fuck was I thinking?

And how the hell did he get me to agree to play on his terms when I know a hundred ways to dethrone Duke without throwing a single punch? In theory, at least. Because that's the frustrating part. In reality, I don't have jack shit on Duke, no matter how deep I dig. Not a single speck of dirt I can use to gain the upper hand with him.

But, fuck, maybe that's a sign. Maybe hacking isn't the route to take on this one. God knows it exploded in my face when it came to Sloane. So maybe the way to best Duke is to rely on the one thing everyone at this school has such a hard-on for: tradition.

"Awesome." Duke's smile widens. "Tomorrow night. Last man standing."

"No way. Hold on." Fenn again tries to grab the reins of this runaway horse. "Come on, Duke. Look at his face. You can't expect this idiot to be in any shape for a fight on a day's notice. What the hell kind of leadership fight is that?"

"He's the one who asked for it."

"Like I said, not too bright. But you can at least make it fair," Fenn argues with some desperation. "How will it look to everyone else if you go out there and pound on some guy who's already broken and way out of his depth?"

Once again, they're talking about me like I'm not in the room.

"Again, not my problem." Duke is smug as he crosses his arms.

"Give him some time to train. A month. It'll make you seem more reasonable, and if you win, it'll be a way more convincing deterrent if you took on a worthy opponent."

He snorts a laugh. "You think you can turn him into a fighter in a month, knock yourself out. I wouldn't be worried if you took six. But have at it."

I might have to side with Duke on this one. I'm not too proud to admit I was thoroughly outmatched the other day, and I can't see how a few weeks changes that. Guess I was planning to rely on fortitude and a little good fortune.

A larger part of me starts to come around to the idea, however. It sounds liberating, knocking Duke off his pedestal of egomania and wresting this school from his authoritarian clutches. Anything to get him off my back and start enjoying a little goddamn freedom.

"So it's settled then," Fenn says. Cautiously relieved.

"Under one condition." Duke glances at me, eyes gleaming. "You have to take a time penalty."

"What the fuck does that mean?" I demand.

"It means, if I'm giving you a month, you have to give me something. So if you lose, you leave school. For good."

"That's not really up to me. Our parents would never go for that." I roll my eyes. "How am I supposed to spin something like that?"

"Figure it out. Or I'll go to the headmaster and tell him you've been sticking it to his daughter."

"Sidebar," Fenn tells me. He holds up a finger at Duke, then pulls me out of earshot. "That's not a bluff," he murmurs. "If he tells Tresscott you've been seeing Sloane behind his back, he'll expel you on the spot. There's no coming back from that. The guy is beyond protective of those girls."

"Then I better not lose," I murmur back.

Fenn sighs.

I stride back to Duke, sticking out my hand. "Deal."

Satisfied and practically salivating, Duke shakes my hand then saunters off. No doubt picking out a spot to hang my skull on his wall.

"So…yeah." Fenn scrubs his palm over the back of his neck, taking stock of what's just transpired. "We've got a month to make sure you don't die."

The next afternoon, Sloane calls my bluff and shows up with her history textbook and a binder full of notes. My mouth goes dry the moment she emerges from the path in that short uniform skirt and white dress shirt…which she immediately unbuttons after she sets her stuff down.

"What are you doing?" I growl.

"Relax," she answers, rolling her eyes. "I'm wearing a tank top underneath. I'm hot."

Yes, yes she is. So hot I can't look at her without wanting to remove the rest of her clothing.

"Eyes up here," she chastises. "We have much to discuss."

I blink my gaze away from her tits. Which is difficult because they look amazing in that tight top. "We do?"

Sloane shakes her head in disbelief. "You agree to fight Duke again and think there's nothing to discuss?"

"Oh, that." I shrug. "I'm working on it."

"Working on getting murdered?" she says dryly.

"On plan B." I hesitate. "I know my hacking is a touchy subject, but I assume you're cool with me trying to find ammo on Duke?" I ask, inspecting her expression.

"Go for it. I doubt you'll find anything. With Duke, it's pretty much what you see is what you get."

Shit. That's what I'm afraid of.

"Maybe you can devise a fun scheme to avoid the whole thing," Sloane suggests in a mock helpful tone. "Lure him into a crate and ship it off to Siberia like some Bugs Bunny shit."

I nod vigorously. "Solid plan."

"RJ."

"Yes, cupcake?"

"You can't fight him again." She sighs. "You can't compete with Duke's level of bloodlust."

"I'll figure something out," I promise her. "Trust me. I always do."

She seems unconvinced, but drops the issue. "Fine. Are you going to come over here and kiss me already?"

When she takes a step toward me, I take a step back.

"Nope," I inform her. Yesterday I made myself a promise to help her keep *her* promise, and damned if I let both of us get sidetracked. "We're here to work. What's your paper on?"

She narrows her eyes. "You're serious."

"As a heart attack." I reach for my own bag to remove my laptop. "What's it on?"

After a second, her shoulders sag in defeat. "European history. I'm supposed to discuss the methods the Spanish used in order to spread Catholicism to the New World."

Christ. I'm almost sorry I'm forcing her to do this.

Out loud, I lie and say, "Sounds interesting."

"Stop lying to me, RJ." But there's humor in her voice.

We settle on opposite sides of the bench with our respective laptops and proceed to spend the next little while in total silence. I work on a new script I'm hoping to unleash on Duke's financial world. At this point I'm running out of ideas about what else to look for.

I've just finished tapping out a few lines when I sense Sloane's gaze on me. I turn to catch her staring at me with what's becoming a familiar gleam.

"No," I say sternly.

She frowns. "No, what?"

"No, we're not fooling around."

Her mouth falls open. "*Someone* thinks highly of himself. I wasn't thinking about fooling around."

"Bullshit." I swipe my tongue over my bottom lip, which always goes dry when Sloane looks at me with kiss-me eyes. "You totally were. And you're not getting a piece of this until you finish your paper."

My firm tone must amuse her, because her lips curve slightly. "What are you, my dad?"

I blanch. "God, don't ever say that again. Although I guess I'd be okay if you called me daddy sometimes."

That makes her throw her head back and laugh. "You wish." Then, with her eyes narrowed, she very deliberately adjusts the hem of her skirt, flashing a hint of upper thigh. Fuck. This girl will be the death of me. "You really don't feel like taking a break?"

"Nope." I'm lying. I want nothing more than to slip my hand beneath that skirt and finger her until she's moaning my name. But I won't.

"You could always sell me one of your online papers," she says, lifting a brow. "Fenn told Casey you've got a lucrative side hustle going."

Swear to God, Fenn doesn't know the meaning of the word "secret." Blabbermouth, that one.

"I do," I agree, since there's no point hiding it from Sloane. She won't tell her dad.

"Then why haven't you offered to help me out? If you did, my essay would be done and we could be making better use of our time…" She trails off enticingly.

As much as I want to pull her into my lap and shove my tongue down her throat, I shake my head at her. "I haven't offered because you're not that person," I say simply.

That startles her. She chews on her lip for a beat. "You're right. I'm not that person," she admits. "I can't cheat."

"Exactly. And since you made a huge deal about wanting to get your grades up, you don't get *this*"—with a crude grin, I cup my package—"until you finish that." I nod toward her laptop.

"You're cruel," she accuses, but I don't miss the flicker of pleasure in her eyes. She likes that I'm holding her feet to the fire, forcing her to accomplish a goal. I get the feeling her dad doesn't push her at all when it comes to this shit. He just assumes she's doing whatever she needs to do.

Fuck, and I totally just compared myself to her dad. Willingly, this time.

But I suppose I don't mind taking an authoritative role once in a while if it helps Sloane achieve her dreams.

Later that night, Fenn summons the brain trust to our room for a strategy session. Turns out, I don't know the first thing about training or preparing for a fight. I figured I'd lift some weights and maybe watch some boxing matches, but Fenn had been horrified by that idea.

"You need resistance training," Silas insists.

Lawson flips through the pages of the school paper. "You'll have to become much faster to be any sort of match for Duke."

"He's got power," Fenn says, as if I don't have first-hand experience.

"Yes, I remember." Silas is nodding.

"Look at this." Lawson holds up a picture from the sports section with a picture of Duke at a recent friendly with the soccer team. "Look at your arms, then look at his."

I'm not out of shape by any means. But I've also never needed to work out too hard to maintain a decent build. Duke probably spends four hours a day in the gym.

"Go ahead and strip," Fenn tells me.

My eyebrows fly up. "Excuse me?"

"Take off your shirt and stand in front of the mirror. Pants too. We have to see what we're working with."

"Damn right," Lawson drawls.

I turn to glare at him. "You know, I'm not some piece of meat."

Nevertheless, I pull my shirt off and study myself in the mirror hanging inside my closet door. I've always had broad shoulders and a trim waistline. But at the pool, I'm one of the least muscular guys on the swim team. I'm built more like a runner.

"I'd fuck." Lawson grins at me in the mirror.

"Not helpful," Silas groans.

The three of them spend the next several minutes nerding out over muscle groups and protein ratios, arguing over the benefits of interval training. It's all nonsense to me, but I appreciate their eagerness to help devise a training and nutrition regimen. I had no idea we were taking it all quite that far. They're all in, though, and write up a whole calendar, splitting shifts with me in the gym.

It takes a lot to keep my surprise in check. Frankly, I didn't know they cared. It's been a long time since I had a group of friends who would stick their necks out for me. I mean, it's a ton of effort for very little chance of reward. Sort of gets me right in the chest.

"So, what happens in the likely event of your demise?" Silas asks and receives glares from the other two. "Will you accept your banishment?"

"I don't know." I slip my shirt back on. "I'll cross that bridge when I come to it."

Either way, I won't be leaving. I'm not getting chased off from here after I just got Sloane back. Despite the bumpy start, I think we could really have something, and like hell I'm walking away with my tail between my legs. If this whole thing goes south, I'll just have to figure out a plan B.

"And if you manage to pull it off?" Silas asks. "Heavy is the head that wears the crown…"

I bark out a laugh. "No way. I'm not interested in being the new Duke. If I win, everyone gets to go back to living their lives however they want. No one is ruling over anything." Because it's damn stupid and this childish tyranny ends with me.

Later, after Silas and Lawson have left, Fenn and I are each in bed on either side of the room. I don't make it a habit to burden other people with my feelings, but something nags at me that I've got to get out.

"Hey," I say, to see if he's still awake.

"Yeah?" He sounds drowsy.

"Thanks. For having my back."

"Of course."

"I figured you for a stuck-up rich boy who wouldn't give a shit about anyone else."

He chuckles in the darkness. "I can see where you'd get that idea."

"But I was wrong. You've been going out of your way to look out for me when you really didn't have to."

"We're stepbrothers. That's what family does. I got you."

It never occurred to me that Fenn would ever feel like family. The way we were tossed together overnight, coming from two totally different circumstances with no chance to have a say in our own lives? The chances of developing an actual friendship were slim to none. But here we are.

"You too, man," I tell him.

I can't remember the last time I truly trusted someone. Despite myself, I realize I've come to trust Fenn.

What a world.

CHAPTER 33
SLOANE

I DON'T GET TO SEE RJ AGAIN UNTIL SATURDAY NIGHT, SINCE I couldn't sneak out Friday to see him because my father roped me and Casey into watching a movie with him. I get the sense Dad knows something's up, because he's been at the house more the last few days and being more diligent than usual in checking up on Case and me. I doubt he has any clue about RJ, but clearly his parental senses are tingling.

The thing that gets me about that, though, is why he even bothers acting all protective. There's this cynical part of me that suspects the only reason he warns all the Sandover boys away from his daughters, particularly me, is because he's worried it could affect his position. Not because he cares about my well-being. With Casey, I get why he's overprotective. With me…it feels forced. Fake.

But maybe that's my bitterness talking. My relationship with Dad has been so strained for so long that I lost clarity about his motives a long time ago.

Thankfully, Saturday he has a dinner with the board of governors. Which means he'll be at some swank hotel emptying bottles of wine with the bigwigs and money people. The dog-and-pony show usually lasts until the restaurant kicks them out, so I don't expect him home before three in the morning.

RJ takes the opportunity to sneak me into the dorm. I was skeptical about coming in the laundry entrance, but he insisted that the housefather would be passed out. All it took was propping the door open for me and stealthily creeping our way through the halls, careful to avoid detection by anyone who might dime us out.

"You sure Fenn isn't coming back?" I ask as I make myself comfortable on his bed.

RJ double-checks the door is locked before coming to sit beside me. "He's at an away game. They're staying overnight."

I find last year's Sandover yearbook on the edge of RJ's nightstand and pull it over to flip through. "What's this for?"

"Research."

"Ooh. Sounds ominous. Is something in here going to help you avoid getting your teeth pulverized into pencil shavings?"

He mock glares at me. "Thanks for the vote of confidence."

"Hey, I just want to make sure you're prepared. And I hope you find that plan B soon, because what happened the first time was just a friendly warning. If you really step into that circle with him, it'll be much worse. Don't expect a fair fight. Duke plays dirty."

"Can we maybe not spend the night talking about your ex?" RJ is adorable when he's jealous. He squeezes my thigh with a little snarl. "I'm more interested in how you play dirty."

"You wouldn't know what to do with me." I bite my lip at him, a coy move that has him throwing me against his pillows and draping his body over mine.

"I'll take that bet."

RJ combs his hand into my hair and presses his lips to mine, plunging his tongue into my mouth like he's been just as starved for attention as I have. The addiction came on strong and sudden. Now I'm a fiend, gnawing on pens and clawing out of my skin. I don't know what it is about the loner boy that gets me all knotted up, but he's done a number on my head.

Nibbling on his bottom lip, I throw my leg over his thigh.

Already I feel his erection pressing against me, and it puts all sorts of ideas in my mind. The other day he wouldn't even touch me, and as much as I appreciated him trying to keep me focused on my goal of not falling behind in school, my current agenda is to kiss him until we both forget our names.

"I still have some groveling to do," he says against my mouth.

"Couldn't hurt," I agree.

Another thing I like about RJ: he isn't shy. Not about us. He pays attention and reads my signals. So when he pushes his hand under my T-shirt to scrape his thumb over one nipple, I arch my back into his touch. He teases me, frustrating my patience until I bite down on his lip.

"You do that again and I'll bite back," he growls.

"I'll take that bet."

Glaring at me, RJ shoves my shirt up to expose my breast and gives it a squeeze. He wraps his lips around the hard peak and gently tugs with his teeth, then lashes at it with his tongue. I can't help but grind against him, feeling the thick ridge of his hard-on through the thin fabric of my shorts. Already I'm nearly out of breath and practically dizzy with the need for release. I try palming him through his jeans, but he pulls my hand away.

"You don't want me to?"

"Tonight's for you," he says, his gaze fixed on me as he pulls my shirt up to expose my other nipple and sucks hard on it.

I could nearly come just from his mouth, the way his hands know me. I realize there's a mirror hanging from the closet door across the room, and I watch him kiss and suck on my breasts, gripping the pillow behind my head.

Then his hand slides lower, cupping me between my thighs. He rolls onto his side to pin my leg down. When he glances up to find me looking beyond him, he turns his head to see the mirror.

"Kinky girl," he whispers.

He watches himself run his hand firmly up and down my shorts, teasing my pussy over the fabric. I follow his hand in the mirror, screaming in my head for him to press his skin against mine. Wanting him inside me.

Instead, he moves between my legs and slowly begins pulling my shorts off with my underwear. He studies my face for a moment to make sure I want this. And I do. I almost grab the back of his head, but I restrain myself. Then he pushes both my thighs open, flat to the bed, and drags his tongue through my slit.

"Yes," I moan.

I want to close my eyes, but I can't tear my gaze away from our reflection. The sensation of his mouth, his thumb sliding over my clit, is almost hypnotic. Seeing his tongue work me over in the mirror is the hottest thing I've ever witnessed.

"Love your pussy," he mumbles against my heated flesh. "You're so fucking beautiful, Sloane." He kisses my clit before gently taking it between his lips. He sucks, then releases the swollen bud when I cry out in pleasure.

"Quiet, cupcake," he warns, his hand coming to rest on my stomach. "Don't want to wake the whole dorm up."

"I hate that nickname," I tell him, even as my hips lift, seeking the warmth of his mouth again.

"You love it," RJ argues, then captures my clit again and gives a sweet, gentle suck.

The blood rushes from my head to throb between my legs. I'm a mess. Biting down on my bottom lip. Muscles shaking. Strung so tight I don't know how long I can take his torturous teasing.

"I think about this every second of the day," he mutters between licks.

"What, going down on me?" I ask between gasps and moans.

"Mmm. Everything." His tongue drags a hot swipe down my slit toward my opening, which is dripping for him. "Having you…" Lick. "Here…" Lick. "Spread out on my bed…" Lick. "Mine for the taking." He punctuates that by bringing one finger into the mix, sliding it inside me with one deep thrust.

We both groan.

"So tight," he growls. "I wanna be inside you so badly."

"Please," I beg, but despite his tormented admission, he doesn't undo his jeans. He stays between my legs, his hungry mouth exploring and devouring and driving me mad with need.

"You gonna come?" He lifts his head, his finger still pushing in and out of me, his wet lips a scant inch from my clit. "I want you to come."

I gaze at our reflection again, shivering at the sight of his finger moving inside me. I don't miss the tiny smirk that curves his mouth before he leans in and flicks his tongue over my clit.

"Let me hear it, Sloane." His tongue moves faster. A second finger slides into my pussy. "Let me fucking feel it."

It's too much. I'm overwhelmed by sensation. By the scent of his shampoo and the heat of his mouth and those two long fingers plunging and curling inside me. My breathing has gone so shallow I feel dizzy. All I can do is lie there and rock against his greedy lips until finally my entire body clenches in release.

RJ licks and kisses me through the orgasm, his fingers slowing, his tongue becoming featherlight as my shudders begin to abate.

Afterward, with his arm over my shoulder while we're lying in bed, he can't hide his smug smile.

"Don't be too pleased with yourself." I poke his ribs, and he flinches at the still-tender bruise. "The only reason I came so hard was because I was picturing what you'll look like with shaved legs."

RJ groans, throwing his head back against the pillow. "I'm still repressing that thought."

"How's it going?" I ask. "The swimming. Are you starting to enjoy it at all?"

"Can't believe I'm saying this, but...yes." He sounds deeply ashamed, and I laugh in delight.

"Uh-oh. Someone likes wearing a Speedo," I tease.

"I like the swimming part," RJ protests. "I hate the Speedo part."

"Surrre."

"Hate it."

"Surrrrrrrre."

He pinches me in retaliation, then tightens his grip around me, holding me closer. We chat for a while as it gets late and the dorm grows quieter, whispering in the dark to make sure our voices don't carry or give away my presence. Neither of us is anxious to say good night.

RJ skims his fingertips up and down my arm, idly tracing shapes against my skin. It's nice like this. Talking to someone who really feels like they're listening, that they care.

I wasn't sure I was ready—I'd still been harboring doubts—but tonight has convinced me RJ wasn't simply playing a character for me. Wasn't creating a persona based on whatever inferred psychological profile he constructed from snooping around in my social media. Despite the super-shitty way he went about it, our connection was genuine. It still is. Being here with him feels so natural and right that my throat closes up, tight with emotion.

God, this guy is making me sappy. But I can't help it. Since I agreed to give him another chance, he's been so fucking sweet. I wake up every morning to a text waiting on my phone. Sometimes it's a funny message, like yesterday's: *Top of the morning to you, gorgeous.* Today, it was a sexy one: *Morning, cupcake. Had a dream I was inside you. Fuck, it was incredible.*

And his good-night texts are equally unpredictable. I never know what to expect with RJ, and I sort of love it. I don't know how he's doing it, but he's slowly chipping away at pieces of my armor and making me feel…fluffy.

Fucking hell. I feel fluffy.

"What about your sister?" he asks, jarring me from my somewhat concerning thoughts. "How's she doing at school? Last time you mentioned it, seemed like things were tough."

"I wish I could say it's gotten better, but it's not," I admit. "Casey smiles through it, though. Doesn't want to be a burden on anyone. She's always been like that. It's enough to convince my dad. But not me. I know she's struggling."

"It's gotta be hell coming back from something like that."

I swallow the lump in my throat. The ache of guilt is always there. The dozens of choices I could have made differently to prevent all of this. I live with it, but never forget.

"I do my best to take care of her..."

"But who's taking care of you?"

"Nobody. That's the problem." I sigh. "I know it makes me sound like a bitch. My little sister went through something horrible and I'm sitting here—"

"You're allowed to have feelings," he tells me, kissing my temple. "It's okay to get tired or frustrated or stressed out."

"It's not her, though. Casey can ask me for anything, any time. I don't mind. But our dad is totally preoccupied with everything else. What little attention he does have is only concerned with her, and I'm supposed to suck it up and be the invincible one. Like our whole world is balancing on a ball on my head while I'm teetering on a toothpick."

My throat tightens again, this time with sadness. Every now and then it'd be nice if Dad showed some interest in how I'm doing. If he had even the slightest inclination toward being a parent beyond scaring off my boyfriends. I know he needs me, but I'm at my wit's end.

"In his mind, it always comes back to that night. She was my responsibility and I let him down. So now it's penance."

I feel RJ stiffen. "Why does he think what happened to her is your fault?"

Because it is. On that much we're in agreement.

"Duke and I were on a break, so I figured it would be fun to bring Casey as my date to junior prom. Dad wasn't thrilled with the idea, so he made me swear up and down that I'd keep an eye on her.

Everything was going fine at first. She was dancing with some of my friends and having a great time. Then Duke cornered me, making his case for the hundredth time why I should take him back."

I swallow again. On the list of massive life regrets, that one goes right to the top. If I'd listened to my gut, told him to fuck off, it would have prevented everything that came next.

"And, well, you know, one thing leads to another. We hook up. We're gone awhile, and when we come back, I don't see Casey. I look around, check everywhere I can think of, but I can't find her. Eventually we all start searching. Silas and Lawson—the guys are all there and they spread out. We're frantically searching for over an hour before I get a text from her phone."

It still haunts me. The split-second of relief followed by the dead-cold panic that rushed through my blood.

"It said there'd been an accident and to come to the boathouse." The memories try to race to the surface, but I tamp them down. Banish them to the deep depths of my psyche. "Needless to say, it wasn't a pretty scene. The cops figured the car was headed to the abandoned boathouse and then for some reason swerved and went into the lake. We spent months begging them to keep investigating, but without a witness to say anything, or security footage, they threw their hands up and closed the case."

I only realize I'm shivering when RJ pulls the covers up and hugs me closer. I'm suddenly exhausted and having trouble keeping my eyes open. Even the memories of that night take it out of me. For months it's like I've been on the other end of a rope, standing at the shore, trying to pull that car out of the water. Grunting and screaming, tugging with all my strength, but no matter how hard I dig my feet into the mud, it's going to sink and suck me in with it.

"None of that sounds like your fault," he assures me. And he's not the first. I appreciate the attempt, but I know better.

"It's killing me. There are so many unanswered questions, and it seems impossible there wasn't a single witness. I can't help thinking there are people I've talked to, who I believed were my friends, who saw what happened and never came forward."

"Listen, don't freak out on me, but…"

I twist up to look at him. "What?"

"I may have done some digging into that too. Your sister's accident. I was curious." There's a slight waver in his voice, as if he's afraid to remind me of his hacking prowess. "I was poking around but didn't find anything useful in the case files."

At least he's putting his skills toward a worthy cause.

"This time it's okay," I tease, before going serious again. "If you want to be nosy, I wouldn't mind the help. We're at a dead end otherwise. I'm not sure how much longer I can keep agonizing about this. Or watching Casey beat herself up trying to remember. We have to know."

"If there's something to find, I'll get to it," RJ promises.

He leans down to catch my eyes. Recently, I've come to understand he's a far more sincere person than he lets on. Even when he's sarcastic, there's a level of truth behind it. So I know he means it when he tells me he'll dig until he reaches the bottom.

"By the way…" I turn to lie on my side and prop my head on his shoulder. "My dad and Casey are going to look at a couple colleges tomorrow. They're leaving first thing in the morning and won't be back until late. You could come over, if you want. Spend the day."

There's hesitation in his pursed lips. "I love that idea. Except I'm not sure we should risk it."

"Since when are you the cautious type?"

"You said he's got cameras all over that house. If he's half as obsessed as you say, he's probably monitoring the feed on his phone. He can get motion-sensor alerts when someone trips a camera outside, you know."

He's got a point. Even if I can't help feeling disappointed he's so quick to blow off a chance to spend several unsupervised hours together.

"Sloane." Sensing my unhappiness, he glides his hands down my ribs and clutches my waist. "I want to. Obviously. I'd eat you out on the kitchen counter if you told me to. But I'd like to keep seeing you. If we get caught, your dad's kicking my ass out of school, and I'll end up shipped off to some cattle ranch in Montana for wayward youth."

"I don't know. I'd need to see you in a pair of chaps before I rule out the possibility."

"Keep dreaming, sweetheart."

When a deep, sudden yawn bursts through me, I know it's time to get home. It's too comfy in bed with him. The second I shut my eyes, I'll be passed out and then we'll have a hell of a time sneaking me out of here in the morning.

RJ checks the hallway is clear before we creep out of his room. I didn't tell him this, of course, but I've tried the window route before and it's not a fall I want to take again. So we're quiet on our toes, my shoes in hand, skimming the walls toward the fire stairwell. We're nearly home free when we reach the first floor. The rear exit is located at the far end of the hall through the laundry and delivery loading dock. Except as we're making our way past the corridor to the main entrance, we see a shadow sweep across the floor.

"Shit," RJ hisses.

"What?"

"Roger's door is open."

"Who?"

"Mr. Swinney. The housefather. He's usually asleep by now. The TV's off."

"I don't understand."

He backs us up to cling to the wall in a tiny alcove that holds a bust of a Sandover founder on a pedestal.

"What do we do?" I whisper.

RJ grimaces, gritting his teeth. He takes another peek around the corner. "We have to make a run for it. Hope he's passed out and just forgot to close his door."

"Okay."

I've got my eyes focused on the exit sign at the end of the hall, ready to sprint like I'm qualifying for state. But the second we poke our heads out, the floorboard creaks, and we run smack into Mr. Swinney in a house robe and pajamas, carrying a cup of tea.

"Miss Tresscott." The plump, unkempt man gives me an admonishing glance. "I don't believe we've been formally introduced. I'm Roger Swinney. And you're quite far from home at this late hour."

I scramble for a suitable excuse. "I, ah, was…"

"Sleepwalking," RJ supplies.

I choke down a laugh. "Right," I confirm. "I must have been sleepwalking."

Mr. Swinney holds up his free hand to silence us, and we proceed to get thoroughly but politely reamed. The gist of which is that Swinney can't wait to report this indiscretion to my father. My stomach drops at the threat—or rather, I think it's a promise—and I can tell RJ isn't thrilled either.

"I trust you can find your way out," Mr. Swinney finishes. He lifts one bushy eyebrow. "Feel free to use the front door this time."

RJ and I take our walk of shame to the steps outside, where I put on my shoes and wonder how I'm going to explain this to my father. Whatever his motives for scaring the Sandover boys away from me and Casey, Dad doesn't make idle threats.

"So, yeah. I'm not gonna sugarcoat it," RJ tells me. "This is bad."

"I know." I bite my lip. "The one time I got caught meeting up with a Sandover guy, Dad expelled him on the spot. With Duke, I had to tell him up front and ask for his permission."

RJ mulls that over. "What are the chances he'll give me permission to date you?"

"Before Casey's accident? Maybe decent odds. Now? Slim to none." I let out a breath. "Maybe there's something I can say. Get to my dad first and smooth it over. I'll tell him I came to see Silas and we just happened to run into each other in the hall."

"He's not going to buy that. Trust me. I'm the first guy he's looking at."

"You forget there's at least one of my exes up there. You're not the only delinquent in the building."

"Skipping over that," he says, because he's had about all he can stand of Duke lately. "No, we have to make sure Roger doesn't talk. That means figuring out what he's getting up to every Sunday night. Figure that out, and we have some leverage."

Beyond RJ's shoulder, I spot Mr. Swinney standing in the window, watching us while he sips his tea.

I release a breath and give a somber nod. "Well, Dad's off campus tomorrow. So whatever you're going to do, you have until Monday morning."

CHAPTER 34
RJ

I watched about three minutes of a boxing match online before I got bored. Because, really, if you're going to call yourself something like Satan's Doberman, I expect more than aggressively sweaty hugging. Now I regret bailing so quickly on my research. I feel ridiculous dancing around this mat in the gym on Sunday morning with Lawson behind me shouting "stick and move" while Fenn tries coaching me through where to put my feet and how to close my angles. Whatever the hell that's supposed to mean.

"You don't want to let Duke close you down. Keep your guard up and try to maintain the reach advantage."

"I don't watch that MMA bullshit. Just speak to me like a normal person."

Lawson sighs in frustration. "How hard is it to hit somebody? You two are killing me."

Silas stands off the mat with a bottle of water and creeping doubt. "Don't listen to him. You can't go in there wildly swinging against Duke. He'll take your head clean off and you'll never land a punch."

"Look," Fenn tells me, bouncing on his toes with his taped hands raised. "You do like this. Arms up. You want to use your forearms to block shots. But also need to take away his target, so you want to circle away. Don't stand still in front of him or—"

"He'll remove my face. Yeah, I heard that part. I have been in a fight before."

"And look how that turned out." Lawson laughs.

My last encounter with Duke notwithstanding, I do at least understand that trying not to get punched in the face is the primary directive.

"Come on." Fenn waves his hand to gesture me forward, bouncing side to side. "Come at me." He wears a cocky smirk as he swipes his thumb over his nose like something he saw in a movie once. "I'll give you the first one free."

"Fine. But I'll feel kinda shitty if I break your nose."

"If you can find anything but air."

I jab him right in the nose. He stumbles backwards a few steps, grabbing his face. "Motherfucker."

"Careful what you wish for." Lawson at least is thoroughly enjoying himself.

"I'm good." Fenn holds a couple bloody fingers out. But nothing appears broken. "All good."

"You sure?" Silas tosses him a towel to clean himself up.

"Yep. I think your jab looks good. No notes there."

Silas grabs his backpack, chuckling to himself. "I have to get out of here anyway. Driving to Ballard to see Amy. Try not to kill each other."

"I'm out too," Lawson says. "I need to fuck."

I can't help but snort. "It's barely eleven."

"So?" He wanders over to pat me on the arm. "You know what, it's okay. When I get back, I'll give you the birds and the bees talk so you're able to understand that human beings can fuck at all hours of the day."

That makes Silas hoot. I don't think I've ever seen him this amused.

"You deserved that," Fenn tells me as we watch the other two saunter off. "Questioning a man's sex schedule. You're better than that, Remington."

"Eat me, Fennelly."

We call it a day after that. Fenn and I get cleaned up in the locker room and change clothes. He shoves a hunk of tissues up his nose to plug the bleeding, which has been reduced to a trickle.

"Sorry about that," I say, genuinely regretful. I hadn't meant to hit him that hard. Just wanted to shut him up for a second.

"Nah, it was good form. No worries."

"You took it well."

He shoves his middle finger at me.

"So listen. I have a little fact-finding mission to undertake. I could use a lookout."

"Oh, yeah?" Fenn takes a seat on the bench to pull his shoes on. "This doesn't involve Duke, right? Because I'd give it good odds he's got his dorm room booby-trapped."

"Not Duke. Tonight's my only chance to find something I can use to keep Roger quiet about catching Sloane in the dorm last night. If I don't figure out what he's been up to, that's my ass out of school."

"All right. So what's the plan?"

"Feel like going for a drive?"

"You asking me out on a date?" He eyes me in mock dismay. "But we're related."

I just sigh.

———

Since Silas is using his car to see his girl, Fenn comes through with a ride he borrows from another senior. And since this is Sandover we're talking about, the car is a Porsche Cayenne SUV with baby-soft leather seats and an engine that purrs like a kitten. That afternoon we wait in the gas station parking lot about a mile from campus on the route Mr. Swinney always takes. Right on schedule, he cruises by in his blue compact. Fenn waits a couple of seconds then pulls out on the road to tail him.

"Gonna have to keep some distance," I remind Fenn. "He'll get suspicious if there aren't many other cars on the road."

"Yeah, I got it."

The compact gets smaller as Fenn drops back and does five under the speed limit to let Roger take a comfortable lead. Hopefully, at a sufficient distance, he won't recognize the SUV or notice the same one is about to follow him down these lonely two-lane roads for the next two hours.

Thinking back to the day I was awkwardly holding my mom's bridal bouquet at the altar while Fenn stood beside his dad with two empty ring boxes, I would've rather leapt out of a window than spend my weekend stuck in a car with him, chasing a man across New Hampshire. We barely said two words to each other the entire trip when our parents first dropped us off at Sandover. Now I couldn't imagine asking anyone else along for a covert recon.

Turns out, I like hanging out with Fenn. And this place is starting to feel like home. Something I haven't felt in I don't remember how many moves. Hell, even the swim team gig is growing on me. Most of the guys are cool. Except Carter. Fucking Carter. But still, it's nice feeling like I belong somewhere.

Suddenly it occurs to me how much I stand to lose in this fight with Duke. If I fail and he makes good on his promise to blow up my spot, it's not only goodbye Sloane. This unlikely series of accidents that's become my life gets yanked from my grasp and I become an outcast again. Shipped off on another second chance to no doubt somewhere far worse.

Guess I better start taking this training shit seriously.

The sun is just dipping behind the trees when Roger's car veers off the county road to climb a winding path into the shadow of the mountains.

"Drop back," I order.

Fenn instinctively turns down the radio and gives our mark a considerable distance. The blue compact is barely a blip crawling around curves ahead of us. I watch the odometer slip from thirty, twenty-five, until we're hardly moving.

"We've got to be close," he says.

"According to his last few trips, it's about a half-mile up and a quarter-mile west still."

"Shit." Fenn slams on the brakes.

I'm thrown forward in my seat. "What? Did he spot us?"

He throws the car in reverse and quickly backs down the road, then tucks the rear end up onto the soft dirt shoulder and conceals us between the trees.

"That was his car parked up there." Fenn kills the Porsche's engine. "I think I saw him walking into the woods. Looked like there was a path."

"Awesome. I guess we're going it on foot." I glance over at him. "They got a lot of ticks in New Hampshire?"

"Only outside."

Wonderful.

With no hiking gear, escape plan, or any idea what we might find on the other side of this forest, we traipse into the woods after Roger, following a trail we pick up near his parked car. I mean, shit. If he can make this hike every week, it can't be that hard.

Fenn picks up a fallen limb and cleans it of wayward twigs to construct a walking stick. "Thinking about the ticks will keep your mind off the hillbillies and hunters, at least."

"Huh?"

"Sure. Wild-eyed doomsday preppers and off-the-grid tax dodgers. Then you've got your run-of-the-mill poachers and Second Amendment dudes."

"Seriously?"

We step quietly, well aware Roger could be lurking just beyond the shadows.

"Oh, hell yeah. You ever heard the horror stories about the Appalachian Trail? It runs through somewhere around there. All sorts of psychopaths and serial killers wandering around stalking hikers to their deaths."

"Fuck off."

"For real."

I know Fenn's full of shit. Still, the darkness plays tricks on the mind. Suddenly I'm imagining movement out of the corner of my eye, the sound of my own breathing like a stranger over my shoulder.

"There was one guy. He was sitting in a shelter when this female camper left her tent and walked to the firepit outside. A few hours later he knocks on the door of some nice old lady in town and tells her to please call the police. He's just chopped the poor girl to pieces with his hatchet."

"You couldn't have told me this—"

"Oh, shit!"

I reach out and grab Fenn by the back of his shirt when he nearly does a header.

"You okay?" I ask him.

"Yeah." He turns on his phone's flashlight to see what tripped him. Growing out of the ground like a tree stump, there's the crumbled remains of a brick wall. "What the…?"

We both turn on our flashlights and scan the area. Everywhere we look, derelict ruins loom as tombstones to once-standing structures. A chimney stack reaching out of the dirt. A wall with an empty doorway. The bare slab of a foundation to nothing.

"What is this?" I mumble to myself, not expecting an answer.

"These mountains used to be covered in logging mills," Fenn whispers, as if signs of a long-dead human presence now means someone's listening.

The buildings are gone, but the traces are there. I study the outline of several perfectly situated houses in a row on either side of what was once a horse road. "This doesn't look like a mill."

"What makes more sense? Going up and down this mountain to work every day, or walking right outside your door and picking up a saw?"

"A ghost town."

"If ol' Rog is dumping hikers and drifters, this would be a good place."

Except I'm not the superstitious type, and I don't get caught up in fantasy and scary stories. Roger's an oddball, but I doubt he's got the stomach for gore. Whatever he's doing out here, it's more of an intellectual pursuit, of that I'm certain.

We press forward until the tree line abruptly gives way to tall grass.

"Dude." Fenn stops me, throwing his arm out to halt my steps. He shines his flashlight at the palm of his hand. "Swinney's growing pot."

His humor soon turns to alarm when we hear voices and a bright searchlight streaks through the grove of marijuana plants. We hit the dirt and creep backward on our hands and knees into the relative safety of the trees.

"I hear maybe four, five guys?" I hiss.

He nods. "That's definitely a generator too."

"They've got to have a trailer back there or something."

"How'd they get it in there?"

The more important question is, what do we do now?

"Let's go back." I tug Fenn as I retrace our steps.

"What, really? Why? We just got here."

"And we found what we came for. So now we'll wait for Swinney by his car and confront him there. Assuming he's alone."

Fenn grins, his white teeth shining in the darkness. "You don't want to get a picture of him coming out of the pot forest like the Field of Dreams?"

"Not a chance. You ever hear of Humboldt County?"

"Huh? No."

We double-time it back down the path, through the ghost town and its leering statues, while I quickly fill Fenn in.

"Years back, Mom and I lived in Northern California. Humboldt was, still is, the pot farm capital of the U.S. Part of what's called the Emerald Triangle. There are more illegal grow-ops there per acre than anywhere else in the country. And the second-highest murder rate in the state. Guys up there, they don't play. They'll shoot you dead and turn your body to compost for wandering onto their property."

"Isn't pot legal in California?"

"Yep. And that only pissed them off. We're not talking granola hippies. These guys are hardcore gangsters with fucking AK-47s and dogs that'll eat your brain right out of your skull. So, no. We're not sticking around to run into some of Roger's business partners. As long as we don't see any other cars down by the road, we'll confront him there. I'm not trying to die tonight."

From Mr. Swinney's phone data that I scraped last week, we know we've got quite a wait ahead of us. So we pull up a log with a view of the car and the trail, and settle into the dense shrubs for a long night.

"I spy with my little—"

I throw an elbow into Fenn's ribs. "Don't even start."

"Then what are we gonna do all night? I need to be constantly entertained, otherwise I'll self-destruct."

"You sound like Lawson," I say with a grin.

Fenn shrugs. "He and I aren't that different."

"Nah, you are. You have a conscience."

My stepbrother's gaze briefly flicks toward me. "You sure about that?"

Before I can answer, my phone lights up with a text from Sloane.

Sloane: How's the stakeout going?

As I tap out a quick reply, saying it's all good, I notice Fenn eyeing my phone. At first I think he's trying to read my messages. Then I note his rueful expression.

"You're using the new space phone," he accuses.

"Oh. Right. Yeah." A sigh of resignation slips out. "Your dad was right—this is the fastest processor I've ever seen in a phone."

Fenn chuckles bitterly. "That's how he gets you, man."

A short silence falls between us, finally broken by Fenn's heavy breath.

"I'm not jealous," he informs me.

I glance over, amused. "Okay."

"That my dad is buying you shit," Fenn clarifies. He leans back, legs stretched out on the dirt. He looks completely unbothered. "It's his way of securing something he wants from you. With me, he used to buy me all this obscenely expensive stuff because he wanted my permission."

I frown. "Permission for what?"

"To let him be a bad father. He wanted me to keep my mouth shut about it, pretend we weren't total strangers, that he hadn't completely stopped caring about my existence after my mom died."

His wooden tone and vacant expression reveal more than any uttered profanities or blazing eyes ever could. Fenn's made himself dead inside, immune to being hurt by his father ever again. I get it. It's a useful cope. I used to do it myself sometimes, before I realized the trick, the *real* solution to not getting hurt: stop caring.

"So, what does he want from me? Approval, right?"

Fenn nods. "Wants to win you over. Make himself look good in front of his new wife. But the thing about my dad is—no stamina."

I groan out loud. "I think my mom might disagree with that."

"Gross." He gives me a shove. "I mean, he gives up fast. Once he sees he can't get what he wants from someone, he bails. No follow-through." Fenn shrugs. "Anyway. I guess what I'm saying is—don't get attached to the guy. I don't want you to get burned."

"I never get attached," I say honestly.

"Bullshit. You've planted so many roots here, you're practically imbedded in the ground. You joined the swim team, for Christ's sake. Face it, bro. You care." He starts to laugh. "Aw man, Sandover turned you into someone who cares about shit. Usually it has the opposite effect."

His laughter is contagious. I chuckle to myself, all the while wondering why his frank assessment of my transformation isn't freaking me out that much. He's right. I *have* changed. I showed up here a loner determined to keep everyone at arm's length, and within a month I ended up with a stepbrother, a girlfriend, and a swim team.

Maybe getting attached isn't all bad.

"That thing you said the other night? About us being family?" I start awkwardly.

"What about it?"

"I guess I don't hate the idea."

I expect him to snort out another laugh, but instead, his voice becomes gruff, a bit shaky. "Yeah, I don't hate it either." He pauses. "Maybe I was kinda lonely before you came along."

It takes a lot for me not to reply with a smart-ass remark. His admission is so heavy and my first instinct is to keep things light. But I force myself not to make a joke out of what is clearly a difficult topic for him.

"I miss my mom, you know? Not as much as when I was little. But enough." He glances over, his pale blue eyes flickering with weariness. "Can't talk to my dad about shit. Gabe's gone." Another pause. "So, yeah, it's been nice having you around."

Another text lights up my screen, and I can physically feel the relief that shudders through the both of us. This chat was getting way too real.

Sloane: If you're bored, just pretend I'm there doing things to your dick.

I groan out loud. This goddamn woman.

Fenn's lips twitch with humor. "You okay there?"

"No," I reply through clenched teeth. "Sloane's trying to talk dirty to me when she knows damn well you're sitting right next to me."

He offers a not-so-helpful suggestion. "If you want to go jerk it behind that tree, I promise to look away and cover my ears."

"Fuck off," I say, while my fingers text Sloane back.

Me: I'm muting your notifications because you're evil. Good day, madam.

"So, what's this all about?" he asks, gesturing to my phone. "I swear, every time I turn around, you're texting love letters to the girl. Are you official now?"

"I don't even know what that means."

"It means we're out here because you two got busted in the dorm the other night. So is this a thing now, or…?"

"We're dating, I guess. If that's what you want to call official."

It's strange to think it's only been a few weeks since she wouldn't even tell me her name. Back then, Sloane was just a hot mystery with a killer set of legs, begging me to puzzle her out. Now, despite a few early blunders, I already feel closer to her than I have to a girl since my fifth-grade crush pulled me behind the tire swings to kiss me then punch me in the nuts.

"Then this isn't just a hookup thing?" Fenn draws shapes in the dirt with his walking stick.

A set of headlights sweeps through the trees and sends my heart into my throat before its engine quickly fades into the distance. "Yeah," I answer absently. "I guess I'm trying to get to know her or whatever."

Fenn grunts out a sarcastic laugh. "Or whatever."

"I like her. Obviously."

I knew when I stood outside her window risking the headmaster confronting me with a shotgun that I had more than a passing crush on her tits. And pouring my heart out at the lake kind of reinforced the severity of my affliction. Sloane's also the first girl I've ever spent any time in bed with after the dirty stuff was over. Whatever emotional attachment was necessary for cuddling never existed before her. But last night she didn't get up to immediately put her clothes back on, and I didn't want to kick her out. I would have kept her there all night if I'd thought we could get away with it.

"You'd better like her," Fenn warns. "In a few weeks, Duke's planning to paint the walls with your face."

"I can't wait until I never have to hear his name again."

Seriously, I'm thoroughly over Duke as a topic. Just altogether exhausted of his existence. And I suppose that's another new and unusual symptom brought on by Sloane. Jealously isn't something I'm too familiar with, and I don't think it's a good look on me. I don't much care for this concoction of rage, paranoia, and inadequacy that's injected into my bloodstream every time she drops a mention of him into conversation. How do people live like this?

"For what it's worth," Fenn says, "I can see it. The two of you. It's not the worst match."

"Oh, good. I was hoping for your approval."

"Yeah, okay. Eat shit, asshole." He elbows me in the rib. "I'm just saying, she's a cool chick. You guys make sense to me."

I'm not sure what puts my next thought in my head. It arrives entirely unprompted. But once it's in there, burrowing through the orchard of my thoughts like a worm, I can't help but wonder.

"You two never…" I trail off.

Fenn stares at me with a creased brow.

"I'm going to hit you again if you make me spell it out."

"Oh." He rolls his eyes and goes back to playing with his stick. "Yeah, no."

Thank fuck. I like the guy, but I'm not sure that would have stopped me from smothering him in his sleep for not mentioning something like that sooner.

Like I said, I'm still learning to cope with this new jealousy thing.

"Hey." Fenn smacks my arm as a beam of light slices through the shadows up ahead. "That's gotta be him."

Sure enough, a second later Mr. Swinney comes walking out of the trees with a flashlight and keys jingling between his fingers. We have just enough time to hurry toward the side of his car before he gets the keys in the door.

His jaw drops at the sight of us. "Shaw?" he barks. "Bishop? What on earth—"

"Evening, Roger," I interrupt, while Fenn grins broadly beside me. "Well, aren't you far from home at this late hour."

"What could you possibly be doing all the way out here?" Fenn adds, downright gleeful.

Our housefather's gaze slides from me to Fenn, then back to me. Our eyes lock, and I see the exact moment he admits defeat.

His shoulders sag, lips flattening.

"Yeah," I say, my own grin reaching the surface. "Here's an idea. Why don't you come take a seat on our little log over there and the three of us have a little chat?"

CHAPTER 35
LAWSON

It's Tuesday afternoon and the thin metal handles of the filing cabinet dig into my spine like tiny rungs of a ladder. His hands push open my blazer and trace the seams of my shirt until he hooks his fingers into my belt and tugs. He's hard against my leg and breathing feral with his tongue filling my mouth.

"You can take them off if you want," I tell Jack.

"Stop it," he grunts. "We can't do this."

"We already have." I lick my swollen lips and look down at the evidence of his erection pushing against his navy chinos. "Might as well make it worthwhile."

"You're my student."

"I'll call you Mr. Goodwyn if it helps."

He backs away a step. Roughly drags his hands through his hair. As if that's helping the situation. Honestly, I don't see the point of feigning moral uncertainty now. We're alone. Reasonably protected within the cozy confines of his office. Once I've seen the outline of his cock, well, there's no putting the toothpaste back in the tube, is there?

"This is wrong, Lawson."

"That's boring." And too late in the day to have to coddle a grown man through a hookup. "Right and wrong are someone else's idea that simple people cling to because they're too afraid to take the most out of life. I'm not afraid."

I reach for his zipper, but he grabs my hands and holds them behind my back while he again attacks my mouth, plunging his tongue down my throat.

"Do it," I mutter against his lips.

He pulls back slightly. Green eyes sizzling with lust. "Do what?"

"Ask me to get on my knees."

I feel him tremble against me. He doesn't speak, just watches me with that tortured gaze, his breathing labored.

"Ask me to get on my knees," I repeat, as my hand drifts between our bodies to capture his zipper again. "Ask me to make you come."

This time, he lets me drag his fly down.

He exhales. Slow, ragged. Then he whispers the words I'm waiting for.

"On your knees, Lawson." He groans softly. "Make me come."

Smiling, I sink down to the floor. Where's the fun in going to hell if you can't bring a few friends, right?

If only Silas could appreciate the virtue of occasional sin. I have no idea who he thinks he's impressing with his practically ancient ideas of purity. I've never seen someone so desperately in need of mushrooms. And an orgy.

"Two weeks from denial to the D. Might be a new record," I tell Silas when I get back to our dorm room later than usual.

He sits at his desk with his laptop, doing homework. "You didn't really fuck him."

"Not yet." Though I can't imagine it'll be long now before he's shoving his hand down my pants while gasping against my ear, telling me how wrong it is. Whatever gets him off. "Let's just say Gwen must be able to dislocate her jaw, because—"

"Yeah, okay. You saw a dick today. I get it."

"Aww, babe." I'm worn out and drop onto the sofa. "What's wrong? Amy still not shaving her pussy for nudes?"

"Fuck off, asshole." He flings a pencil that narrowly misses my head and leaves a tiny hole in the leather.

"Christ. All right. So touchy."

"You can't be so reckless."

"Can and will," I say cheerfully, at which point I remember the snack I'd been saving. I pull off the broken leg of the coffee table and dump out a baggy with two pretty little Vicodin inside.

"Dude, what the hell?" Silas jerks out of his chair. "Tomorrow's the first swim meet."

"Yeah, and I need some recovery." I stretch out on the couch and put a pillow under my head.

"What if they pull you for a drug test?"

"Don't sweat it. I've got the inside track. No surprises."

One of the first lessons I learned about competing: all the top athletes have moles inside the testing authority. At every level. In every sport. It's laughably easy to dodge a piss test with the proper connections and motivation.

"You should take one of these," I tell him, holding a pill out on the tip of my finger. "You need to relax."

"Whatever."

Huffing away with his little tantrum, Silas tears his white button-down shirt off and throws his tie on his desk. I spare a look over the arm of the couch to watch him strip in front of his closet, catching the full-frontal in the mirror while he throws on a pair of lounge pants and a T-shirt.

"What the hell do I know, right?" he says before shoving on a pair of headphones and kicking back on his bed with a book. "Knock yourself out."

I place the pills on my tongue and swallow. "Already there."

CHAPTER 36
RJ

THE POOL LOOKS SMALLER WITH SPECTATORS IN THE BLEACHERS. In the air is a hum of noise, the sounds of six other schools clustered around the pool while swimmers take warm-up laps. There's an anxious, politely hostile aura permeating the building. I catch glances aimed my way. Predators lurking in the shadows, sizing me up. Wondering who's the new guy and does he have teeth. Our first meet of the season has arrived, and it finally dawns on me what I've gotten myself into. This isn't a joke anymore. There are nine other guys determined to walk out of here victorious and they're relying on me to hold up my end of the bargain. Which frankly has me questioning their judgment. I wouldn't want to be on a team that would have me as a member.

Nevertheless, here I am.

"Has anyone ever jumped in and immediately forgotten how to swim?" Carter asks Silas, flashing a sarcastic wink at me when he climbs out of the water.

Silas is probably the best we have on our team, the one who makes it look easy. Carter is proof money can't buy functioning chromosomes.

"We all get jitters." Silas gives me an elbow nudge. Maybe

because he sees the oncoming headlights reflected in my eyes. "You'll be fine."

"Yeah, I know." He doesn't need to hear about the dream I had last night where I lost every last wit about me and started doggy paddling through the relay.

"Glad I swim before you." Behind us, Carter is doing these obnoxious breathing exercises. Huffing out air like he's in labor. "Not swimming through fifty meters of puke."

"That would be a first." Silas shakes out his arms and goes through his stretching routine to stay loose as we stand at the edge of the pool. "I've heard of a couple guys shitting the pool before, but never spraying the water with vomit."

A little eddy of queasiness churns in my stomach. "This is why I skipped lunch."

"Probably not a great start." He tosses me one of his gel packets. "You'll need the energy."

We carry our stuff to our team bench to wait for the first heat to begin. At this point it's just about managing nerves and keeping the muscles warm without otherwise expending too much energy. I don't know what to do with myself other than pace.

Lawson jumps into the pool when it's his turn to take a few warm-up laps. The guy is seriously impressive. The strength and precision of his strokes seem so at odds with his personality.

"Make it make sense," I say wryly. "Lawson consumes more pharmaceutical cocktails than a cancer patient. How does he still show up and swim?" I'm all for recreation, but Lawson takes it to another level. If someone handed him uranium in tablet form, he'd try it.

Silas looks up to watch Lawson make the turn at the other end of the pool. "It's his superpower. It'll never make sense. Don't hurt yourself trying to understand it."

"Half the time I wonder if he knows where he is."

"Half the time he doesn't." Silas gathers up his bag and warm-up jacket as Lawson starts another set of laps. "He's had so many black-outs, it should qualify for a world record."

Silas's nonchalance—or maybe it's indifference—toward Lawson's antics remains somewhat of a mystery to me. I honestly don't get his relationship with Lawson. He takes endless heat for the guy for what seems like little to no reward. Eventually he's got to get tired of eating shit while Lawson dances around his own private pleasure palace.

Which gets me wondering about something else.

"How'd you end up here?" I ask Silas.

"What, swimming?"

"At Sandover. You're pretty much the guy a teacher would ask to house-sit their Fabergé eggs and diabetic cat, so how'd you end up at a school for criminals, pervs, and fuckups?"

My research had revealed he'd been expelled from Ballard, but the report filed by his former headmaster was stingy with the details. Under *reason for expulsion*, all it said was "disorderly conduct." And from what I've seen, there's nothing disorderly about Silas.

Silas shrugs. He doesn't look at me while he goes about another stretching circuit. "It was stupid. We were celebrating after a swim meet sophomore year at Ballard, and I had too much to drink. Next thing I know, I'm slamming the headmaster's car into the goalpost on the football field."

"Seriously?"

"My parents managed to talk the headmaster out of pressing charges, and the police let me off with a warning for the drinking. But I got expelled. Obviously. Ended up here."

"Well. I guess you never can tell about people," I say lightly.

"Wasn't my finest hour."

Wasn't a good story either. As someone who concocted a similar backstory for myself, I don't buy it. Sure, even the All-American Boy can have a lapse in judgment every now and then. Some people can't hold their alcohol. It's all entirely plausible. Except that for no good reason, I know he's full of shit. Which is far more interesting than a little grand theft auto and underage drinking. What is the golden boy hiding?

"Hey, Shaw!" a familiar voice calls from across the pool. "Nice legs!"

Sloane just burst into the building with Fenn. She's wearing an oversized Sandover Varsity Swimming T-shirt with the collar cut out so it hangs off one shoulder. It skims just above a tiny pair of cut-off jean shorts that make me think about the last time I had my face between her thighs.

"Damn, you're shiny." Fenn slides his shades over his eyes as the two of them approach. "They lube you up with baby oil?"

Fuck. Here we go.

"Go ahead and get it out of your systems," I tell them. I knew this was coming. Hopefully they'll tire quickly, and we can all move on with our lives.

"Hey, sweetie." Sloane is now greeting Silas, leaning in to give him a side hug.

He hugs her back, and I don't miss the way his fingers linger on her arm before he releases her. This time, the hot sting of jealousy is accompanied by a pang of suspicion. Silas might have a girlfriend of his own, but it's getting harder and harder not to believe he's lusting over mine.

"Gotta finish these stretches," he says, nodding at us as he heads back to bench.

"I was right about the lotion strips, see?" Sloane drags her palms down my bare chest, and I flash her a warning glare because I cannot be seen sporting a hard-on in a fucking Speedo. "Feel that buttery smooth skin."

And at that I grab my warm-ups and pull them on over my suit.

"You're not worried your dad might catch you with your hands all over me?" I ask, lifting a brow.

Her answering smile is smug. "He and Casey went into town for dinner. So don't you worry, rookie, I can rub your hairless chest as much as I please."

"Save it for the janitor's closet," I warn her.

She gets a mischievous gleam in her eye that both troubles and excites me. "You want to have a quickie next to the jugs of chlorine? I think I read somewhere an endorphin release is great for anxiety."

"I keep telling you, don't threaten me with a good time."

Sloane grins and smacks a kiss on me, biting my lip.

I growl against her mouth. "Don't start unless you mean it."

"Is that a dare?" She arches an eyebrow at me. I know those eyes. The ones that watched us in the mirror when we fooled around. If she thinks I won't drag her into the locker room and throw her legs over my shoulders, she's out of her fucking mind.

"Get a room," Fenn groans and looks away, embarrassed to be seen with us now.

Much as I appreciate Sloane's subtle offer to suck me off before my relay, I should probably harness the sexual angst for energy. The lack of breakfast this morning is starting to feel like poor decision.

A sharp whistle pierces my ears. We all flinch at Coach's voice shouting at us to cop a squat on the bench. Which means the meet is about to get underway.

"Good luck," Sloane whispers against my ear before leaving me with another kiss.

I think Sloane might be more excited about this meet than I am. Or maybe she has more confidence in me. Either way, there's no hiding now. Time to nut up. My old guidance counselor's voice creeps into my head. She used to try getting me to do breathing exercises with her. Self-actualization and meditation bullshit. I can't say it ever took, but apparently some part of me absorbed the information because I fall into a kind of fugue state once we're called to the pool for the four-by-one hundred relay medley.

I understand the concept of practice now. I mean, obviously. But in particular, the automation. Training our muscles to work independently of our minds. When we're tired. When we're sore. When we're nervous or stressed or too busy thinking about a midterm in math. Automation takes over and carries our bodies through the task.

I'm in and out of the water from my first swim almost before I even know it's happened. My split is good, within the range Coach told me to aim for. I come in second on my laps, which is enough to give our anchor the time he needs to overtake first place on the return.

To my complete astonishment, we win the heat.

"You didn't drown." Silas shakes me. He's sporting a huge smile, face red from celebrating.

I don't even remember the race, but I'm glad it's over. I'm thankful I don't have to swim again today and get to watch the rest of our team's heats. A few of the events are close. Razor-thin. All of us anxiously watch the scoreboard for the official times then launch into celebrations when we see that tenth of a second difference. With each win, I feel myself becoming more invested in the team, addicted to this feeling of caring about something enough to feel my heart sucked up into my throat.

I never imagined I'd give a shit.

When it's all over, we've dominated. In the stands, Sloane is going berserk. You'd think we just swam the Olympics, the way she's jumping around and screaming. And I realize she's up there cheering for me. Annoying the piss out of everyone around her and making a complete ass of herself for *me*.

"Never thought I'd see the day." Lawson comes up beside me, following my gaze. "What'd you do to our girl Sloane, Remy?"

I let the nickname slide because I'm still riding the high of victory. "What do you mean?"

"You turned the ice princess into your own personal cheerleader." Lawson sounds impressed. Then his gray eyes glaze over a bit. "Fuck. Look at those tits bouncing up and down like that—"

I elbow him. "Knock it off. That's my girlfriend you're talking about."

"Oh, that's fucking adorable. Busting out the girlfriend card." He chuckles to himself. "Fenn was saying you text her every other second, but I didn't realize you'd gone and wifed yourself up." Lawson claps me on the shoulder. "Bad move, man. Once you give 'em the commitment, you lose all the power."

My gaze returns to Sloane. Bad move? Yeah right. More like the best move I ever made.

A strange sensation takes hold and I'm not sure what to do about it. Looking at this girl, I feel the stupid grin pulling at my cheeks. I'd be embarrassed at myself if I didn't enjoy it so much. Whatever she's done to me, it's in my bloodstream now, thick in the marrow. I'm not sure what to do about it or if I'd want to if I could.

"RJ," Coach shouts. "Let's go. You can sign autographs later."

He's a man of few words and doesn't spend much time stroking our egos with "attaboys" in the locker room. Our transitions were sloppy, and our times were seconds off last week's best. Basically, don't go getting too full of ourselves. Still, the guys are mostly riding the high of victory while we get dressed to leave.

"All right, assholes." Lawson jumps up on a bench. "Some of you owe me money. Empty those wallets."

Silas rolls his eyes. "You don't have to do it right in front of his face."

"He's a big boy." Lawson happily collects wads of cash from most of our teammates. "He can handle the truth."

I eye his winnings in amusement. "Taking bets on me?"

"One hundred to puke in the pool. Five hundred if it came out of both ends." He hops down and stuffs the cash in his bag without an ounce of remorse. "Thanks for keeping your shit together."

"Better put him in a diaper for his fight," taunts a snide voice.

Carter. Fucking Carter. He has a mouth like an overcaffeinated Pomeranian. He could suffocate a room the way he never shuts the hell up. And because he's obsessed with kissing Duke's ass, his favorite thing to talk about these days is me.

"Wouldn't be the first time Duke hit someone so hard they shit themselves," he says, slamming his locker shut. "I wouldn't get too comfortable if I were you." Smirking, he walks up and rips my name tape off my locker. "You'll be packing your bags and heading back to whatever trailer park you crawled out of."

"We're on the same team, man." Silas shoves him off. "Let it go."

Carter departs with a cocky grin and two middle fingers in the air.

"I can't take that guy seriously," I say dryly. He's so pathetic I'd almost pity him if he weren't also such an insufferable jackass.

"Carter's a pussycat," Lawson says.

"It's like he lives off sniffing Duke's farts."

"True. But he makes up for it by giving a serviceable blowjob." Lawson throws his bag over his shoulder and slides his sunglasses on the top of his head.

My mouth falls open. "What, seriously?" I didn't see that coming.

"Sure. After almost every practice. On his knees in the broken handicap bathroom stall. But you didn't hear that from me."

Well, isn't Carter just full of surprises.

"Don't sweat the fight," he tells me. "You've got it in the bag."

I don't believe Lawson is being entirely sincere, but I appreciate the gesture. Frankly, I'm considering exit strategies. Because as much as I hate to admit it, this time I might have gotten in over my head.

CHAPTER 37
FENN

RUNNING INTO SLOANE AT THE SWIM MEET WAS AN ACCIDENT. She's avoided my texts all week. I tried a few times to get five minutes with her, but she had track practice and homework and kept brushing me off. So finding her outside presented the uncomfortable option of pretending we don't know each other or reluctantly agreeing to sit together.

"Sorry I didn't get back to you," she says, still watching the locker room door for RJ to emerge while we wait on the bleachers. "I really wasn't ignoring you. Just busy."

"Yeah, I figured."

Except with this RJ thing and her not-at-all-subtle warning to respect a five-hundred-foot perimeter around her sister, I've been getting the impression Sloane is not keen on me these days.

"So..." She taps out a rhythm with her feet. "Was there something you needed, or...?"

"A couple things, actually. I have a favor to ask."

"Let me guess—it has to do with my sister."

I nod, unhappiness rising inside me. "I was hoping maybe you could talk with your dad. Put in a good word for me."

Her gaze narrows on me. Sloane has mastered the ability to pin a guy with her eyes and put the fear of death deep in his soul. "And why would I do that?"

"Because you care about Casey and like seeing her smile?" I offer a wry shrug. "I know you're not my biggest fan, but you can't deny I'm good for her. I make her laugh. And she's not as depressed when I'm around. You know that, Sloane."

Reluctance creases her features before her head jerks in a nod. "Yeah. I know."

"I'm tired of only getting to see her for like an hour on the weekend. So I figured, it's either I keep convincing her to sneak out to meet me, or you help us out with your father."

She stares at me again. "What do you want with Case? Honestly."

Good fucking question. If I understood that, I wouldn't be tormenting myself by dancing around the edges like a virgin at prom.

"I don't know," I say. "Right now, we're friends. And maybe if you remind the headmaster of that, he'll let me spend more time with her."

Her hard gaze cuts through me like a knife. "Still waiting for a good reason why I should help you sleaze on Casey."

Okay. That one hurt a little. I'll admit my history with chicks is less than honorable, but those girls didn't mean anything to me. Townies. Random self-absorbed prep school chicks trying to piss off Daddy. They're not Casey. She's kind and sincere and probably the sweetest person you'd ever meet in real life. So how do I tell Sloane that without digging myself into a hole?

I swallow. "Casey's not a one-night stand. I know that. And I'm probably the only person who knows as well as you do what she's been through. Trust me. I'm not here to hurt her."

I've spent the last few months doing everything I can to look out for Casey. To be someone she can rely on. The last thing on my mind is turning all that upside down to get in her bed and sneak out before she wakes up. If that was the goal, I'd have been in and out by now. There are easier ways to get laid.

"Fine." Sloane spots RJ coming out of the locker room and stands up. "I'll talk you up to our dad. But don't think that's in any way meant as an endorsement. I still don't think you're good enough for her."

Won't get any argument from me.

"Thank you," I say, gratitude rippling in my voice.

"What's the other thing?" she asks, moving toward the aisle.

"Oh. Right." I trail after her, but she's already climbing down the rows of bleachers.

"Well?" she asks, glancing over her shoulder.

RJ nears the bottom of the steps, his swim duffel slung over one shoulder. He grins at Sloane, who's still waiting for me to finish.

"It's fine," I tell her. "It can wait. Go congratulate my stepbro."

As Sloane dashes into RJ's waiting arms, I smother a sigh and fish my phone out of my pocket. When I find a waiting text from Casey, a smile tugs at my lips.

Casey: Did you talk to my sister?

I type a response as I head toward the exit.

Me: Yup.
Casey: And??
Me: She said she'll work on your dad.

Casey sends the preaching hands emoji, followed by the blushing emoji. My smile falters. Shit. The blushing emoji.

You're playing with fire, an internal voice warns.

Trust me, I'm well aware of that.

But this chick does something to me. I make Casey smile, yeah. But she makes me smile right back.

So if I'm playing with fire, fine. Whatever. Let me burn.

CHAPTER 38
RJ

"If you can't be stronger, be meaner." Fenn keeps his gloved hands raised and close to his face as he circles me on the mat. "If you can't be faster, be smarter."

"I don't think this wax-on bullshit is helping."

Lucas snorts, watching us from a weight bench.

"You better pray it does. I'm your last hope."

"How is this training if I'm not going to hit you the way I'll have to hit him?"

Fenn smacks my elbow. "You're dropping your guard."

"Fuck off with—"

I eat a right hook that knocks the words out of my mouth along with the piece of gum I'd had lodged in my cheek.

"Like I said. Keep your hands up." Fenn's really feeling himself today, having too much fun working me over.

My point remains the same, however. Fenn isn't going to come at me with bloodlust and vengeance the way Duke intends to meet me. I can't train with a bunny rabbit to fight a bear. Besides, it's barely been two weeks, and for all of Fenn's sincere effort, I don't believe I'm any closer to standing a chance in this fight. I've taken a punch from Duke. It tears years from your life.

Which means plan A is a nonstarter. That much was always apparent. In the past, I would've already pivoted to plan B and been well on my way to regaining the upper hand. But I've officially reached a dead end. Either he's the cleanest high school crime boss that's ever terrorized these halls, or Duke is far more sophisticated at covering his tracks than I gave him credit for.

I've spent weeks combing his digital footprint for a compromising morsel I could exploit to give myself an exit strategy. And I've got nothing. Fucking nada.

One question that keeps me up at night remains frustratingly out of reach: Where is he stashing the money he's skimming off the top of all the action on campus? Every racket he takes a cut on. The bets that run through the fights. It's all going somewhere. Like most of these assholes, Duke has a trust that he takes an allowance from, but from what I saw when I hacked his online banking, it doesn't look like he's stuffing his ill-gotten proceeds there. It would attract too much attention from family, lawyers, and the IRS. So where's he hiding his piggy bank?

After another hour of mostly procedural sparring, Fenn and I call it a day. He's got a soccer match against Ballard Academy tonight, and I still need to shower and change.

"Hey, can I catch a ride to the game?" Lucas follows us out of the gym. He's become a near-constant shadow these days, but I don't mind the company. He's chill and keeps his eyes on his own paper. That's good enough for me.

"Sure. But be ready to go in an hour," I answer. "We're swinging by Sloane's place first."

He looks startled. "Does the headmaster know that?"

"Nope, and I can't be sure he'll even let me through the door, so this should be fun."

Lucas snickers. "Awesome."

If it were up to me, Sloane would meet me in the parking lot and her dad would never be the wiser. But she wants, and I quote, "to test the waters." So I'm pretending I'm just the chauffeur, and I guess she's hoping if he doesn't rip my head off at the mere sight of me, it'll serve as a promising omen that one day he might actually let us date.

I don't share in her optimism.

In the dorm I manage to bargain an essay for car keys from a guy on our floor, because I feel weird asking Silas to borrow his ride. We might be teammates, but the two of us just can't seem to click and I've given up on trying.

Lucas and I pull up to the headmaster's cottage on the outskirts of campus with eight whole minutes to spare. I am absolutely nailing this prompt and punctual shit.

Sloane is quick to answer the door, and my heart speeds up when I see her. I am such a goner for this chick. It's like I can't get enough of her. Since we made it official, we've met at our spot every day after school. I text her every morning after I open my eyes, every night before I close them, and pretty much the entire time in between, and yet it's still not enough.

Tonight, she's looking goddamn delicious in a red crop top and a pair of cut-offs. I can barely pry my gaze away from her legs even as I glimpse Headmaster Tresscott in the background set down a coffee mug to intervene.

"If you jump in the car now, we can ditch the kid and skip the game," I tell her.

"Best behavior," she scolds me with a hushed voice, as her dad approaches with a firm scowl in place.

"Where are you off to?" he demands of her, while keeping one mean eye fully trained on me.

"Sandover's playing Ballard," she says with an innocent daddy's girl voice I'd find hilarious if it wasn't so scary how well she pulls it off. "I told you."

"You said you were going with friends." He drills his attention squarely down on me. "I didn't realize you and Mr. Shaw were acquainted."

I give him a placid smile. "I'm just the driver, sir. Fenn asked if I could do him a favor."

Tresscott hums a disapproving sound, arms crossed. As admittedly lenient as the headmaster's been to this point, considering our last meeting, he's made his impressions known. In his eyes, I'm the hacker ne'er-do-well who's been expelled from every school he's ever attended.

If I were him, I wouldn't welcome my presence on Sloane's doorstep either.

"Hey, Dr. Tresscott." Cheerful as ever, Lucas nudges his way to the threshold and offers a jovial wave. "I'm the court-appointed chaperone this evening. There'll be no mischief, shenanigans, or tomfoolery on my watch, sir."

The headmaster's frown dissipates instantly. Lucas has that effect on people. And turns out, he's a clutch wingman.

"Mr. Ciprian. Good to see you. I hear you're working on an exciting robotics project for Ms. Redman's class. I look forward to your presentation."

"Nearly there, sir. Working out the bugs."

As they chat, the headmaster allows us to venture deeper inside. But only as far as the foyer, where a short strawberry-blonde with freckles pokes her head around the corner.

"My sister," Sloane says, throwing her arm around Casey as she walks over. "Casey."

I introduce myself with a nod. "RJ."

She smiles impishly. "I know."

I shoot a glance at Sloane. "So it's like that. I see."

"Being early was a good move," Casey tells me. "Major bonus points. Keep it up."

I tip my chin at her, chuckling. "If you've got any other insider tips for me, hit me up."

Her amused grin grows wider. "I might."

Sloane shushes her, but their father is still well distracted by Lucas's infallible charisma. Like Fenn said, the kid belongs to the exclusive club of guys not at risk of being shot on sight for crossing the property line.

Not that the headmaster isn't justified in his precautions.

It all starts to make sense. Fenn's inscrutable obsession with Casey. She's gorgeous, of course. The genes in this family are fucking insane. But she also exudes this sincere gentleness and charm. I'd know better than to ruin her life if I'd passed her on the street, but Fenn is apparently caught in the throes of an identity crisis where he imagines himself someone who could lie amongst the tulips and still leave the flower beds untrampled. I doubt it, but who I am to say?

And after only a few minutes with the Tresscott sisters, I also better understand the compulsion Sloane feels to protect Casey. I see how Casey smiles past the obvious implication that she's not coming with us tonight because her father won't let her anywhere near the Ballard campus again and Casey couldn't tolerate it if she did. Because beneath that sweet smile are the shy, darting, fragile eyes of someone still guarding their scars.

"Mr. Shaw? A word, please." The headmaster summons me outside while Sloane and Lucas hop in the car. On the porch, his shrewd gaze gives me a long once-over. "I can't say I'm overjoyed to have you arrive on my doorstep like this."

"It wasn't meant to be a surprise, sir."

"Sloane tends to be less than forthcoming about her social activities," he says with a glance toward the car. "So allow me to disabuse you now of any notions you have about dating my daughter."

"Sir—"

"So long as I'm inclined to tolerate such an arrangement, she may carry on a casual and closely monitored friendship. However. If I suspect you have other designs…"

I play dumb. "Designs, sir?"

He turns his back to the car and closes the distance between us. The headmaster doesn't meet my eyes, instead looking toward the tree line with his chin raised. In case I think myself on his level.

"If you make a move on my daughter, I will have you bounced from this school and out on your ass. Am I clear?"

"Crystal."

"Drive safely, Mr. Shaw." He turns on his heel and enters the house.

Well, fuck.

If I thought Duke was bluffing or there was room for negotiation before, I'm now sufficiently convinced otherwise. If I lose this fight and he makes good on this threat to out Sloane and me to her dad, I'm cooked.

I need to find that plan B. And quick.

CHAPTER 39
SLOANE

THE GOTHIC SPIRES OF BALLARD ACADEMY RISE OUT OF THE TREE
canopy as RJ drives through the iron gates on the west entrance near
the sports complex. I used to love this campus. The stone architecture and shady courtyards. Now it roils a pit in my stomach that lifts
acid to the back of my throat.

Last time these halls saw my face, I was loading boxes in the
back of my car from cleaning out our lockers. Casey by then had
stopped leaving her room.

It didn't occur to me until now what a visceral response I would
have to coming back. Or what this excursion might do to Casey's
recovery.

"I thought Sandover was fancy," RJ says. He looks like the new
parents on orientation weekend, in awe of the manicured lawns and
gothic architecture. "It's a shithole compared to this place."

"Ballard is about eighty years younger," Lucas says from the back
seat, where he's been on his phone most of the ride. "Besides, rich
families aren't embarrassed to have buildings named after them when
they aren't funding a reform school for their delinquent offspring."

"Good point." RJ pulls into the parking lot. It's full for the first
rivalry match of the season.

As he kills the engine, I stay rooted in the passenger seat. The what-the-hell-am-I-doing-here-edness of it all slams into me like running headlong into a sliding glass door, and I'm not sure I can get out of the car.

Staring out the window at the students filing their way between the cars toward the entrance, I remember how it felt those last few weeks after Casey's accident. Feeling like we didn't have a friend left in the world.

"Hey, you okay?"

I must look dreadful, judging by the concern creasing RJ's forehead.

I bite my lower lip. "I just realized how Casey might react to me being back at Ballard."

"What do you mean?"

"She still has nightmares. It got bad again after school started, but she's finally started to sleep the last week or so." I gnaw harder on my lip. "What if I just lit a stick of dynamite and chucked it through her window?"

"We don't have to go." Instantly, RJ puts the key back in the ignition.

"You should try giving Casey a little more credit," Lucas says behind me. "She's stronger than you think."

I'm not sure I appreciate the insinuation that I don't know my own sister. He isn't there at three in the morning when she comes creeping into my room. He didn't see the thin, pale ghost of her floating around the house most of the summer. I've got a mind to tell him to piss off.

On the other hand, maybe there's some science to the idea that babying Casey too much can hamper her recovery. One could argue I can be a little overprotective these days.

Besides, Casey and Lucas have spent a fair amount of time together since we got back. It's possible she confides some things in him that she's been reluctant to share with me. For all I know, she's been complaining that her big sister has created a suffocating cocoon around her.

Fine.

"Say the word." RJ reads my face for some clue as to my intentions. It's sweet the way he's concerned.

"We're good. I'm probably being paranoid." A feeling that is unlikely to dissipate anytime soon. I don't think it'll ever go away, the foreboding that slithers up from my subconscious when I think about Ballard and what it represents now.

That dread proves justified, however, when we hardly make it out of the parking lot before getting T-boned by the bad tidings of mortal enemy number one.

I spot Mila sitting on the trunk of a convertible at the drop-off loop in front of the ticket windows. She's decked out in Ballard colors and a ribbon headband. Must be dating a soccer player now. Or doing some student council bullshit. She used to hate that school spirit pep rally crap, so I'm leaning toward the she's-banging-a-striker option.

I try to nudge us toward the edges of her periphery, hoping to slip past while she's otherwise distracted by the impromptu tailgate party. She's surrounded by everyone I used to call my friend before they ripped the masks off to flick their forked tongues.

"You have to buy tickets to a school soccer match?" RJ says, eyeing the lines in front of the ticket booth. "Weak."

"Be glad they didn't charge for parking," I answer. Carefully, I steer our course to give Mila a wide berth, using human shields to evade detection.

"Oh, shit." Then Lucas blows our cover. He nudges RJ's arm and nods over his shoulder. "Incoming."

We both turn to realize not only has Mila noted our arrival, but she's also got company.

Fuck my life.

"Who?" RJ asks, unsure what's got our hackles up.

I'd know that stench of old money and arrogance anywhere. "Oliver Drummer."

RJ stares at us for a more substantial answer. "Am I supposed to know that name?"

"He's the Duke of Ballard," Lucas tells him. "Ordained by God, as far as he's concerned."

"What is it with rich-kid schools and archaic power structures?" The culture shock of the prep school realm still hasn't worn off on RJ. "I swear I'm this close to unionizing you assholes."

We're trapped. It's a slow-motion march to an inevitable collision, until Mila is standing in front of me.

She has the nerve to beam at me. "Oh my God, Sloane. It's been forever."

I flick up an eyebrow. "Not long enough."

To RJ, she laughs like she's in on the joke. "Don't listen to her. She loves me."

It's one of her infuriating little talents. Being totally immune to the bitchiness of others. Like her own bitchiness is so bright that the light of other bitches can't penetrate her corneas.

"If you say so," he responds lightly. RJ's still gauging the interaction, looking to me for cues.

It might have been helpful to conduct a study session for him beforehand. Flash cards or something. These are the people you don't have to be polite to.

"He's cute, Sloane," Mila says, her eyes shining. "Where'd you find him, and can I borrow?"

Over my dead body. Mila's not getting her claws anywhere near my new boyfriend. She's pretty, like men-throw-themselves-over-a-puddle-for-her kind of pretty. And she knows how to weaponize it. After she betrayed me, I had dreams about shaving her head. Taking a baseball bat to her Benz. I settled on ghosting her in the hopes that one day I might casually flip through obituaries in the metaverse and know she died pitiful and alone.

"Not really a freelance gig," RJ quips, while not so discreetly lacing his fingers through mine.

Mila notices but is undeterred. "You want to get airbrushed?" She flashes RJ the Ballard Bengal mascot on her shoulder blade. "We're selling them for charity."

"Nah, I'm good," he says.

Oliver catches me watching his approach and a cold sneer plucks the creases of his dark eyes. If Mila spotted me first, he's no doubt come along to see what all the fuss is about. When his calculating gaze lands on RJ, I know this won't go well.

"Holy shit, Sloane. Check out the big brass balls on you."

I keep my tone cool. "Not sure showing up to a soccer game counts as daring."

Oliver's tall and muscular, with arms bigger than my thighs. He's looked twenty-five since he was thirteen. Freshman year he walked on to the varsity football team and the superiority complex has never worn off.

"Didn't you tell us all to die in a fire on your way out last year?" he reminds me. "Not back to finish the job, I hope."

"Don't tempt me."

He cracks a wry smile that's somewhat impressed, maybe. Only because he lives for the drama.

"I'm Mila, by the way." My former bestie all but writes RJ's name on her tits in lipstick. "You definitely don't go here. I'd notice a six-two king walking down the hall."

I'd tell her to eat a bag of dicks, but she's probably already full.

"Six-three. And I'm just casing the joint." RJ shrugs, but I see his lips twitching with humor. Her rampant flirting isn't going unnoticed.

"I know who this is," Oliver tells her. "He goes to Sandover. Fenn's new stepbrother." He directs his gaze at RJ. "Rumor is the honeymoon's over and you're on the outs with Duke."

"He doesn't appreciate my sense of humor." One of the things I like best about RJ is that he doesn't rise to asshole bait.

Oliver tips his head. "The way I hear it, you've got a title fight coming up. Watch out for that wicked left hook."

"Smart money's on RJ." Lucas suddenly feels compelled to throw himself in the middle of it, and I only wish I could have grabbed him by the shirt collar before he caught Oliver's attention. "Duke will be lucky if he wakes up before Christmas."

"Watch your wallet around this one," Oliver says to RJ with a sarcastic laugh. "How's Gabe liking San Quentin Prep, Lucas? You smuggling him Ziplocs of oxy up your ass?"

Proving he's tougher than he looks, Lucas rolls his eyes. "Yeah, you're so cool, Oliver. I don't remember you talking so much shit to my brother's face."

I give Oliver a shove, which he takes with a pleased smirk. I don't know Lucas well, but I don't like seeing him take shit because his brother screwed up. It's the lowest form of bullying.

"You're such a prick," I tell Oliver. "Don't you have tacks to throw on the handicap parking spaces or something?"

"Ouch, Sloane. Harsh. We're just having a laugh. Right, Ciprian?"

"Whatever." Unfazed, Lucas heads off to find his friends.

"I heard your dad sent you to Catholic school," Mila says to me. The inclination to mention Casey's name is sparkling in her treacherous eyes. RJ must feel my rising rage because he squeezes my hand to hold it tight at his side. "Looks like it hasn't put a damper on your dating life."

"Yep. I'm the whore of Babylon." I put on an indifferent voice. "And this whore's got to powder her nose."

"Can't wait to see if there are butlers in the bathrooms." RJ throws an arm over my shoulder to steer us out of the gravity well of Mila and Oliver's malicious boredom.

A moment later, we grab our tickets and make our way inside the small brick stadium.

"Well, that settles it," RJ leans in to say at my ear. "I'm never asking you for a handjob."

I give him a questioning look. In response, he shows me the fingernail marks and lingering impression of my hand on his as the blood rushes back in.

"That's some grip," he says in amusement.

"Mila's not good people." Which is a profound understatement and far less than she deserves. "And just so you don't get any ideas— she only wants to suck your dick to piss me off."

"I mean, I'm not really political." He immediately throws his hands up in apology to my withering glare. "Easy, tiger. Kidding."

Jealousy is a new one for me. The instant bloodred territorial instinct that arises at the thought of RJ hooking up with Mila catches me off guard. It's impossible to ignore what it means. I think I've known it for a while, but there's no convincing myself otherwise anymore.

I've got it bad for this one.

For no good reason, RJ has wandered into my life and upended everything I thought I knew about myself. My favorite color is black. My favorite food is chicken piccata. And I'm not a jealous girl. Except now I am, apparently. And that's both exciting and a little annoying. Because now he has power. The power to manipulate my heart and tie it in knots while I stand there helpless and entranced.

Luckily, he's not aware of this yet. So I better not blow my cover.

"What's the story there?" he asks. We make our way through the concourse toward the concession stands. I hate this place with a molten passion, but they have excellent soft pretzels. "You two used to be friends?"

It's a trick question. I pause for a beat, wondering how I can distill the experience of teenage girl warfare into a digestible soundbite.

"The short version is, after Casey's ordeal, we realized who our true friends were."

"What happened?" he presses.

"Mila decided it was a better story to start a rumor that Casey made the whole thing up. Popped some pills and plunged our car into the lake. That the pathetic sophomore wanted attention and faked this whole elaborate drama for sympathy clout. Which is total bullshit. But it took hold, and they tortured her. Called her crazy, mental, psychotic. Taunted her about it. Someone put a straitjacket in her locker—my bet was on Mila's right-hand cheerleader Connie."

He whistles under his breath. "Chicks are brutal."

He has no idea.

Guys don't understand the inherent rivalry at play in female high school relationships. Make friends with people you like, yes. But your best friend, she's always the first throat you'd slit when the coup starts. I suppose it was my fault for not getting Mila before she got me.

"They were relentless until Casey finally broke and couldn't go back to school."

"And that's where you left it? Never tried to reconcile?"

Ha. Over my lifeless, rotting corpse. "I was born with a forgiveness deficiency," I inform him. "Mila showed her true colors and can go right ahead and fuck off forever."

"Damn, woman. Guess I must have caught you on a good day for second chances."

"All you did was piss me off. But she came for my little sister. Nobody fucks with my family and gets a pass."

RJ watches me with smoldering eyes. "I'm so turned on right now."

A smile tickles my lips. I swear, this guy always says the right things when I need it most.

We get our snacks, and RJ texts Lucas to let him know where we're going to sit. I remain steadfastly un-fucking-daunted by the moving lips and darting glances in my direction, the conversations that take place in huddled clumps as we traverse the concourse. It's like I never left. They can all choke on it.

I assure myself the worst is over. I survived a brush with Mila and can therefore pretend to understand soccer in peace. Until we head toward the tunnel to the bleachers, where I come up short to a tap on my shoulder.

"Look at you two." Clad in his Sandover soccer uniform, Duke stands with his chin raised, exuding snide indignation. His cloudy gaze is fixed on mine and RJ's joined hands. "Isn't this a little public?"

"You following me now?" I ask my ex.

He scoffs at the question. "I'm captain of the fucking team." He sweeps his hard gaze between RJ and me. "Not afraid of word getting around?"

I must've been testing makeup on bunnies in a past life. Because I'm being punished. "Have you ever known me to be afraid of anything?" I retort. Then I push forward. "Now, if you'll excuse us, we—"

Duke intercepts my path. "We need to talk. Alone."

"No."

His mouth tightens. "Five minutes of your time, Sloane. That's all I need. It's important."

"Dude, she's told you nicely, and now I'm gonna be a dick about it." RJ wraps his arm around my waist to bring me closer. "Take the hint and fuck off."

Duke bristles. "Yeah, I'll see you real fucking soon, man. Don't you worry."

"Do I look worried?"

The two of them look ready to throw down. I'll admit, my reptile brain does get a little jolt from seeing the protective side of RJ. Ready to defend my honor. It's hot, even if it is regressive. But hey, we can't help how society has programmed us for cowboys and roughnecks.

Duke turns to me again. "He's not doing you any favors, babe. What do you think'll happen if someone let Daddy know what you're getting up to?"

"Someone, huh?" I say sarcastically.

He grins, utterly smug. "Never know who might decide to snitch, right?"

"Yeah?" Screw it. I might be engraving my own tombstone, but I'm not living under Duke's ransom forever. "Take a picture, then."

I reach up and grab RJ by the back of the head, yanking him toward me to smash our lips together. It's hot and a little raunchy when he palms my ass. And I'm into it. Shoving my tongue in his mouth and not bothering to control the little moan of arousal that tickles my throat. I know we're both doing it for spite, but I still can't help the overwhelming surge of lust that propels me to keep kissing him longer than necessary to get the point across. Hell, I'd be naked and climbing him already if some part of my rational mind didn't know we were standing in the middle of a stadium crawling with my enemies.

Like I said, I've got it bad.

The game is scoreless at halftime after some plays I didn't entirely follow. A Ballard player was sent off for an ugly tackle that had Fenn sprint thirty yards to shove the guy on his ass. That got Fenn a talking-to as well, but he managed to stay on the field. The foul led to a penalty kick, which the Ballard keeper saved to cheers from one end of the stands and shouts from the Sandover supporter section claiming some infraction I couldn't explain.

I fucking hate soccer.

While the bleachers empty to make a mad dash for the restrooms, RJ and Lucas start chatting about some computer nonsense I don't understand. So I pull out my phone, finding a text from my sister.

Casey: How's it going? Is it awful being back there?
Me: Not too bad. I talked to Mila and Oliver, but nobody else has had the balls to approach me.
Casey: Don't do anything crazy, k?
Me: Define crazy.
Casey: If people are saying anything about me, just ignore them. No need to start trouble.
Me: No promises.

I hesitate, then send another text.

Me: Are you pissed that I'm here?
Casey: What?? Of course not.
Casey: Seriously. It's fine. Just because my accident took place there doesn't mean the school itself is cursed.
Casey: Just have fun with RJ, k?

Easier said than done, because now I'm preoccupied with thoughts of the accident. I sweep my gaze over the stadium, the soccer field, the shadowy outlines of buildings on the Ballard campus. I don't have a line of sight to it, but I suddenly see the boathouse, the image of the abandoned shack surfacing in my mind. The roof covered in years of fallen leaves and pine needles. The black, gaping mouth of its open face that stood over the lake. I flinch at the chills that run down my arms.

RJ glances over. "You okay?"

"Fine," I assure him. But my knees feel a tad wobbly as I rise to my feet. "You mind if I desert you for a little while?"

Worry flashes in his eyes. "Where are you going?"

I release a troubled sigh. "There's something I want to do. And I need to do it alone."

RJ firmly grips my waist when I try to leave. "I don't like it. Let me come with you."

"No." I gently remove his hand. "I'll be fine. Just taking a little walk. I'll have my phone in my hand the entire time, and if anything happens, I'll call you. But nothing will happen, okay?"

Even if it did, I probably wouldn't call him. This is something I have to do alone. Because on the off chance that I fall apart, I refuse to let anyone, even RJ, see me at my most vulnerable.

"Don't be gone too long," he finally says, his frustrated expression telling me he doesn't like capitulating.

And that's how, a few minutes later, I find myself taking a walk down memory lane.

It's a short hike to the lake. There used to be a sidewalk, but weeds have long since overtaken it, and enormous tree roots turned the path into a mountain range of cracked and broken slabs. Ballard Academy hasn't had a crew team in two decades. Not since rumors of a ruthless coach, team hazing, doping, and a freshman found hanging from the rafters got the school banned by the division. Now the boathouse is just a place kids go to drink, smoke, or hook up.

Or to almost die.

That terrifying night still looms huge and daunting in my mind. Stalking me. But I'm hoping there might be something therapeutic in facing it again, reclaiming my sanity from the monster under my bed.

I find my way using the flashlight of my phone. As I walk, I stare at the ground to watch for potholes and to avoid remembering the last time I walked this trail.

Before I know it, I'm standing at the spot where my car once sat after the tow truck had dragged it onshore. Illuminated by the yellow rotating lights of a tow truck, draining water, covered in mud. But that's not the *first* sight I encountered the night I emerged from the trail and reached the lake. No, that was much, much scarier.

The memories suddenly come rushing back. It's like being hit by a tidal wave, images of horror crashing over me, making it hard to breathe.

The first thing I saw was my car half-submerged in the lake. The trunk sticking out of the water with the taillight turning the trees red. Then I glimpsed a heap on the ground at the edge of the water. It was Casey. Soaking wet and shivering.

"Fuck," I choke out, my voice sounding tiny and weak in the pitch-black air.

I remember how I lunged at her. Someone handed me their tuxedo jacket. Duke, I think. I wrapped it tightly around her body, pushed away the fallen strands of hair stuck over her eyes. She was barely conscious and hardly able to speak.

My heart stalls in my throat. My pulse quickens remembering how pale her skin was. The mascara running down her cheeks.

A feeling like dizziness throws me off balance. The strange sensation, I realize, is the adrenaline my heart sends flooding into my blood. Then a low buzzing forms inside my skull while my vision narrows, and I can't catch my breath.

This was a bad idea. I thought I could handle it alone. I believed I was strong enough, but I'm a fucking fraud. I'm not strong at all. And I can't fucking breathe as my hand trembles to pull up RJ's name on my phone. I'm panting hard as I call him.

He picks up instantly. "All good?"

"No," I whisper. "I…" My breath catches, making me wheeze. "Please come. I need you."

"Drop me a pin," he orders. "I'll be right there."

CHAPTER 40
SLOANE

RJ FINDS ME IN THE SAME SPOT I'D FOUND CASEY ON PROM NIGHT. Without a word, he charges toward me and sinks to his knees, completely unbothered by the mud that oozes onto his jeans. I collapse against him, feeling like a child as I cling to his chest, crying uncontrollably.

"Sloane," he says urgently. "Hey. Sloane. It's all right. You're all right."

"She was dead," I hear myself stutter through my shaking fit. "I couldn't even go to her because I was sure she was dead and I didn't want to see it."

"Hey, hey." RJ pulls me into his arms and cradles my head to his chest. "It's okay. You're both okay."

"She nearly drowned. Just like our mother."

"I know," he whispers against my hair.

"I didn't even know she was alive until Duke hoisted her into his arms and shouted for an ambulance. And then later, I sat beside her hospital bed for hours, watching her come in and out of consciousness and then double over in hysterical tears when she remembered it was real." My lungs burn with the struggle of breathing. "Dad arrived in a fit. Delirious with panic. He cornered me outside her room to hiss about how could I have let this happen. As if I wasn't already as traumatized."

Tears stream down my cheeks at the painful memory. The moment when we should have been pulling together as a family, we were coming apart at the seams.

RJ's T-shirt becomes damp against my face, my fingers tightening around fistfuls of fabric. I'm afraid I might sink into the dirt if he doesn't keep me upright. I can't feel my legs.

"I'm sorry," I say, sniffling.

"No. I'm so sorry, Sloane. I shouldn't have let you come here alone. I should've come with you."

I swipe at my wet, swollen eyes. "I didn't think it would be this bad."

"It's fine." RJ rubs small, slow circles down my back. "You're fine. I promise."

"I'm not, though. People always think I've got my shit together. That I'm so impenetrable. Nothing gets to me." My bottom lip trembles, my eyes stinging again. That's always been my defense mechanism. Roar and beat my chest to scare away the predators. Can't let them see me scared. "I think I started to believe my own bullshit."

"Listen to me." He pulls away just enough to swipe his thumb across my cheek and pull the tears away. "This is real shit. You don't have to be okay. You shouldn't be. I know we just met, but from what I've seen, you're tough as hell, Sloane. Never forget that."

A half sob, half choked laugh bursts out of me. "No. I do have to be okay. I have to, RJ. I can't let them see I'm soft inside."

"We're all soft inside," he says roughly, continuing to wipe my tears away. "But I get it. If you let people see your vulnerabilities, that gives them power. Am I close?"

I nod meekly.

"And you don't want that."

"I don't want that," I echo in a weak whisper.

"So you play games."

He does get it. I gulp through the painful lump in my throat. "You do it too."

"All the time. But you know what?" He reaches for my hand and brings it up to his chest, pressing my palm on his left pec, right above his heart. "If seeing you like this right now gives me power, it's nothing compared to the power you have over me. Feel the way my heart beats faster when you touch me? I'm a fucking goner for you."

I smile through my tears. "All this sappiness is a major turn-off, you know."

"Bullshit. You love it."

RJ takes on a contemplative expression. I've come to recognize the crease between his eyebrows and the hundred-yard stare when he's in deep thought.

"What is it?" I ask.

"I was just thinking about something Silas said to me. Right when I first started chasing after you. He said a part of you will always be out of reach. That nobody will ever be able to completely pin you down." My hand is still on his chest, and RJ covers my knuckles with his warm palm. "I think he's wrong. I think I've pinned you down."

With a shaky laugh, I press my cheek against his shoulder. He's not wrong. I *was* out of reach for every guy who came before him. I used to play games because I needed the power that comes with the upper hand.

But, weirdly enough, there's power in letting go and being vulnerable. I understand that now, as I feel his heart racing beneath my palm, as I sink into the strength of his arms.

Whatever doubts or reservations I might have harbored over forgiving RJ for his deceit evaporate as he hugs me tight. Because he doesn't have to be here. There are easier ways to pad his spank bank. He could have hightailed it out of my life a dozen times tonight for all the drama I've thrown in his lap. It feels nice, actually, that the thing that keeps him here is me.

"You good to stand up?" he asks, taking my hand.

I nod, and he helps me to my feet. My legs are sturdy again. My hand is secured tightly in RJ's.

And now that the initial shock of this place has worn off, I dry my face with my sleeve and take a moment to absorb the scene in a new light.

"We should go," RJ says.

I shake my head. "No. I'm good now." *Because you're here with me*, I almost say, but just because I sobbed in his arms like a toddler a second ago doesn't mean I've suddenly transformed into a silly romantic. "It might be helpful if we talked this through. Tried to make more sense of what happened that night."

I move closer to the water's edge, then turn to examine the woods to our left. "The cops did a half-assed sweep of the place after the ambulance left, but they didn't find anything significant. Beer cans and spent joints. More used condoms than I'm sure they cared to find. The usual stuff. But nothing from that night."

RJ clicks on his phone flashlight and uses it to scan the area. "The car didn't come in the same way we did."

"No. There's a road." I point my own light at two wooden posts around the far side of the boathouse that mark where there used to be a gate. The dirt road is now obscured by shrubs, but still passable if you know where you're going. "Whoever was driving pulled the car around this side then went into the water."

"The police report I saw was pretty scarce."

"This whole fucking case is scarce. Casey's drug test at the hospital came back positive, but she insisted she hadn't taken anything knowingly. All she remembered was drinking the punch. The doctors seemed skeptical of her story. But I know my sister. She's not into drugs."

"I assume the police questioned her?"

"Oh yeah. They spent hours grilling Casey in the hospital and afterward. Got statements from most of us at the dance. And through it all, Casey maintained she didn't know what she was given, when she left the dance, or how she got in our car. Only that she had some vague instinct someone was with her, and she was pulled from the car."

I step away from the water, heading toward the boathouse itself. I study the crumbling structure, almost suspiciously, because other than the person who drugged my sister, this broken-down building is the only witness to what went down that night.

"The cops told us there was nothing to pull off the boathouse camera," I tell RJ.

We duck under spiderwebs to step inside. Beside a deserted bird's nest, the camera is still mounted to a wooden beam in the ceiling. RJ pockets his phone and jumps for the beam.

"Be careful," I blurt out, but he easily lifts himself up to straddle it, then takes his phone out again to shine the light on it.

"There's a sticker on here for a security company." He snaps a picture before throwing his leg over to jump down. The landing kicks up dirt and dust that catches in the shards of moonlight peeking through the holes in the roof.

I wrinkle my forehead. "What can you do with that?"

"I've got some ideas."

"Like?"

"I'll let you know. Could be nothing. But I need to check a couple things first and would rather not get your hopes up before I do that."

His vagueness is disconcerting, but what other choice do I have? It's been months since anyone has lifted a finger to help figure out what happened that night. We've been abandoned by the police, the school, and anyone who might have sprung a conscience to come forward with information.

Crazy as it sounds, RJ is my last best hope. And that feeling, *hope*, is something that's been missing in my life since Casey almost died.

I reach for RJ's hand and hold it tightly. "Thank you."

CHAPTER 41
RJ

I NEVER DID FIND OUT HOW THE GAME ENDED. HOPEFULLY FENN won't quiz me about it. But after our adventure at the boathouse, Sloane and I didn't bother heading back to the stadium to find Fenn or check the final score. We'd felt like the parents who'd forgotten to pick up their kid when we found Lucas in the parking lot sitting on the trunk of the car. He was chill about it, though, by the time we dropped him off at the junior dorm.

"Computer lab tomorrow?" I offer as a goodwill gesture.

He hops out of the car with his smile undeterred. "Yeah, sure thing."

Sloane's house is on the opposite side of campus. But when I pull away from the dorm and reach the stop sign, she puts her hand on the steering wheel.

"It's still early. I don't have to be home yet."

She couldn't stop being dead-gorgeous if she tried. But at night, in the colored glow of the car's lighting, she's mystical. It's her superpower.

"What'd you have in mind?"

She licks her lips, and now I'm dying to find out what's happening behind those cunning eyes.

"Fenn will be out with the soccer team for a while," she says. "We could go back to your room. If you're good with that."

Yeah, I'm good with that.

I cut the wheel to take a hard left toward the senior dorm, drawing a soft laugh from her sexy mouth. Not that I'm expecting anything, but Sloane's been throwing some vibes at me since we left the boathouse. I didn't want to respond to it outright in case I was reading the situation all wrong. What she experienced back there was intense, and completely understandable. I'm not the type of guy to take advantage of her feelings after something like that. I might be a dick, but I'm not a dirtbag.

And because I am that kind of asshole, I walk Sloane right through the front door. Ever since Fenn and I discovered Roger's side hustle, the three of us have an agreement of mutually assured destruction.

And fuck Duke. If he's back from Ballard already and sees us, he can eat me.

I'm learning all sorts of new things about myself lately. I like having a stepbrother. I don't mind being part of a team. And given the proper motivation, I'm the guy who picks a fight over a girl. Especially when that girl is a stone-cold ice princess with legs for days and a smile that can drop a man dead.

Upstairs, I watch her walk into my room and throw herself in my desk chair. While I shut the door, she spins around to eye me, and that look makes my mouth run dry. Part seduction and suspicion. I don't know how to take it or how she conveys so much by saying so little.

"What?" I say hoarsely.

She makes me nervous. Which is a strange sensation. Almost nothing does, and I wouldn't like it much if it weren't also sorta exciting.

"You were very decent tonight," she says.

"Was I?" I take a seat on the end of my bed.

Sloane nods, twirling back and forth in the chair. "For the record, I don't have some secret kink for macho dudes."

"Okay…"

"But. It was sexy the way you stood up to Duke. So there's that."

"Noted. Out of curiosity, what are some of those secret kinks?"

Arching an eyebrow, Sloane doesn't answer. Because she's trying to break me. And I'm happy to let her.

"Seriously, though. And then at the boathouse. You were sweet and you didn't have to be."

"I know I made a mess of things at the start, but I meant it, Sloane. I am here for you. That's real. Count on it."

Her lips curve shyly before her gaze wanders off to admire the wallpaper.

I don't often see it, but bashful Sloane is fucking adorable in a heartbreaking kind of way. I knew when we met that there was more to this enigma than the ball-busting headmaster's daughter who wouldn't give me her name. I knew that if I could puzzle her out, I'd get to the core of something fascinating.

"See, it's stuff like that," she finally says, still avoiding my gaze. "It's like you can't help saying the sweetest things to me."

I bite back a laugh. "Should I stop?"

"Yes," she tells me emphatically. "It gives a girl ideas."

"Yeah?" My voice thickens.

"Like, you were already hot. It's overkill at this point."

My chuckle spills free. "Hey, I can keep a secret. You can treat me like a piece of meat in public, and I won't tell anyone the ice princess has a thing for nice guys."

She rolls her eyes. "Shut up."

"You know, for appearances. Got to protect your reputation, after all."

Sloane flashes her middle finger. "I've got your reputation right here."

"That's my girl."

"See?" She cocks her head. "That's what I'm talking about."

I never know what to expect from her one moment to the next.

It's what keeps me hanging on her every word, her every expression. Yeah, I'm fucking thirsty. But no matter how much I learn about Sloane, she constantly slips off another layer and reinvents herself again. So I'm not ready for it when she undoes the first then second button of her cropped shirt. Her attention remains fixed on my face, while mine follows her fingers with meticulous interest.

"You say something nice and I forget to play hard to get," she accuses.

"Forgive me if I don't stop you."

Slowly, Sloane plucks each button open. Slouched in the chair with her legs splayed. She's an album cover. Something immortal. She undoes the front clasp on her bra and lets it fall with her shirt as she stands up. Her perky tits bring a rush of moisture to my mouth. I swallow hard, fighting the urge to haul her into my lap and suck on those cute, pebbled nipples. But this is her show. She's in charge tonight.

Seeing the heat in my eyes, she smiles slightly and walks over to stand between my legs. A shiver travels through me when she grabs the hem of my shirt and pulls the material up and over my head. When her mouth hovers over mine, I lean in to brush my lips with hers.

Her kiss is a fleeting tease. "Not to get all emotional about it…"

"Or do," I tell her, wrapping my arms around her bare back to run my fingertips down her soft, warm skin.

"I think I knew you'd be good for me. That's why I tried so hard not to like you."

"That's fair." I press my lips between her breasts. Feel her heartbeat against my cheek. "I never meant to end up here either."

It was never about sex for me. Never about gratification or a trophy. The first time I saw her, Sloane had this inexplicable quality that begged to be understood. I had to know this girl. Discover her mysteries. Somewhere along the way, she's become the most important part of my experience here. And I can't blow this again. She's put her trust in me, even after I did my damnedest to destroy it. I can't lose her again.

"Do we need to put a sock on the door or something?" I ask wryly.

"Nah. The soccer team never observes curfew. They won't be back before two."

She directs my mouth to one nipple, arching her back when I drag my hands up her legs to palm her ass. I know from experience that Sloane will practically orgasm from a little tit-play alone, but my erection is throbbing against my zipper, and I need her on top of me right goddamn now. She lets me pull her shorts down and slide my fingers between her thighs to feel how wet she's gotten. It's the sexiest thing I've ever seen when she throws one knee on the bed to straddle my leg and push my fingers inside her.

I groan. "Fuck, you're amazing."

Through heavy breaths she kisses me. Deep and hungry. Rocking back and forth on my hand. My other hand squeezes her breast, my thumb pinching her nipple until her head drops forward.

"I want to come with you inside me," she pants against my ear.

I almost weep with disappointment when the warmth of her pussy disappears from my hand. She grabs her shorts from the floor and pulls a condom out of her pocket. Then, before I can blink, she's pushing me back on the bed and attacking my pants.

When my zipper gets stuck halfway, she whimpers in frustration. Her hands become frantic, clawing at my waistband, as she chokes out a pained whisper. "Please," she breathes, "I've been waiting all day for this."

And damned if that isn't the hottest thing I've ever heard in my life. My dick practically tunnels its way through the denim just hearing that.

Chuckling softly, I help her out and manage to shove my jeans down my hips. I'm hard and ready to go, but she crouches and takes me in her hand to drag her tongue up the shaft and suck on the head. I've never been so close to coming so quickly.

"Goddammit," I croak. "If you don't stop that, this'll be over before it starts."

Mercifully, she slides the condom on, then crawls her way up my body to settle herself on top of me and sink down on my dick. I can't help the groan of relief at the fantastic sensation when she begins to ride me. Both of us sitting up, her ass in my hands, watching each other feel this. She cups and squeezes her tits while I kiss her neck. With each deep thrust, the rest of the world slowly fades away until it's just me and her. I catch our reflection in the closet mirror. Her long, dark hair falling down her back.

In the deeper recesses of my mind, while my hands try to learn every contour of her body, it occurs to me that I'm having a sort of epiphany. That before her, I'd been getting off, but never getting the full experience. Of what it feels like to want this girl so much I'm already missing her. She keeps trying to grind herself harder, faster, but I stall her pace, wanting to draw this out as long as I can. Because right here, it all makes sense.

I slide my fingers into her hair and pull her in for a kiss. "I don't want it to end," I mumble against her lips. "Feels too good."

"So good," she whispers back. Her pretty features are strained, teeth digging hard into her bottom lip. Hazy, unfiltered pleasure swims in her gray eyes.

Too soon, her breathing becomes frustrated. She bites into my shoulder, and I know that's my cue to stop fucking around and make her come already. So I flip us over to throw her against my pillow. She watches in anticipation as I slowly ease her leg over until she's on her side. Then, with a filthy smile, I push myself inside her again. On my knees, thrusting hard against her ass.

"Yes," she moans, and gets an answering moan out of me when I see her reach between her thighs to rub her clit.

A jolt of heat sizzles into my balls, drawing them up tight. I've been on the edge of release since she touched me, but I hold out to make sure she gets there first. I breathe through my nose as I feel her muscles tighten around my shaft. Clench my ass cheeks when I glimpse her teeth digging into her bottom lip. Not yet, I warn myself, as my pulse careens and my balls throb. Wait for it.

"You feel so good," I grind out, and that's all it takes to push her over the edge.

I'll never see anything as sexy as Sloane orgasming with my dick inside her.

Afterward, she lies across my chest, tracing the muscles of my abdomen and laughing at the way my stomach flexes under her fingernails.

"You haven't been wasting your time in the gym," she says. "I'd say it's paying off."

"Oh, really?"

"Mm-hmm. Keep it up."

Hell. Between swim practice and training for this fight, I'm honestly in the best shape of my life. If it keeps her all hot and bothered, I'll bench press a Volkswagen for breakfast.

"Hey." She tilts her head up to peer at me. "At the boathouse. Why were you so interested in the camera? Both the school and the police said there was nothing on it."

I nod. "And there probably wasn't."

"But…?"

"There might be a way to make sure."

"What?" She jerks up. "How?"

I'm still reluctant to let Sloane get her hopes up. The footage might not exist. And if it does, there's no guarantee it'll provide anything useful.

But I promised I wouldn't lie to her about this stuff anymore, so I say, "If the camera was working that night, it's possible the footage is still on the security company's servers."

Her eyes are wide and alert. All sorts of wheels spinning. "So how do we find out?"

That's the tricky part.

"The less you know, the better. Plausible deniability is your new mantra, okay?"

"Fine," she concedes. "I'll stop asking. You have my permission to do what you need to do. I just want to know what happened."

I'm relieved she's letting it go for now, because there's no way I'm letting Sloane get caught up in my bullshit. This isn't changing grades or breaking into an essay database. These companies are designed to keep out people like me. They write their business on their ability to protect their clients' digital property. Even if I do manage to muscle my way in, there's always the chance I don't get out undetected. Then I'm facing consequences a hell of a lot more severe than getting expelled. People get charged with terrorism for less than what I intend to do. Hell, they've died in prison for pirating free books.

And yet, lying here with her, I look into Sloane's eyes and have no doubt I'd take a life sentence to help her get justice for her sister and give her family some peace.

"No promises," I tell her. "Like I said, I need to figure out if this is even feasible."

"But you'll keep me posted. You swear."

"Of course."

She's buzzing, practically leaping out of her skin with excitement at the prospect. Awesome. No pressure, right? Sloane's only been dreaming of this chance for months. And I'm the asshole who's going to break her heart if I can't pull this off.

"You know..." Flinging her leg over my hip, she nestles herself closer. I've become oddly obsessed with the way her hair clings to my cheek. "This school will lose its collective shit if you manage to win this fight with Duke."

"If?" I gave this chick a sufficient if not mind-blowing orgasm and she has the nerve to lie here and tell me *if.* Christ. "Wow. Where's the confidence, huh?"

She laughs and kisses my chest as if her mouth can placate this unforgivable wound. "If you wanted someone to blow smoke up your ass, you should have asked Lucas to come over."

"Damn, Tresscott. Harsh."

Her shrug is fully unremorseful. "I'm nothing if not brutally honest."

"Then in the interest of full disclosure, I should probably mention..." I twist a lock of her hair between my fingers. "Duke insisted on a stipulation if I did lose the fight."

Sloane's head pops up. "What kind of stipulation?"

"If I lose, I have to leave Sandover."

"Fuck off." She sits abruptly.

"That's the deal."

"Then fuck the deal and fuck Duke. I don't give a shit what you promised him. You're not leaving."

"I don't plan on losing, but he's not about to give me a choice."

"Then I guess you're in a real pickle, Shaw, because you can't make a girl catch feelings and then leave her high and dry."

I blink a couple times. Muddled in her fiery indignation, it sounded like Sloane just said she more than likes me.

"Feelings, huh?" I can't control the grin that sprouts up.

She rolls her eyes and pulls away from me with an angry little pout. "Whatever. Lap it up."

"You're so fucking difficult." I throw my arms around her and yank her against my chest, kissing the top of her head while she pretends to resist. There's nothing Sloane hates more than showing sincere emotions. The nonviolent kind, at least. "I have feelings for you too."

Her body softens then, and I catch a glimpse of a shy smile tugging at her lips.

"Promise me you're going to win," she says softly. "You can't leave now."

I already hate myself for this, and yet I can't stop those two words from exiting my mouth.

"I promise."

CHAPTER 42
LAWSON

THERE MUST BE PEOPLE WALKING THIS DECAYING ROCK OF GARBAGE and filth who aren't overcome by pathological apathy when they see their mother's name on the screen of their phone. Sadly, I can't relate.

"To what do I owe this intrusion?" I ask politely. I'm between classes, so I'd just stopped off at the dining hall for a drink.

"What? Lawson, it's Mom."

Yes, I'd recognize that shrill tone of inadequacy anywhere. "What do you want?"

"It's loud there. Where are you?"

"It's three o'clock on a Thursday. I'm at a Raiders game," I mock. "Where else would I be?" Sipping my drink, I duck out outside and head across campus to the art building.

"Right." She laughs awkwardly. "You're at school. Sorry. Ah. Anyway. I'm calling because, well, Jeffrey will be stuck in Hong Kong, so I thought perhaps it might be nice to have you visit for the holidays."

"Did you?" Incredible. "You sat down with one of your mindfulness journals and made a little mind map asking yourself if your son would find this offer appealing?"

"Perhaps I caught you at a bad time. I'm not sure what plans your father might—"

"I wouldn't know. And I don't care."

Every time we talk, it's like she's never met me. Which makes total sense considering her total ambivalence when it comes to parenting. Drowning me in the bathtub would have been more humane than leaving me with my father in the divorce.

"It's just I read somewhere recently that the holidays can be especially difficult for people in recovery. That it helps to be with family who can provide a positive influence."

Then it's a good thing I'm not in recovery. I roll my eyes at the phone. It takes more than a couple stints in rehab to break me. Better adversaries have tried.

"Honestly, Mother. What part of our relationship wouldn't make me want to drink? Besides, if you really think I'm in recovery, then you don't want me to come. Trust me, there's probably more cocaine stashed in that house than a drug mule's asshole."

"Lawson."

Right now, she's nervously wondering if I'm serious. How long has it been since the last time I was there? Where could I have hidden it? Can you rent a drug-sniffing dog? With any luck, she'll spend the rest of the week ripping out floorboards with a claw hammer.

"How are things at home?" she asks, as though there'll come a day I provide a different answer.

I snort. "Is that a serious question?"

"Am I not supposed to take an interest in your welfare?"

"Wouldn't that be a first."

She's shelled out for hundreds of hours of therapy I mostly didn't attend. And when I did attend, I just goaded the good doctor through increasingly uncomfortable explanations of my most deviant sexual exploits until they either kicked me out of the office or excused themselves to masturbate in the restroom.

I assume.

Still, as offended as they were by my filthy mouth, those doctors would've been horrified if I'd gone ahead and actually bared my soul to them. If I told them all about Roman, my so-called father, a man who was shooting blanks, so he hired a prostitute to seduce and impregnate his wife to bear him an heir. Except then he'd grown so disgusted with the effectiveness of his own plot that it triggered a deep and unrelenting hatred for that pathetic child. And then there's Amelia, my mother, who took half his empire and ran. The selfish bitch who'd left her defenseless kid in the clutches of a man who would set puppies on fire for fun if there wasn't a perpetual army of activists, lawyers, and government agencies stalking his every move for one heinous crime or another.

You know. Normal teen angst stuff.

"I do try, Lawson. You don't make it easy to be close to you."

I can't think of a good reason why I should. My entire existence represents barely half her life. She blinked and I'm an adult. Meanwhile, I've lived every day of my life knowing I'm nothing more than a vengeful, tragic mistake used as a bargaining chip between two people who'd sooner throw the other off a cliff.

"I haven't talked to Dad in weeks," I answer in a bored tone. "So I'd say, sure, things are great on the home front."

"What about Christine? Are you getting along with your stepmother?"

In a manner of speaking.

"Definitely," I drawl. "She's a real charming lady. Lets me put it in her ass."

On that note, I hang up and pocket my phone to enter my art class. Though the damage is done.

Fuck's sake, the little I ask of her is to simply be invisible. I'm happy to make myself scarce if she can respect a similar boundary of noninterference. I'd rather have a committed absent mother than one who involves me in her bouts of seasonal guilt. Like the Christmas puppy that keeps getting returned to the shelter by Presidents' Day.

Her selfish appearances are brief but destructive, always leaving me unsettled. I'm typically happy to self-medicate in order to clear my head, but today I'm tapped out and knee-deep sober.

Even Gwen and her cute flower-print dress aren't enough of a distraction from the turmoil my mother hath wrought. And anyway, I still haven't won over the missus Goodwyn. She ignores even my most overt advances. But that's fine. All good. I might be questioning my sex appeal if I weren't already getting it on the side from her husband. Which, admittedly, is a big part of the appeal.

This week we're working on clay sculpture. Gwen turns out the lights to put up a PowerPoint of a recent traveling exhibit by a blind Mongolian artist who creates impressionist interpretations of the people and animals of his childhood village. His phallic example of a dragonfly is interrupted by a text from the mister Goodwyn.

Jack: See me during office hours to discuss an extra credit project.
Me: My pleasure.

My phone is suddenly yanked from my grasp.

"Maybe I should hold onto this for you." Gwen darkens the screen, then pockets my device without appearing to look at it.

"Foul play, Ms. G."

She returns to the front of the room beside the projector screen. "No phones in my class, Lawson. You know better."

I flash her a little smile. "I feel it's my duty to warn you. My nudes are on there. You could right now be in possession of pornography."

"Then we'd better turn it off." She shuts off the phone and tosses it on her desk. "You can have it back after detention."

Brilliant. Because my favorite thing about class is staying late. Not like I have anything better to do than clean her paintbrushes when there's an eight ball in my room screaming my name.

But Gwen follows through on the threat. After the bell rings, she waves me over and puts me to work. My first task is to dress the in-progress sculptures in wet plastic wrap then put them in the cabinet.

"All right. What's next?" I have no idea how long this is supposed to last, but I'd like to get this over with as fast as possible. "Ms. G?"

"Huh?" For a moment I'm concerned she's peeked at my phone, but it's her own that she's distressingly hunched over at her desk. "Oh, second period left their acrylics on the back shelf. If you could put them back in the supply closet."

"Yes, ma'am." I collect a couple of armfuls and cart them to the closet, only to find it locked. "Is there a key to this?" I call over my shoulder.

"There was, but the last art teacher lost it." Gwen arrives with a paint spatula to jimmy the door. "I figured out a workaround. There's a trick to it."

A second later, the door pops open.

I chuckle. "Well done. Do a few B-and-Es in your day?"

That earns me a smile. "A girl's got to fend for herself." She takes some of the acrylics from my arms and starts tossing them on the shelf without much attention to order or tidiness.

"Mr. G not the handy type?"

Her expression darkens at the mention of her husband. "Don't get married in your early twenties, Lawson. Live before you die."

My brows soar. Well. Color me intrigued. Is our picture-perfect couple suffering from some marital strife?

"Trouble at home?" I ask lightly.

She seems to catch herself, as if she'd forgotten she said it aloud. "Oh. I'm sorry. I really shouldn't talk about personal matters with a student. It's not proper."

"Maybe you've noticed, but I don't much care for proper." I shrug, playing it cool. "For what it's worth, though…I'm an excellent listener."

She leads me out of the closet, mulling over the offer. I stay quiet long enough for her to fill the silence.

"He says it's nothing," she finally confesses. "But Jack's been distant since the semester started."

Oops. My bad. Probably shouldn't have distracted him with all those blowjobs. "Maybe he's preoccupied with classes," I suggest innocently.

We go around the room gathering the debris of the day's activities and putting away supplies. "It's more than that," Gwen says flatly. "I know him. There's something he's not telling me."

Well, obviously. Jack's in a tricky predicament. How *does* one tell his wife he's engaging in illicit hookups with a student? And a male student at that.

"Have you ever felt this way before?" I ask slowly, because something about the way she's digging her teeth into her lip tells me this isn't a new state for her.

She meets my eyes, rinsing out a rag at the sink. Indecision wars across her freckled face.

"He cheated on me in college."

Called it.

"We were high school sweethearts. He was a junior. I was a freshman. Completely inseparable."

"That's sweet." In a hideously mundane sort of way.

"One semester, there was this girl from class he was spending a lot of time with. They were always studying or working on some project. He'd say it was a group thing, but I'd catch them alone at the library or getting coffee together."

Oh, Jack, you dog. "Did you confront him?"

She nods. "I finally worked up the courage. He denied it over and over until he realized I wasn't going to believe him. Then he came clean."

"Did you break up?"

"I considered it. I even left and spent the weekend at my parents' house. Then he swore up and down he loved me and it was only one time…"

"But you think there were others," I guess.

Gwen shrugs, pulling her wavy red hair down from a loose bun. The moment it cascades over her shoulders, my dick wakes up and says hello. I've always loved redheads.

"I've never wanted to ask," she admits. "But now…"

"I'd ask why you stay if you don't trust him, but I've seen him in a linen button-down, so…" I trail off devilishly.

At that, she cracks a reluctant smile and just the beginnings of a laugh. "Thanks for not telling me I'm just imagining things."

"Definitely not. Go with your gut, I always say."

We carry the last of the materials back to the closet and put away the cleaning supplies.

"Really?" She suddenly sounds pensive. "I thought you'd say something like, 'don't get mad, get even.'"

Careful, Gwendolyn. That sounds dangerously like an invitation.

I grin. "I wouldn't argue with that course of action either."

Gwen leans against a shelf, combing one hand through all that sexy red hair. My dick twitches again. "Thank you. You've been strangely helpful."

"At your service."

"I did wonder if you were feeling a bit under the weather," she adds.

I raise a brow. "Why's that?"

"You haven't tried to flirt with me once today."

Shrugging, I say, "Your lack of interest was well-noted. And I'm not one to beg."

For the first time this semester, something genuinely surprising happens.

Before I can blink, Mrs. Goodwyn plants her lips on mine. And she's not at all timid. Her hands grasp either side of my face as she pushes her tongue against mine and hums the slightest purr into my mouth. It's the kind of blistering hot kiss that sends a bolt of lust straight to my cock.

"Sometimes it's okay to beg," she whispers after we come up for air.

"Yeah?" My voice sounds hoarse to my ears.

"Uh-huh." Her lips travel to my neck, kissing a path toward my jaw and leaving goose bumps in their wake.

"Begging can be fun," I agree. My fingers drift to the hem of her dress.

She stops kissing me and looks down at my hand, eyes wide with interest. I can see her pulse fluttering in the hollow of her throat.

I slowly bunch the filmy fabric in my fist and start tugging it upward. My dick gets harder at each inch of bare skin that gets exposed. When my thumb scrapes a silky thigh, I feel a shudder go through her body.

"Lawson…" She trails off. She's too busy gazing between us, where my fingers are now toying with the waistband of her thong.

"Beg for it," I say softly.

She visibly swallows. "For what?"

"Beg me to get on my knees and put my mouth right…here…" I press the pad of my thumb against her covered clit, and she makes a breathy, agitated sound.

When she doesn't answer straight away, I cup her with my palm while threading my free hand through her coppery hair. I jerk her head up, bringing her mouth to mine again. The kiss makes both of us groan. I love the way she tastes. Why does forbidden fruit have the sweetest flavor?

"Lawson," she chokes out against my lips.

"Mmm? What do you want, Gwen?"

"Get on your knees," she begs, and it requires some effort not to break out in a grin. Took a while, but in the end, she's as weak as her husband.

I get it, though. Gwen needs her own secret. A dirty little lie to indulge her vengeance. The secretive smile over dinner when the mister comes home late from work.

I nudge her toward a low shelving unit opposite the closet door and shove the stack of supplies off it. Items clatter to the floor, but neither of us even blinks. I'm already pulling her thong down her smooth, toned legs, shoving the scrap of material in my pocket as I kneel in front of her. In no time at all, her legs are flung over my shoulders and her pussy is grinding my face, and it's so goddamn hot I'm struggling not to shoot in my pants.

"Oh my God," Gwen whimpers.

I peer up at her and my grin springs loose. She's biting hard on her lip, her face flushed with lust.

Welcome to the modern American marriage, Mrs. G.

CHAPTER 43
SLOANE

"She'll say I never call her, and then she doesn't answer the phone."

It's Monday, and Silas and I meet up for a run before school. He's the only person I know who takes training as seriously as I do. And can function before eight without propping himself up with at least three double espressos. RJ might *say* he likes to run, but, as I pointed out last night after he shot down my morning run offer with "LOL," he clearly lacks the dedication.

"What sense does that make? It's making the problem worse to spite me."

We set a moderate pace, jogging the narrow dirt path embedded with rocks and protruding tree roots. Already I'm drenched in sweat. The overnight temperature never dipped below seventy and it's even hotter this morning. By noon, the sun can practically bake the shirt off your back.

"Amy's mad at me that we don't spend enough time together, but then she skips my swim meet to go shopping with her friends. What the hell am I supposed to do with that?"

I love Silas, but it's too early in the morning for another episode of the unending low-stakes drama that is his relationship with Amy.

It's like watching a shopping cart slowly crawl toward a car's rear bumper. No one expects any lasting damage, and it seems like more effort than it's worth to get involved.

"I've got class till two, practice till six, then dinner and homework until at least ten every night. How am I the asshole?"

I don't know what else to tell him that he hasn't heard a hundred times since sophomore year. This same argument is practically a seasonal occurrence. If he wants to keep Amy, he might figure out a way to treat her better. Otherwise, cut her loose and spare everyone the headache.

"How am I supposed to make time for her if she's ignoring me?"

Amy's a sweet, funny, caring girl who's fully obsessed with him. And for some stupid reason, I think that's a major turn-off for Silas. For the life of me, I've never managed to nail down why they don't work except that he's not that into the relationship despite his absolute refusal to do anything about it. It's like he's in an arranged marriage of his own creation and the sole tenet of his religion is thou shalt not divorce.

"Sloane?"

"Huh?" Shaken from my runner's trance, I stumble over a fallen branch and nearly take a header into the dirt. "Sorry, what?"

"You haven't said anything for over a mile."

"What do you want me to say?" I shrug at him. "Sounds like she's sick of your shit."

"Thanks."

The rising sun peers through the trees to create an opaque yellow fog when the light catches the clouds of dust where our footfalls disturb the ground. Long shadows streak across our path, tall grass and shrubs busy with morning scavengers. I want to make a solid five miles before class, so I push our pace.

"What's up?" Silas breathes harder as he matches my steps.

We take the shortcut across the east lawn, where the old freshman dorms stood before storms in the sixties brought a flood that opened a sinkhole under the building and swallowed the west end overnight.

"Nothing."

"You're somewhere else."

"No, I'm listening. Amy hates you, and you're kind of a dick about it."

"Is that your real assessment or you just guessing?"

"Like sixty-forty?"

"Seriously, though." Silas has incredible endurance, but even he sounds like he's sucking wind through a straw trying to maintain my pace. "What should I do about all this?"

"You know exactly what to do. You just refuse to do it."

He makes an aggravated noise. Then he almost takes a header too, only his near fall is due to his shoelace coming untied. "One sec."

I stop, but keep jogging in place as I wait for him. My watch has been flashing for the past fifteen minutes, so I take this opportunity to check my messages. RJ says good morning and wants to know if I'm still meeting him at our spot later. And then there's three messages from Duke.

Irritation flickers through me. Since the soccer game, Duke's kicked up his calling and texting another notch. He claims he has something important to say to me, but I don't believe that for a second. Seeing me with RJ that night punctured his ego, and now he's going to pull out all the stops to prove to me he's the better man.

"Ugh, he's so obnoxious," I grumble.

"Who?" Silas tightens his laces and rises to his full height. The sweat on his white T-shirt makes the material almost transparent, showing off the chiseled abs beneath it.

"Duke. He's been constantly texting since I ran into him at the soccer game at Ballard." I give Silas a dark look. "Which, by the way, you bailed on."

"I had plans with Amy," he protests.

"Yeah, well, the extra moral support would've been helpful for when I got ambushed by Mila and Oliver."

His expression goes remorseful. "Sorry. I didn't even think about that."

"It's fine," I say, sighing. "RJ was there to keep me from killing them."

We work up to a jog again, our steady breathing the only sound between us for the next little while.

"So, what does Duke want?" Silas eventually asks.

"What else? To win me back." I snort out a laugh. "He's badgering me into meeting up with him. Probably plans to flash his abs and flex his muscles a couple times because he thinks it'll make me want him again."

Silas snorts too. "I mean, it's worked for him in the past."

I give my friend a little shove, but his body is rock-solid and the shove doesn't even disturb his gait.

"Hey, it's true," he says with a grin. "You've never been able to say no to Duke."

"Maybe in the past. But things are different now," I admit.

"Because you're with RJ?" His tone is careful. With a twinge of skepticism thrown in.

"Yeah, I am." I can't stop the dumb, embarrassing smile that arises at the memory of the other night.

"What, like you're exclusive now or something?"

"Hasn't really come up. But, yes, I assume we are."

"For real?" Now he definitely sounds skeptical. "I know you, Sloane. You develop an allergic reaction to a guy the second he talks about trying to lock you down. Like, shit, we're all still recovering from the whiplash of the nonstop on-and-off from the Duke fiasco."

"This is different." I keep my gaze on the path ahead, because I'm afraid he'll see everything I feel for RJ flashing across my face.

"Different, how?" he pushes.

Despite my best effort to control my emotions, I can't stop the sappy confession from sliding out. "I think I'm in love with him."

Silas stops dead in a cloud of dust. "Are you serious?"

I slow down, waiting for him to increase his pace again. "Yeah," I say, and from the corner of my eye, I catch him studying me.

"Well, shit," he finally says. "This is big."

"Huge," I agree.

And entirely unexpected. Never in my wildest dreams did I think I'd fall for the antisocial boy trespassing on my trail. That's just crazy talk. But it happened, despite my attempts to keep him at a distance, making him chase me. I didn't expect for RJ and me to be so damn similar. And then the weirdest thing happened. Those similarities were so glaring it was like a mirror being held up to me, showing me a scary truth: the aloof, always-pretend-you-don't-care attitude might protect us from heartache…but it's the loneliest existence on the planet.

I don't feel so lonely anymore. Opening myself up to RJ messed with my entire worldview, and I'm not sure I mind.

"By the way," I tell Silas, as we push forward, adding another mile to our tally. "Don't say anything to RJ about Duke's constant texting. He's got this whole jealousy thing going on. I mean, it's really hot. But I don't want him thinking I'm starting up with Duke behind his back or anything."

"Of course. I'm your vault, you know that."

Yeah, I do know that. Regardless of the company he keeps—ahem, Lawson—Silas is a man of his word. And since Casey's accident, with every friend we had at Ballard turning on us, Silas has been the one constant. I honestly don't know what I would have done without him.

CHAPTER 44
SILAS

COACH IS ON ONE WHEN HE WALKS INTO WEDNESDAY'S SWIM practice with a whiteboard and an easel. On it are each of our names and best times. With intensity gleaming in his eyes, he tells us we've become complacent, and he's decided to inject a little friendly competition into the team. Inspire us to strive. Because top-four finishes in every event isn't enough to take State. We have to set records.

I don't hate the idea, at least until he throws us into the pool for head-to-head sprints. Out of nowhere, RJ demolishes two guys who've been swimming anchor since sophomore year. Then he nearly conquers Lawson's butterfly time in what would have been a monumental upset. If he'd made it all the way through the bracket to swim against me and won, I might have hung up my goggles.

No one should get that good this quickly.

It's unreal.

He's gotten quicker in the gym too. Fenn can't keep up anymore when they spar. RJ's too fast for him. He's learned to find his reach and time his punches, which lately are landing every time. The guy's looking dangerous and it's starting to get obnoxious.

Admittedly, I thought RJ might have quit the team by now.

Realized it was more work than it sounded and stopped showing up. Turns out, I think he's enjoying it.

When Coach finally dismisses everyone for day, the rest of us are exhausted and dragging ass while RJ's still got some big dumb grin on his face heading into the showers. I know I should let it go. Chalk this shitty mood up to low blood sugar and move on.

Except I can't stop seeing that smile out of the corner of my eye. At this point, it's weirder if I don't say something, right? Like I'm trying to check the guy out or something. Lawson's on my other side giving me a suspicious frown as he walks off to get dressed.

"Come on," I say. "What's with the sudden sunny disposition?"

RJ lathers up his hair and turns under the showerhead to rinse. "Huh?"

"If you get any more cheerful, you're going to burst out in song."

"Oh." He doesn't seem inclined to enlighten me, which is almost more annoying.

"That's all? 'Oh.'"

"Just distracted, I guess. Sloane's supposed to meet me after practice." He shoves hair off his forehead. "She's probably already waiting outside."

Of course. That's why he's turned into a Disney character. His and Sloane's magical new love affair.

I turn to rinse my own hair so he doesn't see my expression. Nothing about that relationship makes sense to me. If you can even call it that. I mean, how can you have a relationship with a guy who barely leaves his room and would rather have bamboo shoved under his fingernails than carry on a conversation? It boggles the goddamn mind.

What the ever-loving fuck does she see in this guy when Sloane could have anyone she wants?

I yank my towel off the hook and wrap it around my hips, eager to get away from Sloane's new boytoy.

Not a boytoy. She's in love with him, chirps the mocking voice in my head.

Whatever. If she thinks she loves the guy, fine. But excuse me if I don't see this thing lasting. She'll get bored of RJ eventually. She always does.

"Shaw," Coach Gibson barks from the doorway. "Come see me before you leave. Need to go over some strategy for your heat next week."

"Yessir," RJ calls back, before glancing at me. "If Sloane's out there when you leave, tell her to wait for me, okay?"

"Sure."

I dress quickly and am out of the locker room five minutes later, eager to grab some dinner and forget about this whole obnoxious day. Just as RJ predicted, Sloane is indeed waiting outside the building for him.

"Hey." She looks up from her phone, her face brightening when she spots me. "Thank God. I'm in desperate need of conversing with someone who isn't Duke."

I smile wryly. "He still blowing up your phone?"

"Yup." As proof, she tilts her screen my way, and I whistle when I see the wall of text on there.

"Someone's desperate."

"I might need to stop ignoring him," she says. "It just seems to make him text more. Ugh. But I'm so not in the mood to deal with Sexy Duke right now."

I raise a brow. "*Sexy* Duke?"

"Oh, no, I don't mean I still find him sexy," she explains, rolling her eyes. "It's just this insufferable smoldering persona he puts on when he's trying to win me back. His seduction attempts always follow the same pattern."

Always work, too, if history is any indication. But I keep my mouth shut. Sloane doesn't like being reminded of her weakness when it comes to Duke.

"RJ's inside talking to Coach, by the way," I force myself to tell her. "He said to wait for him."

She nods absently, once again checking her phone. This time, her expression is more strained than annoyed. "One sec," she says to me, before lifting the phone to her ear. "Hey."

I study the strap of my duffel bag, pretending I'm not blatantly trying to overhear her conversation.

"Seriously? There's really nothing to talk about," she protests. There's a pause, and her gray eyes flicker with unease. "Fine. Okay." Another pause. "Meet me at the bench on the trail to my house. I'll be there in ten." Then she hangs up and sighs.

"Duke?" I guess.

Her jaw tenses slightly. "Fuck." She takes a breath. "Do me a favor and wait for RJ? Tell him I can't meet up, but I'll call him later, okay?"

I narrow my eyes. "Fine, but you owe me one. I'm starving."

"You're a lifesaver." She leans in to smack a kiss on my cheek. "Thanks, Si."

I watch her hurry off, my gaze unwittingly lingering on her ass in those jean shorts. I probably shouldn't be checking out my friend's ass. But it's hard not to. Sloane's body is unreal.

I force my gaze off her retreating back and pull out my phone to text Amy. She's still pissed at me because I told her I couldn't hang out this weekend, but I don't see her offering to make the trek and come *here*. Shit, it's a hell of a lot easier for me to sneak her into my dorm than to break into hers. The Ballard housemothers are way more strict than old Roger.

I decide to point that out via text.

Me: You could always come here...
Amy: How would I even get to Sandover? I don't have a car.

I lift my head when RJ exits the double doors behind me. He glances around, startled to find me standing there rather than Sloane. He wrinkles his forehead. "Sloane show up?"

His visible disappointment raises my hackles for some reason. He doesn't even know her well enough to be disappointed she's not here.

"Yeah, she did, but she said—" I pause abruptly, but disguise it as needing to check my phone. "One sec. Let me send this."

I type a response to Amy, but my mind is elsewhere. It's on Sloane and RJ and this totally pointless relationship they've fallen into. Who are they kidding? Either he'll ditch her when he realizes he prefers to be an antisocial asshole, after all, or she'll crush his heart into dust when she goes back to that jackass Duke. I don't know why they're even wasting each other's time.

Me: I'll pick you up, obviously.
Amy: I guess that could work.

"Silas?" RJ presses. "Sloane said…?"

I keep my gaze on my phone screen, speaking absentmindedly. "Oh, right, yeah. She had to go home and grab something. Said to meet her at the bench on the path."

He claps me on the arm. "Thanks. I'll see you later."

I don't look up until RJ is several yards away. I watch his long strides eat up the grass as he crosses the lawn toward the path on its outskirts. Then I wrench my gaze away and assure myself I'm doing both of them a favor.

CHAPTER 45
SLOANE

HE'S WAITING FOR ME ON THE BENCH WHEN I TURN THE CORNER. He must have just finished soccer practice to beat me here. Annoyance flickers through me as I sweep my gaze over him, the insolent way he stretches his long legs out in front of him, the small flask in his hand, resting on his knee.

"Well, I'm here. What's so important that you threatened to tell my dad about me and RJ if I didn't jump to your beck and call?"

Fenn has the decency to look sheepish. "Come on. You know I'd never do that. Just needed to find a way to get you here. You've been avoiding my texts."

I stride toward him, but don't join him on the bench. I remain standing, playing with the frayed hem of my T-shirt. I didn't realize the thread had started to unravel. Gonna need to throw out this shirt.

"Sloane," Fenn says irritably.

"What?" I grumble, equally annoyed. "I don't know what you want from me. I already said I'd put in a good word with my dad. Casey said he's letting you guys walk down to the lake this weekend, out of view of his precious cameras. Isn't that progress enough for you?"

"That's not why I'm here and you know it."

An icy sensation tickles the spot between my shoulder blades. I gulp, forcing myself not to avoid his resigned blue eyes.

"I tried to talk to you about it at the swim meet last week. I had it all worked out in my head, but now I'm not sure how to broach the subject in a way that won't get me punched in the dick." Fenn mutters a quiet expletive. "RJ asked the question. Came out of nowhere and I didn't know what else to say. So I lied."

My heart stops. Then careens in a reckless pace that makes me light-headed. "Shit," I whisper. "Why the hell didn't you tell me before now?"

His jaw drops. "Are you kidding me? You've been avoiding me, you asshole. And don't pretend it's because you're protective of Case. You knew we'd have to talk about this eventually."

He's right. On weak knees, I walk to the bench and sit beside him. When he passes me his flask, I accept it without a word and take a long swig. The burn of whiskey goes right to my gut.

"Why the hell did you lie?" I ask miserably.

"I panicked. And now it's too late to take it back." Fenn rakes a hand through his blond hair. "So I think it's probably in both our best interests if you don't tell him we hooked up."

"I wasn't going to," I say flatly.

"Right. But if he asks…"

"Why do you care?"

"I care about RJ."

"Since when?" I challenge. "Silas says you didn't bother learning his name when your parents got married."

"Yeah, well, a lot has changed since then," Fenn says, his voice gruff. He sips his whiskey. "I don't know. Whatever. It's stupid. But the idea of having a stepbrother is growing on me. We're getting closer lately, and I don't want something that happened ages ago to mess all that up."

Neither do I.

A feeling of helplessness grabs hold of my throat. God, this is…

bad. I'd barely spared a thought to our unfortunate hookup since it'd happened. Now my brain won't shut up about it. As I sit there ruminating on it, I can't help wondering if keeping it from RJ is the bigger mistake.

I bite the inside of my cheek. "Maybe this is the wrong call, Fenn. It feels pretty shitty to lie to him."

Especially after I made a whole thing about honesty after finding out he'd been spying on me. Okay, the two aren't nearly the same thing, but it's still hypocrisy any way you slice it. RJ made me a promise to be more open. To be vulnerable and let me know him. And since he showed up outside my window that night, he's kept that promise. For the first time, I'm starting to let myself trust someone. It's a dick move to start our second chance off with another major omission.

On the other hand, RJ made it clear he's not interested in hearing about other guys I've been with. If Fenn weren't his stepbrother, there'd be no reason to even mention it. After all, it happened months before Fenn and RJ had ever met. A bizarre twist of fate later, and suddenly a split-second decision made with too much to drink becomes a potentially devastating secret.

"We can't tell him," Fenn says, a frustrated note entering his voice. "Think about it. If you were him, would you really want to know if the girl you're seeing slept with your brother? That's heavy shit, Sloane."

He makes it sound worse than it is. It's not like I was fucking Fenn in the bridal suite while RJ stood at the altar with our families nervously looking at the empty church aisle.

"I don't know." Misery jams in my throat. "If he finds out now from you or me, it's no big deal. But if he hears it from someone else later, then it looks like there was something to hide."

"Who would he hear it from? We're the only ones who know. The only ones who were in my bed that night."

I nod slowly. Gabe had been away that weekend. And if someone did see me sneaking out of the dorm in the wee hours of the morning, they haven't come forward.

Besides, Fenn's already lied to RJ. Going behind his back to tell RJ would only drive a wedge between the two of them. Sure, I'd get to give myself points for honesty, but I'd be pitting them against each other for the sake of my conscience. Maybe Fenn and I aren't great friends these days, but he doesn't deserve that either.

"Maybe you're right," I say. "It's not worth the potential fallout over something so silly."

He nods, visibly relieved. "I don't think Casey should find out either."

I briefly close my eyes. I never told my sister about the hookup. It happened before winter break of junior year, months before the prom and the accident and Casey's subsequent closeness to Fenn. And it's not that I was trying to keep it from her on purpose. I'd just felt stupid and…embarrassed, I guess. Casey always used to tease me about my Duke hookups—my "fuckboy weakness," she'd called it. And then I turned around and fell into bed with yet another guy brandishing that reputation. I suppose a part of me didn't want her judging me.

If I'd told her back then, she wouldn't have cared.

If I tell her now…she'd care.

Fenn passes me the flask again. I drain what's left of it, ignoring the queasy feeling churning in my stomach.

"Okay," I agree, while an unhappy voice in my head insists we're making the wrong decision.

"Nobody finds out," he says, his face grim.

We both jump when we hear footsteps rustling on the path. Half a second later, RJ emerges into the clearing, a dark scowl twisting his lips.

"Great," he says sarcastically. "Now that *that's* settled."

CHAPTER 46
RJ

In middle school, I knew this Navy brat named Sully. He'd lived in six countries on three continents and crossed the contiguous forty-eight states by car before his thirteenth birthday. He said he liked having to move every couple of years. As soon as he started to get sick of a place, they were packing up again. Sully told me the main thing he'd learned was that in any language, people are reliably self-interested. Set your watch by it.

Not sure when I forgot this.

I shake my head in disgust as I look from Sloane to Fenn. They'd been so engrossed in their discussion about how to best betray me that they hadn't even heard my footsteps on the path. Hadn't realized I'd heard nearly their entire conversation until I was standing five feet from their fucking faces.

Speaking of faces, theirs are the same shade of pale. Fenn's lips are pressed in a tight line, shame and remorse swimming in his eyes. Yeah. Sure. Now he decides to feel bad. I still can't wrap my head around the fact Fenn's known all this time that he lied to my face. Apparently I didn't give the guy nearly enough credit for being an ice-cold bastard.

"So, how was it? The sex, I mean?" I ask coolly. The sour sting of acid coats my throat and my jaw hasn't unclenched since I realized what the hell I was hearing.

Sloane slowly gets to her feet. "RJ—"

"Nah," I interrupt. "Let's skip the bullshit apology part."

"It's not a bullshit apology," she says with visible desperation. "I'm so sorry you heard all that—"

"Gee, you're sorry I *heard* it, but not that you said it. Got it."

"That's not what I meant," she shoots back. She shoves a hand through her hair, frazzled. "I'm sorry—"

"Save it." I dismiss her with my gaze, glancing at Fenn again. The anger simmering in my gut homes in on my stepbrother now. "You weren't lying when you said you didn't have a conscience. I mean, dude. You fucked Sloane and then looked me dead in the eye and lied about it."

"Whoa, hey, wait a second." He jumps up too. "The hookup happened almost a year ago."

"And the lying?" I mock. "How long ago was that?"

"Okay, I lied. I know. But just give me a chance to—"

"Fuck chances. Your chance was sitting outside that car in the woods when you swore to me—"

"The hell was I supposed to say? 'I'm sorry I had a drunken hookup with some girl months before any of us ever met?' Cut me some slack." He's panicked, talking fast and circling away from me because we both know what's going to happen if he says something to make me need to hit him.

Sloane, meanwhile, is imploring me with her eyes, clearly wanting another chance to speak. But my heart can't handle her right now, so I keep my hard gaze fixed on Fenn.

"Don't get it twisted. You could have been honest. Maybe I'd get over it, maybe not. Either way, you and I would still be good."

"Okay." He throws his hands up in surrender. "I messed up. That's my bad and I feel shitty about it. But come on, RJ. We're brothers, man. You gotta forgive me."

"We were nothing before we got here and I'm fine keeping it that way." I shake my head to myself. "My first instinct about you was spot-on."

Shame on me for breaking rule number one. Attachments are weaknesses and only create an opportunity to screw me over. I should have stuck to the plan. Kept my head down and did my time until this little exercise was over. This is what I get for trusting people.

"Don't be like that," he says, pleading. "Listen, I'm really apologizing here. You're pissed and I get it. But you sprung that question on me, and I didn't know what else to say. I knew you were getting serious about Sloane. I wasn't about to get in the middle of that." Resignation settles over his expression. "If you need to hate me for a while, okay. I'll do whatever it takes to make it up to you."

He's practically begging, and I couldn't care less. Maybe there was a time I convinced myself having a stepbrother meant something. Thankfully I know better now.

"You did me a favor, Fenn. You reminded me it's only a matter of time before everyone disappoints us. Thank you for being the one who got it out of the way early."

"Fuck's sake, RJ. Don't be like that. I've never had a brother before. This came out of nowhere. I've told you things I've never told anyone. I want us to be friends."

"Grow up, Fenn. Our parents like banging each other. That's the sole basis of this relationship. I'm not your damn wet-nurse."

"Enough," Sloane snaps at me, her gray eyes burning. "You've blown right through justly pissed and veered headlong into fucking uncivil."

"Yeah, well..." I give her a humorless smile. "I'm not feeling especially diplomatic today. Maybe that's what happens when you show up to meet your girlfriend and overhear her and your stepbrother hashing out a battle plan about how to fucking *lie* to you."

"I get you're mad, okay?" She takes a step closer, pushing her dark hair behind her ear. "You have every right to be mad. I'm so sorry. It was stupid of me to even consider lying to you, especially after we agreed to be upfront with each other. That's on me. I own it. But you're acting like a total asshole, and you're really going to regret all this shit you're spewing once you calm down."

I ignore that, instead asking, "So what's your excuse? Why didn't you tell me?"

She tightens her jaw. "Because it wasn't relevant."

I can't stop a low bark of a laugh. "See? I gotta disagree with you there. It would have seemed pretty damn relevant when you had my dick in your mouth."

"Screw you, RJ." One hand flies to her hip, the other shoving more hair out of her eyes. "If you want to be crass and throw a temper tantrum over some territorial dick-measuring bullshit, I am not the one to do it with. You're being a child. Grow up. It was just sex."

"With my fucking stepbrother." Resentment heats my blood. "You can't even keep your story straight. Either it was such a nonissue you didn't think to tell me, or you lied because you didn't want me to find out. Which is it, sweetheart?"

She shakes her head in frustration. "We both know that's not even what you're mad about. And you're right, okay?" Shame fills her eyes. "When Fenn told me he lied to you when you asked, I shouldn't have let him convince me to go along with it. Agreeing to lie was a shitty thing and for that I'm genuinely, sincerely, entirely sorry. And I'll do whatever it takes to earn your forgiveness. But who I hooked up before you *is* a nonissue. It's not like you disclosed the names of every girl you were with before you met *me*."

"I don't give a shit who you sleep with, Sloane. I just don't want to be related to them."

She advances on me. "You can shout and stomp around all you like, but I'm not the only one who's committed a few sins of omission, remember? Wasn't so long ago you were begging me for a second chance. How'd that go? I forget."

"I don't know. Let me fuck your sister and we'll find out."

"Hey," Fenn growls, lunging forward.

Sloane throws herself between us, slapping her palm against Fenn's chest. "Stop," she orders. "This isn't productive."

Fenn goes still, but he's glaring at me now.

Sloane turns back to me, taking a deep breath before speaking. "One day. Very soon," she says between gritted teeth. "You're going to wish you could take that back."

"Don't worry," I say bitterly. "I already wish I could take it all back."

With that, I turn on my heel and walk away.

CHAPTER 47
FENN

SINCE RJ IMPLEMENTED THE SILENT TREATMENT IN RETALIATION for my crimes, the vibe in our room has turned decidedly chilly. The guy has hardly peeled his ass from that desk chair in days. He takes every meal at the computer. I roll over in the middle of the night to the perpetual glow of his monitors. Clacking keys echoing in my dreams. He doesn't so much as grunt at the olive branches I keep extending. I brought him a slice of pie from dinner the other night— it's still sitting on a stack of textbooks at the foot of his bed. At this point, the lifeforms emerging toward sentience on the pie crust might talk to me before RJ does.

"How about we go a few rounds at the gym?" I offer during a pause in his ferocious typing. It's been constant for hours. Probably the manifesto they'll discover after they find my body hanging by a bedsheet out our bedroom window. "Full contact. You can give me your best shot."

Not even a flinch to the sound of my voice. I'm white noise. Deaf to my entire existence.

"Last chance…"

The typing resumes and I sigh, accepting there will be no break-throughs this weekend.

Already dressed for the gym, I decide to skip my workout for a walk instead. This place has a way of suffocating you. Living and going to class with the same degenerate assholes every day for months on end takes its toll. My sanity demands I find an occasional reprieve.

Me: Fancy taking the dogs for a walk? I could use some fresh air.

She texts back before I reach the bottom of the stairs.

Casey: Meet you in 10.

It was a brutal summer, but the deep orange aura of an autumn sun is mild in the late afternoon. I can finally get more than ten steps out of the A/C without my shoes filling with sweat. A slight breeze scatters the first fallen leaves of the season.

Penny and Bo sprint ahead of Casey when we converge on the trail that leads through the woods.

"They're energetic today," I say, trying not to look offended when the golden retrievers snub their noses at my outstretched hand.

While they're perfectly sweet dogs and tolerate most people fine, they've never been shy about their utter indifference to me. Casey's the only person who gets the privilege of their affection, and I think they like shoving my face in it.

"Sure, now. Then they'll be whining for me to carry them home."

"That'd be something to see."

"Sure." She laughs. "I'll just throw one on each hip like a nanny with twins."

I chuckle at the image. Of the two Tresscott sisters, Sloane got the athleticism and her dad's stature. Casey's petite by comparison. More delicate. But that doesn't mean fragile, which is something people tend to confuse. More so since the accident.

"You okay?"

The dogs bark until Casey kneels to offer them treats from a plastic baggy she pulls from her pocket. They body-slam each other to compete for ear scratches.

"Sure. Why?"

"You seem distracted." She narrows her eyes at me. "Does this have anything to do with why RJ broke up with Sloane?" Now her eyes widen. "Wait. Do you know the real reason he ended it? Because Sloane refuses to talk about it. She said he told her he wasn't feeling it anymore. Which, if it's true, is total bullshit. How can he just lose feelings for her out of nowhere? Talk about emotional immaturity."

I let her ramble for a moment to buy time searching for a diplomatic answer. The last thing I want to do is unpack this whole situation with Casey. It's bad enough that RJ is ignoring me, if not also secretly engineering some way to have our parents' marriage annulled.

"He doesn't exactly keep me apprised of his dating life," I reply. Which is mostly true. He wasn't a chatty guy even before he became non-verbal. "I don't know. I'm sure he'll come around." I shrug. "And I guess I am a little distracted. I've been thinking about my mom a lot lately."

Also, not a lie. Memories of her come and go, these patterns of nostalgia.

"It's the weirdest involuntary phantom pain," I admit. "I'll be sitting in class, and for no reason at all, I'll forget she died. And suddenly this immense relief will wash over me, like I'm waking up from a nightmare."

We walk along the path, watching the dogs jump at falling leaves and bark at things moving in the trees.

"That happens to me too sometimes." Casey picks a long weed and ties the stem in a series of tiny knots. "And then reality comes rushing back in, and I remember the nightmare is all there is now."

"You've been good for me," I find myself blurting out. "You

always manage to make me smile. Even when everything else is going to hell. At least when I'm with you, I feel better about myself."

The dogs run up around Casey's legs to nudge her for attention, which she lavishes on them while it occurs to me, I didn't mean to say any of that out loud. Now she probably thinks I'm a complete emotional train wreck. Excellent.

"Good." Casey takes a stick out of Penny's mouth and flings it down the path for the dogs to chase. "I think everyone needs someone to be that person. I'm glad I can be yours." She elbows my ribs, tipping her head to smile at me. "You're mine too. Person, I mean."

The dogs come galloping back to her. Both tugging at the stick to put it in Casey's hand.

"I don't know if I've said so in as many words," she continues. "Since, you know…"

Prom.

We all have our own uncomfortable buzzwords.

The Accident.

Big, heavy syllables that sit in our mouths like stones.

"You put me back together. I don't know where I'd be without your friendship." She urges me to meet her gaze. "I mean that. I cherish it. And you."

The dogs run ahead to chase the wind or some poor creature. A breeze curls Casey's strawberry-blonde hair around her face as she looks at me with these eyes that could melt glaciers. My gut gets the message before my brain does and it screams out at me that something's coming, dumbass.

You better duck.

"We've gotten so close so quickly, you know?" Casey pulls the hair from her face and shyly tucks it behind her ear. "It's weird how feelings can evolve out of nothing."

A siren goes off in the furthest recesses of my mind, getting closer.

"I feel silly saying this. So please don't laugh," she punctuates with a quiet laugh. "But lately when we're together, I can't help wondering why you don't kiss me."

It arrives as a question. Like what happens to us when we die and why are we here? This enormous, unknowable thing. Fucking hell. If she only knew how close I am to hauling her off her feet and never letting go.

For months I've punished myself with this silent desire. And yes, I occasionally entertained the unlikely idea that she might find her way to wanting me too. But then I roundly dismissed the thought.

Casey stares at me with those big, trusting eyes so full of warmth and hope. Completely naïve to all the ways I'd manage to ruin her.

"Okay…" Redness blooms across her cheeks and she drops her embarrassed gaze to the ground. "This got awkward."

This is my fault. I was careless. I should have taken greater care to maintain a buffer zone that would have prevented any confusion from bleeding through. But now I'm wrestling to put a stop to this, a ripple of panic traveling up my spine. No matter how badly I do want to kiss her, I can't.

Because the consequences would be destructive and irreversible. No survivors.

"Case," I start, then stop to clear my throat. "I want to be your friend. I just, ah, don't think of you *that* way."

"Really?" This time when she appraises me, I feel her suspicions slithering through her skull, picking up the debris of clues. "Because I feel like I've gotten to know you pretty well, and it really seemed like maybe you'd thought about it too."

"Sorry, kiddo."

God, I fucking hate myself.

"Well, now I know you're full of it." She's got the nerve to spin around and poke a playful finger in my chest.

"Casey."

"If you're worried about Sloane kicking your ass, we don't have to tell her."

I have done terrible things to this world. I will do terrible things again. But few will be as awful as what I'm compelled to do now.

"We hooked up," I say flatly. "Me and Sloane."

She cracks a disbelieving smirk.

My tone becomes firm. Unmoving. "I'm not kidding. I had sex with your sister."

All humor dissolves from her expression. I have to avert my eyes before the shame knocks me over.

"I'm sorry." I swallow hard, staring at my feet. "I want to be your friend, Casey. But I'm not interested in being your boyfriend."

Even when I tell the truth, I'm still a liar.

CHAPTER 48
SLOANE

IN WAR MOVIES, WHEN THE MAIN CHARACTERS MEET IN BASIC TRAIN-ing, there's always the one guy who catches the drill sergeant's attention. The recruit they're determined to crack and grind into powder to be poured into brass casings. For Sister Ana Louise, I am that recruit.

Wednesday after class, she does needlepoint at her desk with her severe glare admonishing me from across the room. Short of dousing me in holy water and taking scissors to my ponytail, she's once again invited me to join her in after-school detention.

"I can't believe you told a nun to eat your ass," Eliza whispers. She sits beside me in the last row of desks, filling in the blank flesh of her arm with a black ballpoint pet. The flesh-canvas artworks started about a week ago. They'd made her stop wearing combat boots to school, so Eliza mounted a counterprotest. Any day now I suspect we'll be attending an assembly to witness the sisters scrub her skin bare with steel wool.

"Technically, I was talking to Nikki. The sister got caught in the crossfire."

Sister Ana Louise smacks a ruler on her desk to shush the room.

"Either way." Eliza winks at me, revealing a pot leaf drawn on her eyelid. "You showed impressive gusto."

"I'm missing track practice for this," I grumble.

But I guess that's par for the course. I woke up this morning with not a fuck to give and went into the red from there. I've been drawing from a negative balance of fucks all day. Up to my eyeballs in fuck-giving overdraft charges.

That's what happens when you're completely numb inside.

"Your sunny mood have anything to do with hacker boy? You two get back together yet?"

"No," I say weakly. "He's ignoring all my texts." I pause, a jolt of pain stinging my heart. "Actually, that's not true. He responded to one of them."

"What did he say?"

My tone is flat. "*Unsubscribe.*"

Eliza's jaw drops. "Harsh."

Oh yeah. Harsh enough to reduce me to tears, although I luckily got the text in the middle of watching some nature documentary with Casey and our father, so I was able to pretend I was weeping for a poor injured gazelle and not because the guy I love wants nothing to do with me. Then again, I don't think Dad and Casey even noticed my wet eyes. Casey's been acting weird the past few days. Quieter, more subdued. Dad thinks it's the nightmares again, which means he's been extra attentive toward her. Which means I'm once again an afterthought.

And while I know I should be following his lead and tending to my sister to figure out what's wrong, I've been an emotional wreck since RJ ended things.

I should've never let Fenn convince me to support his lies. I hadn't told RJ about the hookup because he didn't need to know all the gory details of my hookup past. But once he asked Fenn that question, all bets were off. I should've just told Fenn to man up. Should've pulled out my phone, called RJ, and told him the truth right then. He probably would've still been pissed at Fenn for telling that initial lie. But at least he and I would be good.

And I wouldn't feel like someone scraped my heart with a dull blade dipped in battery acid.

"I don't know how many more times I can apologize," I mumble, as my eyes start stinging again. God, if I cry in detention, Eliza will never let me hear the end of it.

"Hey." She grabs my arm and scratches DESTROY MAN into my forearm in bold black letters. "If he doesn't know what he's lost, he didn't deserve it in the first place."

Sure. She's right. It's what a good friend tells you. Even when it doesn't help. Because the damage is done and the heartache won't pass for days, like food poisoning that needs to get a lot worse before it gets better. There's that hour or two in the middle of the night when you think it's all out of your system. Then you're doubled over in agony, swearing to any god that will listen to just make it end.

I honestly didn't think losing RJ would hurt this much. Who saw that one coming.

All I want to do when I get home from school is throw on some loud music and sulk in my room, so of course my dad is waiting for me in the kitchen with a perturbed look on his face.

"What?" I say, dropping my bag on the dining table.

"You know I don't like that."

I muffle a sigh. "Can we not tonight? I've got homework."

"No, I think we will, Sloane." He nods toward a chair to tell me sit. All evidence suggests this will be an especially unfun conversation.

"Want to tell me why I watched Casey pull up in an Uber?"

I lean back in my chair, annoyed with the question because it's clearly a pointless one. "I'm going to assume you already know the answer to that."

"St. Vincent's called to inform me you've been given detention several times recently."

"Is that a question?"

"Let's try to dial back the attitude." Unmoved by my clear

indication I'm being involved in this under duress, he reaches for his cup of tea. "What's going on, Sloane? It isn't like you to act out in class."

"How would you know what I'm like?" I demand, laughing darkly. "When's the last time you asked me anything about myself?"

The last reinforcement of my patience snaps. Like the hairline fracture in a bridge support that endures years of relentless traffic, weather, and neglect until it dumps the morning commuters into the ravine.

"You suddenly decide to show up to parenting and start taking an interest in my life like I haven't already become a whole functioning person with minimal involvement from you?"

Teacup still hovering in one hand, Dad is visibly stunned by the outburst. "Where is this coming from?"

"I've got a better question. When's the last time you asked me how I like school? Or if I've made any new friends? Would it surprise you if the answer was never?"

"Sloane—"

"No, you dragged me in here, Dad." I'm hyperaware of the heat soaking into my pores. My ears burning red. Years of neglect and resentment springing up from a deep well of some serious father-daughter shit that's been a long time coming. "You've always made it obvious my feelings don't matter in the house. I'm expected to shut up and play my part. Be the strong one who never asks for help or lets the mask slip because God forbid I not shoulder the burden of everyone else's needs at all times."

His eyes widen. "I've never asked you to—"

"Seriously? 'Sloane, Casey is your responsibility. You're her big sister.' Which is fine. I want to be there for her. Of course. But what's your job in all of this? Who's responsible for me?" I'm mortified to hear my voice crack. "Sure, sometimes you play the part. You act all protective and scare away my boyfriends as if you're actually concerned about my virtue when you're probably just terrified one of those rich boys will knock me up and then you'll lose your job, am I right?"

His jaw falls open. "That's not—"

"But what about my feelings?" I interrupt. "When do those get to count?"

"If you'd come to me," he starts, all furrowed brow and clasped hands.

"I'm not one of your students. I'm not making an appointment to get my father's attention."

"Maybe I've been preoccupied," he admits in what feels like an attempt to placate me, but it still doesn't sound like he gets it. At all. "That doesn't mean I'm not interested. You've always preferred to have your space. Communication is a two-way street."

Right. Of course he'd find a way to make this my fault. Couldn't possibly be a deficiency on his part. No, *I'm* the one who wasn't sufficiently forthcoming.

I stumble to my feet.

"Where are you going? We're not done talking, Sloane."

I sling my bag over my shoulder. If I have to sit here another minute, I'm going to throw something. "Here's an update for you, Dad: I was dating RJ Shaw behind your back. I really liked him. But now we're broken up, and instead of being allowed to be sad and dig into a pint of ice cream, you expect me to put on a smile and pretend nothing's wrong. Well, I'm sick of it. Consider this me clocking out. I'm done."

"I had no idea you felt this way." On a deep breath he clears his throat. "You're right, perhaps. I've always been confident in your ability to take care of yourself. That you didn't need me."

I stare at him, allowing years of resentment to show on my face.

"A girl always needs her father," I say before walking away.

In my bedroom I slam the door behind me. I toss myself on my bed and pull at a pillow until I hear the seams begin to tear and my fingers go numb. Then I bury my face in the stretched fabric and sob.

Confession is supposed to be good for the soul, but mine's shot full of holes. No part of letting my dad see me break felt like catharsis. And every time I look at my phone to see a message from RJ isn't there, I curse myself for giving a shit. I knew better than to fall for the stranger in the woods.

How many times do I have to learn nothing good comes from opening my heart until I'm convinced it'll only bite me in the ass?

"Sloane?" There's a tentative knock on the door. My sister.

"Go away." My voice is muffled against the pillow.

"No. I'm coming in."

Without waiting for an argument, Casey marches inside, pausing only to close the door behind her. Then she's on the bed beside me, pulling my face out of my pillow. "Hey," she says softly. "Are you okay?"

A hysterical laugh bubbles out. "Not in the slightest."

"I guess it was mostly a rhetorical question."

I lift my head to find her lips twitching with humor. I almost laugh back, genuinely this time, until I remember why I'm crying in the first place. Why RJ can't stand me.

Casey must see something in my eyes because her forehead creases warily. "What?"

I exhale a slow, measured breath. "I slept with Fenn in junior year."

There's a beat of silence.

Then she shrugs. "I know. He told me."

Sheer outrage slams me up into a sitting position. "He *told* you?" I growl. "Seriously? He made a huge fucking deal about keeping it from you and RJ—which is why I goddamn lost RJ in the first place!—and now he's going around talking about it? When did he tell you?"

"This past Sunday."

I frown at her. "You've known for three days and didn't say anything to me? Why?"

"I was waiting for you to tell me," Casey answers. Another shrug. "I figured we'd talk about it when you were ready."

"There's nothing to talk about," I admit, shame sticking to my throat. "It happened one time. We were both drunk. And it was long before you and Fenn ever exchanged a single word."

"I know. That's why I'm not bothered."

"I'm sorry I didn't tell you," I say. "Honestly, I didn't say anything after it happened because I knew you'd make fun of me for it. But I should've said something after you two got close."

"So that's the real reason RJ ended things, huh?"

"Yeah. He overheard me and Fenn deciding to hide it from him."

"And I assume all those long paragraphs you've been texting is you apologizing?"

I nod bleakly. "He just ignores them."

"He'll come around."

Hope ripples through me. "Do you really believe that?"

"Of course."

Her confidence triggers a weird rush of emotion. To my dismay, the tears well up again, and I have to blink rapidly to stop them from spilling over.

"It'll all work out in the end, Sloane. It always does." Casey scoots closer and reaches for both my hands, which feel cold and clammy. Hers are warm, and she wastes no time clasping them around mine.

I rest my head on her shoulder. "You don't have to comfort me," I mumble. "It's weird that you're comforting me."

"How is it weird? I'm your sister." I can hear the smile in her voice.

"Yeah, but I'm the one who—" I stop.

"You're the one who's supposed to comfort me?" she finishes knowingly. "Yeah. I know. I overheard some of your conversation with Dad. How you feel like you have to carry all the burdens—"

"You're not a burden," I interrupt. "Let's be clear about that. You are never a burden, Case."

"No, I know. But let's not pretend you haven't spent our whole lives serving as my champion. Don't get me wrong, I appreciate it. I really do. But you don't need to baby me. I'm stronger than I look."

I lift my head and see the fortitude shining in her eyes. "I know you are."

"Do you?" Casey prompts, lifting a brow.

"I do." I bite my lip. "Or at least I used to know that. I guess after the accident I kind of forgot. I was so caught up in my own guilt about letting that happen to you—"

"You didn't let it happen," she interjects, her jaw falling open. "Do you actually believe any of it was your fault?"

"Yes," I say simply. "Because I was responsible for you that night. I know it, and Dad knows it. He blames me too."

"Of course he doesn't blame you."

"Case. I know you mean well. But trust me when I say this— Dad will never forgive me for almost letting you die."

Casey heaves a long, heavy breath. "I don't believe that at all. But that's for you two to figure out." She squeezes my hands. "I don't blame you one bit, for what it's worth. And I mean it, I don't need you to be my protector all the time. Sometimes you're allowed to just be my sister."

A smile touches my lips. "I can do that."

"Good."

"But." I shoot her a look. "I'm not going to stop the verbal beatdowns against Nikki Taysom if she talks shit about you."

"Well, obviously." Casey snorts out loud. "You're Sloane Tresscott. You're going to cut a bitch. You can't not."

"I can't not," I agree solemnly. And then we both start giggling, and for one blessed moment in time, I'm able to forget about my broken, mangled heart.

CHAPTER 49
LAWSON

THE BRIEF WINDOW OF TIME THAT EXISTS BETWEEN THE MOMENT I enter Mr. Goodwyn's class and the next student's arrival has become some of my favorite eight minutes of the day. I feel him waiting for me before I've walked into the room. His hunger and anticipation. The relief when he sees I haven't gotten bored of him yet. Because as much as he wants to hate himself for what we do, he won't let himself stop. Jack's too afraid to admit his conscience is unbothered. Out loud he says otherwise, pretending it's wrong, it can't happen again, it's bad, as if someone's keeping score of all the times he's had my dick in his mouth while promising it was the last time.

His wife does the same thing. Not just the taking my dick in her mouth part, although I'm not complaining about Gwen's skills. Yesterday after art class, for example, was one for the blowjob books. But, like Jack, she's constantly telling me how wrong it is, how we can't, even while her tongue is in my mouth and I've got my fingers inside her.

They're my favorite couple, these two.

"I hope you've done the reading." Jack holds a flimsy paperback in one hand while he writes quotations and page numbers on the board. "I'd prefer it if your participation in class discussion stays on the topic today. We have a lot to cover."

"I might have skimmed it." I toss my bag down at my seat and come around to admire the solid wood desk at the front of the room. It's replaced the seventies-style dented metal hunk that used to sit in its place. "New desk, huh? Looks sturdy."

"Apparently, my petitions have been getting through to the administration after all." He turns around and coyly slips past me to pull his attendance notebook and stacks of homework assignments out of his bag.

"We could break it in," I drawl.

Jack turns to lean on the corner of the desk with an impatient glare. "Take your seat. Your classmates will walk in any—"

"How hot would it be…" I push his legs open to stand between them and run my hands up his thighs. There's a narrow window beside the door that at any moment could send buckshot through his entire life if anyone passing by cared to look. "If I was sucking you off right here for everyone to see when they walked in."

"Lawson." My name is a whispered groan. He grabs my wrists but doesn't push me away. Instead, he slides his hands up my arms to squeeze my biceps. "Not all of us have your endless desire for self-destruction."

"Where's your imagination, professor?"

"Firmly seated in the reality that you're still my student. So take a seat."

I grin at him and return to my desk to sit down. I keep my legs splayed open so he can see the erection pressing against my zipper.

His throat dips as he swallows. Oh, he sees it.

Jack dumps himself into his chair behind the desk, which tells me he's suffering from a similar affliction.

I lick my lips. "How hard are you right now?"

There's a long beat. Then he locks his gaze to mine. "As a fucking rock."

A laugh tickles my throat. "Good. Put your hand on it. Just for a second."

My gaze tracks the downward motion of his arm. The desk

hides his lower body, but I don't miss the way he trembles when he does what I ask.

"Squeeze," I tell him.

His arm moves, almost imperceptibly. He lets out a soft groan. Then a loud one, as he yanks his arm up and fixes me with a dark scowl. "Enough, Lawson. This really can't continue."

"Right. Of course not. You're a happily married man with a lovely wife whom I'm sure adores you. So naturally my involvement in that equation would be completely unneeded."

"Your tactless sarcasm aside, lately I've had a suspicion she might be cheating on me," he says with a grimace.

He says this without the slightest hint of irony. Unfortunately, we don't get to further explore his concerns of the mysterious other man when others loudly clatter into the room.

I'd almost muster some sympathy for the poor, handsome fool if his wounds weren't so pathetically self-inflicted. The man has a voracious sexual creature at home desperate to please him in all the ways he could imagine, if only he'd dislodge his head from his ass. Not that I'm complaining or anything. If Gwen and Jack want to exercise their carnal frustrations with me, I'm happy to oblige. For as long as it takes for these two to compare notes, at least.

RJ is among the last to enter the classroom, and I quickly get up and toss myself into the seat beside him just as his last option to escape is taken. Last few classes he'd been faster and managed to avoid sitting with me. Today I'm a ninja.

"What?" he says, already in one of his typically amiable moods.

"Well, I'm honored to warrant a verbal response."

"And I already regret it."

I chuckle. "Just out of curiosity, how much longer do you expect to employ the silent treatment on Fenn like some petulant child?"

"Piss off."

"Mr. Shaw. Page ninety-two." Jack then casts his gaze toward me. "I'm sure Mr. Kent can find our page as well."

We both dutifully open our books to appease him while he engages in a lecture about some bullshit that could be swimming around somewhere in my head between the brandy and Vicodin.

"Regardless of your little family falling-out," I whisper to RJ, "Duke will still be waiting for you this weekend. You intend to follow through with the fight?"

"Yep." He slouches in his seat, pretending to read. "And I'm planning on losing. Leave this place and never see any of you assholes again."

If my eyes could roll out of my head, they'd be spinning down the aisle between our feet. It seems RJ's not yet entered his cooling-off period since the blowup with Fenn. I'd admire his stamina if it weren't so exhausting to watch this tantrum persist for another week.

"Brilliant," I tell him. "Truly masterful strategy."

"Eat shit, Lawson."

"Honestly, grow up. You can't take everything personally. So his dick slipped and landed in your girlfriend once upon a time. Oh well."

We've never been especially close, me and RJ. But as teammates and a foursome, I do believe we're something akin to friends. And since Silas has been uncharacteristically moody lately, I suppose it falls to me to make RJ see reason.

"How many people will the average person know in their lifetime? A few thousand? Even less we'll consider friends. Some of those orifices are bound to have interacted."

RJ's attention remains defiantly aimed at Jack pacing the front of the room on one of his emphatic literary tangents.

"You're in your feelings now," I tell him, leaning across the aisle between us. "But come on. You don't actually intend to leave Sandover. You know you love it here. And having a brother. You'd miss us. I mean, shit, do you really want to say goodbye to all this?"

He shrugs in response, a thoroughly dispassionate gesture. "I've been alone before. And I'm used to saying goodbye."

I shake my head at him and settle back in my seat. Well, I tried. Anything he does now is on him.

CHAPTER 50
RJ

A LITTLE RESEARCH PROVES MY HUNCH CORRECT. THE SECURITY company responsible for Ballard Academy's surveillance system maintains an automatic backup redundancy for every feed of every client worldwide. The feeds go to a third-party cloud service and are then encrypted and randomized for an additional layer of protection. Which means the first thing I had to do was figure out which sub-folder contained the Ballard feeds. After that, I discovered twelve months of footage from more than two dozen cameras. That meant writing a decryption to let me see the dates and positions, then running another script on the data to eliminate everything but the boathouse on the night of the accident.

Again my instinct was correct. Though the video system on campus was undergoing upgrade maintenance and not downloading to the home server on campus, the cameras that were operational did back up to the cloud. Call it laziness or ignorance, but it seems the local police department didn't bother to ask.

Luckily, I'm more thorough.

I've got a couple of other side projects running as well. One of them, a piece of spyware I wrote to track down Duke's hidden bank account, pings while I'm watching my script populate the video feeds. But it seems like a moot point now. It's Saturday afternoon and I'm hours away from walking into the greenhouse to let Duke get enough good licks in that I can call it a loss and get the hell out of there.

I guess that means there isn't much purpose in tracking down this boathouse footage either. Except regardless of Sloane, Fenn, or anyone else, Casey deserves an answer. If I can give that to her, maybe this whole experience will have served a better purpose.

I grab a Red Bull from the mini fridge just as footage begins downloading. It's a huge file and there's nothing to do now but wait. And waiting is a bad thing, because it gives me time to let my mind wander. And when my mind wanders, it always returns to Sloane and the look on her face when I left her standing in the woods. She tried calling a dozen times that night. And when I didn't answer, she started texting. One apology after the other. Some long, some short, all expressing her regret and begging me to talk to her, to forgive her, to meet her at our spot.

It took a lot of willpower to ignore her messages. I slipped up only once, sending a shitty response that I've since come to regret, but maybe it's good I went nuclear. It succeeded in making her stop. It's been twenty-four hours since her last message, and I suspect she won't reach out again. The notion sends a bolt of agony to my heart, even though I know it's for the best.

Days later now, I still miss her. As much as I try to find solace in my anger, I can't shake the part of me that wishes I never found out about her and Fenn. That I could forget everything that's happened since and return to blissful ignorance.

When Lawson was harassing me about it in class, he was under the impression that I cared about the sex. Except that's not it. Sure, I experienced a jolt of white-hot jealousy when I realized my girlfriend and stepbrother had seen each other naked, but that was nothing compared to what I felt when I heard them deciding to lie to me about it. It was a cross between unadulterated anger, cringing embarrassment, and a weird sense of worthlessness I'd never felt in my entire life. Like I didn't matter enough, to either of them. Like I didn't deserve their honesty.

Still, I shouldn't have lashed out at Sloane the way I did. I could have said a simple goodbye and left it at that. Truth be told, I didn't know I had it in me to care enough to be hurt so badly. Which reinforces my original instinct: there's no upside when feelings are involved. Casual hookups protect everyone. Clean and simple.

Okay, enough. My head's a mess and I can't sit here listening to myself think anymore. Putting my screens to sleep so nosy eyes won't see what I'm doing, I leave the dorm to go for a walk. Maybe the fresh air will help clear out the noise and congestion that's got my head feeling like a soda can full of rocks.

The slightest hint of a chill carries in the breeze. For days now, the weather's threatened to turn toward cooler temperatures, which feels like a cruel tease after we've spent the summer and part of the fall up Satan's asshole. At this point I'd cut off a toe to see it drop below eighty degrees.

I'm planning to head for one of the walking trails that skirts the eastern property line of campus when a couple of rambunctious golden retrievers come barreling toward me. A brief and startling panic swarms through me, expecting Sloane to emerge. Instead, Casey jogs up to quiet the dogs.

"Sorry about that," she says breathlessly. "They get a little overexcited."

I don't how much Sloane might have told her sister, but Casey offers me a warm smile without a hint of resentment.

"What are you doing out here?" I ask, still on guard. Part of me expects Sloane to sneak up behind me and sucker punch me in the nuts.

"I sort of live here, you know."

"Oh yeah. Me too."

It's awkward as hell. We've never had a proper conversation

before, and it's brutally painful making nice when I figure Sloane's been cursing my name all week.

"So…" Casey tosses a tennis ball for the dogs, which sends them sprinting after it. She's got a pretty good throw on her. "Care to explain yourself?"

Yep. Sloane's been talking to her, all right. How much she told her is a whole other story.

"My sister's been moping around the house all week because you refuse to hear her out. Not cool, RJ. Not nice."

Christ. Even in her soft, sweet voice, Casey's got some fire in her.

I release a rueful breath. "I don't know that it's the best idea for the two of us to be having this conversation."

"Why? Because her and Fenn had sex?"

My mouth falls open. Well, I didn't see that coming.

"Who told you that?" I ask, narrowing my eyes.

"Fenn. A few days ago."

That throws me for a loop. It's been a poorly guarded secret for a while now that Fenn's got a self-deluding crush on her. Actually, he's pretty fucking obsessed. Why he hasn't made a move or moved on, I couldn't say. But it seems like the last thing he'd want is to drop an anvil on the potential for them ever getting together. Maybe guilt finally won out? I don't know if that makes him slightly less of a bastard that he'd lie to his brother but not Casey. Judges are still out on that scoring system.

"Either way, this is a strange conversation to be having with Sloane's little sister," I finally answer, shoving my hands in my pockets.

"Or," she says with a daring grin, "I'm exactly the person you should have come to in the first place."

We start walking together. Not saying much at first. I let the dogs distract me when one of them puts the ball in my hand to throw it. With each return, they egg me to chuck it farther. Whatever it is about Casey's presence, she has a calming effect on me. Call it good energy. Or maybe I'm reaching, searching for any excuse to feel a connection that's at least Sloane-adjacent. Tricking myself into believing decaf coffee will settle the craving.

"I'm a good listener," she coaxes, telling me in not so many words she can sense the word vomit backing up in my throat like bile. "If there's anything you want to get off your chest."

She must have cast some clever spell on me because it works. Before I can stop myself, a veritable buffet of my repressed bullshit spills out. I'd be embarrassed if I could stop myself long enough to feel anything.

I tell her about all the schools I'd been kicked out of. I tell her about my mom always moving us around, more boyfriends sneaking out of her bedroom in the morning than she had pairs of shoes. All of them out of the picture before they'd even learned my name.

"It taught me to expect people to leave," I say roughly. "So why bother getting invested, right? Only this time I let myself forget what happens when you let someone get close enough to form attachments."

"You still like her," Casey says quietly.

"Lot of difference it makes now."

"Seems like it makes all the difference."

Except she wasn't there. She didn't hear the way I shut Sloane down and threw everything we'd worked on in her face. It was callous even by my standards.

"I'm pissed they lied," I say with a sigh. "I was totally blindsided, and I feel...I don't know. Stupid, I guess."

Casey wrinkles her forehead. "In what way?"

"Like..." I pause, searching for the words. "I'm the one who always knows everyone's secrets. Information is power, you know? It gives you all the control. But this was one fucking secret I couldn't hack. And it's this big glaring reminder that I'm not in control of a damn thing."

"Control is just an illusion, RJ." Her expression softens. "But

I get it. It's not just the lying that hurt you. It makes sense when you really think about it. You find out people's secrets so you can be prepared going into any situation, right? So you have something you can hurt people with if you need to. And this whole situation showed you there's secrets out there with the power to hurt *you*."

I frown at her. "It annoys me that you're so perceptive."

Casey breaks out in a grin. "Sorry. I like analyzing people."

"Clearly." I purse my lips. "All right, what else? What's the rest of the analysis?"

"Of you? I think that's it. But here's something you should know about my sister." Casey's tone becomes serious. "Sloane hates apologizing when she's wrong. Half the time, she refuses to even admit she's wrong. So it took a lot for her to send you all those messages."

My good humor fades. "Maybe. But that doesn't excuse that she planned to lie to me."

"Of course not. But for what it's worth, we don't know if she would've gone through with the lie, anyway. Maybe she would've changed her mind and told you. Either way, groveling doesn't come easy for her. She knows she made a mistake and she's spent days trying to talk to you. The least you can do is listen." Casey gives me a pointed look. "You know, the way she listened to you after *you* messed up?"

"It's not the same."

"Isn't it?"

"No. I just…" I grumble in frustration. "I'm still so pissed. And jealous. Doesn't matter that I know how pointless that is. I can't help it."

"It's pointless, yeah, but understandable. The question is whether you see any way past it. Are those feelings more important than the people?"

That one simple question is like a punch to the gut. She's right. Is my anger and jealousy and embarrassment more important to me than Sloane? Those emotions will pass and I'll be glad to be rid of them. But the people...do I actually want to be rid of the only girl I've ever fallen for?

Damn. Casey's more mature than I think Sloane gives her credit for, but I guess Sloane can't help seeing her baby sister as someone she has to coddle. Not that anyone could blame her after what they've been through together.

"We should've gotten to know each other better," I tell Casey. "You're a cool chick."

"Obviously." She flashes a cocky smile that is eerily reminiscent of her sister. "And look, I'm not about to tell you Fenn can do no wrong. He's got plenty of screwups to answer for. But he's not a bad guy. Even if he doesn't always believe that."

"Yeah, well, I appreciate the—"

"Before you blow me off..." We stop under a tree, where the dogs plop down in the dirt to take water from a bottle Casey pours out for them. "Fenn's felt alone for a long time. I know what it means when your mom dies and your whole family falls apart. He's been lost, and then you came around and he really fell in love with the idea of having a brother. He wanted so badly for you to become friends. It's meant everything to him."

This girl knows how to lay it on thick. The way she describes Fenn, I feel like I kicked a puppy.

If I'm honest, I do get where he's coming from. I never thought I was missing out not having any family to speak of beyond my mom. I wasn't lonely in the slightest. Figured that was a character weakness I'd taught myself to overcome. Then he smothered me with friendship and a little of it rubbed off. More than I've been willing to admit to myself.

"Just give it some thought. You can't forgive one without the other," she points out with a tiny smirk.

"Who says I'm forgiving either of them?" I challenge.

"Come on, RJ. At least give them another chance to apologize. Especially my sister. She has real feelings for you, and that's huge.

I don't know what she tells you, but I've never seen her be all giddy about a guy. She doesn't do the cutesy hearts and butterflies stuff."

That makes me smile. Yeah. Sloane's always been a tough one to read. Playing her cards close because God forbid anyone get a hint of genuine emotion out of her. A team of archaeologists could excavate miles of sarcasm and never hit bedrock.

"I don't think either of us were pretending," I admit.

"So then, you know she cares." Casey shrugs. "We don't know each other, I get that. So I can't give you many reasons to listen to me. Except for this: if any part of you would rather be talking to her right now, you should be. That feeling's only going to get stronger. Don't let it be too late when it does."

I swallow the lump in my throat. Everything she'd just said, a voice had already been shouting in my head for days. Telling me to call her. To swallow my pride and accept her apology. To offer an apology in return for the way I'd spoken to her.

I'd spent as many hours convincing myself that apologizing meant admitting defeat. But who the hell cares about defeat if I'm the only one in the fight? What's the use in being right and alone? Like, good job, you showed them, sitting by yourself in the dark while everyone else has moved on with their lives. What's more pitiful than being the last one who even remembers what the feud was about?

I lean in and give Casey a kiss on the cheek, which she bashfully accepts with a laugh. "You're a good person," I tell her sincerely. "Do yourself a favor and stay far away from assholes like me."

"If you're wondering," she says over her shoulder as the dogs coax her home, "Sloane's on the track."

CHAPTER 51
SLOANE

IN NEARLY ALL OTHER ASPECTS OF MY LIFE, REPETITION GIVES ME a migraine. I never had the patience for piano lessons or French class. I grind my teeth when Dad wants to subject us to the same Christmas movies we've endured countless times.

Except running. On the track, the endless loops are like meditation. White noise. The way babies fall asleep in a car. When I run, I set my brain to autopilot and practically fall asleep to the gentle repetition of my shoes slapping the rubberized surface.

So there's no telling how long he's been there when I pull up on my final lap at the sight of a mirage waiting on the bleachers. I'm not out of breath until I stop running. Then it's like my lungs are collapsing, and I can't get a clear answer from my brain whether I should entertain this intrusion or ignore him entirely.

Curiosity wins out.

"What are you doing here?" I ask RJ, forcing myself not to get my hopes up. For all I know, he's here to yell at me again.

"There's one thing I need to know," RJ says with his elbows propped on his knees. "Did you use protection?"

"Are you fucking kidding me?" I'm already starting to walk away.

"I am, yeah." He smiles to himself. "I needed an icebreaker and that's the best I could come up with on the walk over here."

"You know, you're not a tenth as funny as you think you are."

His lips are still twitching. "Even so. Still pretty funny."

Insufferable, more like it. But I can't deny my pulse is racing at the sight of him.

"If that's all…"

"No, it isn't. Hey." He hops down the bleachers, chasing me down the length of the fence. "Your sister basically cornered me and said I better come talk to you or else. She had a brute squad with her. And some guy with an eye patch? It was intense."

Casey. Of course. My sister can never leave well enough alone.

I cross my arms and pin him with an icy look. "Get on with it, then. Talk. Or are you still unsubscribed?"

He has the decency to appear repentant. "Yeah…that text might have been out of line."

"You think?" My chest tightens painfully. "I poured my heart out to you in my last message. And you responded with fucking 'unsubscribe.' That hurt."

"I know. I'm sorry." He leans against the fence and runs a hand through his hair. "I regretted it the moment I sent it, if that helps."

"It doesn't, no." I'm having a hard time tearing my gaze off him. It's unfair. How the way he smells reminds me of being in bed together. Or the way I love the shade of his eyes in the sunlight.

"I should probably have come up with a better explanation by now, but I was just an asshole. Not only for the text, but the way I blew up at you in the woods. This is all new territory for me," he says gruffly. "I didn't know how to handle these feelings and I snapped. I said awful things to you that I didn't mean. And it wasn't about the sex, not really. It was the lying. That's the part that hurt. The jealousy and outrage and whatever else, it was mostly a cover for what I was really feeling. Hearing you guys decide to lie to me triggered this wave of hurt I didn't expect."

My heart clenches. Because he's right. It *was* hurtful. I know if

I'd walked up and heard the two people I was closest to make a pact to keep me in the dark about something, I probably wouldn't have reacted much differently.

"I know, and that's why I've been sending you essay-length apologies for days," I say ruefully. "And for what it's worth, it didn't sit right with me at all. I didn't want to lie. But Fenn had already panicked and told you it never happened, so I kind of got put in a corner. I'm not trying to make excuses, though."

"I know. I get it." RJ shakes his head. "I shouldn't have lost my temper like that."

"No," I agree. "But I get it too."

"That conversation might have gone differently if I hadn't let my pride get in the way," he finishes, shrugging wryly.

As much as his words from that day still sting, I do know where he's coming from. Neither of us is overly experienced in functional relationships. Our emotions tend to sneak up on us. We spend so much time fighting them, it comes as a real shock to the system when they burst forward. Like him, I've succumbed to my worst impulses a time or two.

"We have that in common." There's almost nothing worse than showing weakness, especially to someone with the power to hurt you. It becomes a weapon. Which puts us on the defensive. "I blew up at my dad the other day."

RJ raises his eyebrows at me.

"It didn't go well."

"You okay?"

"I don't know."

Truthfully, I haven't felt like myself in a while, so I'm not sure I remember what the baseline looks like anymore. What to compare myself to. This year has been one massive upheaval after another, and it's left me completely scrambled.

"Listen, I can't promise not to screw up again," RJ says. "We know I'm prone to bouts of idiocy. But I can promise not to screw up the same way twice. I won't let my jealousy and insecurities get in the way again. You have my word."

He takes my hand to entwine our fingers, rubbing soft circles against my skin with his thumb. It's a mesmerizing sensation that reminds me how much I miss touching him.

"I still don't think I understand how much I care about you. It surprises me on a daily basis." His features soften. "This isn't anything I've had with someone before and, so far, I'm doing a shit job of handling it. I just need you to understand it's because I'm an emotionally stunted moron and not because I'm not madly in love with you. You're the best thing that's happened to me in years."

I eye him in amusement. "Madly in love with me, huh?"

"I mean. Maybe a little." One corner of his mouth quirks up bashfully, and it's so adorable I can hardly stand it. "Is that something you can get on board with?"

It's impossible to control my pulse. It kicks off in a gallop, making my knees feel weak.

Can I get on board with RJ loving me?

With loving him back?

When I don't answer right away, RJ continues. "I know you think you have to be strong for everyone else, that nobody has your back, but that's not true, Sloane. Your sister's got your back. I do. You've got people in your life who love you. And you don't have to go it alone all the time. If you'll let me, I'd be proud to be by your side."

As I meet his earnest gaze, I remember what's it like when we spend hours talking. How he's the only person who's ever understood me. The only person who seems to really *see* me, who recognizes I struggle sometimes and lets me lean on him. It's this innate frequency we both share. I feel it now and it's like returning to my own bed. Familiar and perfect. I'd know it in the dark.

That's got to count.

I bite my lip to stop the smile threatening to consume my entire face. "I think I can get on board with that."

"Yeah?" His voice is husky. "You sure?"

"Uh-huh." I put on a casual tone. "And maybe I feel the same way." When his smile widens, I narrow my eyes in warning. "Just a little, though."

"Of course." Without another word, RJ grabs my waist and hauls me over the fence to plant a relieved kiss on my sweat-salted lips.

For the first time in days, everything feels right.

CHAPTER 52
RJ

I'VE JUST SAT DOWN TO SCAN THROUGH THE BOATHOUSE FOOTAGE when Fenn returns from his workout. He's gotten used to me ignoring him and doesn't say anything as he grabs a water from the mini fridge and shoves his gym bag in the corner beside his closet. From my peripheral vision I watch him bang around for a couple of minutes until he notices the plastic bag on his bed.

"Where'd this come from?" he says, pulling out a takeout container of wings and onion rings with some of that god-awful bar sauce he loves so much.

"I sent a sophomore into town for it."

"You got me wings?" Forehead creased, he takes the box to the coffee table and digs in.

The guy's always going on about the damn wings, but they don't deliver and he's usually too lazy to go into town himself unless it's to stay long enough to get wasted.

"Call it a peace offering."

"I'm listening."

I swivel around in my chair, meeting his eyes. "I've decided that maybe I overreacted. And given everything, I understand why you didn't want to tell me about you and Sloane."

"I admit I didn't handle it the best," he says, licking his fingers. "I'm sorry I lied."

"Well, you know. I forgive you or whatever."

Fenn smiles around a drumstick. Dude's entire face is already covered in that wing sauce. He possesses little kid levels of enthusiasm when it comes to these wings. "This mean we're good?"

"Yeah, we're good."

"Should we hug it out?"

"Nah." I grin to myself. "This took a lot less time than my talk with Sloane."

"Girls are long-winded," Fenn says solemnly. "They need too many reassurances."

"Right?"

"Guys know how to do it. Keep it short, you know? Maximize all the cool shit you can be doing instead of dragging it out."

I nod seriously. "Maybe Lawson has the right idea about swinging both ways."

Fenn busts out laughing. "I'm telling him you said that. Dude. You know what Silas told me the other day? Lawson's banging two teachers. Two! I can't even get my dick in one."

"Damn," I remark. "Can't wait to see how that turns out."

"Wait." Fenn arches a brow at me. "Does that mean you want to stick around? You're not going to throw the fight with Duke?" At my startled expression, he glowers at me. "Yeah. I heard about that one too. Lawson said you were ready to lose just to get out of here."

"I was," I admit.

"And now?" my stepbrother pushes. "You're ready to face Duke?"

"As I'll ever be."

There's a better-than-zero chance Duke is going kick my ass That nothing I did or could have done over the past month t prepare ever would have made a difference. This is a guy who ge off on inflicting pain and has his entire personality wrapped up being the meanest dog in the junkyard. I can't compete with t'

But I'm not about to hide from him either. I picked this fight. And I'm going to try to win it.

Even if it kills me.

———

A couple hours after Roger nods off to the History Channel, Fenn and I get ready to slip out of the dorm. I do one last thing on the computer before we head out.

"Stop messing with that and let's go," he says from the doorway. "What is it?"

"Yeah, I'm coming. Don't worry about it."

There's a distinct chill in the air tonight, an almost ominous turn in the weather. The night feels darker than usual as we cross campus and wade into the black forest. Sloane texts as we're walking, my screen lighting up the darkness.

Sloane: You sure you don't want me there?

I type a response as I walk.

Me: Nah, you're too delicate. The blood will make you squeamish.

She responds with a dozen laughing emojis. Yeah. My girl is no 'gile flower and we both know it. But it's still fun to tease her.

'oane: Good luck. If you don't win, I'm kicking your ass.

\ at the phone, and Fenn smacks me on the arm. "Focus," he
     n't have you tripping over a rock or something and taking
         of the equation."

          them but hear the whispers and footsteps stalking our
          campus descends on the dilapidated glass building

overgrown with weeds and drowning with fallen leaves. The walls are dripping with condensation from the bodies crushed inside, ready to see the floor painted.

Duke spares a glance over his shoulder when we walk in. He's in his corner, surrounded by Carter and the rest of his most loyal lackeys. I get a few slaps on the back. Guys I've never met telling me I've got this. They're pulling for me. It has an inauspicious air of defeat about it and I don't know why.

"Hey." Fenn shakes my shoulders. "Whatever that look is, get rid of it."

I stifle a sigh. "I didn't think so many people would show up."

"Are you kidding?" Silas hands me a sports drink, as if electrolytes are going to make this difference. "This is the biggest thing to happen to Sandover since that time the European history teacher was arrested for espionage."

"You're their champion." Lawson offers me a bump of cocaine, which I know in his own way is helping.

I decline.

Grinning, Lawson grabs the drink out of my hand, puts a flask under my lips instead, and dumps a burning gulp of tequila down my throat. "Trust me. You don't want to feel what's about to happen."

"It's now or never, new kid." Duke yanks off his shirt and saunters into the center of the room where the crowd parts for him. "Let's dance."

"Oh, good. For a second there, I worried this might get violent."

"That mouth can't save you now." He's too excited about this, sporting a self-assured grin as he waits for me on the dirty concrete slab. "Step up or get out."

Fenn all but shoves me forward with a last *good luck*. I neve really liked pep talks anyway. They sound like loser talk.

"Last man standing," Duke tells me. "The fight doesn't end un one of us doesn't get up."

"I'm familiar with the concept," I say dryly. "Are we going to talk all night? I didn't bring my sleeping bag."

He snorts and shakes his head. "We could've been friends, Shaw."

"I don't think so."

He shrugs at me and takes a step back. We each assume a fighting stance, and when someone yells "Fight!" we both come out swinging.

Duke must land the first blow because almost immediately there are sirens blaring in my ears. My vision narrows. The first several seconds become a blur, and I'm not fighting so much as reacting, operating on full self-preservation mode.

The guy hits *hard*. I'd somehow forgotten how unpleasant that right hook is, but now it all comes rushing back to me. Even still, I get in plenty of my own shots. A few that stagger him, one that busts open a cut on his cheek.

Fuck. *Yes.*

I want this, I realize.

I want to win this fucking thing.

As adrenaline surges through my veins, I come at him hard, giving him everything I have. I won't let Duke drive me out of Sandover. I won't give up Sloane.

I won't give up, period.

I get in another jarring blow that makes his head jerk backward, eliciting a cheer from the crowd. But Duke's been at this a long time, d he can take a punch. And he's even better at throwing one. My feels like ground beef and one eye is nearly swollen shut when he s over the top with a cross that I walk right into.

'nd knocked right out of me, I feel my face skid on the floor. ves plastered in blood stick to the side of my face. I spit at the crowd's feet. Hear their groans and shouts. I try to t Duke's on top of me and I've got nowhere to go.

rself. Because this is where he bounces my skull off the wake up a week later in the hospital having to learn

But the finishing blow doesn't come.

Breathing hard and dripping sweat in my eyes, Duke leans over me, hissing at my ear with my shirt bunched in his fist. "There's an order to things. And it'll always be this way. Losers lose. I'll tell Sloane you said goodbye."

It's her name in his mouth that makes this fun. I cough, finding my voice.

"Six hundred thirty-two thousand four hundred eighty-six dollars," I tell him with a bloody, toothy smile.

Duke flinches. His dirt-smeared face hovers inches from mine. "What the fuck is that?"

"The exact balance of the bank account where you've been stashing all your racket funds." I tongue the open cut on my lip that's still swollen and wet with fresh blood. "Or it was. Now it's in mine. As of about an hour ago."

"Bullshit. You fuck with my money—"

Duke rears back to put his fist through my face, but in his rage he's distracted. I manage to muster enough strength for one last burst of energy and use my legs to flip his body over mine, laying him out on his back. We both quickly climb to our feet, and he lunges for me. I see his uppercut coming and circle away to his weak side, then throw my jab. I feel the crack in my hand when it connects with his jaw. The whole crowd reacts to the sound of bone on bone. A stunned Duke staggers backward as bodies make way. Then his eyes roll back into his skull and he goes down.

A puff of dirt springs up from his landing.

Carter dives for his buddy. "He's out cold," he says in dismay.

The cheers are piercing, ricocheting off the glass.

"Well, look at that," Lawson drawls. "The king is dead." Winking, he shoves the flask in my bloodstained hand. "Long live the king."

CHAPTER 53
RJ

I'VE BEEN IN MOSH PITS THAT WERE LESS SUFFOCATING. WHEN THE fight ends, the crowd crushes in on me. I taste beer and maybe vodka raining down on my head and dripping down my face to mix with the blood filling my mouth. People I've never met are smacking me on the back to congratulate me. You'd think I shot laser beams out of my dick instead of simply knocking a dude out with a punch. Still, I can't deny I'm relishing the victory.

Lucas shoves his way through the excited mass. "Dude, that was incredible. You're my freaking hero."

Fenn hands me a towel and bottle of water. I use them to clean my face up but abandon the task halfway when I spot Duke at the door.

I run to catch him before he slips out to lick his wounds. I find him out back in the glow of his phone, checking his bank account to confirm I'd made good on my threat.

"How'd you do it?" he demands, bewildered, when he hears my approach. He looks like I feel: thoroughly pulverized. I guess it makes me feel better that it wasn't a completely lopsided bout. No matter how it ended. "How the hell did you pull that off?"

I shrug because I'm not one to divulge secrets. "Tell you what," I say instead. "I'll make you deal."

We're not about to bury the hatchet over some bruises and bare knuckles. This isn't that kind of bromance. But I'm also not so naïve to think I can make off with more than half a million dollars scot-free. People die for that amount of money.

"You can have it all back. Every cent."

Skeptical, Duke scoffs. "Why would you do that?"

"I told you. I only wanted to mind my own business. You do the same, and we don't have a problem." I tip my head at him. "That includes keeping your mouth shut about me and Sloane. Agreed?"

"That's it?"

It's ridiculous we had to go through all this to come to a simple agreement.

"That's it."

After a beat, Duke shrugs. "Fine. Deal."

Before we can awkwardly shake on it, Fenn and the guys bombard us to hurl some parting taunts at Duke and whisk me away with some other overenthused seniors to the soccer field, where they are intent on celebrating the supposed revolution. You'd think the Berlin Wall had fallen, the way these idiots rip off their shirts and shotgun cans of beer while hollering and dancing around in the dark. They become primal animals freed from their cages, and, if anything, it makes the case why Duke's regime held so long.

The atmosphere is contagious, however. Maybe it's the liquor Lawson pours down my throat. Or the relief that the entire stupid ordeal is over. I indulge more than I should, basking in my own victorious radiance. It's a party, after all.

I'm not wasted enough to forget my nightly ritual with Sloane, but my fingers are definitely unsteady as I type out a text.

"Stop texting," Fenn orders, trying to smack the phone out of my hand.

"Fuck off. Gotta text Sloane good night."

Lawson busts out in laughter. "Remy. Stop. You're embarrassing yourself."

"For real." Fenn nods in agreement. "You're not acting like the dude who just took out Duke Jessup, you pussy-whipped asshole."

Despite their pawing hands, I manage to hit *send* before they can confiscate my phone, hoping Sloane won't be too upset if I don't acknowledge her response right away. The boys are clearly not going to allow me to duck out early tonight.

"Not gonna lie," Silas says from his spot on the grass. "I was sure he had you beat."

Fenn snorts. "Don't sound so disappointed."

"Duke was felled by his fatal flaw," Lawson drawls. "The guy loves to hear himself talk."

"What shall the crown bestow upon us as his first decree?" Fenn asks me, his tone mocking.

"Don't even start."

I never asked for power, nor do I want it. You'd think a bunch of spoiled delinquents would have a healthier disdain for authority.

After a couple of hours or so, the group thins until only Fenn and I are left lying on the grass, watching for UFOs. Soft blades of meticulously manicured grass poke at my arms. The cold that's threatened to break the relentless heatwave has finally arrived, the chilly dampness seeping into my back.

"I ran into Casey earlier," I tell him. "She said you told her about you and Sloane."

"Had to. She asked me to kiss her." He's got a good buzz on and is still coming down from the elated high, but I can hear the pain in his voice. "Couldn't do it to her."

"That was decent."

"I guess."

His feelings for Casey haven't been a secret. Considering she seemed pretty receptive to him, I'm not sure why he hasn't moved on that. Not that I've known Fenn to be the relationship type. But if anyone were going to tame a famously promiscuous guy like him, it'd be a girl like her.

"I'm glad we're stepbrothers," I say. Because for all we've been through, I don't think I've ever said those words out loud. Given everything, I think maybe it bears mentioning.

He chuckles. "Yeah. Me too."

Suddenly a flashlight sweeps through the darkness. I catch its beam right in the face and squint as I get to my feet beside Fenn.

"Names. Both of you."

Oh, for fuck's sake. The overzealous housefather of the junior dorm comes traipsing across the field. I guess someone should have articulated to Lucas the imperative to not get caught walking in drunk off his ass and smelling of pot.

"Wanna make a run for it?" Fenn mutters.

I couldn't run ten feet right now without falling over. "You first."

As we stand there drunk out of our minds, the housefather calls the headmaster to get here on the double. Within minutes, Headmaster Tresscott is giving us a disapproving scowl while inspecting the obscene state of my face.

"I'm extremely disappointed in both of you," he tells us. He's usually even and reserved, so the anger vibrating in his voice is chilling. "I'll deal with the two of you in morning. Go back to your dorm and stay there."

But after we're dismissed, he doesn't let me follow Fenn. With a sharp nod, he pulls me aside. And I know it's coming. Pack up my shit and be ready to leave in the morning.

Damn. I didn't even make it a whole semester. That's a new record.

"Seems you had quite an evening, Mr. Shaw. Do you need medical attention?"

The headmaster doesn't appear especially surprised by my appearance, which only confirms what Lucas had said ages ago. Tresscott is absolutely aware of the fights. For a guy as obsessive as he is about surveillance, there's no chance in hell he's oblivious. Which means he's clearly chosen to ignore them, same way he ignores most of the illicit activities that take place on this campus.

"Nothing a bag of frozen peas won't cure, sir."

He lifts a brow. "This is the second time I've found you with similar bruises."

"Yes, sir. He had it coming."

There's no mistake between us as to who was on the other end of this masterpiece. And I take it Dr. Tresscott is no fan of Duke because he spares the slightest twitch of a smirk in response. It quickly evaporates, however. Replaced by a stern frown.

"I'm aware of your relationship with my daughter," he says stiffly. "And that you've since broken up."

"Yeah, well. About that." An unwitting smile springs free. "There's been some recent developments in that regard, sir."

He crosses his arms, none too pleased at the revelation. "Do I need to remind you of the discussion we had outside my home, Mr. Shaw? And perhaps you can explain how you interpreted that to mean I was giving you permission to date my daughter?"

"I didn't. Interpret it that way," I clarify. "I, ah, disregarded your orders."

The headmaster frowns and opens his mouth to speak, but I hurry on before he can object.

"But hear me out, sir. Just for a moment. I know this probably sounds rich coming from me, but you don't have to wonder about my ulterior motives. I care about Sloane, and I want to do right by her. So I'm asking you to give me chance. I admit I've been a screwup at my other schools, but that doesn't mean I can't treat her well. She's teaching me," I add with a self-deprecating grin. "I'm trying to be a better person. And I know I can be a good boyfriend to Sloane."

I peer at his face through my one good eye, trying to gauge his reaction to my little speech. Sloane would never admit it, but I know it's important to her that her dad not hate me. Or at least that he give his reluctant permission to our relationship. It's one less thing she has to worry about.

He considers me for a moment before clearing his throat. "Take care with her. She's not as unbreakable as she looks."

Relief washes over me. "Yes, sir. I know."

It's what makes her love so precious. It's extraordinarily rare and almost impossible to obtain. I won't take that for granted again.

I offer a hopeful look, unable to stop from pushing my luck. "I don't suppose this means you'll take it easy on Fenn and me tonight? Given that we're practically family now."

He gives me a solid pat on the shoulder. "No chance, Mr. Shaw."

CHAPTER 54
LAWSON

THE POST-CARNAGE FESTIVITIES FIZZLE OUT WITH A WHIMPER. After all that blood and sweat, and a handle of tequila, I've got a taste for something salty and sweet. Yet somehow I find myself wandering the dark lawns all by my lonesome after Silas managed to sneak away into the night without so much as a kiss good night.

Me: Where'd you scamper off to?

In the courtyard framed by the art and music buildings, there's a garden featuring a small man-made pond. Beside it is a willow tree that freshmen are known to decorate with condoms on Halloween. An orchestra teacher designed the space after an ancient chestnut came down in a blizzard and toppled the south corner of the choir room along with it. It provides a peaceful environment for studying or contemplating nature. Or in my case, a late-night pit stop to do a bump under the cascade of gently fluttering branches.

Silas: Snuck over to Ballard to see Amy.

Boo. No fun at all.

I can't even imagine what they get up to in bed, but I suspect if they were to do their dirtiest on a public bus, even the nuns wouldn't flinch. Silas has spent his entire life restraining his most carnal impulses.

Me: Enjoy dry-humping each other through a blanket.

Still, while his execution may be lacking, Silas does have the right idea about what to do tonight.

Doused in a perfect cocktail of liquor and cocaine, my head is capable of enticing me toward all sorts of bad intentions. The only dilemma is whether I'm in the mood for the warm embrace of soft, feminine flesh or a rough tangle with masculine muscle. In the end, I pick the first Goodwyn I see in my chat thread, because it's too difficult to run through a pros and cons list when you're this fucked up.

Me: You up?
Gwen: It's nearly 2:00 am. I'm in bed.
Me: But you're awake.
Gwen: Can't talk now.
Me: Is he right beside you? Does that make you hot?
Gwen: What do you want?
Me: How about a nightcap? The art room?
Gwen: It's late.
Me: And that isn't a no.

I picture her lying there in some indecent silk nightie, the screen dimmed. Nervous while she watches his chest rise and listens to his breathing. Daring herself to pull the covers back and slide out of bed. All those silent fantasies tumbling through her head.

Gwen: Meet me at the fire exit.

I smile to myself. So predictable.

From her staff apartment, it takes only minutes for Gwen to emerge from the darkness in a pair of old worn jeans, a plain navy T-shirt, and a baseball cap over her red hair, as if she could blend in with the wayward students still whispering their way across campus at all hours in search of mischief. After the first time I met her here after hours, I nudged the camera at the rear entrance to face away from the door, allowing a clear path, so my stride is confident as we enter the building. I did the same thing outside the faculty offices to clear the way for me and her husband.

"You can't text me at all hours," she says, closing the art room door behind us and tossing her cap on a chair. "There has to be boundaries."

"If you say so."

Her hair is bed-messed and soft, and I enjoy the way she frustratingly shoves it out of her lovely face as she corners me against the wall.

"I mean it." Her teeth tug at my earlobe before she explores my neck with her mouth. For a woman who's supposed to be annoyed, she can't keep her hands off me. They're already fumbling for my zipper. "No more of this dare-me-to-get-caught shit."

"Would it be so bad?" I push my fingers up under the hem of her T-shirt and tease skin that's still cold from the fresh chill in the air outside. "Could be overlooking an opportunity."

"Stop talking."

Gwen seals her mouth over mine. She can be quite bossy when she's so inclined. Especially when she's scolding me. That agitated energy releases itself in physical insistence and she becomes voracious. I reach my hand between our bodies to cup her pussy over her jeans and elicit a breathy groan from deep in her chest.

I quickly lose my sense of place and time, the darkened room narrowing to a hazy inference. I feel everything, but on a delay, like I'm watching myself in slow motion. The ground beneath me is unsteady and undulating. I might have gone at the tequila a little harder than I thought. Maybe done one too many bumps too. But I'm not complaining about the ride. My dick is so hard it hurts, pleading for relief.

We stumble toward her desk, where she unbuttons my jeans and pulls down the zipper as her lips leave mine. My hands grip the edge as my head falls forward. She strokes me firmly, making me groan.

"Feel good?" she whispers.

"Not good enough," I say. My body is screaming for release. "I want to fuck you."

Her lips curve in anticipation. "Then fuck me."

It's all I need to hear. Breathing hard, I spin her around. One hand tackles her zipper, the other reaching into my pocket for the condom I stashed there. I knew I'd get laid tonight, but the winner of the sex partner lottery had been undetermined. Now, as I run my palm over Gwen's bare, perky ass before giving it a soft smack, I'm glad I didn't go into town with some of the others. This is exactly what I need.

I lean forward to press my lips to the back of her neck. She shivers at the contact. "You're teasing," she accuses.

"Mm-hmm." I reach around her, finding one perfect breast and giving it a firm squeeze. "You like it."

She doesn't deny it. Just thrusts her ass out, seeking my body.

I'm about to tear open the condom packet when the overhead lights flick on and the room flashes a blinding fluorescent green.

There's a sudden alarming burst of commotion. In my current state, it takes a second to discern what's happening until my vision clears enough to make out Jack standing in the doorway. Gwen's already moved away from the desk, shoving her shirt down to cover her tits while her other hand attempts to pull up her jeans. I register the vague sounds of the Goodwyns trading strained words.

"I pretended to be asleep because I knew you were up to something."

"You followed me?"

"Of course I did! That's the least offensive thing that's happened here, don't you think? You're cheating on me, goddamn it!"

I bust out a laugh that silences the room. Gwen snaps around to meet me with a glare. "Not now, Lawson."

"Nah. Now seems like the time." Still chuckling, I direct my unfocused gaze to the doorway. "Come on now, Jack. Let's not cast stones."

"What does that mean?" his wife demands.

"Hadn't you figured it out?" I glance over in amusement. Man, this night ended up even better than I anticipated. "Jack and I are old friends." I wink at him, and he visibly winces. "I thought maybe this was a kink thing. Both of you pretending it was a secret to spice up the maritals."

"Absolutely not," he growls, aiming his righteous indignation at his now-stricken wife.

"Oops." I neatly tuck everything into place and do up my pants. "Guess I spoke out of turn."

At any rate, I know better than to be the last one to leave the party. And these two have a lot to discuss. So I take my leave and bid them good night. All but teleporting back to my room, where I hardly remember walking in the door before my head hits the pillow and I embrace unconsciousness.

CHAPTER 55
RJ

The bruises and swollen hand aside, I never stood a chance of sleeping tonight. I'm too amped on the aftertaste of adrenaline. No one was more surprised than I was to win that fight. And it keeps hitting me sideways that for a fleeting moment, I had six figures in my bank account. But easy come, easy go.

Checking the time on my phone, I remember my mom and David are in Sonoma for a vacation. It's just after eleven there. Not too late to give her a heads-up the headmaster will be calling in the morning to discuss my latest indiscretion. Hopefully she's three wine-tasting tours deep and will appreciate the irony.

"It's late there," she answers the phone without even a hello. "Is everyone okay?"

"Yeah, fine. No one died."

I hear her exhale, and it catches me off guard, the tone of concern in her voice. For a second there, she sounded like a real mom. I'm not sure where it came from, but I think I appreciate it.

"Where are you?"

"In my room. Everything's fine."

"Uh-huh. So what'd you do now?"

I fight a smile. "Why's it have to be like that now?"

"Because if no one's bleeding or in jail after two in the morning, it means you're probably getting expelled again."

Harsh, Mom. But not altogether unwarranted. I've earned the reputation.

"Well, relax. I'd say it's a ninety percent chance I'm fine. But if you want to have David throw his weight around a little to push it over that last ten, I wouldn't be opposed."

She laughs. "Oh, so now you don't mind asking for favors. Does this mean you're coming around?"

One thing I appreciate about us, we tell each other the truth. About the stuff that matters, at least. I've never been one to filter myself and it's always been obvious I got that from her. So I don't feel the slightest remorse giving it to her straight.

"You know where I stand. I went into this not believing the marriage will last. It's only been a few months, and that hasn't really changed. But maybe I'm getting used to the situation."

"That's something."

I understand this is important to her. And I'm not being difficult just to deprive her of any joy. I've just watched so many of these guys sweep into her life and just as quickly disappear. Every time, she was perfectly happy until she wasn't. Sorry, but these days I have a high bar if they want to convince me this won't end the same way.

"So fill me in," she says. "Let's hear it."

I glance over at Fenn's side of the room. He's dead to the world, snoring in bed still half-dressed.

"I fought a guy. It was sort of a bet? Wasn't pretty, but I won."

Of course, she has to scold me for embracing violence, though she doesn't pretend to be too upset about it since we've already established no one ended up in the emergency room. And I tell her we got busted drinking on the soccer field. Which I suppose without all the necessary context probably sounds like the beginning or the end of a dangerous spiral.

"You'd tell me if you weren't okay. Right, buddy?"

"Sure."

"I'm being real with you. I know maybe we should have had a conversation like this sooner." Mom's voice softens. "A lot of things maybe I should have done different. But if you don't like it there or think that place isn't good for you, RJ, you can come home any time you want. Just say the word. I love you. I'm always here for you, no matter what. We're a team before anything else."

Eighteen years and I don't think I've ever heard these words come out of her mouth. We don't really do heart-to-hearts. And in more ways than not, she's spent most of my life putting herself first, making me feel like an accessory or inconvenience. I was just the result of an unwanted pregnancy, and she never made any significant effort to convince me otherwise. We've mostly tried to stay out of each other's way, but tonight, for the first time, I'm getting a glimpse of what it would be like to have a mom.

"Sounds crazy, but I am kind of happy here," I confess. It's a new sensation, so I'm not about to oversell it. "There's this girl. Sloane. It's been a crazy ride. But she's pretty fucking great. Sort of hates me, so it's fun."

Mom laughs, and I can feel her shaking her head.

"And, you know, Fenn and I are getting along."

"Yeah?"

"We hit a couple snags. But it turns out, I like having a brother. I thought he was an obnoxious rich boy at first. But then I realized he's just been lonely. Just wants someone to care about him."

"Of course we care about him." Mom sounds troubled. "Why would you say something like that?"

"The way he tells it, he thinks David stopped giving a shit a long time ago. Trust me, he feels strongly about it. It's a sore subject."

"I had no idea." She's quiet for a moment, absorbed in whatever's running through her head. "Obviously David loves him."

Sure, she has to say that. It'd be weird if she didn't. Except I hear the doubt in her inflection. Now she's replaying every interaction she's witnessed between those two in the short time we all shared a roof. Recalling conversations that didn't happen. The times David didn't go on for hours about his son with TV-dad pride.

After we get off the phone, I'm no closer to feeling tired enough to shut my eyes, so I hop on the computer to pore through more of the Ballard security footage. For the next hour, I sit there scanning through hours of stagnant monochrome forest around the boathouse. It's goddamn brutal.

Until I glimpse movement in the frame.

I hit play and let it run at speed. It's blurry at first. Dark and out of focus in the corner of the image. As it comes more fully into view, I flinch, startled nearly out of my chair. Confused at first, I double-check the time stamp that the script I wrote didn't pull in a file from the days after the accident. But there's no mistake.

Holy shit.

CHAPTER 56
SLOANE

ON SUNDAY MORNING, I'M STILL UNDER MY COVERS HIDING FROM daylight when Dad knocks on my bedroom door. I'm sure my groan to go away is more than clear, but he lets himself in anyway.

"You've got a friend downstairs."

"No."

This is my one recovery day where I was looking forward to sleeping in. No running or homework or chores to pry me away from my pillow. Whoever it is can make an appointment.

"They brought breakfast. Smells good."

"Tell them to leave it."

"Come on, kid." Dad rips the covers off me. "Up and at 'em."

I hate it when he does that. But whatever. I begrudgingly peel myself out of bed and throw on a sweatshirt. If Silas is ruthless enough to show up bright and early unannounced, he's getting ugly bedhead Sloane.

Dad's waiting for me in the hallway when I exit the room. He shifts his feet. His eyes aren't quite focusing on me. It's obvious he has something on his mind.

"What?" His energy is weird. It's freaking me out.

"I want to reassure you that I was listening the other day." His face suddenly softens with this intense tenderness that I haven't seen since Casey and I were little, still going off on crying fits in the grocery store or in the drive-thru ordering dinner. Those first few months after Mom died, it seemed like we would spontaneously remember she wasn't waiting for us at home and it would crush our hearts all over again. And Dad would swoop in, our gentle savior, wiping our tears and reassuring us we still had him and he would never, ever leave us.

"I realize I need to do a better job of stepping up and being your father. I've depended too much on you to take care of all of us, when this is the time you should be thinking about college and SATs. Getting to be a little selfish and enjoying your senior year." His voice thickens. "I want you to know you don't have to be our rock all the time. You can come to me whenever you need to talk, but I'm going to be better about checking in on you too. That's a promise, sweetheart."

"Thanks." My eyes feel a little hot. "I appreciate that."

He gives me a tight hug, clearing his throat. "One more thing. You accused me of something. You wondered if the reason I don't want any of the boys around you is because I fear for my job." Dad lifts one eyebrow. "That's not the reason, Sloane. I keep them away because whether you like it or not, you're always going to be my little girl. And nobody, and I mean nobody, will ever be good enough for you in my eyes."

I stare at him in surprise.

He chuckles quietly. "With that said, I'm willing to keep an open mind."

Before I can respond and make this more emotionally awkward for both of us, he nudges me along.

"Go see your friend. He's been waiting awhile."

Blinking away the stinging sensation in my eyelids, I head for the kitchen. All ready to take my breakfast back to bed and tell Silas to come back when he's learned some manners. Instead, I see a nervous RJ at the counter beside Casey, who looks absolutely tickled.

"What the hell is this?" I demand.

"As I understand it, you two have patched things up." Dad slips past me to resume making his tea, which he'd left mid-prepara-tion. "I see no harm in you continuing to associate with Mr. Shaw. Provided you respect our agreement. I would have you be where I can see you, rather than behind my back." With his mug in hand, he nods at RJ. "You kids have fun."

Casey gets a good laugh out of that before wandering off, her attention engrossed with her phone.

"Oh." Dad pops his head around the corner one last time. "Mr. Shaw, there's still the matter of your punishment. Sandover cannot toler-ate underage drinking, as you're aware. Make sure you and Mr. Bishop see the dining hall manager after breakfast Monday morning. You'll be assisting the kitchen staff with cleanup duty for the rest of the month."

Smirking, Dad saunters off, finally leaving us alone.

"You've been busy," I tell RJ, letting him tug me into his arms.

There was part of me that wondered if I'd managed to twist myself in knots over something that existed mostly in my head. That maybe my feelings for RJ weren't as deep as my heart kept telling me. But then I see him here mildly getting along with my dad and it triggers all the gooey emotions in my chest. I'm not sure I'll ever understand it, and against my better judgment, I'm silly for this guy. And I know in his lopsided smile, when he reaches for my hand, that he's gone a little silly too.

He winces when I grab his face to kiss him. His lip is still swollen from the fight.

"Careful, cupcake. I'm fragile." RJ, sitting on a stool, holds me between his legs. Fingertips dipping under my T-shirt to skim bare skin.

"It's sexy." I mean, he's a mess. It's like stampeding horses trampled him. But all that ingrained Hollywood marketing has conditioned us for rugged, war-weary cowboy types. We can't help it. "Like, I'm-wetter-than-ever kind of sexy."

Eyes glazing, his tongue comes out to lick the corner of his mouth. "Cut that out. Your dad's going to walk in here and change his mind about me."

Fine. For the sake of not blowing our cover, I take a seat and dig into the pastries RJ brought. "Silas says the fight was one for the ages."

He shrugs. "No one's more surprised by the outcome than me."

"Nah. I think you were grossly underestimating yourself."

That earns me a husky laugh. "I'm going to let you keep believing that."

RJ then attempts to fill me in on some of his heroic exploits over the last twenty-four hours, but I become entirely distracted by the way he draws absentminded shapes on the top of my thigh. Spies be damned, I can't help myself from stealing another kiss, tasting sugar and butter on his tongue. As if he's forgotten his reservations, he yanks my stool closer to deepen the kiss. His tongue tickles mine and we both make a desperate noise.

"I mean it," he whispers against my lips. His voice is suddenly earnest. "This is for real, Sloane. I'm not going anywhere."

"I wouldn't let you."

He's stuck with me now.

When he pulls back to meet my eyes, however, there's something haunted lingering at the edges.

"What's wrong?"

A brief struggle plays across his face before he sighs and pushes his plate to the side. "I got the security footage from the boathouse."

"What, seriously?" My outburst is louder than I intend. I quickly lower my voice while asking, "Have you seen it yet? Was there anything on it?"

RJ gives me a reluctant nod.

"What?" I demand.

"I'm warning you," he says gravely. "It's fucked up."

I don't care what's on it. I have to know. Nothing can be worse than the version in my head that's grown more graphic and terrifying every day for months since that night.

Without another word, I drag him into the den and close the door behind us.

CHAPTER 57
FENN

SHE ASKS ME TO MEET HER AT THE LAKE. AND BECAUSE I'M A masochist, I can't say no. Instead, I throw a hoodie on, shove my feet into a pair of sneakers, and practically sprint all the way there. I'm pathetic. Last time we spoke, I told her I fucked her sister and that I didn't want to be her boyfriend. I burned that bridge. Or at least, I should've. Instead, I'm racing through the ashes of that burnt bridge just to see her.

And what the hell is wrong with her that she's asking to meet? My callous words were designed to push her away and this chick is inviting me right back in.

But of course she is. Because she's Casey Tresscott, an endless well of forgiveness and compassion. It probably took her all of five minutes to forgive me for sleeping with Sloane and deciding our friendship is too important to lose.

Christ. If she only knew she's got way bigger things to forgive me for.

"Hey," Casey says when she sees me emerge into the clearing. She's wearing black leggings and an oversized blue sweater the same shade as her eyes. Her hair is pulled back in a low ponytail, emphasizing her high cheekbones.

"Hey," I say gruffly.

"Thanks for coming."

I shove my hands in my pockets, slowing my gait as I approach her. "What's this about?"

She rolls her eyes. "You know what it's about, Fenn."

A breath gets stuck in my throat. Yeah. I know. "Let me guess," I say flatly. "You don't give a shit that I slept with Sloane."

"Not really, no." She shrugs. "It happened before you and I ever even had a real conversation. Everyone has baggage. And trust me, I'm well aware of yours." Her eyes narrow. "With that said, I don't appreciate that the only reason you told me was because you were trying to hurt me."

I blink in surprise. "I…wasn't trying to hurt you," I lie.

Casey laughs. "Bullshit. You freaked out because you wanted to kiss me and decided the best way to push me away was to drop a bomb like that."

Frustration creeps up my spine, stiffening my muscles. Fuck's sake. Why does this girl have to be so damn smart?

"Listen, I'm sorry for hurting you and spitting the truth out like that, all callous like. But telling you about it had nothing to do with the kissing thing."

She just laughs again.

"It didn't," I insist. Taking a breath, I force myself to reiterate what I'd said the other day. "I don't feel the same way as—"

Casey cuts me off by grabbing the front of my hoodie and pulling me down for a kiss.

Our mouths collide, her warm lips latching on before I can react. And the moment I get a taste, I couldn't stop this even if I wanted to. It's the kind of kiss that fogs your brain and makes you lose track of your surroundings. The lake disappears, the grass beneath our feet, the trees, the sky. It's just me and Casey, her hands on my chest, her eager lips moving over mine.

When the tip of her tongue darts out to tease mine, my entire body clenches and my heart rate becomes dangerously high. I groan, deepening the kiss, all but attacking her with my tongue.

We're both breathing heavily when we finally come up for air.

It takes a second for my body to stop trembling. "Casey," I start, my voice shaky. "We're just friends. I'm not interested in anything more…" I trail off weakly.

She tips her head to look at me, her expression gleaming with satisfaction. "No, we're not," she says firmly. "And yes, you are."

Then she kisses me a second time.

God help me, but once again I don't stop her.

EPILOGUE
SLOANE

SETTLING ON THE OVERSTUFFED LEATHER COUCH, RJ PULLS A tablet out of his bag. I sit beside him, impatiently tapping my fingers on my thigh as I wait for him to play the video. I figure we have some time before my dad notices and walks by loudly clearing his throat.

"Here we go," RJ says grimly.

I lean forward to study the screen. The resolution isn't great. The images are dark and somewhat blurry.

My car speeds through the frame, obviously out of control and traveling toward the lake. It's barely a smear across the screen, but the unmistakable silhouette chills my blood all the same. I haven't seen that car since the tow truck pulled it out of the water, with its front end covered in mud and seeping from every seam.

Minutes later, a person runs away from the scene. They're barely a shadow with the hood of their sweatshirt up, head bent, facing away from the camera. There's nothing to gather about the coward's identity other than their height and build suggest it's a male who's escaping. A dozen faces flash through my mind as I try reconstructing that night, accounting again for their whereabouts while I frantically searched for Casey.

"Wait," RJ tells me when I try to run the video back. "There's more."

He scans the footage ahead twenty minutes. I watch the time stamp roll and am sickened to realize that with every second that ticks by, Casey is stuck in the front seat as the water rapidly rushes in and she struggles to free herself. Or else trapped unconscious and sinking toward her death while I was checking bathrooms and hallways.

I keep waiting to see myself. To glimpse Duke and me rushing in to find her. Finally, there's movement on the edge of the screen. Another figure emerges from the darkness to run toward the lake. It isn't the same person as before returning with help. This one is taller and wearing different clothes. After a few minutes, he again appears in the frame, now carrying a limp and apparently unconscious Casey dripping wet in his arms. Carefully, he lays her on the grass and rummages through her pockets until he finds her phone.

"He's sending the text," I point out. My heart is stuck in my throat. "That's how I found her. I got a text from her phone telling me where to look."

When he's done, he places the phone in her unmoving hand. I watch him lean in to whisper something in her ear. He tenderly touches her face, lingering a moment to watch her. Then he gets to his feet and sprints away.

Leaving her there.

Alone and freezing.

Not knowing if she'd ever wake up or how badly she might be injured.

Just before he disappears into the black forest, as if knowing I would be here, right now, watching him, he glances at the camera and reveals his face. It's only a split-second of grainy black-and-white footage, but it's enough.

Fenn.

This whole time. And he's never said a word.

I sit silently until the video ends and the screen goes black. My hands tremble.

"What do you want to do?" RJ asks tentatively.

I stare at the blank screen for what feels like forever before finally finding my voice.

"I don't know."

READ ON FOR A SNEAK PEEK
AT THE NEXT IN THE PREP SERIES
BY ELLE KENNEDY: *ROGUE*

CASEY

SOMETHING WEIRD HAPPENS WHEN THE GUY YOU LIKE SAYS HE likes you back. Everything becomes hyperreal. Vivid. Those dimples I hadn't paid significant attention to before? They now occupy an inordinate share of my thoughts. I can't stop touching his hair. Can't stop noticing how he always seems to miss one tiny patch of dark-blond stubble on the corner of his jaw whenever he shaves.

Fenn was a stranger for so long. Just another upperclassman my sister occasionally hung around with. Then the accident threw my world into chaos and there he was, with a smile and a shoulder. For no good reason other than he saw I needed someone and decided it would be him.

And for no good reason, I let him in.

After school I throw on my running shoes and whistle for Bo and Penny, who hardly wait for me to open the front door before they bolt down the driveway toward the sun sitting low above the tree line. For a couple of big golden retrievers, they've got engines like racehorses and the patience of caffeinated toddlers. They sprint most of the way to the spot where Fenn is waiting off the forest path between the dorms and my house on the edge of the Sandover campus.

I'm still not tired of the way he always looks deep in thought before his head lifts and his eyes light up. That embarrassed grin he smothers as he wraps his arms over my shoulders and kisses the top of my head.

"Hey," he says. Never more than that. But it's the inflection that makes it our own secret language. Everything we need to say in one sound.

"Hey."

I lock my arms behind his back and stay there awhile. Because even on days I remember my armor, school is exhausting.

"You all right?" Fenn says against my hair.

He's almost a foot taller than me, letting me nestle against his chest. He must've ditched his blazer in his dorm because he's wearing only his Sandover-issued button-down, the sleeves rolled up. He smells so delicious. That boarding school tuition doesn't skimp on the good fabric softener.

"Yeah," I answer. "You give good hug."

I feel his laugh fan over my cheek. "Oh yeah?"

"Mm-hmm."

"'Kay. Knock yourself out."

I give him one last squeeze before I let go, shielding my eyes from the sun to spot Bo and Penny harassing some creature up a tree. "Guys," I shout in reprimand, and they quickly dash away from the tree.

"How long can you stay?" Fenn quickly unbuttons his shirt and lays it down on the grass for me to sit on.

I can't help but roll my eyes.

"What? It's called manners, Casey."

"Any excuse to take your clothes off." Not that I hate it. Playing soccer has given him ridiculous abs. Which he's not shy about.

"Eyes are up here, sweetheart." He winks at me and sprawls out beside me.

"I can't stay long," I answer. "Homework. And Dad's making dinner. So…"

"So I better not waste my time then."

With a naughty grin, he reaches for my hand and pulls me to sit across his lap. My resulting squeak is a cross between surprise and delight. Then my pulse quickens as Fenn catches me around the waist to hold me tight and presses his warm lips to mine.

ABOUT THE AUTHOR

A *New York Times*, *USA Today*, and *Wall Street Journal* bestselling author, Elle Kennedy grew up in the suburbs of Toronto, Ontario, and holds a BA in English from York University. From an early age, she knew she wanted to be a writer and actively began pursuing that dream when she was a teenager. She loves strong heroines and sexy alpha heroes, and just enough heat and danger to keep things interesting!

Elle loves to hear from her readers. Visit her website ellekennedy.com or sign up for her newsletter to receive updates about upcoming books and exclusive excerpts. You can also find her on Facebook (/AuthorElleKennedy), Twitter (@ElleKennedy), Instagram (@ElleKennedy33), or TikTok (@ElleKennedyAuthor).

Don't miss the rest of the *New York Times* bestselling OFF-CAMPUS series from ELLE KENNEDY

THE DEAL

She's about to make a deal with the college bad boy...

Hannah Wells has finally found someone who turns her on. But while she might be confident in every other area of her life, she's carting around a full set of baggage when it comes to sex and seduction. If she wants to get her crush's attention, she'll have to step out of her comfort zone and make him take notice...even if it means tutoring the annoying, childish, cocky captain of the hockey team in exchange for a pretend date.

...and it's going to be oh so good

All Garrett Graham has ever wanted is to play professional hockey after graduation, but his plummeting GPA is threatening everything he's worked so hard for. If helping a sarcastic brunette make another guy jealous will help him secure his position on the team, he's all for it. But when one unexpected kiss leads to the wildest sex of both their lives, it doesn't take long for Garrett to realize that pretend isn't going to cut it. Now he just has to convince Hannah that the man she wants looks a lot like him.

THE MISTAKE

He's a player in more ways than one...

College junior John Logan can get any girl he wants. For this hockey star, life is a parade of parties and hook-ups, but behind his killer grins and easygoing charm, he hides growing despair about the dead-end road he'll be forced to walk after graduation. A sexy encounter with freshman Grace Ivers is just the distraction he needs, but when a thoughtless mistake pushes her away, Logan plans to spend his final year proving to her that he's worth a second chance.

Now he's going to need to up his game...

After a less-than-stellar freshman year, Grace is back at Briar University, older, wiser, and so over the arrogant hockey player she nearly handed her V card to. She's not a charity case, and she's not the quiet butterfly she was when they first hooked up. If Logan expects her to roll over and beg like all his other puck bunnies, he can think again. He wants her back? He'll have to work for it. This time around, she'll be the one in the driver's seat...and she plans on driving him wild.

THE SCORE

He knows how to score, on and off the ice

Allie Hayes is in crisis mode. With graduation looming, she still doesn't have the first clue about what she's going to do after college. To make matters worse, she's nursing a broken heart thanks to the end of her longtime relationship. Wild rebound sex is definitely not the solution to her problems, but gorgeous hockey star Dean Di Laurentis is impossible to resist. Just once, though, because even if her future is uncertain, it sure as heck won't include the king of one-night stands.

It'll take more than flashy moves to win her over

Dean always gets what he wants. Girls, grades, girls, recognition, girls...he's a ladies man, all right, and he's yet to meet a woman who's immune to his charms. Until Allie. For one night, the feisty blond rocked his entire world—and now she wants to be friends? Nope. It's not over until he says it's over. Dean is in full-on pursuit, but when life-rocking changes strike, he starts to wonder if maybe it's time to stop focusing on scoring...and shoot for love.

THE GOAL

She's good at achieving her goals...

College senior Sabrina James has her whole future planned out: graduate from college, kick butt in law school, and land a high-paying job at a cutthroat firm. Her path to escaping her shameful past certainly doesn't include a gorgeous hockey player who believes in love at first sight. One night of sizzling heat and surprising tenderness is all she's willing to give John Tucker, but sometimes, one night is all it takes for your entire life to change.

But the game just got a whole lot more complicated

Tucker believes being a team player is as important as being the star. On the ice, he's fine staying out of the spotlight, but when it comes to becoming a daddy at the age of twenty-two, he refuses to be a benchwarmer. It doesn't hurt that the soon-to-be mother of his child is beautiful, whip-smart, and keeps him on his toes. The problem is, Sabrina's heart is locked up tight, and the fiery brunette is too stubborn to accept his help. If he wants a life with the woman of his dreams, he'll have to convince her that some goals can only be made with an assist.

THE LEGACY

Four stories. Four couples. Three years of real life after graduation...

A wedding. A proposal. An elopement. And a surprise pregnancy. Life after college for Garrett and Hannah, Logan and Grace, Dean and Allie, and Tucker and Sabrina isn't quite what they imagined it would be. Sure, they have each other, but they also have real-life problems that four years at Briar U didn't exactly prepare them for. And it turns out, for these four couples, love is the easy part. Growing up is a whole lot harder.

Catch up with your favorite Off-Campus characters as they navigate the changes that come with growing up and discover that big decisions can have big consequences...and if they're lucky, big rewards.